Also by Matthew Scott Hansen

It's in the Book, Bob! (with Bob Eubanks)
Confessions of an Enron Executive: A Whistleblower's Story
(with Lynn Brewer)
Andy Kaufman Revealed! (with Bob Zmuda)

The SHADOW KILLER

Matthew Scott Hansen

SIMON & SCHUSTER
NEW YORK   LONDON   TORONTO   SYDNEY

SIMON & SCHUSTER
Rockefeller Center
1230 Avenue of the Americas
New York, NY 10020

This book is a work of fiction. Names, characters,
places, and incidents either are products of the
author's imagination or are used fictitiously. Any
resemblance to actual events or locales or persons,
living or dead, is entirely coincidental.

Copyright © 2007 by Matthew Scott Hansen

"Deacon Blues" by Walter Carl Becker and Donald Fagen © 1977,
copyright renewed 2005 by Music Corporation of America, Inc.
All rights administered by Songs of Universal, Inc/BMI.
Used by permission. All rights reserved.

SIMON & SCHUSTER and colophon are registered trademarks
of Simon & Schuster, Inc.

For information about special discounts for bulk purchases,
please contact Simon & Schuster Special Sales at
1-800-456-6798 or business@simonandschuster.com.

Designed by Davina Mock

Manufactured in the United States of America

1 3 5 7 9 10 8 6 4 2

Library of Congress Cataloging-in-Publication Data
Hansen, Matthew Scott, 1953–
The shadowkiller / Matthew Scott Hansen.
        p.   cm.
1. Sasquatch—Fiction. 2. Washington (State)—Fiction. I. Title.
PS3608.A7225S47 2007
813'.6—dc22   2006050491

ISBN-13: 978-0-7432-9473-7
ISBN-10:   0-7432-9473-4

To Mom and Dad, the finest hominids I know . . .
. . . and to Steph and Zane, my inspiration

Acknowledgments

Although I have written other books, the creation of a first novel is singular, so I have many people to whom I must send out bouquets for their forbearance during this longer than long process.

First, my wife, Stephanie Bianca, deserves special thanks for many reasons, not the least of which is her brilliant counsel, tireless editing, sterling ideas, tough love, and cool head under fire. Trust me, you'd want this girl in your foxhole.

If superagent Nick Ellison were simply the best tactician an author could ever hope to have, that would be sublime, but he's also wickedly irreverent and crazy smart. Thank you, Nick, for embracing this book from the get-go. Thanks also to Nick's terrific staff, particularly his director of foreign rights, Sarah Dickman.

I must send out a huge thanks to my team from Simon & Schuster, starting with David Rosenthal for recognizing the value of this story. My editor, Amanda Murray, also deserves particular credit for her unfailing patience and wisdom during the process of putting this book out. Amanda and her assistant, Annie Orr, did all they could to make me look good. I would also like to thank the marketing staff, my copy editors, and the art department for their meticulous attention to detail.

Thanks to Deputy Rich Niebusch of the Snohomish County Sheriff for his assistance in creating a fictionalized version of his fine organization. Thanks also to Tinabeth Pina for sharing her knowledge of television news. My attorney, Nigel Pearson, requires special kudos for his calm British demeanor in the face of all things Hollywood. Thanks to story analyst *extraordinaire* David Bruskin not only for his astute suggestions, but for his eyes and ears.

A large number of friends and family were part of the birthing process of this big, hairy hominid, providing endless support and encouragement, and I must put forth some of their names with my heartfelt thanks. Verna, you were there from day one and read this thing, what, four times? Thank you. And many, many thanks to the gang, Steve and Carol Schneider, Mitch and Jana Hunter, cousins Gregg and Kendall, Alan Erickson, Bill Fitzhugh, Lynn Brewer, Allison Saiko, Mary K. Dean and Walter Addison, Jackie Riggs, and David Brayton. Also, a loving thank-you to my folks, Jim and Grace Hansen, and my sis, Meredith, for listening to my stories from the start.

And finally, thanks go to Emilio, for giving me the motivation to write fiction.

The
SHADOW
KILLER

*T*he Keepers of Fire allowed it to escape. He watched as they let it loose. Then they ran. The Great Fire rose fast, like the wind, climbing the slopes from the floor of the valley, its white orange maw devouring everything it touched. The inferno pushed his tribe back against the high cliff above the river. It came too fast for him to protect them, so he found a place and clung to the rocks, the teeth of the fire gnawing at him, trying to break his grip. It burned him and the smoke stung his eyes but he held fast, knowing the churning rapids were far below. Eventually the Great Fire moved on.

All but he had been consumed in its flames.

He made a pile of rocks to remember them and began walking. He moved north, toward the mountains. Crossing streams and following ridge lines, he relied on his instincts for direction. The farther he journeyed, the more evidence he saw of them. He felt he would soon find many of them. A relentless traveler, he kept moving. He would not stop until he had found the Keepers of Fire.

1

Had you asked him when he rolled out of bed that morning, Joe Wylie wasn't even remotely thinking about being first at anything. Being first had always eluded Joe—in birth order, in school, with women, with jobs, with pretty much everything. Something else Joe didn't think about very often was the fact he'd been married for twenty-four years. His wife Lori's unwavering daily consumption of handfuls of Ding Dongs and Double Fudge Yoohoos had doubled her weight since the day they were married. On top of that his nineteen-year-old daughter was over in Seattle shacked up with some dope-pushing jerk on a Harley and, maybe worse, his son had recently decided a nose ring would be a shrewd fashion statement.

Yet when Joe saw the nose ring, it didn't bother him, and that's when he realized he didn't have strong feelings about anything anymore. His sixteen-year-old had a ring in his nose and Joe didn't give a crap about that or anything else. Finally, he concluded, at forty-seven, it was nice to be all through with worrying. His rapidly receding hairline didn't even cause him the stress it used to, nor did his accumulating Budweiser gut. And he sure as hell didn't worry about his job, which wasn't particularly rewarding but paid well and was pretty frickin' easy. More or less drive a truck around in the woods, look at the trees, then tell your bosses they're still there. Piece of cake.

Uncharacteristically, Joe Wylie was actually thinking about his job as he steered up Access Road Number 4. Logging roads were rarely given descriptive, enchanting names like Pine Lake or Deer Hollow because they were only used to gain access to the seemingly boundless stores of timber owned by multinational conglomerates and, except for the rare logging crew, only people like Joe and kids looking for places to party made use of them. Road 4 was way the hell off the beaten track, high in the mountains, seven miles and four thousand feet above the last sign of civilization, a Weyerhaeuser equipment facility.

The day before, local kids had reported some busted trees up Road 4 and Joe was asked to investigate. Joe guessed it was probably the work of disgruntled, drunken loggers out of Sultan or Gold Bar. Joe had been timber cruising ten of the twenty-six years he'd been with Weyerhaeuser and little surprised him. He imagined the perpetrators were probably just vengeful independents put out of work either by his company or some damn owl or rare squirrel or something. He sort of sympathized with their frustration, but if they wanted to ruin trees, they could kindly go over to the national forest, or better yet, Buse Timber's property.

Joe fiddled with the radio, hoping to receive a Seattle station, but got only static. He remembered he was on the eastern edge of Snohomish County and that he almost never got good radio here. The dash clock's spindly hands indicated six forty. He wondered why the truck's manufacturer had bothered with such a shitty timepiece since it had never worked right. By the angle of the sun he reckoned it was about eight fifteen a.m.

From inside the paper sack on the floor he fished out another longneck Bud. He preferred the longnecks because they were easier to hold while he drove. For Joe they had the pleasant effect of rendering what could be completely stultifying work into the soothing vocational equivalent of easy-listening music.

Seven miles above the equipment station he slowed the truck as his eyes widened in wonder. A typically uneventful shift had suddenly become the jackpot of interesting mornings: ahead was something he had never seen in all his years in the woods. He stopped the truck and stepped down onto the damp hardpan. Clutching his coat tighter, Budweiser vapor swirling around his head, he stood and stared. *Some broken trees, my ass.* For fifty yards every tree on both sides of the road was snapped, maybe ten feet above the ground. Expecting two or three or even a half dozen, he quickly estimated a good hundred trees. *This is crazy. This is big.*

Joe walked down the lane of shattered fir and hemlock and tried to imagine who on earth had done this. And why? He'd seen the work of spiteful, drunken loggers but this was not that. Some of the trees were big, eight-inch-diameter second growth, yet all were splintered, some hanging by fibers, some clean off. Though he was an experienced woodsman, his mind whirled for answers but came up lemons. Brushing aside his dismay, he forced himself to tick off possibilities.

There had been no wind, so he ruled that out. Besides, he knew it would have taken a goddamn tornado to do this and that would have broken other trees, not just the ones facing the road. So his first conclusion was that this was planned. The notion irritated him because it was a waste of good timber, and if loggers had done this, then it wasn't just excusable rowdiness, it was vandalism, maybe even downright *sabotage*. Rolling the word *sabotage* around in his mind, he made a mental note to use it in his report.

As Joe's eyes swept the scene from the cold shadows to the sunlit treetops, he squinted, concentrating hard as to how this maliciousness had been carried out. It was then, despite the intake of several Buds and the fact it was not even eight thirty, that he unscrambled the puzzle. Somehow these really determined timber pirates—as he now labeled them—had gotten a big diesel scissors loader up here and somehow snapped the trees off. He'd never seen a scissors loader do that, and sure, there were a few extra somehows in there, but that must have been how it happened. The fact that the pirates hadn't seemed to have actually *pirated* any timber was another small detail Joe let slide in his solution.

Joe smiled contentedly as he pondered the fate of such vicious despoilers of his arboreal kingdom. But then his smile faded as he realized that all of the faint animal sounds had just *disappeared*. Though he heard the truck purring nearby, suddenly the birds and insects and whatever else that sang and chattered in the woods had fallen silent, as if someone had hit the pause button on the forest sounds tape.

A moment later something even more disturbing happened. At first it was as if sunlight warmed his back, only he knew the sun's rays had not yet reached beneath the trees to touch him. Then Joe realized it was really more of a creeping-up-the-spine force, like someone watching you but there's no one there. He'd felt it before in the woods and had chalked it up to once in a while just feeling something eerie you can't explain. Dismissing things was Joe's path of least resistance, but this time the sensation bothered him, even scared him. He nervously scanned the woods but saw nothing. Suddenly he felt very alone, so he headed toward the safe haven of his truck.

A few yards from the refuge of his beat-up Chevy, a noise behind him caused Joe to spin around. The human mind can identify a threat in a tenth of second and it took about that long for Joe to realize he was in grave danger. And either despite or because of the extreme stress, his brain also reached the rather academic conclusion that in all those years he'd never believed it existed. Until now.

That's when the air and his vision and his thoughts became clearer than crystal, and it suddenly didn't matter if his kid had a nose ring or if his wife had porked out, because everything was about to change for him. Joe suddenly gave a crap again, because you always do when you're about to die. And with that supreme clarity of cognition he also understood he was about to check out in a very bad way, much worse than a car crash or house fire or gunshot to the chest, and a life-sucking chill rippled through his temples into his neck, down his spine, and jumped to his scrotum, which tightened up like a sea monkey in reverse. Joe's knees wavered, then buckled, and the two Buds that had gathered in his bladder drained into his pants.

Because for the first time in his life, Joe was about to be first.

Seven miles below at the equipment station, twenty minutes had elapsed since Chuck Pendleton waved to Joe Wylie as his truck passed. Chuck readied a couple of quarts of fifty-weight to pour into one of the big D8R Cats he maintained in his yard. As he punched the filler spout into an oil can, he thought he heard something. He set the can down and listened. Faint, it sure sounded like a scream. He shrugged, lit another Winston, and picked up the can.

Must have been the gate creaking.

2

Ty Greenwood wanted to die. Or, perhaps more accurately, he didn't want to live anymore. Pondering what were probably the last minutes of his life, Ty stared down that dead-end alley and sipped a little more fifteen-year-old Balvenie, searching for the commitment to make it happen.

And as if to make his case to himself, he made one last push to picture himself happy again and immediately realized it was just another of ten thousand exercises in futility.

Yes. I'm suffocating. He thought about what went wrong. How he had lost everything that mattered to him. *Everything that mattered?* But wait, didn't he have great kids, a woman who loved him deeply, and money and his health? Isn't that all that matters? So maybe it was just his pride that had been murdered. But isn't that *really* everything?

Then he flashed on how his story had turned him into a punch line. Even Leno had made a crack about him. Ty raised his glass. "To the big joke." He took a sip, then held the glass high and addressed an imaginary gathering. "Hey? Who believes in monsters out there? Anyone? No? Okay. So just me, huh?" He took another drink.

His eyes narrowed as he relived the betrayals. His "friends," his trusted coworkers. The company he practically cofounded. Forced out. *Ungrateful bastards. Cruel bastards.*

Or did I quit?

"Doesn't matter." He lifted the heavy cut-crystal glass again and toasted, "To no credibility. To no respect."

The black mist had descended over his mind again and the booze was only adding to its opacity. The bouts with depression had only increased in the last year. Then he remembered the unkindest cut of all—that even Ronnie doubted him. His own wife's skepticism told him that trying to convince anyone else was futile.

I just cannot prove it. Period.

Sometimes he wasn't even sure it had happened. *Did it?* He was too drunk to remember.

The time readout in the lower right corner of his computer monitor said it was 2:41 a.m.

Time to die.

Ty drained off the last of the single malt and cast a blurry eye to the text on the screen. He hit save and looked for the last time at its morbidly informative title, "Why I Killed Myself," then exited the program. Ronnie would be poking around in there some day. It would offer some insight into the pressures he was feeling and the way he arrived at his final decision.

He gave a last glance around the walls and desk in his home office, and each of the photos brought back an overload of memories. Staring at the photo of himself with his current coworkers, a rugged crowd attired in khaki Forest Service uniforms, he saw himself in the context of the other men. Fair-haired, with the same jaw line at forty-two as at twenty-five, Ty felt he looked more racquetball fit than the rest of the guys, who seemed to have earned their muscle on the job. Carded at bars well into his early thirties, Ty felt his boyish face had only in the last few years begun to assume an adequate degree of character. One of the few men in the picture without a beard, Ty was also standing, tellingly, at the edge and to the rear of the fifteen or so people, yet his lean six-foot-two-inch frame was prominent even in the back.

He had never invited any of the Forest Service crowd over, partly because he wasn't really that close to any of them but mainly because he feared the questions his elegant, eleven-thousand-square-foot shrine to state-of-the-art architecture and high technology would elicit from them. It was just too tough to explain. Ty knew the progression of those imagined conversations. He had only taken the job to allow access to something else, something far more important. Like getting his name and his life back.

But his plan had failed miserably. Two years had passed without an inch of progress.

Maybe he'd taken the job as a form of therapy. Maybe he took it to fool Ronnie, since she wouldn't let him search for his specter out in the open. Maybe he'd been fooling himself all along—about finding it, that is.

But he'd gambled and lost and now it was time to pay up. He poured more Scotch and toasted again, "To the late Tyler James Greenwood, former software king and former respected family man."

He drained the silken, fiery liquid into his throat and jumped up, grabbed a fresh bottle of Glenmorangie from the wet bar, and headed toward the front door. On the way he realized that, aside from his eloquent death manifesto, checking out without a simple good-bye would be downright heartless. Ty weaved down the long hardwood hallway with its fifteen-foot arched ceilings toward the kitchen area, behind which was housed Ronnie's home office.

This home was the fantasy he and Ronnie had envisioned years ago, back when they were lowly programmers at a start-up software company, both making twenty-two grand a year and banging off the walls of a cramped two-bedroom, one-bath in Totem Lake with a baby on the way. *A perfect place to raise our kids.* He crushed the guilty pangs and focused on the job at hand. He made his way around the huge kitchen, the center island alone the size of their last kitchen. He passed by the soaring windows, designed by him to allow as much light as possible on those all-too-often gray Washington days. None of these things gave him the joy they used to.

In Ronnie's office, the glowing screen savers on her four computers, the multicolored digital displays from a bank of VHS, CD, and DVD players, along with the assorted red lights from power strips and modulators, all created a sort of Mephistophelean Christmas ambiance. Ronnie's firm, Digiware Microsystems, and its parent company, NovaSoft Digiware Systems, had a current market share of 1.4 percent of all software sales on earth. Ty was profoundly proud of his wife's accomplishments and was heartsick that in recent years he'd only been a drain on her.

You'll be free of me soon enough, honey.

He set down the bottle, plopped in front of the home business unit, and hit a key, calling up the desktop. He stared at the blank screen.

He typed out *I l-o-v-e y-o-u*. It looked stupid, trite.

That's all you can say?

He tagged it with *a-l-l*. Worse. I love you *all*?

He erased a-l-l. Back to square one. He erased *I love you* and then retyped it.

Christ, I can't even get past the suicide good-bye.

He stared at *I love you* and suddenly felt the overwhelming urge to cry. He'd held it in with iron resolve but now he was losing it. He took a hefty pull off the Scotch, sucked up his courage, and left *I love you*. He hyperventilated to regain emotional control, then walked out.

At the coat closet he selected his leather bomber jacket. *That'll be good to die in, kind of a James Dean effect.* He paused at the door and for the last time his eyes took in the soaring entry. Under normal circumstances, Ronnie would have set aside that coming Saturday from her busy schedule to decorate for Christmas. He used to love the holidays but his descent over the last three years had erased that little pleasure. One more time he rationalized that the kids would be well taken care of. He also knew they wouldn't be putting up decorations this year 'cause Dad would be dead. Bummer.

It was really for the best now—dying, that is. The liquor aided in staving off any further doubt. He was ready to rock. He stepped out the door. It was cold—probably thirty-four degrees—but he was drunk enough that he didn't really feel it. Though a long covered walkway connected the far end of the house and the garage, Ty walked out under the huge porte cochere, then across their massive circular plaza toward the six-car structure, clenching the whisky.

He entered the garage's side door and flipped on the lights, revealing a vehicle behind each of its six portals. Passing his work truck, a muddy Dodge Ram with a bedliner, he continued on to his baby, a mercury silver 1956 Mercedes-Benz 300SL Gullwing coupe swaddled in a car cover. Once his dream car, it would now be his longboat to Valhalla. He took off the cover and pulled up its door—the doors on the Gullwing opened upward—and slid down into the buttery, flame red leather. Ty's only concession to modernity had been to install a modern sound system. Ty had a technical mind tempered with the soul of an artist and felt this machine was not so much simply a great car as it was the pinnacle of a mid-twentieth-century ideal expressed by a meeting of art and engineering. He felt it would be fitting to take this car with him, as no one else could appreciate it as much as he did.

As with all Ty's vehicles, the key was in the ignition. No need for high security, given they were on the edge of the foothills of the Cascade range and much farther from civilization than indicated by the thirty-eight-mile ride into downtown Seattle.

Ty twisted the key, and the big in-line six's two hundred and forty horses roared awake. He had considered just sitting there and letting the fumes do the job, but he had another plan. He punched the clicker, and the door in front of the Mercedes rolled up. He sat there and stared into the void beyond his garage. As he put his hand on the gearshift, he paused, and his thoughts went back three summers to when all of his torment began.

3

It had been an unseasonably warm summer in Seattle. But on that Fourth of July weekend in central Idaho, up the middle fork of the Salmon River, it was an oven. When thirty-four employees and spouses of NovaSoft Digiware Systems gathered at the junction of Highway 93 and the dirt track leading them into the Frank Church River of No Return Wilderness Area, there was fleeting talk of fire danger. When a few of the more prudent souls suggested they reconsider (Ty noted they were all spouses, not the gung ho NovaSoft troops), the NovaSoft gang voted them down heartily. For they were invincible.

Everyone who had been with the company much more than five years had long since been anointed as a millionaire, and that included the warehouse guys who wielded rolls of shrink wrap for the UPS shipments. Most of the execs, including Ty and Ronnie, had stock and options worth many tens of millions. The dot-com collapse had hurt many others, and while NovaSoft had taken a slight dip, it had come back strong and lost little since the heady days of the big run-up.

The caravan moved slowly in the wake of a dust cloud up the one-lane fire road toward a place they were told was heaven on earth. Twenty miles of cloudy grit later, the promise was kept. They rolled their dozen vehicles into a dirt parking area. A few yards below them lay the river, a sparkling strand of aqua pura crowned in sunlit diamonds that hurt the eyes. The surrounding forest was a luxurious blue green and the mountains were nearly virgin, having suffered little at the hand of man. Everyone got out and stood silently in awe of the grandeur and dead quiet of the place.

Then the party began.

For two days in paradise the revelers drank and ate and shattered the silence of the woods. Ty and Ronnie had much to celebrate. Nova-Soft had just formed an entirely new company called Digiware Microsystems and Ronnie was the number three player. Ty would assume a new role at NovaSoft as head of product development while retaining his position as executive vice president. The moment was so heady, Ronnie had lightheartedly cautioned her extroverted husband about drinking too much. Ty was always the life of the party, and after a stint of hiking or river rafting or even just sitting around enjoying a cold Pilsner Urquell, he would always egg someone on to break with their tight-ass sensibilities and get wild.

On the third night, while everyone was roasting smores over a massive bonfire, Ty and the company's founder and CEO, Bill Bender, went into the forest up above the camp. Bender and Ty both loved practical jokes. Their current mission was simple: now that everyone was comfortable in the woods, scare the shit out of them. The two techno-nerds knew how to pull a joke that would stick. Before leaving town Ty had made a digital recording and downloaded it to his MP3 player. Now hidden from the group, Ty connected the digital player to some small but ultra-high-quality battery-powered loudspeakers. A bit drunk and trying to conceal his laughter from the noisy crowd below them, Ty put the recording on standby and whispered loudly, "Ready?"

Bender took a big pull off his beer. "What's on there?"

Ty could barely contain himself. "Animals!"

They both broke into booze-enhanced hysterics and Bender gestured, "Let her rip!"

Ty hit the play button. "I left a delay . . . twenty seconds and then *ggrrrrrr!*"

They broke into a run toward the campfire.

No one had missed them as they approached the rowdy crowd, bathed in the dancing firelight. Ty sat back down next to Ronnie and she handed him his beer.

"Where did you go?"

Ty smiled deviously. "Had to see a man about a dog. Or was it a werewolf?"

Suddenly a frightening sound radiated from above in the woods and everyone fell silent. As the eerie growl rose in volume, a collective gasp emanated from the group. Ty fought to hold back a laugh.

One of the programmers, a guy named Don Donovan, was incredulous. "It's . . . it's a bear!"

Another throaty rumble issued forth and one of the wives asked meekly, "Ohmigod! Is it really a bear?"

For more than a minute the terrible bear continued to taunt them from the dark forest.

"Do you think it's a big one?"

"Who cares, a bear is a bear, stupid!"

"Could it eat us?"

"Of course it could eat us!"

The angry bear caused the circle of petrified campers to draw closer to the fire and each other. Then, impossibly, a lion roared.

"Doesn't *anybody* have a gun?" implored someone.

Two women began to cry.

A trembling voice raised everyone's worst fear: "Is that a bear *and* a mountain lion?"

A fearful hush fell over the campers, and Ty and Bender positioned the bonfire between them so they wouldn't start each other laughing.

But when the elephant trumpeted, neither Ty nor his coconspirator could hold it in any longer. The dazed looks on the faces of everyone around that campfire caused the last good laugh Ty Greenwood had. The party dwindled at that point, partly due to the hour, but mainly because many felt the joke had gone too far. Ronnie finally laughed but later in their tent asked Ty, "Don't you think it was in slightly bad taste?"

Ty brushed it off. "C'mon, it was just a joke. And a pretty damn good one, at that."

The next morning the mood in the camp was damaged. A few, mostly spouses, grumbled that if anyone but Ty Greenwood and Bill Bender pulled such a gag, they would have been sent home and probably terminated. About half the gang now thought it was fairly funny, but the other half still didn't see the humor at all.

By around ten a.m. a large group prepared to shoot the rapids, sending several four-wheel drives downriver to retrieve the boats and ferry the passengers back. Ronnie wanted Ty to go, but he was ambivalent. It was already hot, Ronnie looked great in her bikini, and although the mood had risen somewhat since the group's sullen breakfast, Ty could still sense a few cold shoulders among the rafters. Ty kissed Ronnie, urged her to go, and said he was going on a solitary hike. She protested but he'd made up his mind. He hoped that by afternoon the ill feelings from the previous evening would have passed and things would be back to normal.

The rafters departed, leaving a half dozen people in camp, and Ty set off on a trail and began climbing. Though the forest stood tall and dense, the unremitting July sun beat into its heart, the hot air still and fragrant from the heated pitch of a million pine.

A half an hour into the trek Ty stopped to drink some water. The trail was rustic, with various fallen branches and overgrowth forcing him to stop occasionally to determine the path, but he was getting used to it and had a rhythm going. He guessed it was already ninety degrees and reckoned he had the endurance to climb for another hour before heading back. That would put him into camp around one, about the time the river runners planned to return.

After another forty-five minutes he had worked his way around the mountain above camp and finally reached the end of the trail, which culminated in a striking vantage point at the edge of a cliff. A good three hundred feet below was the river at what he guessed was a bend or two past where they were camped. The heat sucked all the moisture from his lungs and he was sweating torrents. With his water running low, the river suddenly looked very inviting and he decided to head back. The soft whooshing crunch of dry pine needles made him turn and look behind him.

In that split second Ty Greenwood's life changed.

Every hair on Ty's body, the skin on his neck and arms, everything clenched in a primeval fear stimulus response. In the thick of the woods not ten yards away stood a creature, manlike, apelike . . . some sort of hairy humanoid, like a gorilla standing upright on long legs. Motionless, it stared at Ty, and Ty froze dead in his tracks.

Jesus Christ, this is Bigfoot.

Ty judged it to be at least seven feet tall. Standing on the slope slightly above him, it was covered with shiny black hair with hints of red in the tree-filtered sunlight. With a conical head like an ape, its face and palms were bare and the hair around its midsection was thin enough to reveal dark skin. Its arms were proportionally long—nearly to its knees—and its face looked . . . sort of human . . . but not fully apelike either. But more immediately frightening to Ty was its massive physique. Its head seemed to sit directly on steep trapezoids that slanted to formidable shoulders that rose well above its chin level. Obviously tremendously strong, its arms were far larger around than Ty's legs and its chest was humongous. In the three or four seconds it took Ty to observe all this, he concluded that it probably had ten or twenty times his strength.

Yet despite his terror, Ty realized it looked more curious than nasty. They stared at each other for what seemed to Ty like a month but was about twenty seconds. Then it made its move—toward him.

That's when Ty bolted. He ran as fast as he could, knowing it was the wrong thing to do but his brainstem had seized control and ordered warp speed away from the threat. Never mind that the threat was undoubtedly faster. Ty imagined its steely grip on his neck from behind. That would be it. It would kill him and his body would never be found.

Death is nothing compared to the wait before it hits. His fright was so vivid he felt at times he was running out of his skin.

But suddenly he knew it was not behind him.

Having covered several hundred yards, he realized it had chosen not to follow him. He screwed up his courage and glanced over his shoulder, then slowed to a jogging pace. It was gone.

Almost giddy, he continued running, making a deal with himself that he would not stop until camp. That meant a solid forty minutes with that thing out there. He kicked back up to full speed. Within ten minutes the dry forest heat had turned his throat into asphalt. He reduced his pace to catch his breath, guessing he'd already covered the better part of a mile but probably had four to go.

As he slowed, he caught a glimpse of movement out of the corner of his left eye, and got the second biggest shock of his life: it was above him in the thick of the trees and pacing him. Suddenly Ty was a mouse with the cat nearby just watching, preparing to take him at any second. He knew he had no control over the situation, and his helplessness caused him to stutter-step and almost trip. He fought to keep his mind and body from giving in to stinking animal panic.

Though he couldn't always see it, he heard it boldly cracking and snapping alongside, just out of view, easily following without benefit of a trail. He heard its massive lungs sucking in and blowing out air like a diesel truck. Ty toyed with the idea of stopping and trying to communicate with it but dismissed that as suicidal. His only hope was to get to camp, doubting it would attack with a group of people around. He prayed the boats would be back with the full party assembled, making noise and welcoming him into their arms.

He thought about his kids, about Ronnie. He didn't want to die. Not this way. After he'd just landed on top of the world, how could God be so cruel as to kill him in this terrible, ridiculous way? He ruled such a cruel death as out of the realm of reality, then two seconds later reminded himself that reality was running somewhere beside him and could do anything it wanted.

For half an hour the thing paced him, even bursting ahead to wait until he passed, then catching up again. Ty's world was coming undone. Nothing else could have changed him as much as the next forty minutes.

Five minutes outside of camp he was beginning to think he might make it. Then it stepped out of the woods directly ahead of him, casually, as if racing past like the Road Runner with time to rest. As it stood astride the trail, its barrel chest barely heaved. Ty was utterly exhausted and knew the end had come. Out of breath, his legs gone, Ty stopped and waited, gasping and soaked in fear sweat, his resolve gone.

It cocked its head and looked at him for another moment, then turned and ambled up the very steep hill into the forest. In seconds it was out of sight. Ty just watched, awaiting its return, before realizing it was really gone.

He ran again, his body operating on adrenaline fumes. He entered camp shouting desperately for someone, anyone. The boaters had not yet returned, but a few campers were stoking the fire for lunch. He was sweat-drenched, scratched, and breathless, but the look on his face frightened them the most. The two women who first saw him later swore to the others that Ty had literally aged years in the short time since he'd left camp.

Once he calmed down, he began to relate his tale of horror. By the time the boaters returned, Ty had recovered his wind. The original re-cipients of the story, sympathetic when he first appeared, soon began having their doubts, and as the rest of the campers trickled back, Ty's tale began to sound taller and taller. Ty's angry insistence put many off, reminding them of the joke he had pulled only the night before.

Ty took Bill Bender aside and told him the story. While Bender pretended to believe him, Ty quickly saw through his act. Ronnie thought Ty was kidding at first, then read her husband's face. She knew he believed it but also knew it was just not possible. That anyone would claim to have been chased by a Sasquatch was totally ludicrous. After all, they didn't exist.

Around the campfire that night, Ty regaled all with the lucid minutiae of his encounter. Ronnie thought it sounded like a really great pitch for a video game, and she wasn't alone. Ty had a reputation as a showman and many felt he seemed to be setting them up, pitching a new product, an entry into the lucrative games market. For a while the whispered buzz was infectious about Ty's thrilling new Bigfoot video game. But as the evening wore on and no title was revealed, no release date mentioned, people began squirming over Ty's seeming de-parture from sanity. Some suggested that if it had really been Bigfoot, it was apparently playing with him and he was likely never in danger. Ty was furious. Someone ventured that the thing might be up above in the woods watching them that very moment. One man was pretty liquored up and suggested they take flashlights and go look for it. He got no takers. Ironically, the people who knew Ty best were the ones who most doubted his story.

Ronnie's troubles with Ty started that night when he insisted they sleep in their Suburban. Ty tossed and turned all night and in the morning looked like a wreck. His continued insistence finally resulted in six men walking the trail for about a mile looking for a sign of "Ty's monster." The men were not trackers and therefore missed myriad bro-ken branches and disturbed debris, but it didn't matter. By the end of the day no one believed him.

The next day Ty angrily informed Ronnie they were leaving. Against her wishes they left and drove the five hundred and some miles back to Snohomish. Ronnie read a book the entire way, not knowing what to say to Ty.

When they got home, Ronnie paid the sitter, then went to bed. Ty went to his office and started drinking. Ronnie found him the next morning snoring in his chair, a glass and a bottle nearby. She went into her office and called a psychologist. Ty woke up and called a press conference. And that's when the circus began.

Whether he was shut away in his office, gone for days or weeks in chartered airplanes equipped with infrared sensors and spy cameras, or off on treks to Idaho and northern Canada, he changed all of their lives. His offer of a huge reward backfired when kooks from all walks of life created a furious blizzard of false claims. And the media were all too eager to mock the ringleader.

All right, maybe it was the way I handled the story that made me a laughingstock. When the media pushed him, he pushed back, and in that contest he was doomed to lose. Should he have just laughed it off? Would it have gone away? The *Weekly World News* had been the first. And typical Ty Greenwood, he had to get in a fight, and that's when the mainstream media got hold of the story like a slathering, fevered dog and wouldn't let go.

But truth be told, from the time he first tasted success, Ty just knew things would go bad. The product of hardscrabble Pentecostals from the Mississippi Delta, Ty had been infused from birth with the rule that no great success goes unpunished by God. For so many years Ty heard his father solemnly spout Matthew 19:24 like a mantra, *"It is easier for a camel to pass through the eye of a needle, than for a rich man to enter the kingdom of God."* Although Ty's faith had long since been shaken, he was still programmed to look for dropping shoes. He had moved away from his roots, literally and figuratively, but his outrageous bounty had brought both a feeling of elation and a submerged sense of dread. Deep in his brain that Trojan Horse virus planted by his father so many years ago told him that getting higher on the mountain only meant you had farther to fall. With depression and whisky working to cement his self-loathing, Ty now accepted his demise as predestined.

Ty comforted himself that he had just relived that awful chapter in his life for the last time. He switched on the headlights, put the Mercedes in gear, gripped the huge, two-spoked wheel, and rolled down their hundred-yard driveway. He accelerated with a low burble from the exhaust pipes and headed into the blackness.

Sleeping with a window open a few inches for fresh air, Ronnie stirred, thinking she heard the far-off rattle of one of the garage doors. Then she heard a car engine, the unmistakable low thrumming of her husband's old Mercedes. Ty liked to fire it up once in a while just to hear it growl. She pushed down the edge of the comforter to see the clock's red numerals: 3:19. Too sleepy to reason out everything that was going on, her mind synopsized that he was depressed as usual and, judging by the varying pitch of the engine, he was going somewhere at three-something a.m. in a car he never drove. Whatever. She'd talk to Ty when she got home from her morning call with a major client in their London office. *Just like the workaholic Japanese to pick a Saturday for a teleconference* was her last semiconscious thought as she drifted back to sleep.

* * *

Ty slowly accelerated down Harrsch Road, a woodsy secondary lane with the occasional mailbox identifying another five- or ten-acre spread. Thick woods shielded all the houses from view. He heard the odd plaintive honking sounds of the Harrisons' emus as he passed them. His kindhearted neighbors had started rescuing the strange birds from various meat ranchers around the country who had discovered that emu meat was not going to be the new pork. Ty felt their hearts were in the right place but he wouldn't miss the shrill cacophony that ensued every time the birds panicked over a possum or raccoon.

His right foot propelled the big coupe down the road, as he worked his way through the gears and up the speedometer. It was a real shot of adrenaline to not worry about safety. In his sodden state he wondered if race car drivers felt any fear at such blurring speeds or if they could just shut off the fear. He decided to enjoy that last rush of utter carelessness, because he was going to die presently, probably by running into a bridge overpass or a divider or whatever good immovable object presented itself.

The needle edged past the century mark and he was now solidly overdriving his headlights as the car floated over the dips in the narrow, black, tree-lined corridor. Reaching to uncork the Glenmorangie and take a pull, he single-handed the wheel at one-ten, a wildly exhilarating feeling. He took out a CD and put it in the deck. The song's instrumental opening got Ty's hands tapping on the wheel. The lyrics evoked an image of the here and now:

> *You call me a fool*
> *You say it's a crazy scene*
> *This one's for real*
> *I already bought the dream*
> *So useless to ask me why*
> *Throw a kiss and say good-bye*
> *I'll make it this time*
> *I'm ready to cross that fine line . . .*

Listening to the song on the way home from work one evening recently, Ty had *really* heard for the first time what Steely Dan was saying. *Drink Scotch whisky all night long and die behind the wheel . . .* What a great, heroic notion. *Forget shooting yourself. Anyway, I don't even have a handgun. Forget pills, that's a woman's way to go. Exhaust fumes? Too passive. That's for pussies.*

"Passive pussies," he slurred and chuckled at the alliteration.

No, go out in style, my man.

They call me Deacon Blues . . . Deacon Blues . . .

Drink Scotch whisky all night long, or at least until you're shitfaced enough to do it, and die behind the wheel of a really fine automobile. No one could say Ty Greenwood didn't know how to kill himself.

They got a name for the winners in the world . . . As Walter Becker and Donald Fagen's words and music filled the car, Ty had another decision to make: where to do it.

I want a name when I lose . . .

He'd drive away from town and run himself into a nice concrete something or other.

My back to the wall, a victim of laughing chance . . .

He'd know it when he saw it. He took another pull off the Scotch.

This is for me the essence of true romance . . .

He wondered what the impact would be like, then realized he had unconsciously buckled his seat belt. He chuckled slightly, unfastened it, and put the Scotch to his lips.

Drink Scotch whisky all night long and die behind the wheel . . .

As he laid the bottle on the seat, Ty caught a flash of brown and a spark of red animal retinas in the distant penumbra of his headlight beams. He instinctively slammed the brakes as hard as he could and the old Benz, without benefit of antilock technology, tried to bite the mist-wetted asphalt. Despite his desire for self-destruction, Ty did not want his last earthly act to be mowing down a hapless doe and her fawns, so he rapidly pumped the brakes to maintain control. The deer family stood fast, as they are wont to do in the wash of headlights, and Ty pulled back on the wheel as if it would stop the car faster. Squealing rubber spooked the deer, but they didn't bolt.

As fast as the crisis was upon them it was over. The car stopped so close to the deer, Ty could see their black, shiny noses—even their long eyelashes. As they casually strutted from his path on stick-thin legs, he honked the horn to speed their departure.

Now they move. "Shit! Stupid goddamn deer!"

The car sat in the middle of the road, wrapped in the dark woods, running lights glowing, exhaust steam quickly dissipating in the frigid early morning air. Ty's heart raced. His hands shook as he grabbed the Glenmorangie and took a slug off it. *Glug, glug, glug.* He was supposed to be on his way to his final destiny and a *near-death experience* had him rattled. Great. What did that tell him?

Easing away at a greatly reduced pace gave him more control over his mental resources, more time to figure out just what it was he was doing. If anything, he wanted some control over when it would happen. *If it happens,* he now thought.

A few minutes later he saw a familiar landmark and slowed. He couldn't believe it but he'd driven the wrong way, and instead of heading away from Snohomish, he'd driven *into* it. At almost four in the morning there wasn't much going on except some men drinking beer in front of a bar that had closed a few hours before.

A half block away, for some reason he wasn't quite sure of, he pulled into the town's only 7-Eleven, sliding in front of the windows filled with racks of magazines. The kid behind the counter made eye contact, probably because he'd never seen a car like that. Ty shut off the engine, took another swig off the Scotch, and slouched as best he could in the low-backed seat.

His eyes went from the storefront to the instrument panel to his hands on the wheel. In the fluorescent glow of the store he examined the lines and veins in them. Good hands, they still looked youthful despite his being technically defined as "middle-aged." They were the same hands that had held his wife when they made love, when he slipped the ring on her finger, when he cut the cord when his children were born . . .

Don't do it. Think of your family . . .

Oh, that's not fair.

Then the trump card. His left brain, in desperate overdrive to make its case for survival, ran footage of the faces of Ronnie, Meredith, and Christopher, shrunken into hideous masks of anguish as they learned of his violent suicide.

Ty lost the battle to die right then and there, and tears began streaming down his cheeks.

No, no, no, I've been over this, I can't live!

But I can't die . . . because of them.

Oh shit. No, no, no . . .

Reason, and all the whys and why nots dissolved into a sea of tears as Ty crumpled behind the wheel of his old German car, sobbing like a man without hope or answers, save for one: he would continue living, yet he didn't have the faintest idea how.

Todd Shelton had been plagued by wicked acne from the time he was eleven. Now nineteen, he liked working graveyard because his acne scars and rampant zits made interaction with other people painful, and at this time of night in Snohomish, Washington, you interacted with very few people. And while Todd had seen some strange stuff working the counter for a year and a half at 7-Eleven, this was really weird. This older dude, like thirty or so, pulls up in a really cool old car, drinkin' right outta the bottle, then bawls like a baby. *Weird, man, definitely weird.*

He kept his eye on the guy and went back to sorting the morning newspapers. That was one thing his boss had been adamant about: "Put the papers out the minute they come in." As he straightened a stack of the local *Snohomish Daily News,* his eyes gravitated to a headline he found a little grabbier than usual.

It intrigued him enough to scan a few lines about some guy who'd disappeared from his truck and left his engine running. Todd wasn't a good reader but the bits of info he gathered made him wonder why a guy would do that. *Weird, man.* He shrugged it off as shit happens and stuck the papers in their slot.

He looked out again and the dude in the cool car was wiping his eyes and drinking some more. Todd shook his head. *That's fucked up, man.*

5

Daylight slowly crept into western Washington, and warm ocean air from Puget Sound glided over the chilled layer from the upper reaches of the Cascades, creating wonderfully buoyant air currents. A western red hawk wheeled lazily a half mile above an asphalt ribbon dividing lushly carpeted peaks. The hawk watched that dark ribbon and followed a small speck as it climbed higher and higher up the mountain track.

Inside the speck, a year-old dark metallic green Jeep Grand Cherokee, Mitch Roberts absentmindedly pushed a Springsteen CD into the dash player, then immediately punched the eject button, mindful of the man next to him, whose arms were crossed, his head bent in a light sleep.

Mitch was clean-cut in a square-jawed, buttoned-up, Christian Coalition kind of way. To kill time and keep his mind busy he invented a mental game of juxtaposing his life with that of his snoozing companion and fellow litigator. Mitch had been married for eleven years and had two kids. Mitch's companion, Jack Remsbecker, had been with Mitch's law firm for about two years and had never been married. Mitch had been with the firm longer and was making partner first. Jack was almost as good as Mitch was but had a few more years before the partners would invite him into the inner sanctum. Mitch's recent promotion was marked by a gigantic suit filed five years prior that had just paid off in a massive settlement. Partnership was a done deal.

They had spent the previous evening in very different ways—Mitch with his family in their home on the west slope of Queen Anne overlooking downtown Seattle, while Jack partied with a girl named Shannon he had met the night before at a bar on Lake Union. Having left Shannon's apartment on Capital Hill only two hours ago, Jack found his way back to his condo in Kirkland just in time for Mitch's five a.m. knock at the door. Now he was making up for lost sleep on the ride up Highway 2.

An avid hiker, Mitch had conned Jack into tackling a trail by Mount Brayton, a seventy-two-hundred-foot knob northeast of Seattle near the loggers' havens of Sultan and Gold Bar. Mitch figured hiking could kill two birds, fostering camaraderie while giving them yet another goal to achieve together.

Mitch steered off a ramp and climbed a dirt and gravel road for about five miles, smiling to himself that the slightly muddy lane-and-a-half was about the most challenge he had given this four-wheel drive since he bought it. To his mental checklist he added a note to wash the Cherokee when he got home. He slowed at the turnoff and pulled onto the apron near the trail head.

Mitch tapped Jack. "Wake up call. Caravan leaves in five minutes."

Jack blinked to a pained squint and glanced at his watch. "Forty-five minutes? You must have been driving eighty."

The rush of cold dampness gripped them as they opened the doors. It was a week before Thanksgiving. Snow had fallen in the past couple of days but had mostly melted off. Thirty-eight degrees at best, gray clouds floated in to block the predawn sky. Mitch stepped to the back of the Jeep, opened the hatch, and pulled two day packs to the lip of the door, knocking his three-year-old Brittney's Barney the Dinosaur doll out onto the ground. He smiled as he tossed it back inside.

Mitch pulled sandwiches wrapped in foil from a plastic cooler. "Chicken or tuna?"

Jack wandered to the back of the Jeep, a lit cigarette already dangling from his mouth.

Mitch couldn't believe this guy, not yet awake and he's hacking a butt.

Jack took a drag. "You pick."

Mitch shoved two sandwiches into a backpack and tossed it to Jack, who stabbed at it with his cigarette-free hand but missed.

Mitch eyed the cigarette reproachfully. "What the heck good does hiking do if you smoke two packs a day?"

Jack proudly displayed his pack of Marlboros. "Low tar. And I don't smoke two a day. One and a half, tops."

Jack fetched a cell phone from his gym bag and Mitch held up a hand. "No phones. We're communing, remember? Anyway, it probably wouldn't work up there."

Jack shrugged and tossed the phone back into the bag and closed his door.

Mitch aimed his keyless transmitter at the vehicle and locked it with a little chirp, then slipped the transmitter into the pocket of his yellow Gore-Tex parka. In the distance a stone escarpment, capped in patchy snow, jutted five hundred feet above the tree line.

"That's it," he said, his finger arrowing at a slight irregularity in the trees that zigzagged across the mountain's face. "Nine miles, there and back."

"Great," said Jack sarcastically. "I can't wait."

Four hundred feet above the two hikers, the hawk spiraled lazily, and from this vantage point his extraordinary eyes could make out the texture of their clothes and hair. Although he had excluded them as prey, he continued to watch them for they did not belong here. The hawk continued to drift on the growing morning thermals in search of movement in the forest below. He was hungry. Catching an updraft, he soared a few hundred feet and used the added altitude to bank toward the flank of a densely forested slope. Sailing toward it he felt a presence, not a movement, not a smell, not a sound. But something.

Deep inside his small brain a circuit was receiving a vibration on the frequency band just slightly above that of his material world. Like the feeling one gets just before something bad happens. The hawk could not know what it was. It just *was.*

He normally would have sounded off with a screech, but his brain told him to fall silent, so he automatically flapped his wings to give himself some distance from the oncoming hill. There was something to be avoided in those trees. But it was not like the human animals.

This belonged here.

6

Ty awakened, and as weak as the dawn light was, it knifed his retina. As soon as he could focus he saw he was in front of a 7-Eleven in the Benz. He vaguely remembered pulling in—when, he couldn't recall. But he did know he felt like warmed-over dog crap and the half-empty bottle of Glenmorangie on the floormat testified why. He lifted the door, painfully slid out, and shuffled into the store.

Todd Shelton noticed the blondish guy in the rad car had come alive and was entering his store. He was taller than Todd expected.

"Hi. Cool car. You okay?"

"Yeah," Ty muttered. "Got some coffee?"

"Right there. Just made it. Uh, what kinda car is that? Is that like an old 'Vette or somethin'?"

"No," Ty said, patting his jacket. Just as he felt a wave of nausea, he realized he'd left home without his wallet. "Shit . . ."

"Is that one of those DeLoreans?"

As sick and hungover as Ty was, that this bonehead had just mistaken a Rembrandt for a Thomas Kinkade touched a nerve. "No!" he snapped, exacerbating his headache. Then he softened his tone, anticipating he might need a favor from this unenlightened, pimply youth. "It's a nineteen fifty-six Mercedes 300 SL Gullwing," he explained patiently.

"Cool. A buddy o' mine, actually his brother, has a Gullwing. But, it's, like, a cycle."

"That's a *Goldwing*. A Honda Goldwing," said Ty as he made eye contact, trying hard to be nice. "Hey, I left my wallet at home. Could you spot me the coffee? I'll come back and pay for it later."

He waited as the kid pondered for a solid ten seconds in blank concentration. Finally Ty repeated, "I'll pay you back." Then, trying to clinch it, "I'm good for it."

"Uh, yeah, okay," said Todd. "But you gotta do it before my shift ends."

"Sure. Thanks," said Ty.

Todd consulted his black plastic Timex. "Uh, I'm off at eight."

Suddenly Ty's stomach failed him. "Bathroom?" he croaked.

"Uh, it's just an employee lavatory, but—"

Ty couldn't wait and leaned over the tall Rubbermaid garbage can adjacent to the Slim Jims and herbal energy drink display and vomited up a jaundiced, ninety-two-proof Scottish barf. Feeling better instantly, he wiped the spittle from his mouth and chin and focused on Todd's grimace.

"Sorry," said Ty. "I don't feel too good. I'll tell you what . . . ," as his eyes dropped to the name badge, "Todd. I don't think I can make it home and back that fast, so I'll bring it back tomorrow with a tip for you. How's that?"

Todd narrowed his eyes suspiciously. "Uh, yeah, okay."

Ty poured a jumbo coffee and as he turned to walk outside, the same news headline that captured Todd's attention caught his eye:

Weyerhaeuser Man Missing
Sheriff Acknowledges Few Clues

A longtime Weyerhaeuser employee, Joseph D. Wylie, disappeared Tuesday morning while working his shift eight miles northeast of Index. Wylie, 47, a timber steward for the company, was investigating a report of a large number of broken trees on Weyerhaeuser land when he vanished. According to police sources, his truck was found on a company-maintained access road, out of gas, with the ignition key in the "on" position. Wylie's supervisor, Jack Kelleher, said that Wylie had been with the company for more than 20 years and was a good employee. "Joe wouldn't just take off like that. There's got to be something wrong," said Kelleher. Weyerhaeuser officials were working with the Snohomish County Sheriff's Department in investigating the matter. A sheriff's spokesman acknowledged the agency had no solid leads in Wylie's disappearance. The police report also mentioned the presence of alcoholic beverages found in Wylie's vehicle. A resident of Monroe, Wylie has a wife and two children.

Ty was riveted by two words: *broken trees.* Badly hungover, he focused hard, reading and rereading the short article, slowing each time to savor those two significant words. Ty wondered if the article was a cruel joke, perpetrated by the gods to tease him at his lowest ebb. But Ty also felt there was something to fate or coincidence and that maybe he was supposed to see this story at this exact point in time.

"Hey, uh, Todd, mind if I take a copy? There's something in here I need."

Since unsold copies of the *Snohomish Daily News* got shitcanned anyway, Todd didn't really care. "Yeah, okay," he shrugged, "just add that on."

This news of the possible misfortune of another had given Ty a reason to live a little longer.

While Jack Remsbecker hated the first five hundred yards of the trail, since it only pointed out how he needed to quit smoking, his hiking partner loved it. Mitch saw it as a metaphor for his career, his life. Things had been grueling in his twenties but then the trail of life smoothed out and now he could manage whatever fate handed him. He enjoyed his life and felt pity for Jack's hollow, bachelor existence. Mitch thought it was a waste not to share your life with those you placed above yourself—a great woman, then great kids. Those who saw such sentiment as a corny, traditional sociocultural cliché Mitch dismissed as cynics, truly believing that love conquered all and that it was a basic human need, like eating or sleeping. Maybe that's what separates us from animals, he thought.

From his vantage point high above, his eyes were cemented on the two multicolored forms moving slowly up the trail. Like the hawk's, his existence generally comprised a series of actions and reactions. When he was hungry he ate, when he was tired he slept. And his waking hours were spent in search of sustenance, of which he required a great deal. But unlike the hawk, he had the power of advanced thought. And unlike the hawk, he could make these two creatures his prey.

A mile up the trail, with Mitch setting a purposely competitive pace, Jack stopped, winded.

"What's wrong?" Mitch asked as he slowed but didn't stop. "You toast already?"

Jack gulped air. "Screw you, I'm fine. I'm just not here to set a record, that's all."

"Okay. I'm warmed up and don't want to stop. I'll meet you at the Y."

"Yeah, okay," agreed Jack. "Give me a sec. I'll be three minutes behind you."

"I won't bet on that," Mitch threw in sarcastically.

"Yeah, whatever."

As Mitch continued up the trail, Jack was irritated that his partner's pace was that of a thirtysomething guy with no vices. *How can you live like that? Guy's married to his college sweetheart and has done everything by the book.* Jack's heaving breath made nice little stratus clouds around his upper body. When he felt short of wind like this, he did the one thing his body demanded and his head knew was wrong: reach for a cigarette. He lit up and that first pull of smoke felt like pure oxygen, his distress instantly relieved. He tarried for a few minutes savoring the taste of the Marlboro Light.

He watched as the small two-legs separated. One continued past him but did not see him sheltered in the trees. The one that stayed behind burned

*something that issued a smell he did not know. He watched it. The small
two-legs were the Keepers of Fire.*

*He did not know how they controlled it, but that didn't matter. They
controlled it and let it loose and they had brought misery to him and his
own. And he hated them for it.*

*The Great Fire had been during the last warm time and he had been
moving since. He was drawn here because he felt he was close to the place
of the small two-legs. After the Great Fire passed, he resolved to kill every
small two-leg that crossed his path. Not for food, but for what they had
done. But now there was something new, something he had not known
about killing them.*

*The first one he had killed only a few suns before surprised him when
its fear spilled out in waves. He felt its mind voice as he would a warm
breeze on his face or a drink from a clear, cold stream. It was then he realized the small two-legs died in a different way than a bear or deer or
salmon, in that their feelings of terror were powerful and their thoughts
were more like his own. Though their bodies were tiny and fragile, their
mind voices were strong. Destroying them, but only after draining their
fear, gave him a feeling that was as strong as anything he had ever
known—like fire, like mating.*

*And as he moved closer to where they lived, he had found that, even
when he was not near them, he could sometimes hear the strange sounds
from their heads, those complicated, confused mind voices. He could even
feel them when they were far away, sometimes as far as a distant valley.
He had never killed anything for any reason other than to fill his belly or
protect his tribe, but now vengeance had taken on something unexpected:
pleasure.*

Five minutes after finishing his cigarette, Jack needed another. He knew
he shouldn't but he stopped, pulled out his smokes, and popped one
up. *So what if I'm an extra five minutes late to the rendezvous point?*

As he lit up he heard a rustling in the trees nearby. Probably a chip-
munk or a raccoon or something. He was hoping to hear it again so he
could report at the office Monday he'd encountered some real wildlife.
He did hear it, only this time it didn't sound like a squirrel. It was definitely bigger. He held a lungful of smoke, keeping as quiet as possible
for fear of spooking some decent fauna like a deer. *Maybe it's a bear.*

Quickly exhaling and stubbing out his cigarette, he began walking. Fifty feet up the trail he heard it again, a faint crackling of small branches and maybe some partially dried needles on the floor of the forest. He heard, even felt something, as if whatever it was had decided to pace him, just out of sight in the trees.

"Mitch? That you?"

He didn't believe this was Mitch's style, but the man was certainly cunning enough and perhaps possessed just a hint of cruelty. Maybe he wanted to scare his pal. He thought he had detected a little passive aggression from Mitch.

"Mitch? Come on out, you jerk. I know it's you."

Nothing.

Jack quickened his pace despite the increasing upward slope. There was definitely something following him. Maybe worse, whatever it was seemed to be toying with him. His mind raced to find possibilities. A mountain lion? A bear?

Another slight crackling sound off trail caused a chill to rocket down the back of Jack's neck. He didn't think a bear would follow someone. It would prefer to just make its move or stay away altogether. It had to be Mitch. Jack stopped and confronted the wall of green.

"Okay, you made your point," he said, stifling his anxiety. "I'll keep up."

Nothing.

Mitch would have shown himself at that point, unless he was perverse in a way Jack had never imagined. Now Jack was scared and started moving even faster. He remembered the stories of people being mauled and killed by mountain lions a few years back in California and got goose bumps. Then he tried to get a grip, telling himself it was ridiculous that a grown man would be frightened by a few sounds.

This is silly . . . fucking nuts, frankly.

Jack stopped again and peered ahead into the forest. For a split second he thought he saw movement, a large shape quickly passing, then nothing. He stared, shaken. He couldn't have seen what he just saw. Or thought he saw. Optical illusion, or . . .

Jesus, it really is a bear. It's a fucking bear.

Yet his mind rejected the possibility because bears just weren't that big. He'd seen them in the zoo and watched *Grizzly Adams* as a kid, and though that was certainly a big bear, it sure as hell wasn't anywhere near as big as—

No, he refused the thought. *Nothing* in the forest was *that* big. *Yet trees don't move . . .*

He watched the small two-leg and felt its rising fear. It pleased him that they were also easy to catch and provided a large quantity of good meat. Once the colorful yet tasteless outer skin was sloughed off, their soft underflesh was savory, better than any other animal he had eaten.

He stood in the shadows of the big trees and watched the small creature standing down the trail and followed the teachings of the old ones: let the hunted come to you.

Jack's radar was on full alert but there was nothing on the horizon. Nothing but that shape he thought he saw. After twenty seconds passed with no other indications, he tried convincing himself he hadn't seen it. He *couldn't* have seen it. Frightened, he turned and started trotting uphill, pulling out his pack of Marlboros as he moved. He'd light on the fly.

Then he had a feeling of something warm on his back. It was such a palpable but bizarre sensation, it caused him to stop and turn. Jack fully expected to see the sun peeking from behind the clouds, but instead the unbelievable figure facing him astride the trail a mere fifteen yards away caused his entire body chemistry to change in a split second. His hand went lax and his cigarette pack dropped.

Jack Remsbecker's mouth fell open and his perception became dreamlike, as if what was happening was not actually happening. It was the body's extraordinary defense mechanism, preventing the mind from sending such shocking distress signals to the organs so as to actually induce heart failure or blackout from shock. Keeping going, despite all hope's seeming gone, was part of a last-ditch effort by the body to save itself. The failure of that safety mechanism, when confronted by a certain, terrible death, can cause some to literally die of fright.

Jack was not so lucky.

He saw it all coming through eyes filtered by absolute, paralyzing fear. As this towering engine of destruction quickly advanced on him, he stood stock-still, his Timberlands glued to the muddy trail. Somewhere, some cognizant brain function ruled flight impossible. The figure moved so fast, too fast for something that big. And he saw the certainty of his death in its eyes.

As it reached him, his muscles crumbled and he fell backward. But it caught him by the face before he went all the way over and held him, the pressure just enough to keep him up. Then it lifted him off the ground. Its massive palm covering his entire face, Jack saw his peripheral vision flash with red flecks as his blood pressure maxed out.

He felt it bounding up the hill, off the trail. It carried him easily and, after a moment, stopped and shifted its grip to the back of his neck. It raised him, and their faces came within a foot of each other. As muscled fingers closed Jack's voice box off, he smelled the awful stench of this thing and stared into its terrible orbs, yellow centers glistening with white rage.

Then he heard—and felt—a popping sound like microwave popcorn. It was his spine.

Jack wanted to cry like a baby but couldn't get his lungs to respond because his neck had just suffered the catastrophic C2-C3 break, rendering his body from his shoulders to his toes into just so much flaccid meat. Then he felt hot breath as this unspeakable demon opened its vast mouth and bit into most of his face like an apple, from his chin to the bridge of his nose. With his vision still momentarily functioning, his severed spine didn't ameliorate the unbearable pain from his neck up or the stark terror of man's worst primal fear—that of being consumed alive by another creature. Jack's last chaotic sensations were unimaginable agony layered upon exquisite horror.

7

Not long after the recently demised Jack Remsbecker had been spirited deep into the woods, then cleaned and consumed like a slaughterhouse chicken, Ty was easing the Mercedes back into its tiled slot. By the clock over the work bench it was 6:52. He knew Ronnie would be up and there would be tension until he explained himself.

He crossed the plaza into the house, hung his James Dean death jacket in the closet, and staggered toward Ronnie's office, hoping to expunge his cryptic good-bye message from her computer. In the kitchen sat his six-year-old daughter, Meredith, in her pajamas, spooning cornflakes as if comatose. Ty knew that she would someday describe herself as "not a morning person."

"Hi, sweetie. Mommy up?"

"Yeah," she managed in a whisper.

"She been in her office yet?"

"Dunno."

In Ronnie's office the screen saver streaked Escherlike images of ducks and reversed ducks, the same image that had played earlier. Ty tapped a key and the message he had typed was gone.

"Shit . . ."

"Hi."

Ty spun to find his wife standing in the doorway, wearing a white terry cloth robe, wet hair wrapped in a towel, her arms crossed.

Ty looked surprised. "Hi."

Ty read her face, and despite her outward calm he saw the slightest bit of concern. As Ronnie undid the towel and tousled short auburn locks, her sloe eyes were cautious, inquisitive. She looked more like twenty-eight than thirty-eight. Her tossed gamine crop and pale, almost pixieish beauty gave the first impression that Veronica Greenwood was soft, even girl-like. Yet Ty told anyone who would listen that Ronnie had the balls of the family.

At that moment Ty desperately wanted her, physically and emotionally, but knew he didn't deserve to even come near her. She just wanted her husband to snap out of his malaise and come back to her. They both feared they would never be able to talk things out because the problem had become too complex. Yet they also acknowledged that very smart people sometimes overcomplicated the potentially simple.

"I love you too. We all do," she said, answering his earlier message. She lowered the towel and squinted. "You look terrible. What's going on?"

As Ty and Ronnie's eyes met, he suddenly felt deep shame over what he had almost done a few hours before. The betrayal and abandonment of his woman and children would have been enough to cast him into eternal damnation, if he really believed in that, which he sort of did. Ty chose to walk out, kissing her cheek as he passed. "I'm okay," he said.

Ronnie watched her husband disappear down the hallway. She had feared for her marriage but now she feared for his life.

Ty entered his office and thought of his Scotch-blurred promise to never return. He sat at his desk, unrolled the small newspaper clenched in his hand, and found those two words, *broken trees,* and reread them again and again, as if someone, an editor at this two-bit local rag had somehow stumbled onto the Truth. This just might be the Rosetta Stone Ty Greenwood had searched for to restore his name and his life.

Unlike anything else he'd seen in three years, this piece of news was alive and right in the neighborhood, and no one but Ty knew what it might mean. He picked up the phone and started to dial the newspaper, then realized they wouldn't be answering at seven ten on a Saturday morning. He hung up and stared at the headline.

Tears came to his eyes as a wave of emotion washed over him. *Please God, don't let this be a false lead.* Ty rarely prayed for anything, but this moment seemed appropriate. *Why did I see this? Tell me this isn't a joke to prolong my agony. Is this my answer?* Ty could wait to make that call. For if this wasn't what he had been seeking, then he would soon be back on that black road to oblivion, and this time he'd get it right.

As a light rain began, Mitch looked at his watch. He'd been waiting at the trail's Y for twenty minutes. After giving Jack ten minutes leeway, he allowed himself to steam over it. Why should he pay the price for this guy's excesses? Mitch didn't go out and get smashed and whore around till all hours in search of some cheap thrills.

My God, can't he move a little faster?

That's why he, Mitch, was making partner and Jack was lucky to get his leftovers. Mitch's brain angrily searched for analogies and metaphors for Jack's failed existence and his own growing success and it all came down to who would be first to the top of that hill ahead. That reasoned out—and after waiting precisely twenty-four minutes— Mitch continued up the trail, his staccato pace matching his irritation.

John Baxter heard the phone ringing as he slipped the key into the lock of the glass door. He scurried, as quickly as he could at seventy-four, to the reception desk. It wasn't even seven thirty and someone was calling, probably to place an ad for their missing dog in the classifieds.

As publisher of the *Snohomish Daily News,* Baxter's pragmatic hope was that a big shot from some outfit like Burger King or Albertsons had finally seen the error of their ways and was caving in and buying a double-truck ad in his humble paper. But he quickly dismissed that fantasy as he picked up the receiver. Too early and it was Saturday. His bet: missing dog.

"News."

"May I have your editorial department?"

Baxter detected a faint Southern drawl. "You got it," he answered.

"There was an article about a missing Weyerhaeuser guy. You know it?"

"Yup."

"You write it?"

"Nope," said Baxter. "A kid who works for me wrote it. A Wazzu intern."

Wazzu was the local diminutive for Washington State University, the state's farm club for journalists.

"Her name's Verna McKay," continued Baxter. "What can we do for you?"

"I'd like to talk to her about the information in the . . . Is she around?"

"No. Won't be in today. Maybe I can help."

"I'm just curious as to what you have on file. I assume you have a file?"

"Yeah, but it's confidential. Why do you need it?"

"I'm sorry, you are?" Ty asked.

"John Baxter, editor and publisher. And you?"

"Ty Greenwood," Ty blurted, immediately realizing he shouldn't be too aggressive. "If you could let me look at the file, I would really appreciate it. I'm with the . . . Forest Service . . . and we're concerned about the disappearances lately."

"There've been others?" Baxter asked, ever the newsman.

"Yeah, a few," Ty lied. This was the first such occurrence he knew of.

"Forest Service, huh?" Baxter figured nobody would make this up. "Yeah, okay, you can come down, but the file stays here."

"Thanks. I'll be down later this morning."

John Baxter hung up wondering why the guy had seemed so excited just to see a file about a logger who'd gone missing. People disappear in the woods all the time.

Mitch got to the top of the mountain, brushed the snow off a rock, sat down, and fished a sandwich out of his pack. He took a bite and thought of that sorry sonofabee Remsbecker. He glanced at his watch and shook his head. Though he hadn't seen Jack for over two hours, he calculated his hiking partner was a little less than thirty minutes behind him.

He finished off the first sandwich and gazed at the holy panorama. There were two nearby peaks taller than his, and the rest of the view was of smaller knobs and valleys of dark green stretching below. He was a few ridges away from the highway and had lost sight of the depression it tracked through. He liked being unable to see the road or any evidence of man.

He sucked in the chill air, which expanded in his lungs like bottled oxygen. Mitch decided to finish his lunch—it was nine thirty already—and head back. He smiled as he pictured Jack at the office Monday, struggling to counter Mitch's version of the hike.

Forty minutes later, Mitch's emotions had run the gamut from irritated to disgusted to worried. He briefly considered that Jack might have gone back to the Cherokee to nap off his hangover but then rejected that because Jack had no way to get inside. Having been out of touch with each other now more than three hours, Mitch began glancing off trail in particularly dicey spots for signs of misadventure. He knew his friend was not as trail savvy as he was; Jack really only went on the hikes to humor him. Mitch felt guilty over his lack of patience and his competitive drive since Jack was only along for the fellowship.

After quickly descending several miles, all the while scanning the nearby slopes and ravines, Mitch seized on a patch of color twenty-five yards ahead. He trotted to it, the small white and gold pack of Marlboro Lights standing out against the drab moist dirt and rocks. Mitch put the pack in his pocket, then looked around, knowing Jack would not have parted with them unless something was very wrong.

"Jack?" He called out, "Jack!"

His voice echoed away and he waited for a response, even a moan.

"Jack! Hey, Jack!"

More nothing, except the white noise of soft rain and occasional rustling of birds and small ground dwellers.

"Jack!" Mitch gazed around. Not prone to cursing, he categorized this situation as appropriate for an expletive. "Shit," he whispered.

Regretting his no-phone rule, he decided to jog to the car and call for help. He'd have either the King or Snohomish County Search and Rescue here in no time and they'd have Jack back safely before dinner.

Now this will be a story for the office on Monday.

It was easy to jog using the trail's steep downward slope. About five minutes into his trek, he slowed and looked around, feeling that the sun had just peeked through the rain clouds. A few yards later, after searching the sky, he realized he was actually having a gut instinct that something was wrong. He increased his jog to a run, his feet now sailing over the ruts and dips and switchbacks in his path. Racing down the trail, he suddenly had the perception he was being *pursued*. He acknowledged it was totally irrational, but there really seemed to be someone following him.

Even though he knew it wasn't Jack—everything told him it wasn't—he stopped to look, to listen. Though the soft whisper of rain had let up for a moment, he was woodsman enough to be aware that what he heard was *nothing*. Not a sound other than air molecules rubbing together. Not a bird, squirrel, cricket, or fly. Nothing. On any other day he might not have even noticed, but there was something ominous about the silence and a slow wave of panic swept over him.

Mitch began to run as fast as he could.

Running at full clip for ten minutes, he saw landmarks that told him he was less than half a mile from the Cherokee. The syncopation of his footsteps on the hard-worn trail beat a steady rhythm, and as he poured on the coal, the snapping of twigs and thudding on hardpan under his feet no longer sounded synchronized with his footfalls. Even in the split second of ground contact he was making, he could feel other, faster, bigger steps. Much bigger steps. It wasn't Jack and it sure wasn't anything he wanted to see. He concentrated on getting to the car and getting the hell out of there.

He was sprinting now, flying. The rain returned, harder than before.

Throwing his stride off slightly, he reached into his pocket and pulled out his keys and the Cherokee's remote transmitter. That little black piece of plastic was a welcome feeling in his hand and gave Mitch the illusion he was safe already. But that warm shell shattered when Mitch heard *the breathing*—metered, regular breaths, but at a volume and resonance that were unreal, like a horrifyingly deep, basso profundo recording someone had concocted in a sound studio and was now playing behind him to frighten his wits from him. And it was working.

And the giant footfalls of the other were overpowering his too. Now there was no doubt something was right behind him, something really big, something . . .

Through the misty rain he saw the Cherokee and readied the door clicker, his thumb on the button—the one-touch, driver-side-only door opener. Closing on the truck, only thirty seconds more and . . .

He was going to make it . . .

He knew it . . .

He was so close. He visualized jumping into the front seat and . . .

It grabbed him.

There were no doubts in his mind as he was stopped short and lifted two, three, four feet off the ground, the transmitter falling out of his hand. A throaty, tearing snort from a maw like Cerberus's told him he was not in the grasp of anything human, and when he was whipped around, his mind froze as he realized he was merely a smaller animal in the clutches of a vastly superior animal.

He was held by the waist and neck, as the process of ending Mitch Roberts began. His body was bent backward like a fragile bundle of sticks into an impossible position, resulting in his nervous system's failing and his lungs collapsing from the pressure.

With calamitous shock buffering his awareness that he couldn't breathe, Mitch made what puny attempt he could at struggling, his arms being the only limbs that still worked. His immense attacker responded with animal fury and ripped Mitch's left arm from its socket, the limb separating from his body in a jet of blood and torn skin, muscle, white tendons, and red and bluish striated ligaments. Mitch looked up at his arm, now flailing above him, as a spray of crimson wet his face. Then he swung his head and looked into the inhuman face of his killer.

8

The young man glided over the forest path like a strong breeze, his feet making just enough contact to create locomotion, his movements the essence of economy. A Native American at the man end of his teens, he wore overalls, a denim shirt, and bulky old boots. Tall and lean, he wore his long black hair tied in a ponytail. The dusky forest through which he passed was sullen, a heavy mist dulling any detail past four or five yards. Although his face was a mask of concentration, the panic in his eyes betrayed the fact that he was running for his life.

A few dozen yards behind him, something menacing, something evil moved through the fog, pacing him. Like the oversized shadow of a normal person projected on a wall, only this shadow had substance.

The young Indian knew its thoughts and it knew his. The huge shadow toyed with him, knowing it could overtake him whenever it chose to. The teenager's only hope was to let it think he was far from safety and let it continue to enjoy the hunt, right up until the moment they came out in the small clearing by the home of his family. He prayed his grandfather would have felt or heard the cries of his spirit or the murderous thoughts of the shadow and would be waiting in the field, his shotgun leveled.

The shadow sensed this deceit and began to close in, slapping the trees in its path. The slapping sent a message to the boy that he would soon feel an open blow from that massive hand, breaking his neck and ending the chase.

Slap, slap, slap . . .

It got closer and closer.

Bam, bam, bam . . .

The sound was louder, the shadow behind him, its breath on his shoulder, his hair . . . his neck. Closer, closer . . .

BAM . . . BAM . . . BAM . . .

Oh-Mah . . .

BAM! BAM! BAM!

"Hey, Chief, you okay? You in there?" asked a muffled voice.

BAM! BAM! BAM!

The Indian awoke, confused, the pursuit over, his life saved by a knock at the door.

"Hey, Chief, you okay?" the young voice repeated through the door as the knocking came again.

The young Indian, suddenly an old man, looked around the dim trailer, getting his bearings, the drapes drawn against Southern California's sharp November sun. He sat up and moved slowly to the door and opened it. A blaze of strong morning light blinded him.

"Wow, I was worried," said the young voice. "You all right?"

The old one, a lanky six three in a chambray shirt and jeans, his long hair now silver but still pulled back as in the dream, slowly focused on the twenty-year-old production assistant two steps below. Behind the PA was a flurry of activity—normal operations for a major motion picture studio. He remembered he was in a Star Waggon outside Sound Stage 27 at Paramount Pictures on Melrose Avenue in Los Angeles.

"Chief? You okay?" said the youth, unsure owing to the chief's lack of response.

"Yeah, no problem," answered the old Indian. "What's up?"

"They need you in makeup, sir. Five minutes."

The man nodded and turned back into his trailer. He went to the sink, poured water into his cupped hands, and splashed his ancient, lined face. He was having the dream from sixty-some winters past more often now. He couldn't even take a nap and there it was. He hadn't been sleeping at all the past week, partly because of that noisy hotel on Santa Monica Boulevard in Century City, and partly because of that infernal dream that wouldn't leave him alone.

The dream had become increasingly vivid and for some reason the dreams were closer calls. *It* was closer. *It* was now almost upon him just as he'd wake up. His greatest fear now was that if it caught him, in the dream, as it almost really had in early 1945, he would never wake up. He was afraid that as old as he was, and since his strength was diminished because he was still smoking two and a half packs a day, *it* would grab him in his sleep and he would go to his death in its clutches. He couldn't let that happen. What was about to happen had been coming for a while and he knew, or rather *felt*, it was finally time. *This is it.*

He shivered at the thought and looked up at himself in the mirror. *Seventy-nine and looking every day of it.* He dried his hands, found his fringed, beaded, buckskin jacket and fished out the pack of Kools. He lit one. The jacket was part of the look he'd cultivated for years. He wore it whenever he traveled because Chief Ben Eagleclaw, as he was known in most of the credits of the many films he had done, would wear a jacket like that. Back home in Eureka, plain old Ben Campbell simply wore windbreakers and sweatshirts.

Ben took a deep, unsatisfying drag off his cigarette and thought of his agent and how he might break the news to him, because Ben Campbell was just about to get Chief Ben Eagleclaw in a lot of trouble—and there wasn't a darn thing the chief could do about it. There was something out there—he wasn't really sure what—but he could feel its pull. He knew some of what drew him were the unanswered questions from sixty years past. But there was something else now, something new, something strong, something *living.* Ben wasn't sure yet if it was simply his awareness of this thing, like a tickling feeling on the edge of his consciousness, or if there was some entity out there, actually *in contact* with him, somehow. Ben couldn't yet fathom the details but he did understand one thing: the decisions he would make in the next few minutes would change everything.

Despite it being ten thirty on a Saturday morning when Ty entered the office of the *Snohomish Daily News,* the place was a bustle of activity. In his best Forest Service uniform, he'd tidied up as much as he could despite feeling pretty much like Morning of the Living Dead.

John Baxter approached and sized up Ty. *Great. Some alcoholic Forest Service guy on a wild goose chase.* It took one to know one: John had been sober fourteen years, two months, and five days.

"John Baxter," he said, extending his hand, then passing Ty an olive green Pendaflex folder. "You can sit here and take notes if you want. Just can't let you walk out with it."

Ty took the folder. "Sure, not a problem. Thanks."

Baxter went back to his office and Ty sat on the vinyl sofa in the open reception area. The low buzz of workers and keyboards clicking faded to nothing as Ty took out a pen and opened the folder. The notes reflected the conversations between the article's author and Joe Wylie's boss, as well as a Snohomish County Sheriff's deputy named Bill Alexander. Though the exact location of the incident was unclear, Ty noted down the approximate area, then wrote down the pertinent names, as well as Wylie's phone number. He decided to call Wylie's wife as soon as he got home.

As he left, he caught Baxter's eye and waved his thanks. Baxter nodded.

John Baxter sat back in his tired-out Clark Kent office chair. His newsman's gut told him there was something familiar about this guy, but he just couldn't place it. He glanced down at the name on the scratch pad he had borrowed from the reception desk earlier that morning.

"Ty Greenwood," he said softly to himself.

He had a suspicion there was more to Mr. Greenwood than Mr. Greenwood was letting on. He tore off the page of the pad and put it in his desk. He thought briefly about calling the Forest Service but decided to wait. *Next time Greenwood appears—and he will—this newsman will do some checking.*

Five minutes after his wake-up call, instead of settling into a makeup chair, Ben was now aboard a Cushman, riding with a PA across the immense Paramount Pictures facility. To get that lift he had lied to one of the assistant directors that a family emergency was forcing him home. The AD summoned the director and Ben repeated his tale of a family crisis. The more he elaborated, the more he believed his own story.

Only when he'd been formally excused by one of the executive producers and given transport to the parking lot did he realize he was setting things in motion that were beyond his ability to analyze. This was real Indian instinct stuff, he thought, blowing off a major picture on a gut feeling and a dream of something that had happened sixty-some years ago.

Crazy Indian stuff.

As their cart made its way down the narrow alleys between sound stages, Ben's mind flew back in time, briefly revisiting the events that had brought him to Hollywood. On returning from the South Pacific in '46, Ben and his unit came ashore in San Francisco. Instead of going home to his tribal lands in Northern California's Humboldt County, he went south with some buddies to see Hollywood.

One night, while he was standing in a crowd ogling Betty Grable and June Haver as they alighted from limos at the premier of *The Dolly Sisters*, a small, sharp-featured man approached Ben and handed him a card. "Wanna work?" he asked. "I need Indians, especially tall ones. I'm in *the business.*"

Ben had heard the Lana Turner myth and had seen enough movies to know which business the guy meant. So, despite the ribbing of his buddies, he made the call the next day and it led to a job as an extra on a Republic serial playing a member of an angry Apache horde. Soon he was in demand, one month as a Shoshone for RKO, the next at Warner Brothers playing a Creek. Neither the directors nor the audiences knew the difference and he was more than happy to take the then kingly sum of thirty-five bucks a day to eat dust, whoop a lot, and get shot by guys like Duke Wayne and Ward Bond.

By the time Ben got his first picture with a screen credit, the man who had handed him the card, an independent ten-percenter named Al Levine—who was now his agent—decided Ben Campbell needed an "Indian" name, so he became Ben Eagleclaw. With Al's promise it would get him more money, Ben went along with it. That years later another Indian, Benjamin "Nighthorse" Campbell, would be elected U.S. senator in Colorado didn't matter much because by then Ben's last name was known to nearly everyone as Eagleclaw.

Flashing forward to the late sixties, and after nearly thirty years at three packs a day, Ben had weathered his face into a finely tuned symbol of Indian wisdom. Al, then eighty-one and still his agent, decided to give Ben a promotion. Having ascended the casting ladder from muscled brave to seasoned warrior to medicine man, Ben was ready, Al felt, to become a chief. He told Ben it could mean his price would go up. It was Al's last earthly strategy, for an hour after their ill-fated lunch at Chasen's, when Al made Ben a chief, Al died.

Ben always wondered if it had been the chili.

Though Al's cavalier disregard for Indian cultural protocol made Ben a little uneasy, he decided, partly out of respect for the dead, to go with the handle of chief. Over the years he had witnessed menacing redskins evolve into noble Native Americans, and though the roles for Indians had dwindled, Ben was established enough to command parts that just needed a sage old guy. Of course, the fact he was a sage old *Indian* guy certainly wasn't lost on Hollywood. Ben thought of the late Al Levine as they entered the Paramount parking lot. He wondered how he was doing in heaven or the Great Spirit Village or wherever old Jewish guys went. Al's partner Sid had retired around ten years back and had given the business to his son, Jay, who had assumed Ben as a client. Ben wondered how he was going to tell Jay he'd just walked off a picture, something he'd never done before. He shook his head.

Crazy Indian stuff. Honest to God, I've got no damn idea what I'm doing.

He muttered softly, "Damn crazy Indian stuff," and the PA driving him, barely more than an embryo, noticed.

"Huh? Did you say something, sir?"

"Oh, just an old Indian chant," he fibbed. "'Bout the past . . . and the future."

The fresh-faced kid gazed at Ben in reverence. "Awesome."

Ben figured the lad had never been anywhere but the womb, his home, school, prom, and this movie studio. Ben smiled inwardly that the kid had bought his bull because he was old, had done lots of movies, and was an Indian.

Then it occurred to him that maybe it wasn't a complete load of crap.

He felt the conflict between the movie Indian, Chief Ben Eagleclaw, and the real Indian, Benjamin Campbell, the Tsnungwe of Humboldt County. The real Indian was running the show. The movie Indian was just along for the ride. This was instinct territory, because the movie Indian was the only one still operating on a conscious level.

It was a little scary because he felt too out of practice for this spiritual Indian stuff. As they arrived next to his rented Chrysler 300, Ben looked at the kid and smiled slightly. All of twenty and this baby had just helped show him something he didn't know.

Old dogs . . .

9

Ronnie was at the office conferring with her Japanese clients when Ty arrived home and found their seventeen-year-old sitter Amy in the kitchen, watching the Three Stooges with Meredith. His daughter was laughing at the television, whereas Amy looked bored. Ty knew his little girl was going to have an interesting future, because any woman, six or sixty, who liked and understood the Stooges definitely marched to the beat of a different drummer. In her less serious days, Ronnie had professed a real love for the Knuckleheaded Triumvirate, and Ty had never told her that aside from her looks, brains, and good heart, her appreciation of the Stooges had gone a long way in convincing him to marry her.

"When did Mrs. Greenwood say she'd be back?" he asked Amy.

Amy started to answer Ty's question, "Uh, I think she said, like . . ."

"One," Meredith filled in, without taking her eyes from the mayhem Moe was perpetrating on Larry and Curly. Ty went down the hall to his office, picked up the phone, and punched in some numbers.

"Hello?"

"Mrs. Wylie?"

"Yes."

"My name is Ty Greenwood. I'm very sorry about your husband. I have a few questions if you've got a moment."

"Sure, uh, who are you with?"

Ty explained how he got the number from the newspaper, then lied that the Forest Service was interested in her husband's case. Lori Wylie seemed okay for several minutes, but then the questions seemed to veer off into a weird area.

"Did your husband ever mention any odd things while he was patrolling the woods?"

"Odd? Like what?"

"Strange things he might have seen. Things out of the ordinary. Sightings of anything, I don't know, bizarre?"

"You're with the Forest Service?"

"Yes."

Lori Wylie was suddenly very uncomfortable. "Look, Mr. Greenwood, my husband is missing. My kids and I are worried sick. I don't have the faintest idea what happened to him and I'm praying he'll come home any minute. I'm doing my best to keep it together but the waiting is killing me. Now you call up and scare me by asking stuff like—"

"Mrs. Wylie, I assure you I'm only trying—"

"I have to go. Please don't call me anymore."

She hung up. Ty immediately called back but the phone was busy.

At Burbank airport Ben decided he'd first go home to try to explain to Doris what had happened. He knew his journey was going to take him farther north, but he first needed to stop off and calm his rather fragile wife. He heard each of her questions in advance as if she were right there.

"What was the emergency?"

"Can you go back and finish the movie?"

"Will we lose any money, Benny?"

"You're going where?"

The young woman behind the Southwest Airlines ticket counter was trying to get his attention as he woolgathered about how his overwrought spouse would take this uncharacteristic AWOL episode.

"Sir? Sir?" she said. "Excuse me? What's your destination?"

Ben smiled apologetically. "Sorry, just gettin' old. SFO, then Eureka. Guess I'll needa connection."

"Yes," beamed the reservation agent, now that she had reeled Ben back. As she typed away she looked up.

"I'm a big fan. I've been watching you ever since I was a little kid."

"Lately, that's what they all say," he joked.

A few minutes later, as he settled his too-tall-for-the-cramped-window-seat body, he looked out over the vast, flat expanse of concrete and contrasted it with where he knew he was headed. Then it hit him. Though the director had assured him they'd shoot around his scenes until he got back, the real Indian just gave the movie Indian a piece of news that shook him:

You're not coming back.

Between the hours of one and five that afternoon, Karen Roberts's mental state went from concerned to worried sick. Her husband Mitch was a creature of habit, and holding to deadlines was as natural for him as breathing.

By six p.m. the fabric of Karen's orderly world was in shreds.

After dialing 911 and being told she couldn't file a missing person's report until Mitch had been absent for twenty-four hours, Karen went bonkers. She screamed at the operator, then phoned half a dozen friends, including Mitch's boss, Seth Olinka. Seth calmed her down, then hung up and phoned a good friend of his, Seattle city councilman Dick Wright, who in turn called a friend of his, the mayor. Within minutes the entire Eastside, from Snoqualmie Pass to damn near the Canadian border, was crawling with alert patrol officers from ten jurisdictions and agencies, all under orders to find a green Cherokee somewhere out in that cold, misty rain.

At five after nine, high above Highway 2, the headlights of a Snohomish County Sheriff's cruiser flashed across a parked green Cherokee. The Ford Crown Victoria patrol car slid in next to it. Through his rain-smeared windshield, Deputy Sheriff Bill Alexander read the plate, then turned on his dome light to read the info he had scribbled down while driving to a fender bender a few hours earlier. It was a match. He still got a thrill whenever he radioed in. It reminded him of the shows he had watched as a kid.

"One david thirty-two, a reg."

The dispatcher answered, "Go ahead."

"Two-seven-five, victor, x-ray, victor."

A moment later the dispatcher came back with her response. "That's the eleven-twenty-four. It's okay to impound."

Bill answered, "Copy."

A moment later, "One david thirty-two?"

"Go ahead."

"Check that impound. We'll eleven-eighty-five. What's your ten-twenty?"

"Copy that. I'm six and a half miles north of the Dillard Road turnoff on Lone Mountain."

"Copy." A moment later, "One david thirty-two, be advised S & R is ten-thirty-nine and will be on scene in approximately twenty minutes. The nine-twenties are Mitchell Roberts and Jack Remsbecker. They may be in the vicinity and may be unable to respond. Use caution."

"One david thirty-two, copy that. I'm going code six."

"Copy."

Bill put the mic back and reached onto the passenger side floor for his rain hat. Outside his safe little cocoon of light and warmth was wet, black isolation, and suddenly he didn't want to leave. It was an out-of-place feeling, especially for a guy who had grown up around these woods. But finding that Weyerhaeuser guy's truck a few days before, door open, engine dead, and keys in the "on" position, well, it was downright spooky. Twenty-five-year-old Deputy Bill had just watched an *X-Files* episode dealing with alien abductions, so finding that empty truck sent his mind racing.

He left the patrol car idling, shook off his anxiety, grabbed his Maglite, and opened the door. The mist kissed his face as he stepped out and closed the door. The patrol car's exhaust swirled around him as he swung the flashlight about the perimeter to get his bearings. He left the cruiser's dome light and headlights on, which gave him an idea of the immediate terrain.

Pointing his flashlight into the Cherokee, he saw a gym bag on the passenger side floor, a jacket, and a Barney doll in the back cargo area. Nothing suspicious. The vehicle was locked. Bill moved toward the trail.

"Hello? Hello?" he shouted.

No echo returned as the moisture-deadened air sucked up the

sound. All he heard was the slight hiss of rain. Moving toward the trail, swinging the beam back and forth, he looked for something, anything.

"Hello? Mitchell Roberts?" he shouted again, this time vainly hoping a name might bring a result. "Jack Remsbecker?"

Slowly heading up the rocky slope, he didn't plan on going too far, given his peculiar uneasiness and the fact that search and rescue would be arriving pretty soon. Less than fifty yards later, his warning system, that unconscious mechanism that keeps you from walking out in front of a car or putting your hand on a hot burner, was going off full-bore in his head. Just as Bill reached his absolute turnaround line, where he was about to lose sight of his car, his flashlight glinted off something. Washing the light beam over his surroundings, he saw and heard nothing else, so he walked toward it. Six feet away he recognized it as a keyless car door opener with a few keys attached.

Deputy Bill looked before touching, searching for clues as to how it got there.

Thrown? Dropped? Dropped on the way out? Way back?

Reaching what few conclusions he could, he picked it up, wiped the flecks of mud away, and pocketed it. Who knows? It might not even belong to the Cherokee.

He swept the area with his flashlight, and a sizable reddish brown stain on the rocks stood out from the grays and browns. He crouched to examine it more closely. It appeared to be congealed blood, a liver-colored spatter about half the size of one's hand. It had been raining all day, so Bill knew that if this were actually blood the original amount had probably been much greater. As he stared at the dissipating gore, he felt a sensation wildly out of place on that black mountain trail in the middle of a chilly, light rain: sunshine. He could swear he felt it all the way through his uniform and his rain slicker.

He didn't stop to analyze it, he just turned tail and ran. As fast as he could.

It was nearly one hundred yards to the cruiser and he made it in record time, jumped in, slapped it into reverse, backspun his tires in the muddy gravel, and took off. He didn't care whether they asked him why he left. He'd make up an excuse if he had to. He'd come back when someone else was with him. Lots of someone elses.

But for now, all he knew was *Screw the hikers, I'm getting the hell outta here.*

10

At the offices of the Snohomish County Sheriff's Department, Mac Schneider was just finishing off the main course of his dinner, a six-inch Subway turkey breast with Dijon dressing, when Karl Carillo leaned over their facing desks.

"Any chips left?" asked Carillo.

Mac had not yet touched his small bag of barbecue chips. He liked to save them for last.

"Go for it," he waved.

Carillo grabbed the bag, tore it open, dropped most of the contents into his hand, and sat back down. Mac rationalized the loss of the chips as less time in the gym. At thirty-three, Carillo had eight years on him and could burn it off faster.

"You washinthehkstmmrrw?" Carillo asked through a mouth clogged with potato pulp.

"Again . . . in English?"

Carillo swallowed. "You watchin' the Hawks tomorrow?"

Mac knew Carillo was a rabid fan of the Seattle Seahawks. Though Mac had moved from L.A. three years earlier, he was still a Rams and Raiders fan, even though both teams were long gone from L.A.

"I hate football."

Carillo eyes went wide in disbelief. Then he caught the slightest twinkle in Mac's eye and knew he'd been had. Mac and Carillo had only been partners six months.

Carillo took a twenty out of his wallet and dropped it on the desk. "Friendly wager. I'll take us, you take the Eagles."

Mac looked out the window at the rain-slicked asphalt parking lot. "I think you got the idea of a 'friendly wager' mixed up. Oh, yeah, and the Hawks are favored by seven. Let's not bet and say we did."

Carillo snorted, grabbed his twenty, and sat down. "Pussy."

Mac was used to Carillo's macho bluster. Although they both carried good-sized caseloads that they worked individually, they often worked as partners. Carillo was an ex-Marine who still sported a jarhead buzz cut. Though four inches shorter than Mac's six one, Carillo loved to pump iron in the gym and spent a lot more time on the firing range. Bottom line, Carillo was just more typical of the man drawn to law enforcement. Sporting a cropped mustache, Carillo drove a sizable pickup truck, rode motorcycles, and drank a lot with the other cops. He'd made detective faster than anyone who had worked their way up the hard way in the department and was tireless at running down leads.

Mac thought cycles were dangerous, didn't like the way he looked in a mustache, and wasn't particularly mentally stimulated when socializing with his brethren in law enforcement. Mac didn't even appear to be a cop. As a sheriff's detective he worked plainclothes, wearing a sport jacket and dress pants just as he had when he was with the LAPD. Black Irish handsome, he came across more like a therapist or even a low-keyed trial attorney and had the attentive air of someone who listened from the moment you opened your mouth. His intelligently sensitive hazel eyes said, *I respect your point of view, I understand your feelings.*

The phone rang and Mac grabbed it. "Schneider."

It was Mel Benedict, sergeant in charge of search and rescue.

"Just got a call from the boss," Benedict said. "Two hotshot Seattle lawyers with friends in high places are MIA on a hike up in east county. Probably nothing, but one of our patrol guys found the car's door clicker up a trail."

"Maybe they just dropped it. Why you calling me?"

"Could you take it? I'd really appreciate it."

"Take it? Take what?"

"We need to make an effort here, Mac, at least till they're found."

"No. No way. MPs are one thing but this is just hikers. I don't do hikers."

"Look, I've got my in-laws. Plus you're the man."

"Please, I'm choking on the smoke," said Mac.

Mac was used to it. He had been a decorated detective at the Los Angeles Police Department's Robbery Homicide Division for ten years. His experience in the legendary war zones of the Hollenbeck and Rampart divisions had bestowed a major rep on him among his fellow sheriffs in his new home in northwestern Washington. He had left the LAPD and moved to the Northwest to join the Snoho Sheriff, and, hopefully, enjoy a little slower pace. Because of his considerable "combat" experience, many in the department turned to Mac for advice or to bat cleanup.

"It would be a huge favor," said Benedict.

"So you want me to go up there and help look for these clowns? A detective looking for hikers?" Mac said, hoping to squirm out of a drive into the rainy mountains.

"Is Carillo there?"

"Yeah."

"What's he on?"

Mac looked over to Carillo. "What're you on?"

"I'm working twenty-two cases. Why?"

Benedict overheard Carillo. "I figured he had nothing to do. Take him with you. You could use the company. This is just for show, Mac. The word came down to make this a priority. I just need someone to steer things. You two go, I'll give you a few deputies, and S & R will be there. Hey, these guys'll probably turn up by the time you get there."

"You owe me," Mac answered and hung up.

Carillo shrugged questioningly.

"Some lawyers went missing," said Mac. "Hikers, probably just lost. But they're VIPs. Wanna take a ride? Benedict says I could use the company."

"Shit, I thought it was something good."

Mac smiled. "They can't all be drug busts. Let's roll."

Carillo grabbed his jacket, then paused, looking at the wall-mounted television. It was tuned to the Saturday ten o'clock news. A reporter, a drop-dead gorgeous blonde, had just appeared, doing a report from a rain-soaked location.

Mac read his partner too easily and rarely missed a chance to mock him. "I didn't know you ever watched the news."

"Fuck the news," gasped Carillo, "You see her? What a fox!"

Mac shook his head. "Don't you get enough at home?"

Married with two kids, Carillo ignored Mac's question. "Man, I'd tap that," he leered.

"Put it back in your pants, Romeo. The sooner we get there, the sooner we're done."

Carillo took a last look and headed toward the door. As he was exiting the office, Mac stole a quick glance at the television. Carillo was right. The reporter was beautiful.

As he ascended the soft soil of the sheer grade in five-foot strides, the nocturnal buzz of small animal noises dimmed in his path. He could feel the presence of others, a gathering of the small two-legs. He reached a flat spot and followed it around the curve of the hill.

Moments later, many hardshells with colored fire on their backs came into view below him. As the hardshells arrived, they closed their night-fire eyes and small two-legs climbed out of their insides. His visual acuity was superb, and he saw other small two-legs walking between the hardshells. He did not know what power the small two-legs had over the hardshells, but he began to think the hardshells were either creations or servants of the small two-legs.

On first encountering hardshells he thought them living beings, but since he could feel the mind voices or vibrations of all creatures on some level, it was strange these had none. They seemed to be under the control of the small two-legs and, as the small two-legs were his new prey, knowing that about their relationship with the hardshells might be useful.

He knew the small two-legs had come for the ones he had killed. He sized up the assembled figures, watching as more hardshells came and many more small two-legs scurried about. His count of the small two-legs was two hands and four fingers. He visualized attacking them, knowing the waves of fear from so many would be a very strong sensation. Upon them so fast none could respond, he could quickly kill them all. The thrill of snuffing out so many of those frightened little mind voices was enticing. But his intelligence allowed him to imagine one or two escaping in their hardshells to warn the other small two-legs. And he knew there were others out there. Like rocks in a stream, many, many others.

No, he would watch. His belly was full and he would wait. Small two-legs were easy to take. He was closer to where they lived. He could take some when he was hungry, or take some for the pleasure, whenever he desired. He was beginning to enjoy his revenge.

He sat down to watch the activity.

11

So with this big front moving south, it looks like Puget Sound will be in for plenty more rain," cheerily intoned the stunning blonde who had just snagged the attention of the two detectives. "Reporting from a very soggy Bothell, I'm Kris Walker, Eyewitness News. Back to you guys in that dry studio. Jerry, Trish?"

A tinny male voice issued from their small monitor speaker.

"Thanks, Kris. Looks like you could use a blow dryer," observed Jerry.

Kris gave a ten-thousand-watt smile, her icy pale blue eyes sparkling despite the fact her fine flaxen hair had wilted like lettuce in the rain. The cameraman chopped his light and Kris Walker lowered her mic.

"We off?" she asked, still holding a smile, but now a notch lower.

"Yeah," said the cameraman, quickly striking his equipment to get out of the rain.

"Fuck yourself, Jerry," said reporter Kris Walker to her now disconnected associate in the dry studio twenty-five miles to the south. In one second Kris's stunningly pretty face had evolved into a cloud of anger. "Now get me the fuck out of here."

The news crew was fearfully silent as she tossed her microphone to the umbrella assistant and headed for the van. Climbing into the pas-

senger seat, she pulled out a pack of cigarettes and lit up. Her cameraman, Rick Kititani, a stocky man of around fifty, was at the sliding door
with his assistant, stowing their gear.

"Hey, Kris, I've asked you before, please don't smoke in the van,"
Rick pleaded. "It stinks and it's bad for the equipment."

Kris took a big pull off her cigarette, then exhaled into the van toward Rick.

"It's raining. You want me to stand outside and smoke? You've had
me outside for twenty goddamn minutes already. My hair's flatter than
shit and now you want me to stand outside? I don't think so."

"No," gritted Rick patiently, "I just don't want you to smoke in the
van. If you have to, I'll pull around the corner, we'll find a building, and
you can smoke under the eaves."

"Yeah right," she snorted, "and that'll *ever* happen."

At that moment, Rick wanted to strangle this girl. When he first
met her, the seemingly humble, supposedly green recruit from the Fox
affiliate in Tacoma, he concluded she was the best-looking woman he
had ever seen in person. From her soaring cheekbones to her ruler-
straight teeth and hair, Kris had a genetic endowment which others
paid fortunes to replicate but never quite realize. But if the eyes were
the windows to the soul, those limpid sapphires betrayed a powerful,
aggressive, and perhaps even malevolent intellect. Now, three weeks
after being charged as her cameraman, director, and occasional men-
tor, he couldn't stand her and had discreetly begun referring to her as
"the Asshole Goddess." Very discreetly, of course. She was the kind, he
feared, who would file a harassment suit in the blink of one of those
hypnotic eyes.

Kris was tired of the bullshit happy-talk stories they gave her. *"Go up
and report that it's raining in Bothell, Kris." Fuck that. Of course it's raining in Bothell. This is frickin' Seattle. It RAINS here! What a waste of my
talent. Give me some hard news.*

She fancied that a big crack bust in the Central District would give
her more credibility. Or the powerful theater of a guy crushed by a
crane down on the docks that would show off her talent for verbally re-
creating the horrific. Better yet, her imagination conjured a family of
six killed in a horrible, bloody collision with a cement mixer. She pic-

tured the emotions of the moment and how she would wring out every last drop in her report. Now those were stories she could sink her teeth into.

She knew Rick hated her, so she'd already begun laying the foundation for his demise with a few choice comments here and there to the right people. And as far as the "right people," she was actively cultivating her connections to them. Soon, she felt, she would have the power to drop the boom on anyone when the need arose. In her short but meteoric career Kris had evolved into quite a tactician in undermining fellow employees, then making them go away. She recalled her favorite *Twilight Zone* episode, during which an evil boy, when displeased, sent people to the "cornfield," a kind of horrific limbo where you ceased to function as a living entity. Kris enjoyed knowing that when crossed, she would find a way to send the offender to the cornfield. And it took very few slights for her to begin mobilizing a plan.

The slamming door of the Eyewitness News truck jarred her from her reverie of revenge. Rick plopped into the driver's seat, angry that Kris had lit another cigarette while lost in thought. She took another luxuriating drag and exhaled it toward her middle-aged, Japanese-American cameraman. She pondered the day when Rick entered the cornfield.

"Oh, sorry, Rick," she said mockingly, "I guess I couldn't wait for that shelter you promised."

As Rick pulled away from the curb, while formulating a comeback that would in no way be perceived in a court of law as sexist, harassing, or otherwise offensive, the radio connecting them with the station in downtown Seattle squawked.

"Hey, Mobile Five? Rick? Kris? Pick up," said a female dispatcher's voice.

Rick and Kris exchanged a glance. She was smoking, he was driving. A test of wills. Rick caved, grabbing the microphone. "Yeah, go ahead."

The woman's voice crackled over the speaker, "We've got a story for the eleven. Two missing lawyers. Went on a hike early this morning. Sheriff found their car. Rumor is they or their boss are good friends with the mayor of Seattle. You're the closest field crew. It's up Highway Two, above Gold Bar. Head that way, we'll get the exact location and feed you. Kris there?"

Rick handed the mic to Kris, who rarely exchanged pleasantries.

"Anything you've got, shoot to my Palm Pilot. Then get somebody in graphics to do a map. Who's on scene?"

Despite the energy she put into taunting, intimidating, and eviscerating her coworkers, first and foremost, Kris Walker was a newswoman.

"Yeah," the dispatcher replied, "Snohomish sheriff. You're slotted for a live at around eleven ten, so shoot your tape to us by ten fifty or you'll have to feed your own. I'll call back when I get the exact locale."

Kris put the mic back.

"Now we've got something," she said, looking heavenward to a Higher News Authority. "Oh please don't let them be found till I get my story."

Rick shook his head slightly but certainly not enough so she'd notice. God forbid.

Although Carillo hadn't been too thrilled about working in the mountains in the rain, when the Eyewitness News van arrived and that beautiful newsgirl alighted, he brightened considerably. Nudging Mac, he nodded toward the approaching blonde in the rain slicker. Mac had no time to react as Kris held out her hand.

"Kris Walker, Channel Seven. You in charge?"

Mac took her hand. "Yes."

Despite the wet chill her hand was warm and soft and she allowed it to linger in Mac's a bit too long. *She's even better-looking in person.* Mac forced himself out of his trance.

"You looked in charge." Kris smiled slowly. "Your name is . . . ?"

"Mac Schneider, detective, Snohomish County Sheriff's Department. This is Detective Karl Carillo."

Kris shook Carillo's hand. His grip and eyes told Kris he was married and on the make. She warmed to the other guy, the strong, quiet alpha dog.

"I'm doing a live report"—she looked at her watch—"in about twenty-five minutes. I need to get some background, shoot a tape piece, then get ready to go live with an interview. Is that okay?"

"Interview? Who?"

"You."

"No. Talk to our PIO."

"Oh, c'mon. I just want someone to confirm some of the facts that are known. I can't wait for your PIO."

Procedure was to have the public information officer make any press statements, but to Mac this seemed pretty simple. And that she was so damned good-looking helped.

"There's not much to tell."

"Maybe." Kris pulled out her Palm Pilot. "'Mitchell Roberts,'" she began, "and Jack Remsbecker, litigators, Addison, Olinka, and Cothran. Big law firm. Connections to the mayor, governor, yada, yada. Roberts, married, two kids, Remsbecker, single, both thirty-six.' Okay, so these two guys get lost, not one or the other but both, and there's no snow for an avalanche, so what happened? How do two guys, lawyers of all things, just get lost? I mean, the map shows there's only one way up and back."

Mac and Carillo's eyes met briefly as they realized she knew more than they did. Kris noticed their reaction and decided the situation might allow a more ratings-friendly interpretation, since so few facts were known.

Ronnie sat at the kitchen counter sipping herbal tea. It had been a long day. When she got home a little after noon, Ty was nowhere to be found, Amy the babysitter was on the phone with her boyfriend, and six-year-old Meredith was launching sponges in the pool with two friends. The so-called retracting pool cover was broken at half-retract, exposing a lot of open water—a natural but potentially deadly playground for unsupervised kids. After rushing out and scolding the little girls, Ronnie shuddered as she pictured one or more of them falling in and getting trapped under the cover. That clinched it: Ronnie decided they needed a live-in.

She was also beginning to regret her insistence on having the pool. When they planned the house, she wanted a pool and Ty reminded her that in this climate they'd be lucky to use it two months a year. She found a solar heating installer and handed Ty the brochure, assuring him the pool would be cozy year-round, costing next to nothing to heat. Ty used his proposed wine cellar as a bargaining chip. He wanted a formal, fully stocked cellar under the house, with a secret passage, just like one they had seen in a castle in Bavaria. Ronnie dismissed the wine cellar as pretentious, citing the marginal amount of wine they consumed per year, but Ty held firm. So Ronnie got her pool and Ty got his wine cellar.

Now the pool was ice cold ten months of the year because the solar heating system lacked one critical item: continuous solar radiation. Meanwhile Ty stocked the cellar with more than $40,000 worth of wine, and in three years they had cracked open exactly sixteen bottles. But the kids loved popping open that hidden door just off the kitchen, running down the stairs, and hiding from each other among the Château Margaux and Lafite Rothschild.

She glanced at the clock on the microwave, saw it was 11:05, and picked up the remote for the plasma TV on the kitchen wall and clicked on channel 7. She'd focus on someone else's problems for a few minutes.

12

The fridge was empty and that pissed off Russ Tardif. Back when he was married, it was always magically full of Cokes and Miller Lites. He shut the door on the apartment-sized cooler and contemplated that long walk to the house. He decided he'd do without a soda. It was a little after eleven, raining cats and dogs, and he wasn't up to the hundred-yard uphill trek for one lousy soda.

He could tell how hard it was raining because Cold Creek was roaring below. His little utility shop was perched so close to the edge of a fifteen-foot-high cutbank that Russ was afraid the creek would someday eat away the bank and topple the shop and all of his treasured equipment into the water.

A tattooed, thirty-one-year-old machinist, Russ commanded either a precision gap bed tool room lathe or a CNC bed mill at Boeing's Everett facility eight hours a day. The massive aircraft plant, the birthplace of the 747 airliner, was a collection of outsized buildings encompassing nearly one hundred acres *under roof*. After work, Russ would make the long drive home, then trudge down the hill to the ramshackle shed he called his shop to operate even more machines, changing his medium from aircraft aluminum to wood.

Russ's obsession with woodworking led to the undoing of his marriage, but married life wasn't all it was cracked up to be. Regular marital sex turned out to have more disadvantages than jerking off, and on top of that his wife's constant nagging about going into Everett or Snohomish for some damn thing like dinner with people he couldn't stand or stupid swap meets eventually got on his nerves. He'd heard time heals all wounds, and truth be told, the only thing Russ really missed was the full fridge.

He shrugged it off, picked up a two-by-ten and reached for the switch on his DeWalt table saw. That's when something on his ten-inch television grabbed his eye. This total knockout reporter was talking and the little map above her left shoulder looked like his neighborhood—if you could call the middle of the woods a neighborhood. He walked over, brushed sawdust off the volume knob, and turned it up.

"... *were last seen this morning around five a.m. I'm with Snohomish County Sheriff's Detective Mac Schneider, who is heading the search. Detective, what efforts are being made to find the hikers?*"

The camera panned slightly and a man stepped into the frame next to the pretty reporter. She held out the microphone to him as a superimposed graphic identified him. Streaks of light sparkled as rain traced through the bright light mounted on the camera.

"Search and rescue is on scene and we also have a canine tracking team," said Mac.

"What are the odds of the men surviving overnight?" Kris asked.

"Hopefully they'll be found before that, but we understand they're experienced hikers and dressed warmly, so we feel the odds are good."

"You also have another sheriff's detective on scene, right?

Mac nodded. "That's correct, Detective Karl Carillo."

"So why are two detectives in charge of looking for missing hikers?"

"Standard procedure. We're just filling in for search and rescue. That's all."

"I understand you found a door clicker and some keys. Plus one of your deputies said he may have seen some blood," she said. "So I assume you suspect foul play."

"No, the facts absolutely do not warrant any such conclusion. Contrary to what you may have heard, no blood was found."

"So," she continued, "if this is so routine, why did they send two detectives? Wouldn't such a show of high-powered investigators be more in keeping with a homicide investigation than a simple missing persons report?"

Mac angrily set his jaw. He didn't need to tell her on live television they'd been sent because of politics.

"Two people," Mac said, grating each word, "are overdue from a hike, and yes, the car door opener was found. They might have simply dropped it. There *may* be blood, but so far there's been no sign of it. Extrapolating foul play from those thin facts would be the height of irresponsibility."

Mac turned and walked away.

"Do you suspect foul play, detective?" she yelled as he walked away.

Mac kept moving and didn't look back.

"Detective Schneider, do you suspect foul play?"

Kris was impressed. She'd never heard a cop use the word *extrapolating*. This guy was different from the cops she'd met. She gave Mac a few more dramatic moments to retreat from her interview, then repressed a huge cat–who-ate-the-canary grin and turned back to the camera as grim as she could fake. "So, apparently the search team will work for at least a few more hours to locate the two missing men. If they are not found by then, the search will resume at dawn, although we hope they're found soon, safe and sound. Kris Walker, Eyewitness News, reporting live from the mountains high above Gold Bar."

Russ Tardif turned down the sound. He wondered why the cop had been so rude to the gorgeous babe reporter. Then he thought about the hikers. They seemed to have gotten lost just a few miles over the hill, and around here that was damn near next door. He flipped the switch on the saw. Maybe they'd show up at his door. *Well, I sure as hell got no sodas or beer to offer 'em.*

Mac turned away from Kris and headed up the hill toward deputy Bill Alexander, the discoverer of the Cherokee. Mac was angry for two reasons: first, he'd been set up by the reporter, and second, he had a funny feeling she might be right. He'd arrived on the scene with an attitude of irritation almost as bad as Carillo's, knowing they were just babysitting the scene while S & R did their thing. But now that they were here, Kris Walker's supposition suddenly didn't seem so completely out of the realm of possibility. It made him mad that he'd been asleep at the switch when she abruptly reminded him things might not be what they appeared to be. The deputy said he may have seen some blood, but whatever he may have seen had long since been washed away in the rain. Mac was irritated with the young deputy for leaving the scene before securing the evidence but shrugged it off after recalling the frequent mistakes that fellow cops made when he was with the LAPD.

Kris watched Mac walk away. She handed her microphone to the soundman and set off on the detective's heels. She was delighted he'd played into her little drama, but she realized she also had an opportunity to act the victim. She wasn't sure he'd fall for it, but she had nothing to lose.

"Hey, what the hell's with you, walking out in the middle of my interview?" she yelled.

Mac didn't slow his pace, nor did he look at her. "You asked me before we went on the air and I said your theory was irresponsible. Then you asked me on camera."

"You walked away."

Mac stopped and she caught up with him. "You blindsided me," he started. "Two detectives from the Snohomish Sheriff are here heading a standard department search. The head of our search and rescue team was unavailable, that's it. Normally he'd be here running this search, not us. We're here as a courtesy. Maybe you don't realize this, but 'missing' is a helluva long way from 'presumed dead,' or worse, 'presumed murdered.'"

"I can surmise anything I want," she returned.

"And I can refuse to acknowledge your idiotic speculation," he shot back and started walking again. "You're only hurting yourself, lady."

"Look," Kris said, following and radiating as much sincerity as she could summon. "I'm sorry, but I was just looking for a story. Missing hikers, important guys, two detectives checking it out . . . What am I supposed to think?"

"Don't think, report," he snapped.

"Give me a break," she said. "Listen, I'm not stupid. If I think there's something you're not telling, I have to speculate."

Mac stopped again and they stood toe to toe. He was aware there had been what many considered a degradation in the quality of news reporting in the past ten years. If the lead story wasn't big enough, make it big enough by lots of hyperbole and speculation. This reporter had an incredibly irritating approach, but as she brushed the hair out of her face with her left hand, he saw she was not wearing a wedding or engagement ring. Mac set his jaw.

"Two guys are missing a few hours—"

"Twelve hours."

"Okay, twelve hours, and you want to make this into a much bigger story than it is," he said. "These men have families and friends, and until we have something solid, I don't want anyone scaring the crap out of them with their half-assed theories."

Kris felt he was stonewalling her. That's when she noticed he had no wedding band.

Married and hiding it, or divorced? My guess is divorced.

"Okay," she said, "then just tell me why you're here."

Mac turned quickly to avoid her question and almost ran into Deputy Bill Alexander.

"The search team's been up a couple miles and got zip," Deputy Bill reported eagerly. He'd never done a TV interview.

"How many trails could they have taken?" Kris asked. "I thought there was only one."

Mac shot her a "Don't talk to my guy" look, but she ignored it and turned to Deputy Bill.

"Yeah, only the one," said Bill. Then he added, "There's a Y up a ways, but it all goes to the same place. The top."

"Have you searched off trail?" she asked.

Bill looked to Mac, unsure how to answer since they hadn't. Mac didn't want to answer the reporter's questions but also didn't want to look like they were hiding something.

He sighed. "It's too dangerous. It's pitch-black and even with flashlights the trail's dicey. If they don't show by first light, we'll bring in a chopper and a much bigger team."

"You been up there to confirm that the trail's dangerous?" she asked Mac.

Mac fixed her with an impassive gaze and said nothing.

Kris turned to Bill. "So you tell me why two detectives are running a search for hikers."

Bill squirmed as if it were a trick question. Then Kris started laughing, breaking the tension, and Bill followed her lead and broke into nervous laughter although he had no idea why. Mac smiled to show she didn't scare him. He knew that Kris Walker was nothing but trouble, made all the worse by his attraction to her.

Carillo joined them, shaking his head. "No sign of them. We're waiting on the last search team and the dogs before we check out. Looks like we'll be back at seven or so if something doesn't happen pretty quick."

Mac didn't relish rising early on what would have been his day off.

"Call in and see if they've shown up anywhere," he said. "The map shows some roads on the other side of the mountain. Maybe they got to a house."

Carillo left and Deputy Bill snugged his jacket around him, feeling the chill, partly from the cold, partly from the memory of the very unsettling feeling he'd had a few hours before when he'd stood alone on this very spot.

"This is kinda like the other guy that went missing Tuesday," Bill offered.

Mac and Kris lit up at the remark.

"What guy?" Mac asked. He didn't like the fact that a pushy reporter was privy to this information but at least she didn't have a camera running.

"A Weyerhaeuser guy. This timber cruiser. I found his truck. Keys in it, door open. Engine had been on but it had run outta gas. Guy just disappeared. Real strange."

Kris smelled a story. "Where was that?"

"Oh, a valley or two east of here. Just this side of the National Forest."

Mac wasn't surprised he hadn't heard this. His department had more than three hundred employees and covered a piece of northern Washington that was in between Rhode Island and Delaware in size. The county stretched from the ocean to remote mountain reaches and within its confines lived more than three-quarters of a million people. That some guy had disappeared and he didn't know about it wasn't all that unusual.

"You do any follow-up? Any reasons why?" Mac asked. "Personal problems, maybe?"

"No, doesn't look like it. Talked to the wife. Seemed like a happy family. Kid had a nose ring, though."

"Huh?" Kris tripped over the non sequitur.

"The missing guy? Son had a nose ring."

Mac guessed this young deputy sheriff didn't see a lot of nose rings and found it worth throwing into the equation as a possible reason a man might leave his family.

"Was there evidence of foul play?" Kris asked.

"Foul play? No, not a thing." Bill paused a moment. "'Cept maybe the trees."

"Trees?" Mac repeated.

"Yeah." Bill knew he had a good story going when a reporter for a major TV station and the top detective in his department were hanging on his every word. "The trees around where I found the truck were all busted off. Up high, maybe ten feet. Snapped in two like a freak wind or something."

Kris narrowed her eyes. "Sounds like an 'or something' to me."

A rugged, bearded man in a Mariners ball cap appeared out of the darkness up the trail, three bloodhounds dragging him by their leashes. Deputy Bill recognized the dog man and yelled, "Hey, Harley."

Harley Quivers looked uneasy as he strode up, his three dogs quiet, their tails held low.

"Been trackin' for years," he said, spitting Skoal-blackened saliva for effect. "Men, bear, cougars, you name it. But I ain't never seen no dogs spook like that. Picked up a scent but they just wouldn't follow it, not into the woods or any further up the trail. I'm history."

As Harley Quivers and his chickened-out dogs passed them, Bill Alexander fell silent, knowing only too well that feeling. Kris looked to Mac and their eyes met briefly. The revelations of the missing logger and the scared dogs posed questions neither could easily answer. Mac acknowledged to himself that Kris Walker's notion of foul play might have just taken on a little more credence.

Ty wandered into the kitchen and grabbed a Diet Coke. Tired, he didn't want any deep discussions but they hadn't really spoken all day.

"How was the meeting?" he asked.

"The usual." Ronnie muted the TV weather report predicting intermittent rain all week. "When I got home, Mere and her friends were out by the pool and Amy was on the phone."

"She uses our phone more than we do," Ty quipped.

"Well, it's the last time. We need someone full-time, like a nanny or au pair."

Ty knew Ronnie felt slightly threatened abdicating some of her motherly duties, but she would do anything to protect her kids.

"How would we find one?" he asked.

"I asked around. One agency was highly recommended."

"So, we interview prospects?" he asked.

"Yeah. If that's what we want to do. We've got a couple of rooms we could put someone in. What do you think?"

"Sure," he said. "Let's do it."

Ronnie hesitated. "Shouldn't we talk to the kids first?"

Ty smiled affectionately to himself. Ronnie was a team player and brought the kids in on decisions when Ty thought they should just be told: *I outrank you, therefore you'll do as I say.* In this case she was right, since it was the kids who would be taking orders from someone other than their parents.

"Yeah, let's tell them what we have in mind," Ty suggested. "I'll bet they go for it. It'll give them someone new to torture."

Ronnie smiled wistfully. "Okay." His simple, light remark reminded her she wanted the old Ty back, the man who used to crack jokes and laugh and make witty retorts and smile a lot. She desperately wanted to reach out and touch him, but there was a wall between them, as tangible as if it were made of steel.

Ronnie picked up the TV remote and pushed the off button. "I'm sleepy," she said. "You coming?"

Ty nodded. "Right behind you."

Ronnie reached over the counter and put her cup in the sink.

"It's Sunday," she said with the tiniest hesitation, "wanna sleep in?"

Ty knew what her coded words meant. Intimacy was a lot to ask of him right now, despite part of him wanting it so badly. He decided he'd try.

"Yeah. Let's sleep in."

Ronnie blew him a kiss and exited for the stairs. Ty sipped his soda and looked at the tall black windows, following rivulets as they streaked the glass.

* * *

He watched the small two-legs moving below. Some had climbed the trail and passed him in the darkness. He knew the dogs sensed him. He felt their fear. Their fear was dim, like a cloudy day, different from the sunshine fear of the small two-legs. But it was still fear. They did not follow him.

When the last of the small two-legs climbed inside their hardshells and the hardshells opened their night-fire eyes and ran away, he moved up the hill. He mostly slept by day and traveled by night, and though a night rain usually found him seeking shelter, tonight he was restless and not cold.

Easily ascending a slope that would have left a small two-leg scrambling on all fours, he moved for a while, first upward, then steadily down, into a valley. He drank from a strong flowing stream, then followed it, the cold water soothing his feet.

Eventually, something caught his attention: fire. He kept his eyes on it; it grew brighter as he moved farther down the stream. Then he saw that the fire was coming from inside the wood cave of a small two-leg. He had seen other wood caves of the small two-legs, and this one was smaller than most.

He sensed a presence within.

He moved closer to the wood cave, which rested a few strides above him on top of the bank. A screaming came from within. It was a wounded animal noise, like the squeals some animals made as he killed them. But he realized no animal could cry out that long and, searching his thoughts and senses, felt no waves of distress from a living creature. All he felt was the small two-leg, and its thoughts were calm. He decided the small two-leg was somehow making the noise.

He was not hungry nor was he particularly curious about the shrieking sound from the wood cave. But in his mind was the earlier vision of all those small two-legs milling below him and his abandoned plan to kill them. Then his mind flashed back to the Great Fire and why he was here and his anger rose. He took stock of the fragile little wood cave, pictured the noisy small two-leg within, and reached a conclusion: this one was trapped.

13

Not content to wait on her political connections or the police, Karen Roberts had stayed on the phone through the night, calling friends for help or advice. One of those she reached was Steve Keener, a take-charge senior partner from Mitch's firm. Promising her he would find them, twenty minutes later Keener left the comfort of his waterfront town home in Madison Park and headed out to gather other members of the firm.

Mac glanced at his watch, not surprised it was nearly midnight. He ran a hand through his thick, black hair, soaked from the chronic, misting rain. He looked over at Carillo, a dozen yards away scribbling in his notepad, then at the Channel 7 van. The crew was nearly packed and ready to roll and Kris Walker sat relaxing in the passenger seat, door open, smoking a cigarette as she made notes.

Mac loathed cigarettes but suddenly the vision of a beautiful woman with a burning white cylinder between her fingers seemed intensely sensual. Kris made eye contact and gave a slight nod, as if to acknowledge that earlier she had only been doing her job and it was nothing personal. At least Mac decided to take the gesture that way.

* * *

Kris's eyes discreetly followed Mac the cop. She liked tall men, being five nine herself. And with those smart eyes and the slight wave to his jet-black hair he had a kind of Russell Crowe thing going. Putting aside thoughts of the cop for a moment, she felt she was on to an interesting story but didn't want to go as far as admitting it could be *really* interesting. She felt this might be more than just two lost hikers and a logger on an unscheduled vacation. The dogs with their tails between their legs, Barney Fife's story about the missing guy, the door clicker and possible blood, and then these two lawyers. She didn't have a full equation but it looked . . . interesting.

Carillo approached Mac. "I'd say it's time to get outta here."

"Search teams all in?" Mac asked.

"Yeah."

Mac watched the news van back up and drive away, then noticed Deputy Bill Alexander speaking with the two other deputies and a guy from search and rescue.

"What do think of the Weyerhaeuser guy?" Mac asked.

Carillo looked over at Deputy Bill and snorted derisively. "He's tellin' me the story of finding the guy's truck and I swear he's gonna piss his pants. And his so-called blood never panned out. I suppose if these guys really are missing, it's worth looking into."

Down the road, headlight beams cut through the streaks of rain and turned the corner. A gleaming new Range Rover lumbered up and four men got out. The group crossed to Mac and Carillo, led by a lean, athletic-looking man in his late fifties.

Carillo looked them over with suspicion. "Can we help you?" he asked challengingly.

"Is this where Mitch Roberts and Jack Remsbecker went missing?" asked their leader.

"You friends?" Mac asked.

"Friends and associates," he said, extending his hand. "Steve Keener." Then he gestured to the others, who responded in kind. "Alan Erickson, Adam Olinka, John Cothran."

Mac and Carillo obliged in a flurry of handshakes.

"We're with the Snohomish County Sheriff's Department," said Mac, "and we're just shutting down for the night. We've called back the search teams. This terrain is too dangerous at night. You guys are welcome to help us at first light. Probably around seven, seven thirty."

Keener shook his head. "Thanks, but we're going to take a fly now. They might be hurt."

Carillo rolled his eyes. He didn't need any more missing lawyers. "We can't let you do that. Too risky."

One of the other men, Adam Olinka, an intense young man in wire-rims who appeared fresh out of Harvard Law, took up the gauntlet.

"Look, Deputy—"

"Detective," Carillo corrected.

"Detective," amended Olinka. "These men are both our friends and colleagues. We promised their families we'd look for them. And legally, you really can't stop us. Sorry."

Carillo didn't like this trim, clean-cut young lawyer. Sure he was smart, but he was soft. Maybe he played basketball or was in a spinning class at the gym, but had he ever had his life threatened? Would he know if his life were in danger? Of course not.

Carillo spun on his heels. "Fuck it, pal. It's your funeral."

Mac knew Carillo detested successful men, and these guys wore their superiority as proudly as they did their expensive REI slickers, Gore-Tex–lined boots and Panerai watches. He nodded toward the trail. "Guys, just be careful. I've been up there a few hundred yards and even with flashlights it's tricky. The trail'll make abrupt switchbacks along the edges of some hairy drop-offs. Watch out. It's definitely a trail for daylight."

Keener nodded, then asked, "Any evidence of what happened? Where they might be?"

"No," Mac answered. "We found the keys to the Cherokee, but nothing else. All of our patrols in the area, both on this side as well as the other side of the mountain, have been alerted to keep their eyes open. And like my partner said, we'll be back in the morning with search teams."

"Thanks," said Olinka, patting Mac's shoulder patronizingly. "Bring us some coffee then, would ya?"

With that, the men headed up the trail, their boots generating the dull scraping sounds of hard rubber on wet gravel and dirt. Mac watched their powerful flashlights crisscrossing the darkness as they slowly receded up the trail. A moment later the lights disappeared and their voices dialed down and out. Mac went to the car and climbed in.

Carillo was steaming. "Now we'll have to save their sorry asses too."

"Maybe. I think they'll be okay."

Carillo slammed the car in gear and dug out, spinning gravel onto the Range Rover.

"Sorry motherfuckers! I hope they die. It'd make me happier'n a pig in shit to zip that smart-ass bitch with the glasses into a body bag."

Mac looked over at Carillo. The man could be insensitive but this went beyond the pale.

"You don't mean that, Karl. It's bad karma."

Carillo looked over angrily. "Fuck karma."

14

Whether crafting 7000 series aircraft aluminum or dimension hemlock, Russ Tardif possessed impressive focus. His thoughts were as linear as a belt sander when determining which cut to make next or whether he had the correct setting on his lathe or bandsaw. Not one to waste valuable time on pastimes like reading, Russ loved one thing above all else: turning raw materials into finished products.

The television report on the missing hikers had long vacated his thoughts and he now brought his mental resources to bear on a particularly difficult miter cut. It was nearly two a.m., but he was not worried about the time since he didn't have to get up in the morning. And not only was it Sunday now, but this weekend was the start of his two-week vacation.

Russ completed the cut on the molding and held it to its mate. Perfect, naturally. He reached for another piece of molding and out of the corner of his eye saw something move past the window. He quickly turned, staring at the small four-light, double-glazed window he'd installed himself. The glass was night black, a few clinging raindrops sparkling from the shop's interior lighting. Russ shrugged off the motion as flying debris, maybe a cedar bough. The fact that it wasn't windy never entered the equation. Russ turned back to his miter saw.

* * *

He sensed few thoughts from the small two-leg in the wood cave. Glancing inside, he saw that the screaming animal sound came from something the small two-leg was using that looked to be made of stone, only shinier. He did not want the small two-leg to see him yet. He first wanted to create some confusion. He would let the small two-leg's anxiety build to panic, then terror, streaming out of its mind in waves like driving rain. With that the kill would be more satisfying.

Unaccustomed to earthquakes, Russ took several seconds to conclude that an earthquake must be why his shop was shaking. Although it wasn't a violent motion, he nevertheless had to discontinue making a cut because of the movement of the floor and walls. But as equipment hanging from nails on the walls—saw blades and jigs, old goggles, some T squares, and various other items—all bounced up and down, Russ realized the floor wasn't actually moving. As he quickly discounted the earthquake theory, his new assumption was even scarier—a slide. Suddenly the recurring nightmare of his little shack toppling into the rushing water below was enough to motivate him to step outside to investigate.

That is, until *the sound.*

Russ took one step toward the door, and the air outside the shed shattered with what sounded to him like the massive industrial cutters at work as they slashed through giant stacks of sheet aluminum. The tearing-sheet-metal wail came forth with such ungodly volume and resonance it actually vibrated Russ's vulnerable little building—vulnerable because whatever had just let go with that ghastly, inhuman roar was right outside his door.

Russ's heart rate jumped from seventy to one twenty in two seconds. His bugged-out eyes scanned the windows. He was hoping to see something . . . and desperately hoping *not* to see *anything.* He knew in his heart that whatever was out there was not a falling tree or meteor or a secret government test of a new death ray, but rather *a living thing.*

His mind raced for answers as he fixed upon defending himself. He remembered he had a gun in the shop, but in his panic couldn't recall where in the cluttered twelve-by-twelve interior it lay. Throwing everything off his workbench, he began searching frantically for the little nine-shot Harrington & Richardson .22 revolver.

As he furiously swept tools, trimmings, and sawdust onto the floor, the feeble balloon-framed building shook again. Then another sound, not unlike the subwoofer effect from Russ's stereo, began to build. This new sound was an unmistakable animal growl, deep and resonant, like that of a tiger or a bear, but with a wholly different articulation. It was a visceral rumble that quickly climbed into a terrifying, raging roar. Russ knew with heart-stopping certainty this was an animal *nobody* had ever heard of.

Movement in the window again caught his eye and against his conscious will he looked directly at it. Russ knew the top of the window was exactly six feet ten inches. To his horror he saw what looked to be a massive torso pass by, hairy red-black, with arms swinging, but *no head*. Whatever in God's name it was was so tall its shoulders were well above seven feet. Tears welled in Russ's eyes and nausea radiated from his stomach outward. The monster outside his little dwelling was unknown, obviously hostile, and horribly big. In his terror, he convinced himself it was a bear. It was gigantic, hairy, and made *that sound*. Had to be a bear. He tried calming himself, remembering the movie *The Edge* about the guys being chased by a killer bear. Russ knew if he stayed in the shop, he'd be okay.

Then they made eye contact.

Russ looked at the apparition in the window and its face nearly filled the two-by-two aperture. It was no bear . . . definitely *not a bear*. Russ stared at it dumbfounded, uncomprehending, as they locked eyes. It was a face from Russ's worst nightmare, not because it was alien or misshapen, like some heightened bogeyman from a Hollywood horror movie, but because it was so huge . . . and *almost* human. It was the *almost* part that turned Russ to stone. The monster sized him up and curled back thin, black lips, revealing immense, even, yellowed teeth, flanked by thumb-sized canines. Its eyes, as gold as a cat's but with circular pupils, were framed by a low sable brow, angled down in fury.

Russ stumbled backward, away from the petrifying vision in his window, fell over his table saw, and tumbled to the floor. He flashed back to the window . . . and it was gone. Wiping sweat from his forehead, Russ suddenly appreciated everything he'd ever taken for granted because now he truly feared it was all about to end.

As he frantically scurried to locate the gun, part of the roof imploded and a black fist, larger than his portable television, appeared. Unfurling massive ebony fingers tipped with dirty, squared-off nails the size of matchbooks, it clawed away at the shattered shingles and tar paper while splintering the two-by-six rafters like balsa wood.

Russ spun around and made it to the door just before the entire wall caved in behind him, taking most of the roof with it. Russ turned to see his gigantic opponent wade in after him. Effortlessly tossing aside the two-hundred-fifty-four-pound table saw as if it were made of Styrofoam, the creature reached toward him. Russ suddenly knew exactly what it was that was about to seize him.

In a last futile effort to save himself, Russ pulled open the door. But in a flurry, giant fingers wrapped around his neck, and the wall in front of him—door and all—collapsed outward as he and the beast blew through it. Russ was stunned by the trauma and disoriented by his brain's now constricted blood supply. His last sensation before he lost consciousness was the wet night air on his face.

The devastation to the small building was total. Amid the ruin a couple of damaged electrical wires crossed. The resulting sparks met a receptive pile of bone-dry sawdust, and with a moderate *whooofff,* the shed began to blaze. The fire grew too fast for the rain to stop it.

When Russ came to, still somewhat stunned, he saw off in the distance what appeared to be a bonfire. Then he realized he was being spirited away by this devil-giant, the way a child lackadaisically carries a doll, thumb and forefinger curled around the neck, arm at its side, dragging the doll's feet. Russ's feet were ice cold as they passed through the creek, upstream, heel-first, involuntarily kicking stones and floating branches.

Russ was not a religious man nor had he ever really been a churchgoer but, like most people at the point of death, he started pondering what lay beyond this mortal coil. He began a silent prayer that he might die quickly. Unfortunately, in a seemingly pitiless world of Darwinian cruelty, Russ's prayers weren't answered. It wasn't because Russ was being punished for an unexamined secular life, nor was it because, following that simple axiom of the animal kingdom, little fish get eaten by bigger fish—and metaphorically Russ was just a little fish. No, Russ's misery was part of a larger plan of retribution.

High in the hills above his home, Russ had an interminable hour of anticipation to consider the big questions about life and death. When they finally reached their destination, his captor quickly broke his neck to immobilize him and then tore off his clothes. Once that final humiliation was complete, the monster ripped open his guts and yanked out his intestines, which he stuffed into his mouth as Russ's vision mercifully faded to black.

15

Mac was back in the department by 6:35 a.m., five minutes later than he and Carillo had agreed upon too few hours before. Now in charge of the search for the lawyers, Mac phoned the department before leaving home to see if they had been found. They had not. He poured a cup of coffee, then punched up some info on his computer to corroborate Deputy Bill's story about the missing logger. Reading the report, Mac was irritated with the young patrol officer not only for leaving the scene of the lawyers' disappearance before it had been secured, but also for the confusion over the so-called blood evidence. He decided to take the green deputy aside later and reacquaint him with proper procedures.

Mac had a personal collection of area maps, mainly the beautifully detailed USGS survey maps of the wilderness areas north and east of Seattle. His job occasionally took him into those regions, but he enjoyed studying the charts in his free time, a habit that caused his fellow detectives to jokingly christen him Map Nerd. He had begun collecting them after moving from Los Angeles. He loved maps, and this was a way to familiarize himself with his new home as well as his beat.

He pulled out a map of the area where Joe Wylie had vanished. Using his finger, he traced the logging road to where the contour lines leveled out into a flat section, the place where Deputy Bill Alexander indicated the timber cruiser's truck had been abandoned. The report mentioned some empty beer bottles strewn about the floor of the cab. Mac shook his head slightly in disapproval. Though Wylie was apparently an alcoholic, he was married and had a solid job. Mac's gut told him this guy didn't fit the profile of someone running away from his life. And if he was going to do so, why drive up into the middle of the woods? You'd catch a ferry or disappear from Sea-Tac Airport. This just didn't make sense.

Then he thought about the tracking dogs from the night before. They weren't just scared, they were *terrified*. He'd never seen any dog look like that, let alone such experienced trackers. Things were not adding up and that intrigued Mac, who prided himself on being able to quickly categorize almost any situation. He remembered a line from Shakespeare: *The game's afoot.*

Mac had long ago learned to trust his instincts, tempered with his own form of crime-solving algorithms. These seemingly unrelated events of the three missing men, the dogs, and Deputy Bill's broken trees caused him to search his memory banks for correlations. He arrived at no rational answer.

"This is fuckin' ridiculous," Carillo spat as he entered the work area, strode to his carrel, and threw down his keys.

"And good morning to you too," deadpanned Mac.

"They find those dickhead lawyers in the twenty-five minutes it took me to drive in?" Carillo asked as he crossed to pour some coffee.

"Nope."

"Shit. So I guess we gotta go back up there? You know, this is all just political bullshit. Putting us on some missing hikers just because they're rich and connected and—"

"I'm not sure we'll find them," Mac stated, halting Carillo's tirade.

Carillo, pouring coffee, stopped and turned, midcup.

"Whaddya mean?"

Mac Schneider was cerebral whereas Carillo saw himself as action-oriented. Carillo knew Mac had made some amazing busts based on hunches when he was with the LAPD. Mac stood and responded to Carillo with a shrug.

"Don't know. Just a feeling. Let's go."

Carillo wondered at times if Mac had some sort of psychic ability.

* * *

The first rays of morning light were far kinder to Ty than they had been the day before. Waking from strange, inexplicable dreams, Ty stared at the soaring ceiling of his bedroom for a moment. The memory of the dreams washed away from his mind like a sand castle in a tide's path as Ty slowly narrowed his focus, straining to make out the wood grain of the ceiling twenty feet above. He rolled his head toward Ronnie, her head mostly buried in a pillow, dead to the world.

Ty studied the visible corner of her face. The hurricane of depression that had propelled him to his car thirty-some hours before had passed. It now seemed like a week ago, maybe another lifetime ago. Ty reached out and gently brushed a few locks of hair clinging to her eyebrow, and as he did, he was struck by the softness of her skin. It was a sensation he hadn't stopped to savor for a long time. How soft she was. How much he loved her. *God, I love her.* His fingers moved over her head, now caressing her hair, ever so slightly so as not to wake her. He wanted this moment to last, gazing at the love of his life without dialogue, without conflict.

Ronnie's head turned slowly and she inhaled deeply as she awoke. As her eyes opened, the first thing Ty read in her smiling, sleepy face was her vulnerable love.

"Hey," he whispered.

She smiled again, still not completely awake, and crawled the two feet to him, wrapping her arms, her legs, her body, around his. Their lips touched delicately, then again, with a bit more energy. After a few minutes of light pecks, Ronnie was more awake, more aroused. She rolled them both slightly, positioning her head on Ty's pillow, with Ty above her. Running her hands through his hair, she pulled his face to her, opening her mouth for a longer, more passionate kiss.

Their tongues intertwined, their tastes and smells mingling as the intimacy of the moment grew. They kissed deeply, powerfully, passionately, with the intense blending of their souls that only time and limitless love can bring. Ty pulled off Ronnie's T-shirt and threw back the bedcovers as their body heat climbed. He tossed the shirt to one side of the bed and drank in the beautiful nakedness of her body. As she lay beneath him, she exulted in the moment, stretching out her arms and spreading her legs as if making a snow angel. Then she reached up and drew him down to her, the skin of their chests touching, her nipples unyielding with arousal, then his lips finding them, encircling them, her eyes closed, breath hitching in ecstacy.

At the other end of the vaulted, sky-lit hallway, Meredith had been playing in her bedroom for more than an hour. Having roused uncharacteristically early, she decided it was a good place to spend the quiet time before her parents and brother awoke. The walls were gaily decorated in colorful graphics and the images of cartoon and movie characters. Her room was spacious, with a play loft at one end.

Still dressed in her Snoopy pajamas, Meredith began a stage play starring Barbie and Ken. In her script Ken and Barbie were having problems, an unexplained alienation brought on by something traumatic that had happened to Ken. He had seen something weird and people made fun of him and it hurt his feelings. As a six-year-old she was an existentialist by experience and did not completely understand or account in detail for causality. Ken had made himself an outsider because, well, he just did.

Playing the scene for a few moments caused her to ponder the real-life characters upon whom she based her little drama. Suddenly she needed them. She needed them to hold her and to tell her they loved her . . . and loved each other. For if they didn't love each other, how could they really love her?

As Ty's tongue flicked back and forth, bringing Ronnie closer to orgasm, her gasps of pleasure didn't quite mask another sound, a discord with the sound effects of love, a . . . knocking . . . at their door. In the split second it took to realize it was one of the kids, Ronnie was off him, scrambling for her T-shirt. Across the huge master suite, one of the double doors slowly creaked open. Ronnie, now out of bed, shirt in hand, saw Meredith's little face peering around the edge of the door. Her daughter had seen her naked before and Ronnie felt there was no shame in the human body, but nevertheless she also felt there was a time and place for certain things and quickly slid the shirt on. Ty found his underwear and, with his midsection masked by the rumpled mound of comforter, managed to get them back on.

"Are you guys okay?" came the tiny-voiced inquiry.

Ronnie unconsciously straightened out the bedding.

"Sure honey, we're fine. Did the Mad Bo scare you?"

The Mad Bo was a fantasy creation of Meredith's, a creature that came in the night or any other time she needed attention, giving her an excuse to go running for her mommy or daddy. Ty guessed his daughter had seen a cartoon "mad bull" on television a few years back and the Mad Bo had become her phonetic version.

Meredith took her mother's question as an invitation and slowly entered the room.

"No. It wasn't him. I just wanted to see if you guys were . . . there."

Ty smiled, pulled back his side of the comforter and patted the bed.

"C'mon, sweetie. Wanna get in with us?"

The little girl shuffled across the room toward them, her pixie face trying to suppress a smile. This was what she wanted. She arrived at the bed and climbed in her mom's side, and Ty and Ronnie fluffed up the pillows, nestling their daughter between them. Ty looked at his wife and daughter, and his nostalgia instantly soured into a flash-forward of another reality, one that didn't happen but very nearly did. Instead of being in bed with her husband, Ronnie was reeling as she made arrangements to deal with Ty's remains. And instead of snuggling in between the two most important people in her world, his daughter was trying to understand the biggest, most shattering event of her young life.

Ronnie smiled to herself. Though robbed of an orgasm, this moment was still pretty good. Despite her prestigious career and all that came with it, the only things that mattered—really mattered—except for that little boy down the hall, were right here with her.

She bussed her daughter's cheek and felt like grabbing a little more sleep. Looking over at Ty, she was startled to see tears in his eyes. Not wet in the corners, but streaming down his cheeks. They made eye contact and he wiped his face and looked away but it was puzzling enough to worry her again. She suddenly felt helpless, a desolation inside that reminded her of problems that just might be beyond her powers of understanding. She closed her eyes, hugged her daughter tightly, and escaped into sleep.

16

Ben sat up in the bed and the cheap head-board dug into his back until he got one of his pillows into the right position. Lighting a cigarette, he muted *Meet the Press* and looked out from his room in the Comfort Inn over the flat expanse bordering the Columbia River. A United 757 emerged from a gray cloud bank on its approach to Portland International, and Ben acknowledged it was a typical late November day for Oregon. He had shot a TV movie here a few years before and the weather was just like this, except it was May. He remembered Oregonians liked to brag—or despair—that they had webbed feet.

Ben had only a shred of a notion why he was here. He had blown in and out of Eureka so fast, not really thinking about where he was going—other than it was going to be north—that his explanation to poor, sweet Doris had been thinner than thin. He had met her questions with a lot of incomplete thoughts and equivocation, and when they had kissed good-bye, her confused, maybe even frightened look didn't make him feel any better.

He tried to sort between what happened sixty years ago and the dream that had been replaying lately. He was beginning to wonder if the event he so vividly remembered was really just that—a dream. He puffed his cigarette and tried to unearth the real events by sifting through visions and personal mythology, straining to separate hard truth from the fiction of memory. Old, old memory.

He reminded himself that this was something that, *if it really happened,* happened a long time ago: *before* VJ Day, before television, before Orson Welles was fat, let alone dead. Sometimes he felt that after nearly eighty years his brain was worn out. Then he'd surprise himself by being just as sharp as when he was twenty.

But did this happen? This dream chase that at times seemed so real . . .

Did it happen?

Why had he thrown away a good paycheck, maybe even damaged his credibility, *his career.* Why had he jeopardized so much on this whim? Sure, he had SAG insurance and a great pension and would never be out on the street, but Doris was the loose cannon that kept Ben constantly worrying about money.

His wife of fifty-three years was a very sick woman. Like a zombie under the most pernicious mind control, poor Doris sat in their living room all day long, staring dutifully, even compulsively at their Zenith television. It was a special television, a television manufactured in the Twilight Zone, a receiver that seemed to carry only one station: the Home Shopping Network.

Doris wielded Visas and MasterCards like Hank Greenberg handled a bat, and though Ben had put his foot down many times, she'd go right back to buying with abandon. Ben eventually had to rent a large self-storage unit to house all of her acquisitions. When Ben called the credit card companies and asked them to reduce their limit, they did— but then turned right around and approved her purchases that went over limit and charged exorbitant over-limit fees. He finally gave up, partly because he loved her, but partly out of pity.

On top of that, a few years back, Doris had involved them in a real estate investment scheme that had gone very bad and cost them a boatload of money. Ben had made a small fortune over the years but had never been a great financial manager. Doris's habits had made a sizable dent in their nest egg. Ben still joked that he was probably the only guy who lost money in the real estate boom.

Doctors at the dawn of the baby boom had told Doris she would be unable to bear fruit, and her answer to the theft of her motherhood had been to become a spendaholic. They had considered adoption but Ben seemed to be on location more than he was at home and the timing was just never right. Ben had plenty of guilt about certain parts of his life and most of it centered on Doris. He wasn't sure how he could have changed it for her but felt he might have done better, tried harder.

He found himself lighting another cigarette and as he did so, it hit him again. The subconscious Indian inside his head, the *real* Indian, whispered another message: *Quit.* Only this wasn't a quit-because-it's-bad-for-you message, it was something far more profound. Somehow Ben understood he had to quit because he was on his way to battle and needed his strength. He stubbed out the fresh cigarette as the voice told him to focus on his task.

Purify your mind, your body.

But I'm damn near eighty, he shot back at the inner voice.

Doesn't matter. To beat it you must be strong, you must be clear of head, strong of limb. There aren't exceptions.

Ben wondered if he was losing his marbles, but this voice seemed so damn clear . . . and familiar. The words were as loud in his head as if he were wearing a Walkman. Ben grabbed the pack of cigarettes on the nightstand. Before he could talk himself out of it, he went into the bathroom and threw them in the toilet. The powerful torrent from the motel toilet swept the cigarettes away, and it suddenly became clear how he would play this: pure instinct. He would trust his intuition, operate by gut feelings.

Then the voice spoke again. *Use your inner eye to take you to that which you seek.*

Ben hadn't thought of that term "inner eye" since he was a kid. Now he was wondering if he was hallucinating.

The voice came again. *Use it, find it, it's there . . . What you want, what you need is within . . . and all around.*

Ben's father had been a stubborn, pragmatic man who never much believed in Indian mysticism, dismissing it as a romantic construction of white men to entertain themselves and to assuage their guilt for what they had done to his people. But Ben's grandfather had been a spiritual man and, when Ben's father died in a hunting accident, he took the boy under his wing. He treated young Ben not only as a son but as a student, teaching him things that today would fall under the esoteric realm of metaphysics. Ben's grandfather explained to him that there was much about the world we didn't understand, but we had all the tools necessary to do absolutely amazing things: we just had to trust they were there and let them work.

Your inner eye will take you . . .

He got up, walked over to the window, and opened it. A rush of heavy, chilled air rolled in and passed over his feet. He took a deep breath, scanned the horizon, then closed his eyes. He put all thoughts of Doris and filmmaking and credit card bills out of his head and tried to focus. Though he'd been just ten when his grandfather first showed him how to send his mind out, the knowledge soon came back to him as if the instructions had been given the day before. For fifteen minutes he stood there, settling himself, leveling his mental power on the words of his grandfather.

"Turn your eyes in, Benjamin, turn them in. Find your clarity, seek a oneness with all things. When you find it, you will have the key in your hand, and you will be free. Your mind is your spirit eye, your eye of true sight. Use it the way it was truly intended and you will see everything."

Now in an instant he was ten again and felt his grandfather at his side.

After a few more minutes of concentration, the cold bite of the window air had vanished and the mental effort lifted like a weight. He felt a peace that he couldn't have experienced as a child or younger man and he knew that it was an essential element of making this work. Ben's thoughts multiplied and soon the images in his head—places, faces, bits of his life—were racing, faster and faster like a speeded-up film, until the images blurred. Then, despite the incredible speed at which they were moving, he began to divine a pattern, or more accurately, *an understanding.* It was as if thoughts were taking identifiable forms and shapes in his mind, like letters to a reader, but in Ben's case he was reading, with complete understanding, a language he hadn't known ten minutes before. It was a language of pure thought, some sort of elemental truth, the unlocking code for which was either already in his mind, lying dormant, or was something he somehow conjured.

Ben's mind swirled and sparkled with flashes of light like metallic confetti tossed past a strobe light. The image clarified and suddenly he had the sensation of flying, climbing, transcending time and space. Weightless, bodiless, he first let the vision carry him, enjoying for a few moments the sensation of flying without benefit of a machine. Then he found he could exert control over this journey, to give it a purpose. He could now see his dark dreams, the thing in the forest chasing him, off to the side of the main field of view, and he consciously pushed his thoughts to take him to whatever it was he had been sensing, the thing that was drawing him to it.

His journey through space and time made a turn as if it had some-how gotten the scent, and it now bore him north, through clouds, rain squalls, even snow. Then he burst into blue sky, the sun actually hurt-ing his dream eyes. Below him spread an endless forest, white-capped mountains, alpine lakes, dirt logging roads . . .

He swooped into a valley, flying low over the crowns of towering hemlock and fir, his inner eye registering minute detail. To Ben all forests had their own characteristics, even personalities, like people, and this forest was not in Oregon, he knew that, and it wasn't in British Columbia, he'd worked on location there four or five times. No, but this forest was somewhere north and near a big city. He knew that too; he *felt* it.

His mind eye swooped down into the trees and dodged around huge trunks, through the soft, filtered light at the forest's floor. He knew he was still in his hotel room, but in another way he wasn't. He knew he was going somewhere, swept along by these mystical winds, his mind as open as it had ever been. He was being taken or taking himself, he didn't know which, but he let it go, allowing this crystalline daydream to play out.

Cresting a ridge, he plunged, like one of those dizzying Imax shots, into a steep ravine and leveled out over a creek, emerald green from snow runoff. Along the rocky banks he flew, down the middle, ma-neuvering the twists and turns like a helicopter. As the surrounding walls steepened, and the morning light just didn't have the energy to go that deep, his visual clarity dropped. But the vision was so vivid it took his breath away. He also could sense his hands hanging on to the win-dow frame but he felt displaced from them, like his body was in one place and his consciousness was somewhere else.

Around a corner, passing over a bend in the stream that had ac-cumulated a tangle of driftwood amidst a natural cairn of river rock, he saw a shape ahead, the form of a person standing in the rippling water. But as he drew near, he knew it was not a man. In that dim light at the bottom of the canyon, surrounded by forest that came close to the water's edge, this huge shape turned and in an instant he saw its face . . .

Not human . . .

Oh-Mah.

Its eyes found his . . . and its thoughts were—

Ben's eyes jerked open, wrenching him back from his journey. In the safety of the hotel room he instinctively looked for a cigarette and remembered they were gone. He sat down on the edge of the bed, shaken less by his success at hurtling his consciousness out of his body than by having connected with this creature. And this one was just like the thing that once chased him. In that short contact it had all come back. What happened sixty years ago was no dream and he knew what he had to do next.

He took deep breaths to get his pulse back down. Rattled not only by the vision but by the certainty of what it was and what it was doing—and would continue doing—and with the image of the beast's surprised, rage-filled face burned into his mind, Ben also knew he would need all the help he could get.

He knew he must continue north. While still at Paramount he had understood that his answers lay in the north, but now he was dialing in *where* in the north he was going. Seattle. This thing was near Seattle. How exactly he knew that he wasn't sure but when he pictured flying into Seattle, something felt right. *Remember, you're on instincts now.* This creature, this Oh-Mah was near there and Ben's future was tied to it.

After a few moments he had gathered himself enough to make plans. First, he needed a base of operations, so he phoned his nephew David, an IT technician who lived with his wife and two little girls south of Seattle in Burien. David not only idolized his uncle but also shared Ben's interests in myths and legends. David was thrilled Ben was coming and said he'd get Ben's room ready immediately. Ben then called the airline and booked the next flight to Sea-Tac Airport. He knew what he was heading toward and it was no movie effect, no guy inside a suit working armatures. This was all too real, and though it scared him, it thrilled him too. And what thrilled him was being an Indian again—something he'd left on his own cutting room floor so many years ago. No more could he deny it was in his blood, and that blood was compelling him north to a meeting with his past and with his destiny . . . whatever that might be.

The vision of the old, small two-leg had been strong, so much so, he turned and looked down and around the creek for it. He felt it, its mind voice. It was old, it was different. It was one of the small two-legs the elders told of. The special ones who could hear his mind voice as he heard theirs. The ones who lived in the forest, the ones who named him and his kind. He had learned that long ago but it had never mattered until now.

And this one, this old one was far away. He knew that now and his anger subsided. But he knew something else: this old one was coming.

17

Mac and Carillo arrived at the trailhead to resume the search. The Range Rover was still there with two Snohomish County Sheriff's cruisers next to it. No one was visible.

"Told you they'd die," Carillo said, only half joking.

"Let's hope not," Mac said as he climbed out of the car. "Then we'd have a ton more paperwork. Not to mention the hell we'd catch for letting four more friends of the mayor disappear."

The sky had cleared slightly but it was still cold. Mac reached into the backseat and grabbed his parka. Following the trail upwards a few hundred yards, Carillo took the lead at a wedding march pace so as not to miss a thing.

After about forty minutes Mac stopped to stretch his back and Carillo continued on. Surveying the vista, Mac vowed to get away from work more often and enjoy this slice of paradise that lay less than an hour from his condo in Edmonds. He sucked in the chill pure air and let his eyes wander the area, more to relax and regroup than to look for evidence.

Then he spotted something curious.

A couple of yards away, where the side slope met the flat trail, an out-of-place depression caught Mac's eye. Walking over, he saw it was a relatively fresh, scoop-shaped indentation about ten inches across. A small spring had softened the ground there and the base of the hole had filled with a quarter inch of water. He stared at it for a few moments, then looked up the slope.

Climbing away from the trail, he edged his way up the steep hill, his footing shaky over the mat of small bushes and fallen flora debris, forcing him to resort to all fours to maintain balance. In about five yards or so the ground evened out and paralleled the trail right below it. Mac walked along the level ground, looking for something. For what, he wasn't sure. But he'd know it if he . . .

Almost stepped on it. He jumped back as if he had come upon a rattlesnake. He refocused his eyes to make sure this was no trick, no illusion, that what he was seeing was really, truly there. This was not what he had been looking for. This was incomprehensible. Mac Schneider, formerly one of the toughest street detectives in the Los Angeles Police Department, a man who'd seen pretty much everything, shuddered. Instinct caused him to warily scan the forest. Then he looked back down at his discovery. The chill that ran through his body had nothing to do with the frigid air. He continued gazing at this thing, as if staring at it long enough might make it change into something he could accept. Until this moment Mac had surmised the scooped-out soil down below had been made by someone, a boot or shoe at an odd angle that might explain the size. But this?

Carillo was visually sifting the trail when he heard Mac call for him. Irritated, he waited until Mac called again before breaking his concentration to walk back down the trail. *Who knows? Maybe he's got something.*

Carillo rounded the corner to find Mac crouched by the side of the trail, pointing at the ground.

"Hey, check this out."

Carillo walked up and looked.

"What do you think that is?" Mac asked.

Carillo looked at the scooped depression in the soft ground at the trail's edge. He shrugged. "A hole?"

Mac motioned for Carillo to follow him. "C'mere."

Carillo watched Mac climb the steep grade and shook his head. "This better be good."

A few yards later Mac stopped and looked down at the level ground.

Carillo stepped up next to him and his eyes followed Mac's. "Fuck me."

They were looking at what appeared to be a perfect, complete, humanlike footprint, but it was absolutely gigantic. Mac pointed at thick fir branches above them. "The trees shielded the rain. That's why it's still intact."

Mac looked at a partial impression almost four feet away. "Looks like another one."

Carillo quickly sized up their find. "It's a fucking fake."

Carillo's words were almost a relief for Mac. For a few moments he had started to believe the unbelievable. Fortunately his partner was a man who possessed a blessedly narrow view of the world. Carillo was suspicious of everything and everyone and because of this simplified outlook could cut through a lot of bullshit and often hit the nail on the head. Mac liked that about Carillo and knew that it was a quality that made him a good detective. It also made him a bit dogmatic at times, but this was one of those times Mac welcomed his certainty. "You think?"

Carillo fixed Mac with a "What the fuck else could it be?" look. "So some jerk-off went to the trouble of making big, fake feet, but for what reason? This other track here?"

Carillo stepped over to the other, partial print, to make his point. "See? It looks like the guy was trying to make it look like whatever made this was really big but he slid or something . . . didn't make a complete impression. Too far to step and he lost it. Totally fake. I mean give me a fucking break."

"Is this related to the hikers?" Mac asked.

Carillo's eyes analyzed the scene. "Shit . . . who knows? Another thing, we don't even know yet if these assholes are really missing. Do we?"

Mac stared at the print. "No. But if this is in some way related, then why? Like you said, what purpose would it serve?"

Mac knelt by the print while Carillo crouched to get a closer look. Mac pointed to the edge of the print. "It's fresh. Yesterday, tops."

Carillo pushed the soil nearby with his fingertip and furrowed his brow. "How did they get it that deep?"

Mac shook his head. "Either way, we need to pull this, get a cast."

Carillo looked at him. "You want to waste a forensic tech's time on this shit?"

"Do we have a choice? I mean it's right next to the trail and we've got no idea if it's related. Can we take a chance?"

"All right," said Carillo, "but here's how we have to play this. We keep this quiet. If we have to bring in a CSI, then they keep their fucking mouth shut. If this turns out to be related, then maybe it's our ace in the hole, but the downside is it's kinda weird. I'd say we keep this tight, partly to avoid any shit from anybody. We tell Rice and Barkley, that's it."

Mac nodded. "I agree." Undersheriff Tom Rice and his boss, Sheriff Rick Barkley, were the only others who needed to know. Mac gathered some fallen branches and gently laid them over the impression to protect it. "Let's go."

With Carillo leading they carefully descended the steep few steps to the trail. Despite Carillo's confidence that the footprint had been hoaxed, Mac reached in his jacket and touched his handgun for reassurance. Then he cast an eye on the woods around them.

Later, at the trailhead, Mac and Carillo found a milling crowd of about two dozen volunteer searchers. Someone had erected a Red Cross–style aluminum-framed shelter under which two women dispensed coffee, doughnuts, and other snacks. It looked like the group was just getting organized. To Mac and Carillo's surprise the four earnest rescuers from the night before were also present, considerably less fresh-pressed than they had been eleven hours before.

Mac approached Steve Keener, their ex officio leader. "Any luck?" he asked.

Keener shook his head, looking more downcast than tired. "Nope. Not a sign."

"How did you guys get back here?" asked Mac. "We've been on that trail a few hours."

Keener pointed to the peak above them. "Got to the top, then came back. Must've found a false trail in the dark. Ended up bushwhacking down the mountain when we got off trail. Lucky we didn't fall off the damned thing." The bravado of the previous evening gone, he added, "We screwed up."

Mac felt sorry for the guy. He came to save his friends and almost became a statistic himself. Mac stepped by, patting Keener's shoulder as he passed. "You got guts. Go eat."

Mac noticed a distraught young woman who he assumed was Mitch Roberts's wife. She was speaking to some of his department's search and rescue members. Breaking into their conference, he introduced himself.

The rescue workers headed off to do their job and Mac spent the next twenty minutes questioning Karen Roberts. In his heart he hoped it was not an exercise in futility and did it mainly to allay her fears, at least for the time being. He understood that getting used to her husband's being gone would be a process better served by time. He certainly didn't mention what he and Carillo had seen above the trail.

Carillo and Mac hooked up after his chat with Roberts's wife and exchanged notes. While they talked, the Channel 7 news van arrived and the crew piled out. When Kris Walker alighted, Carillo tapped Mac's shoulder. "Go for it, tiger."

Kris and Mac made eye contact and she headed toward him.

"Hi," she said. "What's the latest? Any luck?"

"No, nothing. But now that it's daylight, hopefully the teams will find 'em soon. I'm told the choppers are on the way."

Kris looked around, as if wanting to speak confidentially. "Can we talk? Over there?" she said in a lowered voice, pointing to a spot about ten yards from the growing group.

Mac nodded and they walked out of earshot. Kris turned to Mac, keeping her eye on the people in the background. "I don't think they'll find them."

Her statement drew a curious expression from Mac.

"This kind of search," she said, "is usually presupposed on the notion someone wants to be found, like they're hurt or something."

She looked him straight in the eyes. "I've been thinking about this. I have a theory."

Mac could not stifle his patronizing smile. "A theory? Don't hold back, I'm all ears."

Kris ignored his amusement. She was working a carefully contrived plan. "Look, I've gotta do this report right now, then fly. Can we talk later? Tomorrow, maybe? I've got some ideas I want to bounce around."

Kris had a feeling this might be a great story and she wanted to be the one to break it. She knew he was interested; she read men pretty easily. She also knew it was critical for her to gather more information to support her theory. She needed to know what he knew.

Mac knew she was trouble. Had he been happily married, he would have been less vulnerable and dismissed her advances. But he wasn't.

"Yeah, okay," he said. "Maybe tomorrow. Call me."

As they walked back to the crowd, she handed him her card.

"You're a busy guy. Call me when your schedule opens up. This has all my numbers and I wrote my home on the back."

Kris walked away and Mac looked at her card. He doubted she wrote her home phone on all her cards and wondered when she'd written it in anticipation of giving it to him.

He sang softly to himself, "Eee-eevil . . . woo-man . . ."

By early afternoon, Mac and Carillo left the scene in the hands of search and rescue and went back to the department. Mac did some paperwork, then headed back into the mountains. He volunteered to go back to the scene to meet the forensics person since he knew her and was asking her for a favor. Back at the trailhead parking area Mac saw the same crowd milling around, then noticed an attractive Asian-American woman in her early thirties huddled in her Acura. She saw Mac approaching and got out.

"Hey, Suzy," said Mac, "sorry I'm late."

"No sweat," she said. "What's with the cloak and dagger? You and Carillo running some kinda special operation? If Miller gets wind of this, I'm in the shit and so are you."

"I appreciate you not telling anyone. Don't worry about Miller. Carillo and I'll clear it with the big man and he'll take care of Miller. You got your casting kit?" Mac asked.

She reached into her car and withdrew a tackle box and a paper sack. "I'm ready."

"C'mon," said Mac, gesturing toward the trail.

Suzy Chang was not only the department's assistant head of forensics and crime scene investigations, but Mac considered her a friend. A former Angeleno, she and Mac first bonded over their love of L.A. and the peculiarities of its culture. They climbed the trail past the searchers, reaching the point where Mac found the indentation.

Mac pointed at the caved-in trail edge. "What do you make of that?"

Suzy shrugged and crouched to examine it. "I don't know, could be several things."

Mac pointed at the slope above them. "Follow me."

They quickly reached the pile of branches Mac had used to cover the footprint. He picked them up and looked at Suzy. She stared for a moment, then her face clouded in anger.

"Goddamn it, Mac!" she said, looking around at the nearby woods. "Carillo!" she shouted. "Carillo! You're a dick!" She looked at Mac. "And you are too! I was going down to Edmonds, have brunch, watch the game. This isn't funny. Where's Carillo?" Again she yelled in no particular direction. "Okay, you can come out, Karl! And turn off your camera, you dick, the joke's over!"

She looked at Mac and his expression was even, perhaps slightly solemn. Suzy calmed down then fixed Mac with her gaze. He didn't flinch.

"Okay, that's the wrong reaction, Mac." She looked back at the footprint. "Don't even tell me . . . Don't even frickin' tell me."

Mac squatted next to the track. "Carillo thinks it's fake."

Suzy got down on her hands and knees. "Jesus, now Carillo's the voice of reason? I'm not sure what's scarier, that or this being real." After she examined it for moment, she looked up at Mac. "What about you? You think it's fake?"

Mac nodded. "Yeah, definitely," but his voice betrayed his lack of certainty. Suzy stared at him for moment trying to read his face, then looked back at the track.

"Well, all I can say is, somebody's got a sense of drama. Could this thing be any bigger? I mean if you're gonna fake it, at least try and make it believable. You really want me to cast this thing? I hope I have enough plaster."

As Suzy readied to make the pour, Mac pointed at the other, partial print. "How do you explain that one?"

Suzy got up and examined it. She touched the ground in several places. "That's easy. The ground is soft there, not soft here. The guy could only get one print to stick and luckily the tree boughs protected it. Plus he tried to stretch and it looks like he slipped or something."

"Or something? Aren't you the track expert?"

Suzy laughed. "Tracks? Not really. Give me blood, biologicals, trace, I'm scary. Tracks, no."

"So," Mac asked cautiously, "you think it's fake?"

Suzy looked over the print. "Of course." There was a pause. "But I'd like to know how the guy got the impression so deep. That's wild."

Mac was circumspect. *Wild is not the word I'd use.*

18

The Monday before Thanksgiving, Ronnie set the wheels in motion to find an au pair. She left work late in the afternoon and headed home for her first au pair interview. Hurriedly parking her Lexus, she left the garage door open and walked to the house. She had barely had time to hang up her coat and sort through the mail when the doorbell rang. She opened the door to find a creamy-complected redhead, probably four inches taller than her own five seven. A classically attractive, brown-eyed Valkyrie, the young lady beamed warmly as she held out her hand. Ronnie thought she looked a whole lot like some actress, whose name didn't come to her immediately.

"Mrs. Greenwood? I'm Greta. Greta Sigardsson."

"Hi. C'mon in." Ronnie detected the slight accent. "Swedish?"

"Yes, I am. You have a very beautiful home. It's really . . . uh . . . uh . . . huge."

Ronnie smiled at the young woman, amused by her stumbling to find an adjective. They both giggled and felt an instant bond. Ronnie liked a woman who could laugh at herself. Ronnie pressed the intercom and summoned her kids. Ronnie introduced them all, then excused herself to make a business call. When she returned, she saw that Greta was truly the Swedish Mary Poppins: the three were already playing.

Ty walked in, looking tired, his soiled Forest Service uniform—at least to an outsider—incongruous for the owner of such an immense, sparkling house. It represented a long story that Ronnie could never summon the energy to tell anyone. Ty pecked Ronnie, tousled Chris's hair, then leaned down and kissed Meredith's head. He and Greta made eye contact.

"Hi," he said, moving to the fridge for some juice.

"Honey, this is Greta," said Ronnie. "The agency sent her over. She and the kids are getting to know each other."

Ty turned and shook her hand.

"Hello, Mr. Greenwood," she said, her face flushing as she giggled nervously. Ty smiled tightly and left the room, while Ronnie's eyes enlarged ever so slightly as she woke up and realized this was a beautiful young woman who obviously found her husband attractive. Ronnie suddenly saw Ty as the other woman did, a handsome, virile man with Redfordish dirty blond hair, in a snug uniform, his face rendered just a bit more rugged by two days' stubble.

That's when Ronnie noticed it was seven twenty and the next recruit was on the way to their home. She quickly ushered Greta to the door, thanked her, and said they'd be in touch. When the next au pair arrived, Ty was upstairs showering. This young lady was Danish but shorter and zaftig. Ronnie wanted to like her, but this one didn't really hit it off with the kids as well as Greta. Then her presumption did her in: "I can't wait to drive the Lexus!"

Ronnie thanked her as the door hit her in her zaftig ass.

Several hours later Ronnie climbed into bed. She looked over at her husband as he read a book and visualized him back in uniform.

Ty took a break, set his book on his chest, and closed his eyes for a moment. It wasn't that late but he was tired, mentally tired. Suddenly he felt Ronnie's hand slide over his chest, and his eyes opened, his passion of yesterday morning now replaced by the old, poisonous feelings of insecurity. After some uncomfortable kissing, Ty gently pulled Ronnie's hand away.

"I'm beat, baby. Maybe in the morning," he said, then rolled over.

She picked up a book, read for a few minutes, then got up and left the bedroom.

Ty felt bad about turning Ronnie down. He knew she was going downstairs to work on her computer for a while, then lock herself into one of the five main floor bathrooms and find her own satisfaction. He thought about the au pair and her schoolgirl reaction to him. He knew Ronnie had also seen it and he didn't need any more tension between them. It did massage his ego slightly to know a girl of nineteen or twenty found him a hunk, but with the tension between himself and his wife he took little satisfaction from it.

The next evening Ty got home, showered, paid the babysitter, then went to his office. He was irritated that another day had passed with no progress. Maybe he'd quit the Forest Service and secretly set up an office in Snohomish. Ronnie would probably never know the difference. Problem was he'd never lied to his wife and wasn't about to start. Sometimes he didn't tell her the whole story, but lying? No. He couldn't go there, even for this.

When the dark time came, he followed the stream for a while and saw more signs of the small two-legs. He found a few scattered wood caves, all larger than the one he had destroyed, and some hardshells waiting near the caves to do the bidding of their small two-leg masters.

He came down from the hills to learn more about his enemies, their habits, their ways. He was curious. He found pleasure in the kill, and knowing them better would make him stronger. His feeling that there were probably many, many small two-legs was strengthened by the spread of their signs the farther into the flat land he went.

The mountains were his but it seemed the flat land belonged to the small two-legs.

He crossed several hard black trails, the paths of the hardshells. He knew the small two-legs had made these black trails and there were many of them. He had never been this close to the places of the small two-legs and he could see their marks, their spoor, everywhere. That they left so much to show their presence told him they felt no fear, yet they were weak.

He passed by a large wood cave, this one burning from within by the special fire that the small two-legs controlled. This firelight came from many openings in the wood cave. Though the small two-legs controlled it, he knew well that they sometimes allowed their fire to escape.

He thought of the Great Fire, and how he had survived, clinging to the rocks. He thought of his tribe and how they had all died that day—his mate, his offspring. He could still see them, consumed in the flames, their death cries drowned out by the roar of the fire. Now he was left with nothing but rage.

His journey had taken him over many mountains and he had continued until he came to this place. His desire for revenge knew no limits, and with his discovery that the small two-legs were a good source of meat, he knew he had found his new home.

Passing through a stand of trees, he entered a clearing near a large wood cave. From the openings in the side of the wood cave he saw fire glowing within. The small two-legs were the Keepers of Fire and he sensed them inside, their chaotic mind voices noisy in his head. Nearby were two smaller wood caves but he felt no small two-legs inside them. Three hardshells waited near them. Never having been that close to a hardshell, he approached the largest of the three.

Its skin was harder than he had imagined and cold to the touch. He sensed no emotions from it and, after examining it, was convinced that it was not a living thing. Pushing gently on the skin, he rocked the hardshell slightly. The upper parts of its flanks were open but the openings were hard, like air that had frozen into ice. He touched this phenomenon, trying to understand.

It was also cold, but not as cold as ice. Looking into the guts of the hardshell, he saw it was hollow. He pushed on the warm ice with his fingers and it broke. This told him more about the warm ice. He looked at the inhabited wood cave and realized the openings through which the controlled fire glowed were also covered in warm ice. He reached inside the hardshell and grabbed a round thing and pulled. It also broke. After a few more minutes of poking at it, he decided to leave.

But first he would let the small two-legs know he had been there.

Ricky Allison was getting ready for a date pretty much the way any other seventeen-year-old did. Once dressed, he'd gone into the bathroom to prod a pesky zit. After failing to pop it before making that telltale red welt, he was now trying to cover up the damage with some of his mom's foundation. It had only been a few seconds after his mom yelled he was going to be late when he heard it.

At first he wasn't sure what the sound was. It was noisy but didn't track with anything in his audio experiences. Like maybe a sort of muffled crunching metal sound. It came from out back where the cars were parked. He left the bathroom and passed through the rec room, where his parents were just sitting down to eat, the music from the television heralding the opening sequence of *Wheel of Fortune*.

"You guys hear that?" he asked his folks.

His dad, Deke, didn't even look up from the pork chops, apple sauce, and potatoes au gratin that had just landed on his TV tray. "Hear what?"

Ricky entered the laundry room and called back, "Some big noise out back."

Deke looked to his wife, Marge. "You hear anything?"

She shook her head and dug into the food on her plate.

Ricky flipped the switch on the big mercury vapor lamp located at the top of a twenty-foot pole he and his dad had installed the year before. They'd been having a problem with deer eating his mom's garden, so the light, which put out more photons than a white dwarf star, was perfect for scaring off any critters and also illuminating the entire back area, including the garage and utility shed. Deke loved the light but found he still needed a flashlight because the intense, directional light also created jet-black shadows.

While the light flickered briefly before coming to full power, Ricky slammed the back door and leaped over the two wooden steps to ground level. As the light popped to one hundred percent, Ricky took in the parking area and his jaw did a Roger Rabbit. He didn't take another step because what he was looking at both confused and scared him.

Why would anybody do that? Who would do that? How did they do that?

"Dad! Hey, Dad! C'mere. You gotta see this!"

Then Ricky whispered to himself, "Fuckinay . . ."

Deke and Marge pushed their trays away, alarmed by the urgency in their son's voice. When they stepped onto the back porch, they saw why. Everything was normal save for one thing: illuminated in the ghostly blue-white light was Deke's pride and joy, his metallic indigo blue Chevy Tahoe, with the LT preferred equipment group, the running boards, and the heavy-duty towing package. It was pretty much where he'd parked it that evening.

Except now it was reposing on its roof, tires in the air like a toes-up dead dog.

Ricky, Deke, and Marge were frozen in their tracks. After a moment of nonplussed gaping, Deke kicked into gear and started barking commands. "Son, get the thirty-thirty and my Python. And a flashlight. Margie, get the sheriff out here."

A moment later Ricky returned, huffing, with the requested items. Deke hefted the rifle and slid the big Colt revolver into his pants pocket. Now braced by weapons and a flashlight, they cautiously moved toward the topsy truck.

Deke waved the light around the shadows as they approached it, sweeping over the vehicle and off into the trees for signs of the vandals. Then Deke flashed on the idea that maybe his son had crossed some bad boys at school.

"Any ideas who mighta done this?" Deke queried.

"No," Ricky answered, still incredulous. "I mean it musta taken like twenty guys."

Deke looked over with a cocked eyebrow. "Know who mighta?"

Ricky realized the implication. Ricky was *very* cool with everyone he knew. This was like big-league mayhem, like biker shit.

"No way, Dad," he denied emphatically. "I don't have any idea who would do this."

Deke knelt and looked into the Tahoe and saw that someone had literally ripped the steering wheel off its post. *Unbelievable.* Sobered by the thought of the forces necessary to do such a thing, he was nevertheless infuriated by the mindless destruction.

Marge yelled from the back door to report that the sheriff was sending someone. As Deke started to rise, his flashlight revealed something in the shadows beside the truck. The driveway's drainage was pretty good but the rain had softened some parts of the apron where he parked his vehicles. What he made out in the mud sent a powerful chill down his back.

Ricky noticed his dad tremble and it shocked him. "What?"

His dad, even in the unearthly light of their security lamp, suddenly looked bone white. Now Ricky was really scared. "What?" he demanded again.

Deke pointed the light on the track in the mud. It was clear enough: a complete footprint.

Ricky whistled, "Jee-zus . . . ," and gingerly put his size ten Reebok next to it for scale.

The fresh print dwarfed his shoe.

Without a word, Deke and Ricky headed toward the house to wait for the sheriff.

19

everal minutes into Ty's Internet search, Christopher knocked and entered. "What're ya doing?" he asked.

Ty had been neglecting his kids so he waved his son over and pulled up a chair for him.

"Some research. Want to help?"

Chris brightened. "Yeah. What are you looking for?"

"Newspaper articles."

"On what?"

Ty paused for a moment. "Missing people."

"How come we don't get the paper, Dad?" asked Chris. "Everybody else does."

Though Ronnie got a copy of the *Seattle Times* at the office, Ty didn't want to try to explain his disenfranchisement with the news media. "Don't need 'em."

Chris looked on as Ty punched in his inquiry. Chris knew his dad had gotten in a lot of trouble a few years before, not like with the police or anything, but adult trouble he, Chris, didn't really understand. Some kids gave him a hard time about his dad being a weirdo, but Chris just let it roll off his back. The kids were stupid. Chris thought his dad took their harassment harder than he did. Those kids didn't know how smart or cool his dad really was, so Chris wrote them off.

Suddenly something on the screen got his dad's attention. Chris looked at the screen.

"Dad, what is it? What did you find?"

His father didn't answer and his face looked like he was in a trance. Chris scanned the screen for clues to what had so completely captured his father's attention. He saw an article about some missing lawyers.

"Did you know those guys?" asked Chris.

Ty shook his head, engrossed in the article. "No . . . no I didn't," he answered, a million miles from his son, for at that moment he was planning a drive into town in search of some newspapers.

When the 911 call came in to the Snohomish County Sheriff's Office, the panicked woman was practically screaming that someone had destroyed her husband's SUV. The dispatcher calmed her, then assured her that a car was on its way. With a few hundred patrol cars spread over a pretty large territory, the dispatcher put out a general call with the location to see who could respond. Deputy Bill Alexander wasn't too far away, so he took the call.

The unsuccessful search for the lawyers not only depressed him, it also worried him. After being alone on that mountain, and having felt that . . . whatever that feeling was, he wondered what he was up against. He had some ideas—maybe some good ones—but didn't want to voice them, not even in his imagination. The vandalism call sounded like a good way to get his mind off such things. He had a name, an address, and a description of the vandalized item. No problem.

The call took him out to the eastern half of the inhabited part of Snohomish County, up one of the myriad side roads that wandered through towering stands of cedar and fir. The night was moonless and there were few lights out this way, just the way the residents liked it. They didn't live this far outside town just to rub elbows with any neighbors. Most of the lots were at least five acres, with long, often unpaved driveways leading to the homes.

At a tilted mailbox with some stick-on house numbers and letters spelling *Allison,* Bill turned in. Following the roadway to the back of the house, he came upon a strange sight—a big sport utility perched on its roof. He recognized it as a Chevy Tahoe, a truck he coveted but was reluctant to try and swing on forty-six grand a year.

A man carrying a rifle came from the back of the house, accompanied by a teenager. Bill radioed he was on scene and got out. As the two approached him, Bill noticed the man's pants sagging under the weight of a sizable handgun in his front pocket.

Deke held out his free hand. "Man, am I glad you're—"

Bill interrupted him, "Sir, I'm going to have to ask you to put away the firearms."

Irritated by the request, Deke handed the artillery to Ricky. "Take 'em inside, son."

As Ricky left, Bill opened his notepad. "When did you discover the vandalism?"

"'Bout a half hour ago," said Deke. "My son heard it get rolled over."

Bill walked slowly around the truck.

Deke followed, watching the deputy. "Goddamnedest thing, huh?"

Bill didn't answer. Something had just caught his attention. He shined his light on the side of the truck not illuminated by the yard light.

"This truck wasn't rolled over."

Deke looked at him like he was nuts. "Whaddya mean?"

Bill's flashlight danced over the truck's unabraded flank.

"See? It's clean. Whoever did this *flipped* it over."

Deke looked and nodded softly.

"Well, shit howdy. Don't surprise me, though."

Bill didn't hear Deke's second comment. "Huh? What was that?"

"Said, 'It don't surprise me.'"

Bill looked at Deke. "So, you saw the vandals?"

Deke didn't answer; instead he motioned for Bill to follow. On the spur of the moment Deke decided to come clean with this deputy. He figured the guy should know what was going on. They walked around the truck and Deke clicked on his flashlight, spotlighting the giant footprint. Bill looked at it for a moment, registering no emotion. As Deputy Bill's gaze continued with no reaction, Deke wondered if he'd made his point or maybe the deputy was too stunned to talk.

Bill closed his notepad. Another shiver. *So much for relaxing.*

He looked at Deke. Both men knew the implications of the footprint. The turned-over truck and a bare manlike footprint so big as to be ridiculous meant only one thing. Both men had grown up in the area and had heard the stories since they were kids, but neither had ever really believed them. Bill had an anthropology degree and had read extensively about these things on his own. There were a number of scientists who had gone out on a limb by saying they thought they existed.

Now the decision was upon them whether they would join all the rest who had come forward with myth-come-to-life stories. Neither man wanted what he feared would happen should they open their mouths. Deke visualized hordes of news crews and the nightmare of trespassers day and night looking for this thing on his land. Bill saw skepticism and a diminution of his credibility, both at work and in his personal life.

Bill finally spoke, indicating the muddy print. "I can't tell what that is. Can you?"

Deke automatically started to disagree, "It's a—," then shut up, realizing the cop was telling him, not asking.

Bill repeated, "I can't tell what it is. Can you?"

Deke eliminated the impression with a few swipes of his shoe. "Nope."

Bill nodded approval. He took some more information, and then they shook hands. He walked to his patrol car, having written in his report that the truck was "rolled over by unknown perpetrators." He stopped and looked back at the Tahoe. "What's that thing weigh?"

Deke eyed his damaged baby. "Fifty-four, fifty-five hunnert."

Bill nodded again, then let his eyes patrol the perimeter established by the Allisons' powerful backyard light. "I'd keep that flood on," he warned.

Deke's agitated eyes followed the same path. Deputy Bill's advice went without saying. That thing might be watching them even now. Bill opened his door and started to climb in, then paused. "Was that an aught-six?" he asked, referring to Deke's rifle.

Deke shook his head. "Thirty-thirty."

Bill cast another wary look at the tree line. "I'd maybe go with something with a little more stopping power. That is if you got it."

Deke didn't appreciate the ominous suggestion that he might not have enough firepower but still waved halfheartedly as the cop closed the door and drove off. Ricky came back out of the house and joined him.

"What'd he say?" Ricky asked.

Deke didn't answer for a moment, then said tightly, "That we should move."

Ricky snorted at the joke, then saw his father wasn't joking.

20

After dinner, Mac slid into his leather lounger, turned on the TV, and pondered the unusual item covering most of the end table next to his chair: a plaster cast of a giant footprint. Mac had taken Undersheriff Tom Rice aside that morning, showed it to him, and told him he and Carillo were keeping its existence quiet for now. Rice agreed since it was uncertain what had happened to the hikers. "Plus," he said, "you let stuff like this out and you'll have all kinds of unwanted press, not to mention crazies." The official position was the casting was a confidential piece of evidence. *Evidence of what?* Mac stared at the plaster casting and a little tingle ran up his back. The phone rang, jarring him from his thoughts.

"Mac Schneider," he answered.

"Mac? Kris Walker," came the sultry voice on the other end. "You busy?"

Mac's eyes went to the casting. "Just doing some homework."

"The hikers?" she asked.

"No," he lied. "Something else. So, you still have a theory?"

"I do. Can we meet?"

"When?" he asked.

"I'm near your area."

"How do you know that?"

"I'm a reporter."

He smiled to himself. "Okay," he said. "Down the street, the Mexican place. The bar in ten minutes."

"I'll be there," she said. "See yah."

Mac wrapped the casting in newspaper and set it aside. While getting his coat, he realized he was still wearing his gun, preferring to pack a shoulder holster instead of the tidy belt job most guys seemed to favor lately. As he slipped off the gun, he was pleased he was nervous about seeing her. Since the stress of his job in L.A., the turmoil in his former marriage because of it, and his move north, there had been little life in his love life. That a woman could get his heart rate up was a long lost sensation. He decided he might even have a margarita.

Mac walked into the restaurant eight minutes later, expecting to see Kris in the bar, assuming she would have beaten him there since she was on the way. Mac realized he should have known better. Kris would have to make an entrance; that was the kind of woman she was. His speculations continued until she arrived, twelve minutes late.

"Sorry," she said, dropping her coat into the booth, "I got held up on the phone with the station. I'll be right back."

As she departed for the restroom, Mac noticed most of the eyes in the crowded bar following her, both male and female. Those who didn't recognize her were just staring at a head-turning woman.

She returned, her makeup freshened. Those piercing blue eyes and bang-cut platinum locks reminded Mac of an English movie from the sixties about a village full of perfect blond zombie kids. He decided she was the best-looking woman he'd ever seen in person. Maybe anywhere. The waitress appeared. "Coupla specials?"

Mac nodded and the waitress left.

"I could use one," Kris said. "I've been doing an investigation into crooked transmission shops and we just had a guy come forward who trained managers for a chain. He's got some unbelievable stories. They actually teach them how to screw customers. It's great."

She grabbed a chip and munched as she continued. "This story will kill some jobs, maybe even put some people out of business."

Mac noticed that the prospect lit up her face and voice. He liked busting criminals too but it often left him with a hollow feeling. There were always two sides to every story, no matter how indefensible the other position seemed to be.

"You like being a reporter," he observed.

"I love it. You like being a cop?"

"Less than I used to. Hard to walk on the wild side that long and not have it affect you."

"How long?" she asked, surmising again about his age, now pegging him as a young-looking thirty-eight.

"Twenty next year. Joined out of college."

She recalculated: a youthful forty-one or two. Impressive, she admitted, nary a wrinkle or hint of gray.

"Married?" She asked despite knowing the answer.

"No. Divorced. We're still friends."

Kris deducted a point. No one should ever stay friends with an ex. "She live around here?"

"Los Angeles. Teaches college. How long you been reporting?"

"Since I was at Wazzu. Did an internship. Bounced around on the way up. Landed here. Just another stop on the road to the network," she said.

Their swimming-pool-sized grande margaritas arrived, and as the waitress walked away, Kris shook her head. "Wow, I finish this and it'll finish me."

They hoisted their huge drinks and sipped. Mac stirred his with the Mexican flag that flew from a lime quarter.

"So, you're not staying in Seattle?" he asked.

"Probably not," she said. "This is a great city, but I want to take my career as far as I can. That's either New York or D.C. Maybe CNN in Atlanta."

"Family?"

"My folks live in Spokane," she said. "I'm an only child."

"See 'em often?" Mac assumed an unmarried woman in her mid to late twenties was probably pretty close to her parents.

She shrugged. "When I can. I'm not all that close to my dad anymore."

Mac could have followed that up but let it drop. "Going home for Thanksgiving?"

"I wish," she answered. "No time. Got the investigation, then I'm on call over the long weekend. You? You have family you're visiting?"

"No," he said. "My family's in Arizona. This Thanksgiving I'm working the early shift, then I'll go home and kick back."

Kris balanced her hefty margarita in a toast. "To working stiffs on Thanksgiving."

Mac raised his drink and they clinked glasses.

"To working stiffs on Thanksgiving," he said, noticing her hands. They were strong, with long fingers and short, sculpted nails covered in clear gloss. Practical. He looked into her eyes as the first blast of tequila hit his brain. His desires welled. Afraid his face would give him away, he moved the subject over to business. "All right, so what's your theory?"

She leaned forward as if anyone in the noisy place could actually hear them. "A serial killer."

Mac casually took a sip and ate a few chips. Finally he said, "Three missing men, two probably unrelated to the other, and you think it's a serial killer?"

She nodded. This was not quite the reaction she had hoped for. "They were all in the same general area. The broken trees? It sounds like it could be some kind of cult. I checked it out. Supposedly there were at least a hundred trees . . ."

"You saw the trees?" Mac interrupted.

"No, but it's in Barney Fife's report. I read it."

"Okay," he said, signaling her to continue.

"The truck guy, the logger? Just vanished. The hikers? Same thing. The dogs? They sensed the killer—or the cult members."

Mac smiled. "Sorry to blow your scenario, but those are tracking dogs we're talking about. Some crazy religious cult members on the lam aren't going to scare them."

"Maybe. But I did some research. Years ago, it was the midseventies, a cult in Idaho was stopping motorists, kidnapping, then killing them. They were pretty scary."

Mac nodded. "Yeah, I know, I read about it. Near Rathdrum, but it wasn't proven that it really ever happened. Some say it was just another urban legend."

She sat back, fiddled with her Mexican flag for a moment, then struck back. "Okay. What's *your* theory?"

Mac smiled. *I have no theory, but I've a got a huge fake footprint and two lawyers who probably fell off a cliff, one trying to save the other.* "It was the Dominicans."

Kris wrinkled her brow. "Huh?"

Mac laughed. "*The Exorcist.* Sometimes I make obscure film jokes only I laugh at."

"Never saw it. Okay, so who made these guys disappear?"

Mac took a big sip. "Here's what happened. The lawyers met a bear and the bear had never heard that shark joke about professional courtesy and ate them. And the logger saw his kid's nose ring and bolted, afraid the other loggers would mock him for having a gay son."

Kris slumped in her seat. Mac saw she was not as amused as he had hoped.

"All right, number one," she said, "having a nose ring doesn't mean you're gay. Tommy Lee has about eight of them and he's not gay and so does Lenny Kravitz. Not gay either. And bears eat salmon, not lawyers. Lawyers are low on omega-three. Bears know that."

"So who's playing with who?"

Kris playfully fixed him with an intense gaze. "Who's playing?"

They spoke for another half hour about everything but business. Then Mac began to feel the effects of the alcohol and the long day. He didn't want to look tired, so he made his excuse.

"Early morning tomorrow," he said. "Gotta go."

"Any serial killers to catch?" she asked.

"Maybe. I have a strong lead on a cult of religious nuts operating up in the mountains. Apparently they're targeting hot television reporters."

"You think I'm hot?"

Mac's smile told her to quit fishing for what she already knew. He rose and threw down a twenty to cover the drinks.

She held up her glass. "I feel so safe knowing you're protecting me."

"You should," he said, then turned to leave.

Kris's eyes followed him as he walked away. Initially, she'd called him to pick his brain about the missing men, but now she was intrigued. Here was a guy who walked away from *her.* Men didn't do that to Kris Walker. Ever. Then a thought so terrifying as to be unspeakable flashed though her mind: she was becoming attracted to him. Kris knew that couldn't happen because she was convinced relationships were career killers: once you got unfocused from the main task, you would be lost in starry-eyed bliss and then your competition would eat you alive.

She flagged down the waitress, ordered a shot of Cuervo, and unfolded her phone. The station's newsroom had wound down but an intern named Gwen answered. Kris instructed the eager young lady to dig up backgrounds on the lawyers, the logger, and a Snohomish County Sheriff's detective named MacDonald Schneider. She also told her to find anything she could on missing persons in the last year, particularly in eastern Snohomish County.

Kris was still Christine Walkowski in college. Quickly moving up through the television sequence at Washington State University, she became a communications department star with her iron tenacity, competent work product, and stupendous looks. She was also fine-tuning her sense of whom to throw under the bus and when.

Immediately after landing her first reporting job at a hick station in Yakima, she reinvented Christine Walkowski and became Chris Walker. From the moment she arrived, she did everything possible to get enough usable tape to move up the food chain. Taking every assignment she could, she gave them all the "Chris Walker edge," as she dubbed it. Her "edge" was an abrasive, almost confrontational style of reporting that landed her in several unpleasant meetings, first with the news director, then the station manager.

Those run-ins fanned the flames of her desire to get out of there as fast as she could. Two months into the job, while watching herself on a monitor during an edit session, she suddenly saw a major piece missing from the assembly of the Chris Walker persona: she needed to dial in her look. She had a natural beauty, but if she was ever going to go to the network, she needed to look big-time. At that moment, she looked too Yakima.

She drove to Seattle and maxed out her new Visa with a salon makeover and the genesis of a drop-dead wardrobe. It was a big financial roll of the dice for a rookie reporter making twenty-four grand in a top 500 market, and definitely a gutsy play for the daughter of a lowly milk route driver from Spokane. But it paid off a few months later with a job offer in Tacoma at triple her Yakima salary.

That's when Chris made another decision. She heard a story that inventor George Eastman so liked the hard-palate sound of the letter *K* he coined the name Kodak to represent his new company. Agreeing with George that *K*s ruled, notwithstanding the fact she already had the *K* sound, Chris became Kris. On that day, as Kris gazed into the mirror at her new look, and bolstered by her new *K* name, she saw a future anchor and swore to herself that *nothing* would stand in the way of her goal.

Kris thought about the risks she was going to need to take to get where she wanted to go. Although Kris was not one to build a large circle of friends, she did acquire relationships when they could help her achieve her goals. She smiled as she pictured her most recent "insurance policy" relationship, as she liked to refer to it in her thoughts. She knew that she was about to test its limits.

As the young waitress delivered Kris's shot of tequila and lime wedge, she asked sweetly, "Does your . . . husband want anything?"

Kris had noticed the waitress's attraction to Mac and decided to give her a quick lesson in reality. "Oh, that guy? He's gone." She picked up the salt shaker, licked the back of her hand, and tapped a little salt onto it. "Anyway, he's not my husband."

Then, without taking her eyes off the waitress, she licked the salt, knocked back the shot, and bit into the lime. "He's just a cop I'm gonna have to fuck for a story."

Kris handed the shot glass back to her stunned server and flashed a dazzling set of teeth. "Thanks."

21

Mac lied to Kris that he was working the day before Thanksgiving. He had planned to take the day off to do some research. That morning after spending a few hours online in his home office, he decided to stretch his legs and go down to the library. He had uncovered some interesting source books on various sites and wanted to see if he could find them in the library. The footprint casting had given him a possible answer and now he wanted to understand the question.

Searching through the aisles, Mac dug into a number of increasingly esoteric archeological and anthropological tomes. He read about the fossil remains of beings that were neither ape nor man. *Gigantopithecus* seemed to be the direct antecedent of whatever might have made Mac's footprint. *Gigantopithecus* had been reconstructed by anthropologists using the teeth, jawbone fragments, and a few other fossil relics. Said to be well over nine feet tall, its place in evolution fell somewhere between humans and the other great apes.

Anthropologists had traced *Gigantopithecus* back to within a few hundred thousand years, in China. What struck Mac was that here were nine- to twelve-foot-tall manlike creatures that had really existed and—in terms of the record of living creatures—within very recent memory. And the land bridge that had connected Asia and North America at the Bering Strait during the last ice age could have given such beings an opportunity to cross over and evolve over the intervening forty or fifty thousand years.

A rational case began to gel in Mac's mind for the existence of large humanoids living deep in the forests along the West Coast, from California up into British Columbia. He was surprised to discover that whole skeletons of humanlike beings had been unearthed in the Southwest, some more than ten feet tall. Yet in almost every book, anthropologists insisted that modern humans, called *Homo sapiens,* were the only hominids—that is, upright-walking primates—remaining on the planet. Mac smiled to himself. *Maybe not.*

As he delved into sightings, one continuing theme in most of the firsthand accounts was that these creatures were generally shy and harmless. He even found a few instances where they had saved people. But he also read enough stories to indicate they weren't always gentle. Some women in Southeast Asia had apparently been kidnapped and partially eaten back in the early fifties. The tale also grimly related that one village woman had been raped by a pack of nine-foot-tall beings that walked on two legs.

After a while Mac logged on to the library's computer and took a piece of paper out of his pocket. It was the code number for his department's LexisNexis account. He punched in the numbers and surfed related newspaper articles. He found several concerning a Snohomish man a few years back who claimed he was chased by Bigfoot while vacationing in Idaho. What interested Mac was that the guy had been an exec with a major software company and not some fringe crackpot. Ty Greenwood's reception from the media reinforced Mac's concerns about making a big deal about the footprint. Mac printed out the articles to show to Carillo, thinking that Greenwood might be of some help.

Ty entered the *Snohomish Daily News* office clad in his freshly cleaned uniform. He was ready to continue his official charade in the interest of gathering more information. He asked for John Baxter, who appeared a moment later.

Ty extended his hand. "I read about the missing lawyers and was wondering if you had any further information—"

John Baxter, his face set in anger, didn't take Ty's hand. "Why have you been bothering Lori Wylie?" he demanded.

Ty was taken aback. "I only made a few calls . . ."

Baxter stepped closer, despite Ty's considerable height and age advantage. "Look, the woman is distraught enough about her husband disappearing, then you start wigging her out. You got her number from my file. Lose it."

"I just wanted to—" started Ty.

"Lose it." Baxter walked away.

Shaken, Ty left. Baxter returned to his office. Passing his secretary, he paused.

"Sally, get me the number for the Forest Service regional office," he said. "I want to know why they're so concerned about missing people."

The name Ty Greenwood still stuck in his mind and Baxter remembered his plan to check the man out on the Internet. Just as he was about to log on, Sally buzzed him.

"John, it's the *National Investigator*," she said with a smirk.

Baxter picked up his phone, assuming she was joking. "Baxter."

"Mr. Baxter, Joyce Hyde with the *National Investigator*. We monitor papers all over the world and we found an interesting piece in yours and I was wondering if you'd elaborate on it?"

First Greenwood, now this. "Which one?" he asked.

"The one about the overturned truck."

"What about it?" he asked, wondering why anyone would give a hoot about some guy's toppled sport utility.

"Well," she continued, "according to our research, that vehicle weighs five thousand three-hundred and thirty pounds, yet your article says the victim didn't hear anyone in his yard."

"Probably a big yard."

"But the son only heard the truck tip over, not who did it. We estimate it would have taken fifteen to twenty men to put that truck on its roof. We also checked the weather reports and there was no wind in your area that night."

Judas priest, and this is a tabloid? I wish my people were that thorough. Then he remembered his reporter saying something about the victimized family being reluctant to talk. He didn't need to fuel the fires by mentioning that.

"What's your point, Ms. Hyde?" he asked.

"It sounds very strange. Do you have any thoughts on this?"

He was too old to be coy or even overly civil. "No. How will you characterize it? Aliens or Satanists?"

"I'm just trying to do my job," she said defensively.

"And I'm asking, What is that job? Irresponsible speculation? You're not a reporter, you're a fiction writer."

"Thanks for your time," she said curtly, then hung up.

John Baxter shook his head. *Whatever happened to the good old days of news gathering?*

Sally entered and handed him the number for the Forest Service. Baxter nodded and picked up the phone. He was in a feisty mood and looked forward to chewing someone out about invading people's privacy.

Ty stopped by the 7-Eleven to reimburse Todd Shelton for the "loan." Todd wasn't in, so Ty gave the clerk an envelope containing a note and a twenty-dollar bill. Then he drove over to Everett to the sheriff's department and asked to speak with Deputy Bill Alexander. Deputy Bill was out, so Ty left a message including his cell and pager number. Sitting in his truck, he flipped through a copy of the day-old *Snohomish Daily News* he'd grabbed from their office.

He read a brief police blotter entry about a vandalized truck. It merely gave the name of the victim, the fact that the truck was a Chevy Tahoe, and a quote by the victim's teenage son, who said he didn't hear anything until the truck hit the ground. Also, the truck hadn't just been turned over on its side but was found resting on its roof. And again, Snohomish County Sheriff's deputy Bill Alexander had responded.

Ty thought back many years to when, as a freshman at the University of Southern Mississippi, he and some drunken buddies had turned over an old truck in a field. A postwar Ford that weighed nowhere near what a dreadnought like a Tahoe weighs, and still twelve shitfaced frat boys needed all their strength to put it on its side. Ty remembered it was a very noisy process and took a while. How did this happen with the family sitting nearby in the house? Unfolding his laptop, he searched the Internet for the address of one Donald R. "Deke" Allison.

22

By the time the librarian passed by and quietly informed him it was closing time, Mac was beginning to fully embrace the notion that he might be dealing with something extraordinary. The only thing he had to do, the last step in his chain of matching evidence to reality, was to confirm or disprove the footprint. He didn't want it to be real because that opened up a can of worms he didn't want to try and imagine. He assured himself that Carillo was right and that the print was a great fake. But another voice within told him to get a second opinion.

One of the names that surfaced repeatedly in the reports was of a potentially sympathetic scholar at the University of Washington. Back at his condo Mac phoned the school's anthropology department. After he explained to the secretary that he needed to consult with Dr. Wade Frazier as soon as possible about police business, she put him on hold a moment, then returned, informing him he had an appointment in two days, the day after Thanksgiving.

His gut as a cop told him the mountain trail was where he should continue his search, but a stirring uneasiness made him rationalize a reason to put that off.

* * *

Ben's nephew David and his family lived in the approach path for Sea-Tac, and with jetliners drifting overhead every few minutes, the noise was disturbing what little otherwise undisturbed sleep Ben could get. Ben was also feeling a pull to be closer to the mountains. He couldn't put his finger on the feeling but knew it was his instinct talking. Ben studied maps of the area and settled on Bellevue, which had all the amenities of a decent-sized city and also gave him relatively close access to the forests to the northeast.

He packed his bags and made his excuses to David, who pledged to help him any way he could. Ben did not use a computer but recognized the benefits of research on the Internet. When they parted, Ben asked David to poke around online and fax him whatever he might find on the subject. His nephew was a fellow believer and Ben trusted him to be discreet with the family.

Ben gave Doris a call from his new hotel to inform her of the change. She was disappointed that he was going to miss Thanksgiving with the family.

"Honey, what're you doin'?" Doris asked plaintively. "The agent called, then the movie people called, and they all wanted to know where you were. I said I wasn't sure."

Ben was slightly annoyed she hadn't followed his instructions to simply say he was away tending to personal business.

"When you comin' back, Benny?"

The worry in her voice caused Ben's heart to ache for taking off so abruptly and not explaining anything to her.

"I don't know. Maybe it'll be soon," he said, then added, "I miss you, Dorrie."

"You too, Benny," Doris said, sounding depressed to the point of tears. "I love you."

"You too," said Ben, who had always been uncomfortable responding to that declaration. In all their years together he had told Doris he loved her once or twice but regretted not saying it more. They wished each other happy Thanksgiving and hung up. As Ben unpacked his things, he wished he could have spent Thanksgiving with Doris. Then he regretted not telling her outright that he loved her, knowing it was something she longed to hear.

23

After the extensive background check on Greta Sigardsson came up spotless, Ronnie phoned the agency to approve her as the new live-in supervisor of her children. She had already prepared one of the bedrooms in the south wing—down the hall from the kitchen and TV room—a nice ground-floor room with tall bay windows. She hoped Greta could start that evening. Greta had boasted of her advanced cooking skills, which Ronnie planned to put to the test the next day. Ronnie left work early and the agency called on her way home to inform her Greta was very excited and would be dropped off by seven.

Ronnie arrived home excited to get things ready for Thanksgiving. She was spinning the logistics of the next twenty-four hours when she punched the button on the answering machine. There were six messages, four of which were from Ty's boss. Three were from that morning and one was from early in the afternoon and in all he expressed his concern that Ty had not shown up and was not answering his cell or pager. After that she assumed he had given up or found Ty. Either way she was curious what Ty would say about it.

Deputy Bill Alexander got Ty's message at the start of his shift. He looked at the message and tossed it. If there were two subjects Bill didn't want to talk about, one was the "missing lawyers" and the other was the "incident with the vandalized truck." He assumed this Ty Greenwood fella was probably some kook looking to interview people for some sort of *Stranger than Fiction* cable access show or something stupid like that. Bill wasn't going to end up in a damn sideshow. No way.

Clinging by one hand nearly twenty feet up an aluminum extension ladder, Ronnie lost her grip on an elaborate wreath, sending it plummeting to the floor of the entry. The crashing wreath caused the kids to titter and Ronnie to fume. As she was about to punish her kids for laughing by sending them upstairs for a box of more Christmas flotsam, the doorbell rang.

Chris opened the door and Greta was thrust into the middle of this small emergency. Seizing control, Greta calmed Ronnie, made a joke to the kids, and was cleaning up before Ronnie could get down the ladder. In moments the crisis was over and Greta even managed to resurrect the shattered wreath. Ronnie took this as a good omen.

Now holed up in his office, Ty had been evasive when Ronnie mentioned his boss's repeated calls looking for him. When she asked where he'd been, he told her that as he was driving to work he'd decided to take the day off. He told her he'd later checked in with his boss and squared everything. Ronnie let it go but was worried. Ty had always been relentlessly responsible, but now, if you likened their family to a vessel with him as captain, he seemed to have cast off in heavy waters and gone down below deck to sleep off the storm.

Ronnie hated confrontations, but if the need arose, she could hold her own. She felt such a blowout was coming with Ty. He had taken his public lashing far harder than she expected. She had sought counseling for them, then full-blown therapy, but Ty had soon dropped out, saying he was fine. His current behavior was beginning to indicate otherwise.

Greta ushered the kids into the kitchen to start dinner.

"Oh, we were just going to order a pizza," said Ronnie.

Greta waved her hand. "No, please, I was planning on cooking for you." Just as Ronnie opened her mouth to resist, Greta's eyes twinkled. "Sorry, you have no choice. And contrary to popular belief, Swedes can cook more than meatballs."

Down the hall toward the kitchen Ronnie pushed on the hidden door to the little-used wine cellar. It popped open, seemingly from a plain, uninterrupted wall. Descending the stairs into its cool recesses, she selected a '98 Dalla Valle Vineyards Napa cab and went back upstairs. Ronnie was disappointed Ty was not sharing festivities with the family, but as she looked for a corkscrew, she was philosophical.

What the hell, I'll have my own party.

Hours after Ronnie and the kids and the new au pair went to bed, Ty studied the USGS maps on his desk. He was searching for a relationship between the locations of the three missing men and the upside-down truck. His visit to the Allisons had not gone well. Deke Allison was less than enthusiastic about talking, and when Ty began examining the damaged but now righted Tahoe, Allison exploded and told him to leave. He was convinced Allison was hiding something because he was too jumpy. Ty was also angry that other people weren't talking to him. John Baxter's scolding for calling missing logger Joe Wylie's wife jarred him. He was getting a run of people who were overly suspicious or easily antagonized. Yet he vowed to himself to keep pushing until he found out why.

He needed help holding it together, just a little longer; he knew that now. He was on to something. He felt he was about to answer the question that had haunted him for three years.

Ty thought back to that first year and how Ronnie blamed the circus atmosphere he had created for taking him away from her and the children. One night after his return from a five-week expedition to the Northern California counties of Humboldt, Del Norte, and Trinity, Ronnie sat him down in his office. Waving a massive stack of invoices and receipts for services and equipment totaling more than $1.7 million, she proclaimed that he was destroying the family. She admitted that what set her off was the discovery of the invoice for "that gun." "Are you insane?" she yelled. Ty thought about that gun, now in the garage where Ronnie had banished it.

For her the dollars were tangible evidence of an obsession, but her real worry was the family. She told Ty she "hadn't planned on being married to Ahab." Putting her foot down in no uncertain terms, she swore she didn't give a damn what anybody thought about Ty, she loved him, the kids loved him, and that's all that counted. "Stop this insanity right now," she said. And then her exact words that followed were "You can't find it because it isn't there." That sentence still haunted him.

The next day a chastened Ty called off all of his investigations and announced the withdrawal of the reward. First he'd been an obsessive nut; now he was an unstable, obsessive nut. Ty sulked for days, then sought a doctor's advice. The doctor started him on an antidepressant. When the Scotch and antidepressants went sideways on him, Ty found a doctor to write him a prescription for OxyContin. He dropped the antidepressants and used the combination of liquor and painkillers for about a year. When the prescription ran out, he found a Mexican pharmacy to supply his pills. Then one day he just went cold turkey. But after about a year the depression came back even stronger than before, and that's when he renewed his partnership with Oxy and fine Scottish whisky. He knew the mix was potentially deadly but he was a desperate man who required desperate measures.

He reached to his drawer, the one he kept locked, and inserted the key that always stayed with him. He opened it, took out the pill bottle, and tapped out three times his normal dose of OxyContin. He splashed some whisky into his glass to wash them down. Lately, he'd been upping his dosage since the drug wasn't working as well as before.

I'll get it together, I just need a little time. That's all.

He put the bottle of Oxy back in the drawer and locked it. He often recalled the remark his father reflexively spouted when things had gone bad for him, "No good deed goes unpunished." Ty had long since realized he had inherited that gene of negativity from his father. "You can only fall *down*, son."

Well, I sure as hell did, Dad.

Ty leaned back in his chair and closed his eyes for a moment, and the dream tape of the chase in Idaho played yet again, and he felt the gooseflesh on his arms and neck. For a second or two he allowed himself to see the thing that had chased him in Idaho coming up his driveway. He shivered, set his drink down, and headed to the garage.

In the garage, at a tall storage locker off to the side, he pulled out a key from under a box and unlocked the padlock. Inside were some boxes and two tall, flat cases, one black plastic and the other, larger one, polished aluminum. He opened the plastic case. Inside was the tranquilizer rifle and another plastic case, about the size of a small first aid kit. Inside were six darts, whose bodies were tempered glass receptacles filled with a honey-colored, fast-acting sedative. As the large animal handler from whom he made the purchase said at the time, "These'll literally stop an elephant."

He picked up one of the darts, examined it, then put it back in its slot. Then he sorted through one of the boxes filled with hardware, including state-of-the-art infrared monocular night vision goggles and some motion sensors. Ty spent a few moments refamiliarizing himself with the gear, but he was anticipating the real reason he opened the locker. He pushed the equipment aside and gazed at the large aluminum case for a very long beat before reaching for it.

The beautifully finished case was nearly six feet long, fifteen inches wide, and six inches deep. A small gold plaque impressed into the metal near the combination lock carried the inscription Holland & Holland, London. He worked the combination and flipped the lid back. He stared, almost in supplication, at what was inside, then reached in with both hands and removed a massive rifle, its English walnut stock like so much richly grained brown glass. The nearly twenty-pound rifle was cumbersome as Ty caressed the wood, then hefted it to his shoulder. He put the crosshairs of the 8x scope on a leaf blower hanging from the wall twenty yards away.

"Boom."

He lowered the rifle and reflected on the trouble it had caused him. When he had begun his search for these creatures, he had strongly felt he needed a weapon. Several veteran searchers tried to talk him out of it, then just gave up, insisting that the beings were benign. Ty would hear none of their arguments, feeling he required practically supernatural protection like an Excalibur or the Spear of Longinus. Ty had settled on the gun maker's legendary Royal double rifle in .700 H&H Nitro Express. It was a gun intended for such robust game as bull elephants, Cape buffalo, and rhinos.

Ty had phoned the company and immediately put in his order for the spectacular bespoke firearm. Months later, not long after the handmade gun had been delivered, Ronnie discovered that it had set the Greenwood finances back by a little over £115,000, that is, around $200,000. That was one of the few times Ty had ever seen Ronnie lose it. The firearm had immediately gone out to the garage, but worse for

Ty, the incident had precipitated Ronnie's overall meltdown and the end to his quest.

Ty examined the only cartridge he had ever obtained for it, from a gun store in north Seattle. By chance he had gotten in a conversation with the owner and had mentioned he had the rifle. The guy gave him the single round, which he had purchased as a gag for his display case to dwarf other calibers. He had told Ty, "I think you need it more than I do." Ty had never once fired the rifle. He cringed at the thought of Ronnie's reaction if she found out he'd brought the thing back in the house. He closed the case and picked it up. He remembered a space in the back of his office closet where it would fit perfectly.

24

Thanksgiving day broke and Ty awoke early. He left Ronnie in bed to sleep in and headed downstairs for some coffee, then hopefully an hour or two alone in his office. Hearing a noise in the kitchen, he expected to see Christopher and came face-to-face with Greta as she assembled breakfast ingredients on the counter.

"Good morning," she said brightly. "Want some breakfast?"

Ty rarely ate breakfast. "No thanks, I don't really . . ."

"Oh please, let me cook you something," she pleaded. "I found the eggs and some cheese. I'll make you an omelet. And toast. The kids just wanted cereal. I'm a good omelet maker. Please let me make you a real breakfast."

"No, really," Ty protested, but not vehemently.

"Please," she said, turning her mouth and eyes down, a feigned sadness that appealed to Ty. She was certainly pretty. A beautiful young woman with a face animated by intelligence. Ty figured she was new to the household and didn't need to discover how dysfunctional they were right off the bat. He reluctantly pulled up a bar stool behind the counter.

"Make it wheat toast."

Later Ty finished the last bite and set his utensils on the plate, which Greta whisked away.

"Was it okay?" she asked.

"It was delicious," said Ty, wiping his mouth. "Hey, you drive? You have a license?"

Greta nodded. "Yah, I have a Swedish license."

"C'mon," he motioned, and slid off his stool.

She followed him to the front of the house. They arrived at the entry just as Ronnie appeared at the top of the stairs in her robe.

"Good morning, Ronnie," Greta said.

Ronnie descended the stairs. "What's up?"

Ty opened the front door. "Greta might need a car for errands."

They crossed the large plaza between the house and garage and Ty opened the side door and they entered. Greta's eyes widened at what looked like the motor pool for a small embassy. They arrived behind a fairly new red Suburban.

Ty swung back the driver's door. "Crap." The interior of the Suburban reeked of gasoline. He'd forgotten to remove the full gas can he'd gotten for his mower.

He punched the garage door opener to air out the space, then put the gas can under the workbench. He gestured to the Suburban.

"When you can breathe in it again, you can drive this."

Ben called Doris to wish her and the family happy Thanksgiving, then went downstairs to the Red Lion's restaurant for an early lunch. Even in his nondescript windbreaker a few people recognized him, and two kids, a boy and a girl of about ten, asked for his autograph. He obliged, then picked up a couple of local newspapers to search for interesting stories.

The waitress approached and handed him a menu. "Hi. My name's Cindy. What can I get you? Would you like some turkey? We have a Thanksgiving special."

Ben pondered the notion of Thanksgiving with some bemusement. White men had come to the "New World," had broken bread with his forebears . . . then over the next four hundred years had taken away most of what they had. Thanksgiving? For whom? He handed her back the menu.

"Cindy, I want the biggest, juiciest burger you've got. Hold the onions and put some cheese on it. Okay?"

She nodded, started to turn, then paused. "I really like your movies."

Ben smiled graciously. "Thanks."

On Thanksgiving morning Mac put in a few hours at work, then was back in his condo by one. He paid some bills and straightened stuff before putting his tri-tip in the oven around two. Then he decided to kick back and spend the afternoon catching up on the mountain of research on the desk in his home office.

As the smell of roasting beef wafted through his condo, Mac lounged comfortably with a book. He was engrossed in a story told in the 1890s by a crusty old woodsman named Bauman to President Teddy Roosevelt about an encounter he had back in the 1840s in a remote location in Idaho. Bauman related how he and a fellow trapper were terrorized at their camp for two days by a huge unseen creature that walked on two legs. When Bauman's partner was horribly murdered by the creature, Bauman fled for his life.

Mac got a chill as he put himself in Bauman's shoes 160 years ago, all alone in the middle of nowhere and coming upon the body of Carillo, his neck fang-torn, his head twisted hopelessly, his eyes open in terror but unseeing . . .

The phone rang and he jumped. "Schneider."

"Mac, Kris Walker. This a bad time?"

Mac realized he was breathing hard from being startled. "Uh no. I just ran to the phone. What's up?"

"I was wondering if another Thanksgiving orphan wanted to go have dinner somewhere."

"Actually I was making dinner—" he started.

"Oh sorry, I didn't realize you were—"

"No," he stopped her, "what I meant to say was why don't you come over? Have a home-cooked meal. It's just me, so come on over."

"A guy who cooks Thanksgiving dinner for himself? This I gotta see."

When they hung up, Mac changed from sweats into casual pants and a golf shirt, then quickly set another place at the dining table so she wouldn't feel she was intruding. Flipping on the stereo, he popped in a Joyce Cooling CD, then uncorked a nice zin and set it on the kitchen counter to breathe. He was ready.

Soon there was a knock on his door. Smiling to himself, he realized she had probably been well on her way when she called. Even without traffic his condo in Edmonds was at least thirty-five minutes from downtown Seattle. She was a sly one. As he crossed through the living room to the door, his eyes fell upon what was, at least for the moment, a top secret item. Sitting on the end table by his recliner was the giant plaster foot, left out in contemplation of his meeting with the anthropologist the next day. He quickly hefted it to the entry closet and buried it under some rubber waders he used when investigating river deaths.

He opened the door to find Kris bundled in a long black coat, its fake fur collar contrasting with her natural, almost white-blond hair. She held up a bottle of champagne.

"Happy Thanksgiving."

Mac took the bottle and waved her inside. He helped her with her coat and nearly reopened the closet.

"I love your place," she said. "This is really spacious. Give me the tour?"

They wandered down the hall and he glossed over his office, not turning on the light in hopes the shadows would conceal all the books on his desk that a reporter might find interesting. In his bedroom Kris went to the sliding glass door.

"I like this. Hey, look at that. You can see the Sound from here."

Mac nodded. "Just peekaboo."

"Nice. You decorated?"

Mac looked around, seeing it through her eyes. "Yeah. When I got divorced and moved from L.A., I started over with new stuff. It was kinda fun."

Kris noticed he still had her coat under his arm. She pulled it away and tossed it on the bed. She smiled and headed to the living room. There was sly promise in the quick, confident flash of her eyes.

Ty had a list of people who had been involved with the three missing men as well as the truck. He had some phone numbers but they weren't panning out. Ty still needed to talk to the deputy, Bill Alexander, as he seemed to be a connecting link. He wondered if he was working on Thanksgiving. Just as he picked up the phone to try the sheriff's department, Ronnie pushed open his office door and leaned against the frame.

"Can you cut the turkey?"

"Yeah, sure," he said. "I'll be right there."

"Ty, honey . . . what are you doing?"

"Just some research."

She looked around his office and noticed he had recently pinned up some maps and newspaper articles. "Please tell me this is a hobby not an obsession, right? Are we going to go through this again?" she asked, her voice rising slightly.

Ty shut off his computer and approached Ronnie, who stepped back slightly.

"Well, are we?" she demanded.

Backing her into the wall, Ty wrapped his arms around her. "I wouldn't do anything more to hurt this family. I love you, baby, and I love our kids. You three are everything to me. Okay?"

Ronnie didn't answer but just looked at him, praying things would be all right.

Ty took her hand and led them out to the hall. "Now let's eat some turkey."

He hadn't really answered her question. Nor would he, she feared.

25

From the moment they arrived at Nikki's folks' home for Thanksgiving dinner, Skip Caldwell had been bummed. She had totally roped him into the Thanksgiving dinner, and to an athlete who ate selectively, it promised to be a total clusterfuck of cholesterol, starchy carbs, and junk calories. Her promise had been to have him home by two because his daily workouts were essential, given it was three weeks to a major event in Arizona and he always got nervous as they approached. A world-class mountain biker, Skip had just signed a sponsorship with one of the hottest sports bike companies around and he needed an edge. Or a miracle.

His primary competition was reigning world champion mountain biker Dewey Devlin, and now the pressure was on Skip to show his sponsor that their faith and money were well placed. This was, by far, the most pressure he'd ever been under, so just to make sure everyone at the dinner knew that, he pouted the whole time, enough so that Nikki finally decided to bail the moment everyone else had finished gorging on turkey. On the way home, his mood lightened as hers sank. To get his adrenaline pumping he fished out his favorite death-metal CD, *Heartwork* by Carcass, pushed it into the player, and turned it up to eleven.

Back at their apartment in Monroe, Skip quickly loaded his downhill bike onto the bed of his Ford Ranger while Nikki flipped the tailgate closed, already missing her boyfriend. Skip kissed her long and hard, then pulled back and touched her nose with his finger.

"Back by seven, tops. Bye."

She nodded, then watched him drive away, wondering if he was pushing a little too hard. It was already three fifteen, so she guessed he had less than two hours of light and worried that he'd probably ride until it was pitch-black. But there was nothing she could do about it, so she went back inside their apartment.

Deke, Marge, and Ricky Allison were interrupted three times during the day, once during the NFL game and another time during their turkey dinner, by real estate agents showing potential buyers through their home. The fire-sale price on the house had real estate people climbing all over them, even on Thanksgiving. They all showed interest and Deke quietly told each of the agents to "make an offer, *any* offer" as soon as possible. Deke's biggest fear was that they'd walk the property and come across a giant footprint. Actually, his biggest fear was that the prospective buyers and agent would walk out behind the house to the property line two hundred yards down the trail and not come back.

He moved to a new place overlooking the low areas where the small two-legs lived. He marked it by breaking off the surrounding trees. This spot was flat but elevated, and after breaking the trees, he fashioned a shelter. He could sleep under trees, but when staking out an area, he preferred to make himself more comfortable. He was always careful to conceal evidence outside his area—his droppings, his tracks, and the remains of his kills. The old ones taught that the small two-legs were clever and might use such things against him.

He thought of those teachings, and though he followed them by instinct, he wondered why he should be careful of the small two-legs. They were fearful of him and easily killed. He was questioning the old ways, but habits were hard to break, so he built his shelter far above where a small two-leg could go.

The small two-leg from the little wood cave filled his belly for two suns, and after burying the remains of its body and arms, he carried its legs for two more suns. But he had eaten those just before turning over the hardshell. Now he was hungry again. With the dark time coming soon, he decided to go down from the mountain and hunt. Then he felt a presence. He rose, concentrating on where and what it was.

It was a small two-leg. And it was near.

Skip Caldwell was having the kind of run only a world-class mountain biker could have. He'd been on this trail once before but had made the mistake of splitting off on a fork too soon that dumped him down onto a cream-puff single-track. This time the run promised to be epic as he continued to climb, up past the fork, higher and higher. He guessed his elevation was about forty-five hundred feet, but he still didn't yet see daylight in front of him, just more hill, more trees. He hoped he would gain another several hundred feet before peaking. He'd heard the track on the backside was damn near vertical. He couldn't wait. It was getting darker but he guessed he had maybe thirty minutes left. But so what? Once he hit the top, he'd do the two-mile drop in less than five minutes.

As he climbed, pumping his muscled legs in his lowest gear, he started to feel he was being watched. He glanced around for other bikers, hoping to find some guys who had the *cojones* to run with him and to demonstrate his prowess as a downhiller. But he saw no one and refocused on the difficult task of cranking uphill without slowing enough to fall.

Coming upon what he guessed was the crest, he pistoned his legs harder, anticipating the rush of seeing the valley and trail below him. Then he saw something disturbing, a quick glimpse of what seemed to be a form, moving in the trees and high underbrush ahead. And despite the endorphin blast that had him at one with the universe, he suddenly felt very uneasy, because as he approached the trees, their increasing scale implied the form he had seen was definitely not a person. Too big, way too big . . . and shaped . . . well, wrong.

He pedaled harder, hoping to quickly pass the place where he thought he had seen the shape. Then he'd be at the crest and he'd fly. As he wheeled to the place, there was nothing there now. Ahead, the edge of the ridge beckoned, and he spun toward it.

Then, at most a few yards behind him, the air molecules came unglued, shattered by a rending scream as if all the machines in a factory had broken simultaneously. It was a horrid, grating metal-on-metal, louder-than-loud sound like a lion and a tornado and Metallica might make if they were trying to drown each other out.

Skip Caldwell didn't look back. He pedaled for his life.

While Mac busied himself in the kitchen, Kris found a stool on the other side of the counter.

"Where did you learn to cook?"

He rummaged in the fridge for a tomato. "Was married to a woman who hated to cook. Like getting thrown out of the boat. Learn or starve. You?"

Kris leaned on the counter. "I was Daddy's little girl. He wanted a son but he got me. The only cooking I ever learned was frying fish over a campfire and the only grocery shopping I ever did was helping tie a deer onto the roof of the car. I'd help dress it, then I'd tend the smoker."

"You said at the restaurant you two weren't that close anymore."

Kris took a sip of wine and paused for a moment. "When Daddy's little girl started looking more like a young woman, Daddy took an interest in her."

Mac quit prepping food and looked up while Kris reflected for a moment before continuing. "Anyway, it went on until I was sixteen. I never told my mom. He finally stopped when we reached an understanding."

Kris saw the question on Mac's face. "When I was sixteen, we were bear hunting and I pointed my crossbow at him and said, 'You ever touch me again and I will use this on you.' He saw my point, pun intended. Anyway, until all that went on, I'd been quite a tomboy."

Mac was somber. "I'm sorry."

Kris laughed to lighten the mood. "Hey, it's ancient history. I'm past it. I think it all made me tough. Do you think I'm tough?"

Mac continued dicing his tomato. "Yeah, you're tough. You like that label?"

Kris finished her wine. "I do."

Mac poured her more wine. "I prefer strong. That's how I see you."

Kris smiled at that. "Strong? Hmmm. I think I like that more than tough."

She held up her glass and Mac touched it with his. "To strong," said Kris.

"To strong," seconded Mac.

The trail blurred as Skip dodged rocks and roots and bobbed into ruts and water-cut trenches. With that thing behind him, nothing mattered but escape. Skip had passed through the can't-believe-it stage in about a microsecond. When he'd seen the shape, he'd had suspicions, but that otherworldly primate bellow told him exactly what it was.

Skip Caldwell needed every bit of his considerable skills as he plummeted down the slope. With potential catastrophic failure presenting itself several times a second, those seconds telescoped to seem like minutes as Skip's eyes and mind settled on just getting down—*fast*. For a damn near vertical drop his speed was appropriately insane.

Three hundred yards downtrail Skip took a dip, hunkered down behind his seat to keep his center of gravity low, then zoomed up, getting some big air. As he looked for a landing spot, within a half second he knew he was screwed. He was headed toward a snake basket of deep ruts with no way to avoid it and no way to stay rubber down.

He took it like a man as his front tire clipped the rise between two of the scars and then hit the wall of the next. His big downhill shocks crunched down all the way and that's when he lost it. His front wheel jerked right and dug in, sending Skip flying over the handlebars, the bike coming with him because his lock-in shoes were married to the pedals and he'd had no time to kick out. In three seconds Skip was on his back, the bike on top of him. Stunned at having gone from thirty to zero so quickly, he forced himself to shake it off and scrambled to get to his feet.

That's when he got a really good look at his pursuer in the waning light, and the sight took his breath away. Less than fifty yards above, the thing was bounding toward him, its exaggerated body moving with a sprinter's grace, taking eighteen-foot gulps of the hillside at a stride. Skip's heart rate exploded as he threw the bike upright, leaped on, and shoved off.

A half revolution of the wheel told him it was bent.

He pedaled anyway, the bike now fighting dips with its Flint-stone front wheel. Gaining speed, Skip knew he had little control. A lesser rider would not have gotten ten feet, but Skip was a gifted biker. He heard the thing thundering down on him and knew by its ferocious expression and fervent pursuit that if it caught him, it would kill him.

Another hundred yards with a crooked wheel and the beast was now three or four seconds behind him, its huge lungs venting like a steam train, both of them bouncing up and down on the rocky track, a man on a broken bicycle losing ground to an unstoppable colossus now but three inhuman strides of the hill behind.

That's when Skip fell again, this time tumbling ass-over-teacup, the bike flying away, his forearm smashing hard on a coffee-table-sized rock. Despite the injury he managed to get up and start running, but his narrow bike shoes with the snap-in bindings weren't suited for hiking, let alone trail running, and he slipped within ten feet and crashed onto his back. His broken arm sent blinding electric sparks up and down his body as waves of nausea rolled through him. Sliding on the slope, he turned and looked around. Expecting the thing to be upon him, Skip was stunned by his impossible fortune: it had stopped to study his bike.

Skip stood and ran, stretching his legs until his groin muscles nearly tore from their moorings. It was as if the governor had called just as the executioner put his hand on the switch. He would outrun this thing somehow. He would do it. He would live to tell about it. Live to marry Nikki and have kids. Live to beat Dewey Devlin.

Tears streamed from the corners of his eyes. Skip Caldwell was going to live.

He watched the small two-leg flee in fear down the trail as he picked up its tool. The small two-leg had ridden on this shiny thing's back. It had round legs like those of the hardshells but smaller, thinner. He tested it in his grip and found it gave, but not easily. He exerted more force and twisted it until the two round parts met.

Below, the small creature tripped and stumbled its way down the hill, adding distance between them. He watched it for a moment, its fear glowing like fire at night. He knew it was injured and in pain. He particularly enjoyed the increased chaos of their thoughts when they were scared and hurt.

His hooded gaze followed the frantic little animal, then scanned far ahead of him, finding two landmarks, a large rock and a dead tree. He tossed its shiny tool into a gully and calmly decided which of those points he would let it pass before continuing his pursuit.

26

ac poured the last few drops of the Veuve Clicquot into Kris's glass and realized his initial misgivings about her had vanished. Her vulnerability earlier had surprised and even touched him. There was a lot more to Kris than he first imagined. It had been a while since his last sexual encounter and he suddenly felt a little rusty. A tingle went up his back as he looked into her face. He had a feeling that it would be just like riding a bicycle. He also didn't think Kris would allow him to be rusty.

Kris's attraction to Mac was beginning to transcend the value he represented to her in terms of information. On the way over to his place she had decided they would get the food and small talk out of the way and then have sex. Kris prided herself on a raw sexual appetite she felt exceeded that of most men, and as the champagne tickled her nose, she had already visualized the steps that would put them into his bed. They leaned toward each other and began to kiss. It quickly became passionate, fevered. Just as Mac undid her bra and had a nipple softly trapped between his fingertips, a pager beeped. They stopped kissing and looked around.

"Is that yours?" asked Kris.

Mac started to look for his pager while Kris jumped up, rummaged through her purse, and found her pager. "Shit," she said. "It's work."

She pulled out her cell phone and punched buttons.

"This is Walker. What is it?" There was a pause as she received information. She looked at her watch. "It's only six. Can't you get someone else?" Another pause, and she replied with slight resignation, "All right. I'll be there."

She flipped her phone closed and reconnected the front snap of her bra. As she adjusted her breasts, she looked at Mac and shook her head. "Chain reaction car crash on the five a little north of Lynnwood. Fog rolled in, thirty, forty cars involved. Gotta go. Sorry."

Mac sat back and gave a wry smile. "Yeah, but not half as sorry as I am."

He sighed while she worked the buttons on her blouse.

"This page was prearranged, wasn't it?" he joked. "Look, I know you're pissed because I served beef instead of turkey. It's still early. We can go out, pick up a turkey—cheap I'll bet—and have it in the oven in no time. While it's cooking, we can . . ." He trailed off as those perfect rises of creamy flesh bunching under her bra vanished behind the last two buttons.

She looked around. "My coat?"

"Bedroom."

"Right." Kris nodded and headed back to get it. As she came back down the hall from the master bedroom, she peered into his darkened office, then quickly stepped in, snooping about in the shadows. On the desk were books, mostly anthropology it seemed. *Guy's kind of an egghead.* Like she first concluded, not your typical cop. She quickly exited, having learned little.

Mac walked her to the parking lot and kissed her delicately one last time before she got in her car. From that parting kiss she knew he'd be an attentive lover.

"Watch me on the news," she said, and closed the door.

He held up his hand. "Well then, thanks for stopping by."

She smiled back, allowing herself a brief fantasy that they might end up together. As she drove away, she flashed on a college philosophy class and something Karl Marx said, and she paraphrased it to fit her own beliefs: *relationships are the opium of the people.*

Thanksgiving at the Greenwoods had gone well. For Ronnie it was a magical few hours, just like the good old days. She thought Ty seemed in high spirits, buoyed by the moment, the wine, and maybe even the attentions of their young Swedish au pair. But Ronnie didn't concern herself with the reasons as she and Ty settled into bed.

She knew he'd played hooky from work, and although the whys were in the back of her mind, she didn't want to spoil the moment with an interrogation. She resolved to take the good times when they presented themselves. At that moment all their problems seemed played out in another lifetime. She felt they had a real chance at gluing their eggshell back together. Ty put down his book and turned off his bedside lamp. Ronnie leaned over to kiss him good night.

"'Night, sweetheart. It was a great evening," she whispered as she kissed him.

Instead of doing what she expected him to do, which was to receive the kiss and roll over, he surprised her by kissing her back, hard.

"The evening ain't over till it's over," he said, with a mischievous smile.

Ty wanted things to be like they'd been in the good times and regretted that this one important piece of their past had been missing lately. He also knew Ronnie had picked up on signals from their naïve young au pair, sent via glances, body language, and overreactions to his few jokes. He wanted Ronnie to know he was a one-woman man, so he proceeded to finish what he had left undone the previous Sunday.

27

Carillo was at his desk when Mac entered the office at eight forty that morning. Mac could tell Carillo was excited about something because he rarely got animated before nine a.m. Carillo sailed a piece of paper toward Mac. "Check this out." Mac reached for it but it hit the floor. "Another MP. Mountain biker. Took off yesterday afternoon and his girlfriend says he never came home. Same general area as the others."

Mac picked up the missing persons report. "Two hours old. Is there another search?"

Carillo stood to pour more coffee. "Yeah. S & R's up there now."

Mac continued reading. "Where is this?"

"Just above the two," Carillo said, referring to Highway 2. Mac's wheels were turning, given the proximity to the other incidents. He read the report, trying to find a reason to relate it.

"Live-in girlfriend said he's a pro biker. Maybe he pushed the envelope too hard."

Carillo rode motorcycles and considered bicycles to be for wimps. "How bad could you get hurt on a *bicycle*?" he asked, as if the potential level of injury were a gauge of a sport's merit.

"Those things get going pretty fast. I've watched downhill bike racing on ESPN."

Carillo took a slug of his coffee and set down his cup. "You would. Let's go."

Mac grabbed his coat.

They saw the search and rescue trucks as well as two patrol cars and some civilian vehicles before they saw Skip Caldwell's blue Ranger. They got out and approached a burly man in his late forties.

The man turned to them. "Hey, it's Larry and Moe. Where's Curly?" he quipped.

"You're Curly. So that's the thanks we get?" said Mac.

"Thanks," said search and rescue head Mel Benedict. "Because of you two I had to put up with my in-laws. Anyway, looks like I did you two a favor. This guy plus your hikers and the logger makes four people in about a week. I'm no detective but this smells like a pattern."

Carillo scanned the area. "Whaddya got?"

Benedict pointed at Skip's truck. "Guy left it there, 'proximately three forty yesterday afternoon. Pedaled his bike up that trail"—he pointed his finger—"and how the fuck he could ride a bike on that is anyone's guess . . . Anyway, he heads up there . . ." His hand swept upward indicating the mountains looming above them. "That's it. No sign of him returning to the truck. We've got people looking but so far, nada."

They spoke to Benedict for a few moments, then headed up the same trail as the rest of the search team. After a few minutes they found a trail branch that followed the horizontal curve of the hillside. Neither said anything as they moved in that direction.

About five minutes into the trail, Carillo's foot slipped in some mud and his dress shoe got caked. "Shit." As he reached for a stick to clean off the mud, he spotted something. "Well goddamn . . ."

Mac looked and felt an electric jolt up his back. Carillo just shook his head and laughed. "Sonofabitch . . ."

"This is some kinda joke, right?" was Sheriff Rick Barkley's reaction when Mac set the huge casting on his desk. Mac and Carillo shook their heads in unison.

"Well, could they have made it any bigger, for Chrissake?" asked the sheriff. Barkley was a former major in the Airborne Rangers and a Vietnam vet. A rough-hewn sixty-two, he had crisp, steel-colored hair and a jawline that could give you a paper cut. Rarely raising his voice, he was one of those men who by their strength of personality could instantly command respect. Mac, Carillo, and Undersheriff Tom Rice watched as Barkley hefted the slab of plaster and examined it. "So, you found more of these just now? This is the one you pulled from the hikers' scene?"

Carillo nodded. "Right. Two hours ago we found probably three good ones and a couple smeared. Whoever he is, he's good. Seems to be trying not to be too obvious. We didn't bring in another CSI because—"

"Well, I'm glad as hell you didn't waste any more of their time," grated Barkley. "So let me get this straight: men are disappearing and now it seems some asshole is planting these things in the vicinity. Why?"

"We don't know yet, sir," agreed Carillo.

"Mac, whaddya think?" asked Barkley.

Mac was as unsure as he had ever been. And he wasn't so sure about sticking his neck out either. He decided to float a trial balloon to gauge their reaction. "I'm not necessarily sure someone is planting these."

Barkley did an uncharacteristic double take. "What? Mac, don't tell me you think this damn thing's real?"

Mac looked at Barkley. "There's a way to find out."

Barkley stared back at Mac for a moment, reading his expression, then the tight seams in his craggy face loosened as he burst into laughter. This caused Rice and Carillo to follow with guffaws. Mac seamlessly joined in. Barkley set the casting down and slapped Mac's shoulder. "Jesus, you had me going there for a minute, Mac. I thought we were gonna have to transfer you back to La La Land."

After the light chuckling subsided, the sheriff fixed the other men with his intense slate gray eyes. "Okay, here's what we're gonna do. Investigate this for what it is, or what it's starting to look like: abductions. You guys were smart to keep this casting under wraps; that was heads-up police work. We absolutely do not need this piece of the puzzle getting out. First of all, we don't need the media making a big goddamn joke outta this, and worse, we'd have every nut between here and Cle Elum comin' in with everything from tips to confessions and all kinda shit. There's not enough hours in a day for you boys to sort through all that crap. Keep it clean, and work this by the book."

A few minutes later Mac and Carillo returned to their desks. Mac handed Carillo a manila folder. "Newspaper articles I dug up. A local guy. If this thing"—Mac looked around to make sure no one was listening—"is going in this . . . weird direction, he might be able to help us figure it out."

Carillo set the file on his desk. "Thanks." He grabbed his coat.

Mac put a file in his briefcase. "Where you going?"

"Wylie, the logger, his wife. Lives in Monroe. May be some connection with the lawyers, maybe the biker too. Probably talk to the biker's girlfriend too. You?"

Mac shrugged. "A lead. May be nothing."

Carillo turned. "Later."

Mac was relieved Carillo hadn't pressed him about his "lead." Given the climate of the meeting they'd just come out of, Mac didn't want the substance of his next interview to get around . . . just yet.

28

D r. Wade Frazier took the call from the department receptionist that Mac had arrived and told her to send him up. The university had instituted high security in the building a few years earlier after a disgruntled student arrived for an unscheduled meeting with his professor to discuss the low grade on his anthro term paper. The student decided a convincing argument for a higher mark was a wasted effort and instead came armed with a nine-millimeter pistol in his quest to lobby for an A. The crazed young man got off three wild shots before another professor came to the rescue and brained him with a half-sized plaster bust of Aristotle. The blunt force of Aristotelian logic saved the other professor, the unconscious student went to the pokey, and the bust-wielding Dr. Frazier became something of a darling in the local press. Mac recognized the older man as they shook hands. He decided the guy looked every bit the classic professor—salt-and-pepper beard, unkempt hair, and eyes like an owl—overly alert and very wise.

"Thanks for meeting with me, Doc."

Dr. Frazier eyed the standard packing box Mac held under his arm.

"Brought us a lunch, huh?" cracked the doctor.

"More like lunchtime conversation," Mac retorted.

He followed the doctor into his office, observing the three walls of overflowing bookshelves, windows with Post-it notes stuck to them, and every bit of available floor space stacked with books, files, and paperwork. The desk was somewhere under piles of paper. *So this is how genius works.*

Mac recognized the famous Aristotle bludgeon resting on the computer monitor, a chunk missing from the back of the philosopher's head. His trained eyes swept the bookshelves and quickly scanned myriad titles, many regarding cryptozoology, the paranormal, and the unexplained, some of which the good doctor had authored.

"How may I assist the Snohomish County Sheriff, Detective?"

"I need some advice."

"Fair enough. I am always ready to render it, requested or not."

Dr. Frazier gathered up a mass of books and paperwork from a chair and motioned Mac to sit. Instead, Mac set the box down on the chair and withdrew something wrapped in newspaper. He pulled off the paper to reveal a thin plaster cast of a normal human foot, about half an inch thick. He handed it to Dr. Frazier, who pulled out his eyeglasses, took the object, and quickly glanced at it.

"I'll go out on a limb, detective, but my guess is human."

Mac's even expression told Frazier to play along.

"Hmmm. Very well, I'm no ichnologist, but I'd say *Homo sapiens* male . . . , slight pronation, axial eversion. The medium was damp soil; I see a matting of marginal litter and evidence of arboreal accumulation. Perhaps forest floor loam with a silty subsoil?"

Mac nodded. "Bingo."

Frazier continued, "Eighty kilos, probably around one point eight five meters."

Mac shook his head. "Sorry, Doc, as a cop I know kilos, but the rest of my metric's rusty."

Frazier sighed at the failings of the American school system. "Approximately one seventy-five and six feet or so," he said. Then leveling his gaze at Mac and tipping up his glasses to his forehead, he continued. "You have back problems, Detective. Your foot turns in and puts pressure on your lumbar plexus. I suggest you see a chiropractor for an adjustment. So, did you venture all the way from Everett to get my osteopathic diagnosis?"

"Not exactly," Mac said as he rewrapped the cast of his own foot and set it on the floor. "By the way, I'm impressed. Now tell me if this one has back problems too."

Mac reached into the box and pulled out a far larger object, also bundled in newspaper. He unwrapped the enormous plaster foot impression and watched Dr. Frazier's eyes widen slightly, his demeanor changing instantly from restless to rapt. Mac handed the heavy casting to him. This plaster mold was more than three inches thick, but like the other had been poured to the ground level of the indentation.

Dr. Frazier looked at it closely for a few moments. "My my, this is a big boy, detective."

Dr. Frazier set the casting down on the paper-strewn desk and hurriedly rummaged, quickly producing a small tape measure. "Five hundred twenty-two millimeters . . . a very big boy . . . ," his whisper trailing off. After taking several measurements, he hefted the massive plaster foot and examined it again.

"A fairly competent casting. Police issue?"

"One of my people."

"My compliments," Frazier said, then picked up a magnifying glass. "A credible pour. Hmmm, you even captured some dermal ridges and sweat pores. Impressive." Without taking his eyes off the object in his hands, he asked, "Where did you pull this?"

"The woods."

Dr. Frazier smiled sardonically. "As they say, 'classified police business'?"

"Something like that."

"And you had the presence of mind to make a casting of a known foot for comparison."

"Uh-huh. So what is it?"

"You tell me. You're the police officer."

"Let's not play games," said Mac. "You're the expert. What is this thing?"

Frazier's guard was up since he'd been ambushed once by what turned out to be a tabloid reporter, with the wildly misquoted article causing him embarrassment. But after handling the largest casting he had ever seen, he was torn between caution and candor. He had seen the sketch of the Pitt Lake, B.C., footprint, which was purported to be sixty centimeters, and he once examined both Bossburg castings, that unique crippled right foot and the four-hundred-thirty-seven-millimeter left foot casting, but this one . . . this one was *magnificent,* in not only its detail but its size.

And it was authentic.

"Well, Doc, what is it? Is this thing fake or not?" Mac repeated, his tone conveying a tinge of frustration.

Dr. Frazier relented. "Very well, no, it is not. Fake, that is."

"How can you tell?"

Frazier pointed to parts of the casting and began a stream of thoughts. "These sweat pores, these ridges . . . whorls, these anatomical structures, the toes for instance, their sizes and relationship to each other, the heel impression, the ratio between the length and the width, the leverage point of the ankle, the pads on the ball of the foot, I could go on and on, but show me the man who manufactured this foot and I'll show you a gifted colleague, because no one having anything short of my credentials would know how to re-create such structures. No, Detective, this is a casting of a real, living foot, the foot of an unidentified and very, very large hominid."

"Hominid?" Mac queried, having read the term but wanting Frazier's description.

"Hominid," Frazier repeated, condescending as if to an Anthro 101 class. "Man or manlike, bipedal, that is, non-knuckle walkers. Currently the only known members of that club are us, Detective. Humans."

Mac's hope that Frazier would pronounce it fake and he'd be happily on his way had just been crushed. He took a deep breath and asked the question he'd been fearing. "Okay, so what made the print? Describe it. What have I got here?"

The doctor was still wary. "What part of 'unidentified' did you not understand, Detective Schneider?"

Mac respected the man but the coyness was wearing thin. "Is this Bigfoot?"

Dr. Frazier crossed the office and closed the door. "I truly abhor that term."

"Look, people are starting to turn up missing, I've found these prints nearby, and I can't explain why. I need to rule out—or rule in—all possibilities."

"So, your superiors have yet to hear your . . . theory?"

Mac smiled wryly. "Oh, they've heard it."

Frazier looked at him. "Hmmm. Interesting."

Mac leaned forward. "I was hoping to get a world-class expert to back me up."

Dr. Frazier motioned for Mac to sit as he waded around book piles to his well-worn leather swivel chair. The scholar sat down, found a half-finished bottle of orange juice in an open drawer, and took a pull off it.

"First, there are no experts on this 'thing,' as you call it. Since we've never actually found one, there are many people who speculate about what it might be. A few of us are formally educated in related fields, most are not. Which leads me to my second point. Since I am a scientist, my standing in the scientific community, ergo my livelihood, is dependent upon one thing, my credibility. And that credibility stems from my degrees, my published works, and years of exacting research. Though I have written many books and papers on the subject we are discussing, I have never once officially written or uttered the phrase *they exist*. Officially I have said they *may* exist."

He drained the juice and pegged the bottle into the overflowing trash can. "If you perceive my actions as overly cautious," explained Frazier, "then understand that unscrupulous pseudojournalists caused me great embarrassment among my peers. I am comfortable speaking to you, as you might say, off the record, but I will not be quoted nor marched over to your headquarters to bolster your position with your superiors. If you need such involvement, there is a very competent and respected man in Idaho, a professor like myself, who might be able to help you. As for me, what I tell you goes no further than this office, and should it do so, I will deny it heartily. What I am about to tell you is to be used solely as an aid in your investigation and for your own edification. It is not the solution. Are we clear?"

"Yup."

"Very well. Now, what made your casting? An exceptionally large hominid, uncatalogued by science. It is a relative of ours but is neither man nor pongid. That's a great ape to you, Detective."

"Is it the missing link?" asked Mac.

"That's a discredited term that has been bandied about by laymen. There is no 'missing link,' per se. This is something else. Though bipedal like ourselves, it has pursued a wholly different evolutionary path, tangential to its relatives, that is to say, us and the other great apes."

"So you're saying this thing is—"

"Our first cousin. And as with the other great apes, this creature possesses intelligence probably approaching our own yet has been blessed with the advanced mesomorphic characteristics of our mutual cousin the ape. That is to say, it is muscular in the extreme, resulting in a density that renders it proportionally quite heavy for its stature in comparison to us puny little *Homo sapiens.* Did you read the story from a few years back, Detective, where two male chimpanzees nearly tore a grown man to pieces?"

Mac nodded.

Frazier continued. "At the time the press credited an average chimp with having five times the strength of an average man. That is absolutely true. These chimps were large but weighed no more than one hundred fifty pounds, and yet the man was as helpless as a kitten with them. As to our beast, he's omnivorous—"

Mac interrupted, "You think it's a male?"

Frazier nodded. "Yes, yes, I think that's safe to assume, given the size and what seems to be a predatory pattern. As I was saying, he does not hibernate, has no known form of speech or communication—*known* being the operative term there—is more or less nocturnal, and generally, and I say that with a grain of salt, avoids contact with human beings."

Mac absorbed this for a moment. "So to capsulize, you're saying they exist?"

"Absolutely. There is sufficient fossil evidence to confirm that an immense hominid known as *Gigantopithecus* actually existed in recent evolutionary history. So the question is not do they exist, but do they *still* exist? That such a formidable apex predator could have survived until today is well within the realm of possibility. Some of my colleagues argue it was a homi*noid*—that is, an ape—while others, like myself, say it was an actual hominid, a full biped like ourselves."

"So this *Giganto,*" said Mac, thinking out loud, "you're saying he's probably Bigfoot?"

"Anthropologically, he is the proverbial dead ringer. In regards to *Gigantopithecus,* all the evidence for their currency is far too compelling to dismiss. I believe there are colonies of them in very isolated locations around the world. Sometimes we stumble onto them or their spoor. But science is the ultimate doubting Thomas, Detective Schneider. We must put our hands in the wounds before anything can be said to exist."

A puckish smirk crossed Dr. Frazier's face. "And since I am being completely candid, allow me to put forth that there is compelling anecdotal data, however slight, suggesting these beings may control some form of enhanced reception to the electrochemical emanations of other creatures, human beings included. It may help explain why they are so elusive."

"You're saying they're psychic?" Mac's brow furrowed. *Now we're getting out there.*

"I prefer extra sensory perception, but remember, I said *may*," continued Frazier, reading Mac's expression. "We all have some sort of ability to read each other, Detective, we just don't know how it works. Have you ever experienced that moment where you and another say the same word or express the same thought and you realize it transcends coincidence? We don't fully understand the mechanics of it, but ESP is generally accepted as fact. These creatures may have developed it over time, like any other sense, allowing them an edge in finding food. Such seemingly bizarre abilities are commonplace in the animal kingdom. Sharks have receptors in their chins and can feel the electrical emanations of prey buried under the sand of the sea floor. Certainly, given how large this creature is, it would need prodigious amounts of food, both flora and fauna. Is the theory unscientific? That there is solid information to support animal and human prescience opens the door to its possibility. How does a dog know its owner is in danger a thousand miles away? Such stories, while inexplicable to known science, are documented. As to your suspect, it is definitely male, ten to eleven feet in stature and, roughly estimated, possesses a mass somewhere on the high side of five to six hundred kilograms—"

Mac's eyes fluttered slightly at the bogglingly huge metric equation.

"—that is to say, probably at least twelve to thirteen hundred pounds," Frazier added patronizingly. "That would make him roughly eight or nine times the size of those killer chimps. A frightening notion indeed, that is, if he were of a disagreeable nature."

"Why so heavy?" asked Mac. "If it's only four or five feet taller than a man, then why is it five or six times heavier?"

"Since it is larger in three dimensions—not two—its mass increases in a cubic progression," explained Frazier. "A three-foot-tall child might weigh forty pounds, whereas a six-foot-tall ultra mesomorph such as a bodybuilder could easily have a mass five or six times that."

"Okay, I get it."

Frazier pointed at the large casting. "Notice the length of the toes?"

Mac nodded.

"These are typical of what I have seen on such castings. It indicates a creature capable of grasping the ground with the toes and negotiating very steep terrain. This is an adaptation a being of this magnitude would need to possess, given its locale and needs."

Frazier slid his finger along the instep of the huge cast foot. "And this arch? I find it quite fascinating. I have never seen such a pronounced structure."

Mac looked on. "Meaning?"

"Well, it may mean this individual represents a newer development on the evolutionary continuum, the higher arch representing an improvement over previous, uh, models. The arch would likely make this creature more mobile and fleet of foot than its non- or less-arched cousins. Certainly an extraordinary advancement, if so."

Dr. Frazier waved at the shelves of his works. "Detective Schneider, here is my problem. My books have speculated for years on our friend here, but until you bring me one, I cannot state categorically to my peers that he and his kind are anything more than the quaint folklore of every Indian tribe in North America, or the fantasy of the many thousands who have seen, heard, and gathered evidence, such as you have here. Until that time, they are little green men."

"People are disappearing, Doctor. If these things are responsible, then I need your help. Could your *Giganto*-whatever be doing this?"

"I don't know."

"Have they been known to abduct people?"

"On occasion."

"Kill?"

"On occasion."

"Why would it do that?"

"Detective, this is not Harry and the Hendersons we're discussing. He is a creature seemingly more human than ape. Less than two percent of our DNA differs from that of chimpanzees and scarcely more for gorillas. He could be closer to us than even the chimps. Like us he has wants, needs, emotions. He is subject to behavioral anomalies just as humans, chimpanzees, and gorillas are. He is both cunning and spectacularly strong, likely as unafraid of us as an NFL lineman would be of toddlers. He may feel we are encroaching on his territory and be resolved to stand his ground, not defer to human progress anymore. He may just be ill-tempered. Or you may have a rogue predator, motivated by his own reasons."

Dr. Frazier rose, signaling the end of the meeting. "And, of course, these disappearances all may be coincidental and have nothing to do with . . . your friend there. I have no idea."

He came around the desk and extended his hand.

"But please let me know when you make an arrest. I will have many questions for him."

29

The Channel 7 newsroom buzzed with the usual morning din as the noon anchors readied to report on the day-after-Thanksgiving crush at local malls. Kris was assigned a mall in north Seattle and saw it as an inconvenience since she was trying to put together a follow-up piece on the missing lawyers. Kris wanted something provocative, like making a connection between them and the logger, but she just couldn't connect the dots. She sat down at her desk to do some work before her crew assembled when one of the news writers passed by.

"Hey, Kris," he said. "What about that missing biker? Sounds like you got a series."

Kris leaped up from her desk. "What biker?" she demanded.

He stepped back slightly, startled by her intensity. "Uh, I thought you knew. Last night some mountain biker from Monroe disappeared up near where your lawyers and the logger did. Thought you'd be on your way out there by now," he said, walking away.

Kris was delighted someone else had vanished but angry she'd let such an important piece of information slip past her web. She felt a slight sense of panic at losing her edge. *I need to quit screwing around and make this my goddamn story.* But the panic quickly gave way to fury at how she had wasted her evening at a commonplace car crash that had only killed two when the real story—more missing people—was transpiring at the same time. She also missed out on getting laid and that only added to her aggravation.

This missing mountain biker was the switch to her lightbulb. Kris knew it was now or never to make her move. She grabbed her phone and pressed a three-digit internal code. Without even a hello, she launched, "Rick, get your crew together, we're going to Monroe."

Rick Kititani sighed on the other end. "Kris, you're supposed to do the mall shoot at Alderwood and I'm going to White Center. Find another crew."

Kris was tired of his attitude. He was a cameraman, she was a reporter.

"Fuck White Center," she said, knowing his story was only the dedication of some stupid magnet school. "We're going to the Eastside. We'll leave in twenty."

"No, Kris. No way."

Kris simply disconnected him and dialed. Someone answered and Kris looked around to make sure no one was eavesdropping. "Can you talk?" she asked, barely above a whisper. "I've got a problem."

Twenty minutes later she left the station, bound for Monroe. Her camera crew was headed by the angry Rick Kititani.

When he arrived at work that Friday, Ty got chewed out for his unauthorized absence and unofficial inquiries. While his bosses took turns reading him the riot act, Ty bit his lip and tuned them out. He caught bits and pieces of "diminished work performance," as well as "wildly overstepping his authority" and "investigation using his uniform and association with a government agency," but he didn't care.

After the pummeling he crept off to the motor pool, climbed into a truck, and sat down to think. After promising himself it was only a matter of time until he quit the Forest Service, he climbed out of the truck and went back in to get his day's assignment. He could last long enough to plan his next move, but what he feared far more than Ronnie's concerns or reaction crossed his mind. *What if this isn't what I think it is? Then what?*

* * *

Mac was just settling in at his desk when he got a call from Undersheriff Tom Rice summoning him to his office. When he entered, Mac was surprised to find Carillo and Sheriff Rick Barkley. The three men were standing and Carillo looked nervous.

"What's up?" Mac asked.

Sheriff Barkley leveled a finger at Carillo. "Your partner was on the noon news today."

Then an irritated Rice weighed in. "We've got Channel 7 saying there's an ongoing investigation of four *murders*? What the hell's going on here?"

Mac was confused. "Four murders? Who said that?"

"That blond bitch," said Carillo sullenly.

Before Mac could respond, Rice jumped back in. "They're accusing us of not doing our job. I don't like it. And this man next to me really doesn't like it."

All eyes went to Sheriff Barkley. "When a reporter goes on the air and not only says we're dragging our feet but insinuates that what we're calling disappearances are actually four confirmed murders and we're not telling the public—"

Mac shook his head. "Where do they—"

The chief continued, "—then I have a problem. And now my problem is your problem. I want this handled. Follow all leads, turn all stones. I want you to find the asshole who's been putting those footprints out there and squeeze his balls. If he's got something to do with this, then sweat him and find out what. Do what you have to because I don't want the FBI or any other agencies sticking their noses up my ass because we can't take care of our own backyard."

Sheriff Barkley fixed his intense eyes on Carillo. "And no more goddamn interviews. What the hell were you thinkin', Carillo?"

Carillo hung his head. "Sorry, Boss."

The three men left the sheriff's office and Rice turned to his detectives. "Put together whatever you've got and come down to my office. Let's map this thing out."

As Rice walked away, Mac faced Carillo.

"What the hell happened?"

Carillo's eyes were dark with anger. "That reporter. She fuckin' ambushed me."

"Who are you talking about?" Mac demanded. "I thought you were going out to talk to the logger's wife."

"I did. Then I went to interview the biker's girlfriend. That's when that bitch showed up. She tried to make it look like we were covering up something. She acted all friendly at first, then as soon as the camera was there, she made me look like a total asshole."

Mac cringed, although he knew that what Kris claimed probably didn't matter because if what Dr. Wade Frazier told him was right, then she didn't have the important half of the story. But then neither did Carillo. Yet Mac had to keep that part quiet for the moment. He just wasn't sure when that moment would come. He was worried that if he started spouting what Frazier told him to Carillo or anyone else in the department who would listen, he'd be off the case in a New York minute and probably assigned to cold cases, pending a psych exam. Maybe the truth was he didn't quite believe it himself.

"Man, she fucked me good," grated Carillo. "I thought we were cool, she's askin' regular questions, then she brings up the lawyers, claiming we abandoned the search early, then she throws in this shit about the mountain biker. Christ, the guy's not missing twelve hours and we're responsible. What an asshole."

Mac started walking and Carillo followed.

Carillo continued, "So tell me you got something with that lead."

"Not really. Not yet."

Carillo dodged into the men's room and Mac continued back to his desk. He picked up the phone as he fished around in his organizer for the card Kris had given him. Her cell went to voice mail, so he tried the station but she was out on assignment. He called her pager, then her home. The message he left everywhere was short: *call Mac Schneider ASAP.*

30

Ty left work early, complaining of a stress-related headache. Since no one would tell him where the incident with Joe Wylie had taken place, he managed to hack into Weyerhaeuser's internal computer and found the incident report. It wasn't very informative, making no mention of the extent of the damage. Things didn't look too promising until Ty came across an e-mail memo from a higher-up commanding one of their divisions to "harvest the damaged timber as soon as possible" and to officially blame the event on "wind damage." That was enough to send Ty's curiosity into overdrive. It was either some kind of cover-up or just lazy procedure. As much as he wanted to believe the former, he suspected the latter.

He headed his truck east into the mountains. Within forty-five minutes he passed the Weyerhaeuser equipment facility and proceeded up Access Road Number 4, the same route Joe Wylie had taken that fateful morning a week earlier. After about ten minutes the road made a turn and straightened out as it flattened, just as described in the report. Ty expected to have to look hard for the few broken trees. He was stunned. Four loggers, busily at work with chain saws, had cut nearly half the broken trees down to stumps, but there were enough left to drop his jaw.

This was the evidence Ty had been waiting for, praying for. Tears came to his eyes. *I'm not insane. This thing was here and this hapless log-*

ger crossed paths with it and paid with his life. He parked and pulled his Sony digital camera from his pocket.

Kris received Mac's messages but ignored them all. She had other problems. Her news director had called her in the van on the way back from her attack on Carillo and his department and screamed at her for implying that a series of missing persons had suddenly become a murder investigation. He also yelled at her for accusing the local police of keeping the threat of a serial killer from the public. Though he threatened to take her off the story, if not outright fire her, by the time she got back to the station, he simply ignored her, and that told Kris her guardian angel was probably working his magic.

Because she'd created the serial killer theory, no one else in Seattle had the story, and she assumed that management would at least wait until the next day to check her ratings. If they were strong, she was probably in the clear. She was sure her news director had confronted the station's general manager and probably been told, "If you want to chew her out, fine, but then leave her alone, she's good for the station." GM Lyle Benson was a corporate hack from the home office in Provo, Utah. A relentless bean counter, Benson didn't give a damn about news, accurate or otherwise. He cared only about ratings and Kris was supplying them.

She briefly thought of the men who had vanished. *Now all I need is one of them to appear alive and fuck up my career.* She would deal with Mac later. It was serendipity that she had come across his partner at the apartment of Skip Caldwell, the mountain biker. After hearing of the biker's disappearance, Kris had rushed out to interview his girlfriend and run into Carillo. Taking the fourth missing man as a sign from on high, she had played her boldest hand yet with both the murder angle and her accusation that the sheriff was afraid to call it what it was.

The sheriff's official position was that the men were missing. While no real evidence of foul play had surfaced, Kris had just enough inside information to think there was more to it. But for a lone reporter to suddenly change the course of this whole thing and yell the *M* word meant there would surely be ruffled feathers, not only in every law enforcement agency involved but in television stations across Puget Sound.

When she made the decision to aggressively corner Carillo, without any facts to back up her charges, her rapid-fire attack gave the illusion of substance and heightened the impact of Carillo's caged rat behavior, his quick denial and scurrying retreat from Rick Kititani's camera. It was answer enough, not to mention wonderful television. As Kris relived the moment, she reveled in the heat between her thighs. That inspired her to conclude this might be a good moment for a win-win, a quick interlude that might satisfy her momentary needs while making a payment for a recent favor. She made sure no other employees were within earshot. She picked up her cell and dialed.

"What're you doing?" Her voice was low. "I know you're busy, but how busy? I'm very, very horny. I dunno, fifteen minutes? Ten? I can do that."

Sorting through newspapers in his hotel room, Ben knew he was looking for something but was not sure what: it had become the classic case of "I'll know it when I see it." He was more than a little frustrated to be sitting in a hotel room in Bellevue, Washington, looking aimlessly at every regional newspaper he could find. The TV blared in the background as he turned page after page, one publication after another. He looked at the sheets of newsprint strewn over the bed and thought the room looked like a hobo had been sleeping there. The ringing phone was a blessed distraction and he grabbed it.

"Yeah?"

"Ben?" It was Jay Fine, his agent. "You okay?"

"Yup. I'm okay, Jay. Thanks," Ben answered.

"Look, I don't want to add to your problems, but the production company can't keep rescheduling your scenes much longer. Any idea when you'll be back?"

"No, I wish I knew," Ben said, deliberately giving him as little information as possible. Ben knew agents were very persuasive people, and he didn't want to give Jay any ammo the agent could use against him. "But I appreciate you calling."

"Ben," Jay said, lowering his voice for gravity, "I want to keep you on this picture." He paused, then continued, "I know you may need the money."

Ben smiled to himself. Just like he thought, a little info, a little ammo.

"Thanks, Jay. I know you care about me."

They continued the conversation a moment or two with small talk, then hung up. Ben put Jay's comments out of his head and thought about Doris. Despite the fatalistic voice he had heard at the airport about not coming back, Ben was concerned about the future. How would his decision to drop out of the movie hurt him and Doris?

As he weighed those thoughts, the TV anchor began a "humorous" wrap-up story entitled "Dueling Tabloids." Apparently a local man recently suffered damage to his truck, and one national tabloid blamed extraterrestrials while another laid it on Bigfoot. Ben's ears perked up. He grabbed the remote and jacked up the volume. The piece was over in a flash, but suddenly a police blotter report from one of the newspapers came back to mind. He started digging through the pile of papers.

Unable to contact Kris, Mac knew she was avoiding him for good reason. He chided himself that if he had any sense, he'd avoid contact with her. She was dangerous as well as reckless. By calling these events a series of murders, she had dug herself into a hole. Mac smiled to himself at the irony that she was probably right but would never know the real reason why.

At nine that evening, a small Web site containing several photos, some text, and an alleged conspiracy by the Weyerhaeuser company and "quite possibly by Washington state law enforcement agencies" went live. Ty knew the first claim was probably a stretch, and the notion that the police were covering up anything—let alone even *knew* something—was a real reach.

But he had been emboldened by the six o'clock news when a Channel 7 reporter got the ball rolling, saying the police were downplaying murders by calling them "disappearances." Nothing sells like a conspiracy. Ty rationalized his attack on the police and a gigantic multinational corporation as a necessary evil. The site vigorously charged both with concealing information about a recent abduction of a company employee by an "unknown nonhuman hominid." His only goal was to stir things up and get some answers.

He knew his proof was thin, three photos of a dirt road and some damaged trees, broken, according to the Web site, "by the hominid as it marked its territory." The site went on to speculate that the hapless logger had happened upon the creature and "was abducted and probably killed." He questioned why the trees were cut down and why the police had never spent any resources investigating the damaged trees. Clearly, he said, the trees were key evidence. The site asked for any information and offered a $10,000 reward to anyone who might help uncover what and where the perpetrator might be. To facilitate the visibility of his site, Ty fed Internet search engines keywords such as *Bigfoot, Sasquatch, unexplained disappearances,* and *cover-up,* among many others.

Ty was proud of his site, which only took him around two hours to design. He left his computer and went down the hall to the TV room to watch a video with the kids. Greta joined them, settling onto the huge sectional next to Chris. She put her arm around the boy and her fingers brushed Ty's shoulder. She looked over, slightly embarrassed. Ty knew she had a schoolgirl crush on him. Fifteen minutes passed and Ty got up, figuring he didn't need Ronnie coming out of her office to find him practically snuggling with the au pair. He went back to his computer to check his site. After such a short time in operation he already had one hundred and thirty-six hits. Though he had no e-mails, he felt his nascent site was performing well. The word would get out. For a split second he hoped the men weren't just lost but had been killed, and in the way he described. Ty felt a twinge of guilt. In that fraction of a second, his mind had laid out the stakes: *them or me.* If they were alive, then he would soon be dead, because this would all have been a false alarm and he'd be back to plotting his own demise.

Ty ruminated about one other thing he'd learned from previous experience in such matters: if you open your mouth, make sure you're in the back of the crowd. He made sure his name was not mentioned on the site, but if it got enough positive attention, he might eventually add it. After all, he thought with soft bitterness, on this subject it had some value.

In the few days she had been living with the Greenwoods, Greta felt the tension in the house and was curious about her hosts and the secrets they seemed to be keeping.

Chris turned off the satellite and turned on a DVD movie. He skipped to the part he liked near the end.

"What's this?" she asked.

Chris unfocused from the screen and looked to Greta. "*The Beast from 20,000 Fathoms,*" he said. "It's an old movie but pretty cool. My dad really likes it."

Greta recognized it as one Chris often watched. "So, how long has your father worked in the forest?"

"Since he saw Bigfoot," Chris said matter-of-factly, turning back to the screen as the rubber monster decimated a scale model of Coney Island.

Greta was puzzled. "Bigfoot? What's that?"

Chris looked at her in disbelief. "You don't know what that is? Didn't you see *Harry and the Hendersons*?"

Greta shook her head and Chris conceded she was foreign. "Bigfoot is this thing that lives in the woods. He's big and looks like a gorilla." He looked back at the screen. "Or at least that's what people say."

The sad, faraway tone of his last sentence told Greta that the implications of this story to the Greenwoods were big.

"He saw this thing? Really?" Greta asked.

Chris just shrugged.

"Why didn't he tell someone?" she wondered.

Chris took a moment to answer. "He did."

"And?" she asked.

"Nobody believes him. 'Cept weirdos."

Greta got the gist of the problem. "Your mother . . . she believes him, doesn't she?"

Chris just stared at the TV.

Greta tried another tack. "Do you believe him?"

Chris's face became set but he kept his eyes on the screen. "My dad doesn't lie."

Greta just had some of her questions answered. She was fascinated that people with so much could let something as silly as a mythical forest ogre come between them. She figured there had to be more to it than that. *Bigfoot? What a funny name. Sounds like a character from a cartoon.* She was surprised practical Americans had such folktales.

31

J. D. Watts and Errol Rayburn met at the state penitentiary in Monroe. Both twenty-nine, J. D. was doing three years for burglary, Errol a five-spot for pushing smack. They were both paroled within two weeks of each other and the bond that had formed behind bars remained on the outside. Though forbidden by their parole conditions to associate with known felons, including each other, nevertheless they rented a ramshackle home near Duvall owned by J. D.'s ex. There they set up a respectable commercial venture in under-the-counter pharmaceuticals. Rock cocaine and pot were their profit lines, but homemade glass, a.k.a. crystal methamphetamine, was the blue chip foundation of their gross sales.

When a low-life scum named Leon Newburg took them for five hundred bucks, they were appropriately unhappy. Newburg was a biker who had been assigned a distributorship by J. D. and Errol and one day reported he'd had two lids of bud ripped off. When a drug associate told them Newburg had been bragging that he'd been the one doing the ripping off, J. D. and Errol took the news badly. That night they went to Newburg's home and, in a meth-inspired rage, beat the dogshit out of him.

When Newburg finally copped to the deceit, J. D. Watts went nuts and reached for the closest instrument with which to teach him a lesson. Unfortunately for Newburg, it was an Easton thirty-ounce aluminum bat. After J. D. had applied a few judicious blows to Newburg's head, Errol Rayburn set down his beer and put an end to the attack with the startling announcement, "Shit, J. D., you killed him."

This news was particularly alarming as it implied a trip back to prison, this time for quite a longer hitch than the last, so they decided to conceal their crime. Loading their late employee into the trunk of Errol's Buick Skylark, they headed into the hills to find a final and very remote resting place for Mr. Leon Newburg.

Kris knew she was in for a battle with her news director. But balancing that out was her conviction that people loved serial killers, and by the eleven p.m. news, the story was their lead-in. Since first breaking the idea at noon that murder was afoot, Kris had added an angry Karen Roberts to the circus, along with the red-faced Snohomish County undersheriff furiously denying anyone had been murdered and claiming "there was absolutely no evidence of any such crimes." She also had plenty of time in edit to make the brooding Carillo appear even worse with a voice-over that made him come across like his organization was so taciturn they might even have the Roswell wreckage locked away.

Her piece had been elevated to an "investigative report" since the six o'clock newscast, and Kris was asked to stay around to do a live wrap at the news desk with the eleven o'clock anchors. As soon as she finished, News Director Doug Gautier took her aside. He was fuming.

"If you're wrong about this, I don't care who's protecting you, I'll have your ass in a—"

She waved him off. "I'm not, Doug. People are being murdered. And we're the first to break the story."

"Don't bullshit me. So far, all we really know is that these are random disappearances. There're practically a million people in Snohomish County and people go missing every day. I've had the head of every law enforcement agency involved in this calling me and screaming in my ear. They're calling press conferences to denounce us. Bottom line is if you're wrong, I take some heat but you're fucked. Understand?"

She nodded indifferently and Gautier stormed away. Kris got a delicious grin when she visualized the moment he'd been ordered to run with a story he didn't believe in. Gautier, a former star reporter turned distinguished anchor turned news director, took his job deadly seriously. He was always doing these stone-faced "editorial stand" pieces just before they went to the network news. She knew he fancied himself the *face* of the station, and as the senior newsman as well as news director he had a responsibility to keep the reporters in line to protect his own integrity. She also knew he was right about her. If this thing didn't take the right turn, and soon, she might have a problem.

Kris plopped down at her desk and acknowledged a few congrats from passing newsroomies until her phone rang. She figured it was Gautier wanting to yell some more.

"Yes," she said flatly.

"So who did it? That's what I want to know."

She was surprised but recovered quickly. "That's your job."

Mac's voice sounded slightly amused, not enraged like she'd expected.

"Four murders?" he queried. "Wow. Helluva story. My partner's not too happy about how he came off. You blindsided him, then cut his legs off."

·She put her feet on her desk. "More like his balls. But they say life's hard, then you die."

"So, you thought we were holding out?" he asked.

"I guess so. I went with the story, didn't I?"

Mac chuckled. "You sure did."

"Where were you? I thought you two were twins."

"Oh yeah, sorry I missed Carillo's roast but I was doing a little . . . investigation. But then you already know a crazed serial killer is out there, so why should I bother you with that? Right?"

She guessed he either knew something she didn't or was just psyching her out as revenge for his partner. Whichever it was, she didn't like it.

"Are you saying you know something you didn't tell me about?"

"Who? Me? No, not at all," he said. "You've got it figured." She could hear his smile.

"So what? You're saying these guys weren't murdered?"

"Well, at least the lawyers. They're back home, safe and suing people."

The color drained from Kris's face. "What?"

"Just kidding. But you were supposed to say 'Thank God,' not 'Oh crap.'"

Mac could hear Kris exhale sharply and grinned that his arrow had found its mark.

"You're being a total jerk," she said, trying hard not to give away her anger and relief. "No, make that an asshole. You're being a total asshole."

"Funny, that's what Carillo said about you. But just a thought . . . What if next time I'm not making that up?"

"Why did you call? I was feeling pretty good until you called," she said, hoping some sympathy might flush out whatever he knew.

Mac saw through her ruse but still wanted to help her. "I just called to say I saw your story and to say you've got guts. That's all."

"Thanks so much. And tell your partner it was nothing personal."

She didn't give a rat's ass about Carillo but wanted to give Mac the impression she cared.

"If you've got any leads, call me," Mac said. "We'd really like to solve this case."

"Funny," she said, hanging up. She knew he was onto something. He wasn't bluffing, she was sure of it. He wasn't that kind of guy. For a split second she wished she was a normal woman with normal ideals because she'd be looking for a nice guy and he might be the one. But she wasn't, so he wasn't. She'd find out what he knew. Partly because it was good reporting, but mainly because her career hinged on it.

Mac pressed the mute button on his remote and the sound came back to the Channel 7 news just in time for him to hear that a storm was moving in. He exhaled long and hard, as his burden was now twofold: first, he was becoming attracted to the newly sworn enemy of the department, and worse, he had what he was beginning to believe was crucial evidence in a major case and his partner and bosses were not going to allow him to use it. He looked into his future and saw himself as a rent-a-cop, defending gated communities. *Damned if you do . . .*

The six cylinders in Errol Rayburn's Buick Skylark wheezed their way up the dark and lonely mountain road. Trying to obey the laws for a change, given the body with the smashed head residing in the trunk, Errol carefully watched his speedometer, not that there were any cops out this far anyway. Since J. D. Watts had done some hunting in the area, he was assigned the job of navigating.

"Turn up here," said J. D., indicating a small side road ahead. The Skylark wheeled around the turn and continued to ascend, this time leaving the broken asphalt for hard-packed dirt. After a few miles and a gain in altitude of a thousand feet or so, the men began looking for a place to pull over to the side of the narrow road. Another mile passed through the corridor of trees and a cutaway in the roadbed presented itself. Errol wheeled them to a stop and left the lights on to provide some illumination against the abject blackness.

J. D. pulled his ropy six-three frame out and lit a cigarette. Errol walked to the trunk.

"Gotta shovel?" asked J. D.

"The fuck I'd have a shovel for?" said an angry Errol, still furious that his hothead partner had offed a guy over two lids of weed. He opened the trunk and began hauling out the corpse.

"Hey," said J. D., "why don't we just drop 'em over the side o' the road? It's steep and he'll roll down a ways and the animals'll eat 'im."

"Animals'll eat 'im? Well, that's just fuckin' dandy!" raged Errol as he dropped the body to the dirt. "Got any other smart ideas, dumbshit? Man, we're gonna fry for this! You are just a fuckin' idiot."

"Hey, the dude burned us. He got what was—"

"Shhhhh!" said Errol suddenly. "What was that?" he asked in a whisper.

"I didn't hear—"

"There it is again."

"What?"

"Hey!" shouted Errol at the curtain of night around them. "Hey!"

As a YY chromosomal male, Errol was not afraid of what he had heard, just livid. How someone had gotten up here and was now walking around in the woods above them was not his problem to figure out. The *trespasser's* problem would be surviving when Errol Rayburn got his hands on him. J. D. killing that piece-of-shit thief Newburg was one thing, but someone trying to catch them in the act of disposing of a body—well, that really deserved the death penalty.

"Come out, you fuckin' coward!" he screamed at the woods above them. He turned to J. D., keeping his eyes on the trees. In a voice loud enough for the intruder to hear, Errol yelled, "J. D.? Get my piece outta the glove box."

J. D. Watts dutifully walked to the passenger side and slid in.

"Hey you!" screamed Errol into the night. "I'm fuckin' talkin' to you!"

As J. D. opened the glove box and put his hand on the butt of the cheap .32 automatic, he heard a rapid series of sounds that were at first confusing, then disturbing, then downright terrifying. The first sound was Errol saying "Hey," yet it wasn't in his commanding voice but more muted, as if surprised. Then J. D. heard and felt a thudding beat like a pile driver. But when Errol screamed like a girl, J. D. froze, then grabbed the gun and stepped out of the car.

For the first time in his life J. D. Watts couldn't believe his fucking eyes.

In the soft red glow of the taillights, his partner was in the grasp of a huge manlike thing, covered in hair and maybe twice as tall as poor Errol. As Errol Rayburn made a sick, strangled, gurgling sound, the giant man-thing leveled its gaze at J. D. For a moment or two J. D. was mesmerized by the glint of its eyes as it stared a hole right through him.

Snapping out of it, J. D. leaped into the car, knocking off the rearview mirror with his head as he scurried to climb over the console into the driver's seat. Thank God Errol left the keys in the ignition, and J. D. twisted them—he was still not fully in the seat—then slid in and floored the gas pedal. The tires spun and the doors closed with the momentum.

He accelerated to about fifty—which was twenty faster than prudent on that road—and continued uphill. He knew he was bottled in. Roads like this didn't make loops. Sooner or later he'd hit the end and have to turn around. J. D. Watts was so far beyond scared he'd actually pissed his pants. He'd been gang-raped in prison twice but that was nothing. This thing, well, it was right out of a goddamn horror movie. He decided then and there that if it was behind him and about to catch him, he'd drive off the road and kill himself before he'd meet the same end as Errol. And he knew Errol Rayburn had met his maker.

Abso-fucking-lutely.

Five and a half miles up he hit a turnaround. Dead end. Afraid to stop, he managed to turn the car without backing up and continued back down the road. If it tried to stop him, he'd plow right into it. He didn't know if the car could take it. That thing was even bigger than the grizzlies he and his uncle once hunted. He kept his foot on the gas and plummeted down the road, barely staying away from the deep ditch on one side and the drop-off on the other. When he thought he was at the point where they were attacked, he saw nothing. Then a hundred yards further he saw the actual turnout. Still nothing. He pressed a little harder on the gas, half expecting the thing to leap onto his hood. He steeled himself to the idea of suicide. After a mile had passed, he relaxed a little. Whatever it was had run off not only with Errol but with Leon Newburg's body too.

When he got home, rather than deal with how he would solve all his problems, like what happened to Errol and the blood in the trunk and the terrible thing he'd seen, J. D. Watts smoked a big joint, drank a third of a bottle of Black Jack, threw up, then collapsed into bed.

32

When Chief Ben Eagleclaw walked into the Snohomish County Sheriff's Department the next morning, heads turned. Ben knew that would happen and traded on it. After signing a few autographs, then relating a cockamamie story about a documentary on the paranormal he said he was hosting for The Learning Channel, he got what he came for. Within ten minutes he was walking out with Deke Allison's address.

The television news piece and the article in the paper about the topsy truck were enough to inspire his curiosity. Using a map the sheriff's people provided, he made his way outside town and up into the foothills. The farther out he got, the more he felt . . . it. Though he was reluctant to try and reconnect with the Oh-Mah, he still had some sort of residual sense of it. The feeling wasn't as strong or vivid but it was there, like listening to a distant radio as opposed to actually talking to someone.

At the Allisons' mailbox he saw a real estate For Sale sign and followed the long gravel drive to the house. It was midmorning and he wasn't sure if they'd be home. Parked by a shed was an old Chrysler station wagon and a Honda Civic wagon with the silver paint fading away, but he saw no damaged truck. A middle-aged woman came out of the house, wrapping her arms around herself against the cold.

"May I help you?" she asked. Then she recognized him. Ben knew it was like a "get out of jail" card. She smiled. He smiled.

"Chief Ben Eagleclaw," he said, with a slight wave. "Hello."

"Uh, Marge Allison," she said, slightly awed. "It's a pleasure."

They shook hands.

"Maybe you can help me," he said. "I'm lookin' for the people who had the problem with the truck. I'm doin' a documentary on . . . uh, strange things. And I wanted to talk to them. Is that you?"

Marge had been told not to talk to anybody: Deke had been very specific. But this old man was a movie star. He was famous and famous people know stuff the rest of us just don't know. At least that's what Marge figured when she gestured him inside.

"My husband Deke's not here, but . . ."

Ben smiled. "I don't wanna be a bother . . ."

"Oh no, it's no bother at all. He'll be home in a while. He just went into town to get something."

Marge went to the kitchen to make coffee while Ben waited in the living room. She reappeared a few minutes later with two mugs of instant Folger's. Ben pointed at the pictures on the wall.

"Nice-lookin' boy. Yours?"

"That's Ricky, our son. He'll be eighteen in a couple weeks, December twenty-second actually. My Christmas present," she giggled.

Ben nodded. "You're movin'?"

Marge's face sagged a little and there was pain in her voice. "I guess so. We moved here when I was carrying Ricky. Goin' on nineteen years now."

"Movin' to a better place?" Ben asked.

Marge shrugged resignedly. "I hope so."

The phone rang and Marge went to the kitchen to get it. The bits of conversation sounded to Ben like it was her husband. When she lowered her voice, he knew they were talking about him. A few moments later she returned.

"Well, that was Deke. He's getting his new truck worked on." She seemed nervous. "It's actually not new. The insurance company wouldn't buy him a new one. Anyhow, he's probably gonna be a while, so . . ."

Ben took his cue and stood.

"No problem. Listen, if you don't mind, may I take a look around your yard? I'll be out of your hair in five minutes."

"Well, uh, okay. Sure, I guess that's fine," she said, unsure but assuming this celebrity Indian of all people would be safe poking around. Plus, they might get in the movies.

Ben thanked her and went outside. Following the perimeter of the parking area, his eyes examined every nub of dirt and rock. He wanted to know . . . to feel . . . if it had been here. He needed to find out, to reconnect with it here on its turf, not from a hotel room two hundred miles away.

Marge watched him for a few minutes, then he disappeared behind the equipment shed. Suddenly a moderate wave of panic came over her, the same one Deke got when real estate agents brought customers. Deke warned her that their "dark secret" could blow the salability of their home. On the phone he had been less than enthusiastic about the old Indian poking around but had deferred owing to the siren song of maybe being in the movies. But now that concern dogged Marge as she watched from the window.

What if the old guy doesn't come back?

Ben followed an overgrown path back about fifty yards, then stopped. He could no longer see the Allisons' home, just huge cedars that blocked much of the light from above, and dense undergrowth that could hide anything ten yards away. He cleared his mind, trying to conjure those specialized senses he needed right now. He let his thoughts drain and took a deep breath of forest air, something he had not tasted in many years. He had only quit smoking a few days before but was already getting more input from his nose and taste buds.

From the hotel room in Portland he had summoned his connection with the Oh-Mah with seeming ease, but he just couldn't do it again. He wondered if his failure was because he hadn't really expected it back then and now he did. He badly needed a cigarette and thought the nicotine fits might be interfering with his concentration. His eyes wandered the woods, looking for anything. He walked a little farther and stopped again. In his fleeting contact with it he had felt its thoughts, its intent. Ben knew he was here not only to come to terms with a very old trauma, but maybe to even try and stop this thing.

He suddenly knew it had been here. It was a subtle sensation, like your vision refocusing when you're reading and you look up at something in the distance. He heard the voice from within: *it was here.* Now on automatic, he moved off the trail, cutting his own way through the tangled ground cover. He didn't know how he knew, but he knew it had come this way. He noticed a high broken branch, a freshly snapped rotted limb, some scuffed moss. His eyes were seeing what they were taught as a boy: he was reading the woods.

Another thirty yards and he stopped. It had tarried here, perhaps to smell the burning alder of a fireplace, maybe to make out a distant light. Ben crouched, his old joints crying in pain as he ran his hand over the pliable forest floor. It had covered itself well . . .

But not completely. He saw what he was looking for. Pulling back a fern, he looked down at a heel impression. It had stepped over a fallen log and its heel had dug in. Looking at the dented soil, he judged the size of his adversary. He knew the print was fairly fresh because the decaying soil had two different tones from oxidation, one old, one newer.

Ben sat on the lower end of the log it had stepped over. The log was at an angle and the point it had crossed over was easily five feet high. Ben's breath made clouds and he thought again about a cigarette. He directed his mind back to his foe. This one was big, much bigger than the one that had chased him all those years ago.

He rested a moment, warily eyeing the woods, then went back toward the house.

33

Kris's desk phone buzzed and she picked up the handset. "Walker."

"Miss Walker?" The voice was slightly officious. "Jason Kupperman. I'm the assistant district attorney for Snohomish County. You've made some claims in your newscast and I'm beginning an investigation into their nature."

Kris's mind raced to determine if this was a stupid joke. She thought Mac Schneider might have put up some friend to torment her. "Ever heard of the First Amendment?"

"Miss Walker, I'm a lawyer. Have you ever heard of obstruction of justice? How about making false statements? You could very well—"

Kris interrupted him. "I'm not under oath, so I can say anything I want."

"Aside from issues my office is pursuing, I am going to contact the FCC and demand that they sanction your station for your irresponsible behavior."

Kris didn't care if this were a joke or not. "Go for it."

"My sheriff wants your head on a platter and I'm going to give it to him. You've abused your position by making knowingly false statements regarding the missing men. Aside from the havoc with law enforcement, consider the grief you've caused the families of those men."

"I speak regularly to them and they want to know what the hell you're doing to find their bodies. And their killer." Kris threw in that last sentence to piss him off. And it worked.

"Good day, Miss Walker. Your station will be hearing from my office very soon."

She hung up the phone and considered what had just happened. If that really was the Snohomish ADA, then she had several things on her side. First, the Constitution. Second, the climate of the day: reporters were wrong all the time and nobody seemed to give a damn until some other news outlet exposed them. Even then the issue would blow over fast. And third, her gut said she was right. And if she was, then the DA could kiss her ass. If she was wrong? She'd have bigger worries than the toothless district attorney.

She glanced at her desktop and found a message to call Mac. She'd call him back but not right away. She was saving him. She wasn't sure how, but she felt he might help pull her feet out of the fire. She knew she still had a hold on Mac. Then Kris looked heavenward and thought of the four missing men. *Please let them be dead.*

Ty fingered the keys of his computer like a Mozart without music. He hadn't spent this much time at his computer in a long while but it came back like the proverbial bicycle skills. His Web site had already garnered more than sixteen thousand hits and dozens of responses, but nothing worthwhile. A lot of traffic in his e-mail was from afar, places like Indonesia, Bulgaria, Ukraine, and Arkansas, where kindred spirits sympathetically recounted their experiences with "large hominids." For many others, the notion of a corporate cover-up or police incompetence resonated. Ty didn't really believe either were the case, but he acknowledged they were the necessary cornerstones of his site. Ty flashed over the e-mails, and if they didn't have something to do with his current concern—the forests above his home—he deleted them.

He was emboldened by the response and began adding more fuel to his site, including additional information gathered on the four missing men. He also reported two other disappearances that he did not yet know were unrelated. But the drain on his time from his job, the pressures at home, and the opportunity he saw slipping away were taking their toll.

His focus on uncovering the mystery had been narrowing the past week, along with the desperate hope that its solution would—like the Enterprise blasting an asteroid from its path—solve all his problems. Each day he believed that more and more. Wanting to quit the Forest Service, he conjured up various scenarios to sell Ronnie on why he should, but he knew none of them would work.

Looking at the computer screen, he considered telling his story, exactly as it happened, on his site. He'd told it once before to a so-called respectable reporter, but that interview got so chopped up that he sounded like those misguided fools who killed themselves over the Hale-Bopp comet some years back. He never told it again, not even to Ronnie. He sipped some Scotch and decided against it. He rocked back and stared at the monitor, the cold, wet glass in his hand the only feeling in his body.

34

Mac braked his sheriff's issue Chevy Malibu to a stop and looked down at the USGS survey map on the passenger seat. He accelerated slowly to a dirt turnout and parked. The place looked familiar. It was where Skip Caldwell's truck had been found and not far from where he and Carillo had found the other footprints. The map showed he was about six hundred feet in elevation above Highway 2 and that this quiet mountain road ended some miles ahead, deep in the foothills of the North Cascades mountain range.

Mac and Carillo had now been assigned this case full-time. That meant they needed to follow any and all leads to solve this thing soon. It also meant they would have to split up at times. Mac drew the duty of investigating Skip Caldwell's trail. Mac was blasé in the office but now that he was here, all alone in a lonely place, he was experiencing the slightest creeping feeling. He tried ignoring it but the feeling simply went into a corner of his mind and waited.

The owner of a bike shop in Monroe told Mac about the trail, and since Skip Caldwell's truck was found at the trailhead, it was assumed he must have taken that route. The bike guy acknowledged that this trail's degree of difficulty was legendary.

"Yeah," he said, "people have gotten busted up pretty good on it over the years, but if anybody could run it, Skip could." He drew Mac a map on the back of a bicycle brochure with the caveat, "Probably accurate, but I can't guarantee it."

From his car Mac sized up the area around the trailhead. The large search over the last few days had turned up only one clue, tire tracks that likely matched those on the bike Skip was riding. Other than the few footprints that Mac and Carillo had discovered during the initial search, no others were found. But the ground had hardened again after the last rain, and as the searchers ascended the trail. The higher they got, the harder the soil got. Soon the tracks disappeared.

Mac's finger followed the trail on the survey map to where it ended. But the bike store owner's drawing contradicted the survey map, indicating the trail actually continued and then returned, making a circuit. It made sense to Mac. And if the store owner's drawing was correct, then the circuit dumped onto the road he was on about three miles farther up. Mac deduced that Skip would have started here, climbed the trail, run the downhill, then taken the asphalt road three miles back down to his truck.

Mac started his car and continued climbing, driving slowly. After around two miles he watched for any indication of the trail, or single-track as bikers call it. He crossed a river spanned by a wooden Army Corps of Engineers bridge. About three miles later he noticed a dip on the side of the road.

He slowed and saw what looked like a path. He parked and got out. He hung his binoculars around his neck and adjusted his shoulder holster for a hike. He checked his cell phone's battery charge; it indicated full. *Not that it'll even work up here.* The overcast was thick, so he wrapped a scarf around his neck, tucked it into his coat, and headed out.

Mac had been laboriously navigating through the trees for about twenty minutes, wondering how anyone could ride a bike on a path that was barely visible. But when he exited the stand of trees and stood on the brink of a sweeping clear-cut, he suddenly understood how someone with Skip Caldwell's skills could probably ride this trail down from the top.

The trail continued far above him and his eyes followed its course, finally losing it near the top, which he guessed was easily three thousand feet higher than his position. Through his binoculars he traced the route to the top, where the slope melded into a fir-covered butte. Though more than a half mile away, Mac's twelve-power Nikons found what appeared to be a pattern of broken trees. He wasn't sure but he could almost swear it was so. He recalled from his research that broken trees were a possible sign of an upper primate marking its territory. He strained his eyes, hoping to confirm that the damage was intentional and not wind-aided, but he couldn't.

He continued on and every step of the way his eyes darted back and forth between the trail and several yards off trail, fearful he might find more mammoth footprints. Unlike Carillo and their two bosses, Mac was now pretty sure the prints were real. His meeting with Dr. Frazier had left him a bit rattled. Frazier did not have a shadow of doubt that the print maker was a living, breathing creature, and that excluded a joker, or killer, with huge wooden feet. And as he made his way farther into the wilds, Mac's thoughts drifted to the proportions of the entity Frazier had pictured. Mac shivered slightly and shook his head. *No way. Nothing's that big.*

Far below he felt a small two-leg. It was searching. Its thoughts were strong, clear. Again, the small two-legs were looking for their own, this time for the one on the shiny thing, and perhaps two of the three from a few dark times before. Of those three, one escaped in their hardshell and he let it, so distracted was he by the idea that the small two-legs could kill each other. He sensed the dead one had been killed by the other two and was perplexed by this.

Far below he saw the small two-leg who sought him. He knew it and any other small two-legs who searched would never find any of their missing ones, for he always took them to places no small two-leg could go. The searchers were small and weak and needed their paths. His trail was not their trail.

He knew this one was looking. His hunting skills told him not to warn it. He gazed down from his dominion and his eyes followed the tree line to the bottom. He could go that way, staying in the trees, and cut the small two-leg off. Once he was between it and its escape, this small two-leg would be his.

He turned and moved downhill, hidden from below by the trees.

Mac panned his binoculars across the hill for a few moments, trying to find any trace of Skip Caldwell. Then he glimpsed something, a dull glint, out of place amid the horizon of green and brown. Something metal in the distance, on the side of a ravine. Using his unaided eyes to get a wide perspective, he tried to gauge his chances of getting to the object. It appeared to be at least a thousand yards away, and the steep terrain in between was a formidable rampart of gouged earth, stumps, and overwhelming deadfalls. Not a seasoned hiker, he allocated at least an hour and a lot of scratches and torn clothes to the round-trip trek.

Just as he was deciding whether to hike to it or just report it, he felt something quite strange. Glancing at the sky, he noticed the cloud deck was so thick he couldn't tell where the sun was. A thinking man, Mac didn't often dismiss things out of hand, and he had definitely felt an odd sensation. *Was it heat?* He wasn't sure, then as fast as it was upon him, the feeling was gone. But his uneasiness wasn't. Again he didn't know why, but took one guess. *Instinct? Telling me what?* Mac stood motionless for a moment, trying to get a handle on what, if anything, he was feeling. Just as he was about to dismiss it, it hit him again, an odd tingle he couldn't put a finger on. But given where he was, it was alarming. He turned and started walking, fast.

He knew now what his gut had been telling him: *get the hell out of here.*

He heard the mind voice of the small two-leg. Sensing its rising fear, he knew it felt him. And though its thoughts were confused, it knew enough to flee for its life.

He reached the flat at the bottom and moved through undergrowth like it was a runner's track. This was his world, and when he sensed prey, nothing could stop or even slow him.

* * *

As Mac left the clear-cut and headed back into the forest, his senses were telling him things he couldn't reconcile. Anxiety and the feeling of being watched, or maybe . . . pursued? He thought maybe all of his reading had planted the seeds of fear in him, but something in his environment had suddenly changed and the fact that he didn't understand it didn't mean it wasn't real.

Mac moved quickly, his apprehensions escalating to a controlled panic. Unable to see anything in the trees around him, and with his feeling of being stalked so perceptible, he gladly erred on the side of prudence and started running. Until this moment it had all been speculation, a theory. Now he felt something closing in on him. Mac was irritated that as a veteran cop he would allow such fear to well up and smother him. Yet as much as his rational side told him this was crazy, his instincts told him to keep running.

Frantically brushing back small branches and trying not to trip over fallen limbs, he drew his gun and racked the slide. If this thing was real and if it was going to jump him, he'd likely go down but not without a fight. He'd try for a head shot, but he knew from safari hunting accounts he had read as a kid that sometimes big game—really determined and *very big* game—continued to attack even after receiving a mortal wound. He wondered if that were true.

He felt the small two-leg just ahead. It was so slow, staggering along, out of place, scared. He thought of the shelter he had built, far away from the reach of the small two-legs, marked by his trees, at the summit of his new land. He would take it there, where he took the others. Then he would kill it and eat well.

Mac recognized a big moss-covered widowmaker and knew the road was close. But just past the dead tree he heard a limb crack, then some rustling branches. It was right behind him. *Is something really there or am I imagining it?* He beat down the impulse to turn and look.

Mac broke into a panicked sprint, hopping over deadfalls and bounding across small springs that crossed his path. As the trail rose in the last fifty yards before the car, he knew it was close, close enough to know he wouldn't make it to the car. *There is something behind me. It's really there.*

Closing on the small two-leg, he saw it ahead, desperate to get to its waiting hardshell but knowing it would not make it. He didn't understand their trait of giving up when they seemed to have no escape. Other animals fought to the death, no matter how small or weak. But these animals were different. More fear, less fight.

Suddenly the small two-leg raised its arm and three sounds—loud, sharp, and deep—ripped through the air. He stopped his pursuit, not knowing what it was. They were power sounds like thunder.

The small two-leg continued toward its hardshell and he watched it vanish into the thicket ahead. What was that sound? This was new. He knew they controlled the hardshells, larger creatures with no thoughts, no life. And they were Keepers of the Fire. But this power sound, this thunder was something he could not explain.

Then he remembered something from long past, something the old ones taught: this thunder might hurt him.

Mac leaped into the car, his keys sailing from his hand and landing on the floor. Taking his eyes off the woods for no more than half a second, he retrieved them and shakily found the ignition slot. Bringing the engine to life, he backed the Malibu three hundred yards down the road at top speed before deciding it was safe to turn around.

35

Deke Allison was not a poker player. He didn't even buy lottery tickets. So it was no surprise that Deke wanted no surprises. When the movie Indian was at his home, Marge correctly reported to the old man that Deke was out overseeing the repair of his truck. But he was also performing another errand, one devoted to the security of the Allison commonwealth. Even though his plans involved a family relocation in the very immediate future, Deke had just spent nearly nine grand on laser motion sensors and CCTV cameras to be deployed all around his property. He rationalized that they would make his home more salable.

When the electronics salesman asked if it was wild animals he wanted to detect, Deke automatically answered yes. But when the guy started assembling a system designed to recognize small creatures, Deke suddenly backpedaled.

"I need something that'll only trip when something . . . er, somebody maybe seven feet or so comes through."

The salesman looked puzzled. "Seven feet?"

Deke quickly shook his head. "No, no, I meant six feet, maybe six five. I think it's a neighbor kid, he's real tall, I think he plays basketball for the high school."

"Which kid?" asked the shopkeeper, being a fan of local prep hoops.

Deke shrugged, mumbling that he didn't want to name names, concerned over the blight on the record of a "nice kid." Nevertheless, he wanted to know if the kid was around.

"I know exactly what you're talkin' about," said the surveillance guy, "a peeper." The man nodded knowingly. "We'll set the receptors at six feet, avoid any false triggers."

The salesman set Deke up with the best perimeter intrusion detection system this side of the Dugway Proving Ground or Area 51. And it had consumed a mere six hours to install, align, and hook up.

Now Deke sat in his rec room, eyes flicking between Jerry Springer and the two black-and-white monitors trained on the back and side yards. His quasar-level floodlight made the motionless, grainy wide-angle images very contrasty. Anything larger than a vole or wood rat would grab his eye faster than if his satellite TV screwed up and the Spice Channel came on. Next to the monitors was the control console with eight red LEDs that would not only indicate a breach on his grid but would tell him where. Like a bargain basement nemesis of James Bond, Deke settled back into his Barcalounger for dinner, surrounded by an array of surveillance gear. Marge appeared, gently moved the rifle off his lap, and set his TV tray in front of him.

"Seen anything?" she asked, trying hard to be cheerful.

"Zip," Deke grunted.

After spending all this money, he almost hoped the big sumbitch would show up so he could shoot at it. Almost.

Just as Mr. Springer was waxing philosophically on his final thought, a red light began winking on Deke's control console. Something had just broken the beam directly behind the sheds. Something at least six feet tall. Suddenly confronted with the very real possibility of standing toe to toe with whatever made those footprints, Deke surprised himself.

He dialed 911.

The Kinko's copy center on Bellevue Way was bustling that evening. Everyone from students at Bellevue High and Bellevue Community College to eager job hunters was banging out multiple copies of term papers and resumés as they crowded the dozens of machines. Ben made his way to the will-call desk. A cute girl of about eighteen greeted Ben with a huge smile.

"Welcome to Kinko's. May I help you?"

Ben smiled. Despite his incognito windbreaker, his rangy six-three frame and distinctive face caused many heads in the place to turn.

"I think I got some faxes," he said. "For Campbell."

Ben used his real surname when conducting personal business. The girl sorted through the will-call stack and found a thick folder.

"Campbell? Here it is. Wow, it's a lot. You here doing a movie, Mr. Campbell?"

Ben was amused that so many young people recognized him. Ben still did two or three films a year but had also recently been "rediscovered" via a series of widely popular commercials.

"No," he said, "just takin' a vacation. I like your town."

He looked into the folder, filled with his nephew David's cyberspace research. A quick glimpse at the pages left Ben amazed at what you could find on the Internet.

"Maybe you'll move here?" offered the counter girl airily.

Ben handed her his Amex card and smiled again. "Maybe."

Twenty-five minutes after Deke Allison's agitated phone call was routed to the Snohomish County Sheriff's Department, Tyler James Greenwood was in custody for criminal trespass. In Deke Allison's excitable state he had no problem agreeing to press charges, since he had fairly warned the man the first time he'd caught him on his land. Ty was quiet on the way to the jail, his mind spinning with what he would tell Ronnie.

36

That evening Mac walked into Olson's Gun Exchange in downtown Everett. Though it had been nearly three years, the guy who sold him his current gun recognized him. Tall, tattooed, wiry with wire-frame glasses and sporting the name tag "Ray," the man approached. At first glance Ray appeared slightly bookish, but on further examination he projected an edgy, survivalist vibe. If you made the mistake of assuming he was a weakling, a glimpse of the big Colt .45 auto on his belt caused that perception to vanish.

"Hey man, how're ya doin'?" Ray said, remembering the face but not the name.

Mac shook Ray's hand. "Hi, Ray."

Since Ray had just smoked his dinner and momentarily forgotten he sported a name badge, he was surprised the cop remembered him. Mac released his grip.

"Mac. Mac Schneider."

Ray's face brightened in recognition. "Oh, yeah, Mac. Sheriff's department. You had just come up from L.A. I remember that. What's happenin', man?"

The guys who worked at the gun store liked real cops because most of them were police wannabes and would stay that way because never in a million years could they pass the background check or drug screen to be one.

"I need a gun. Bigger than this one," Mac said, pulling back his jacket to reveal the Sig pistol Ray had sold him when he started with the department.

"What's wrong with that?" Ray asked.

"Nothing. Just need more knockdown power sometimes. What do you have?"

Ray looked conspiratorially at Mac. "This for official use?"

Mac's face was impassive. "Not necessarily."

Ray loved anything that reinforced his belief that the government was doing shit off the books. "How big?"

"Big. Real big," answered Mac.

Ray motioned for him to follow as he strolled to the end of the glass display cases. Ray reached down and got his hands around two handguns—an enormous, gleaming stainless steel semiautomatic pistol and an equally massive revolver. Ray's lips tightened and he puffed out his chest as he went into his pitch.

"Desert Eagle, fifty magnum action express, made in Israel," he said proudly. "Three hunnert and twenty-five grains of jacketed lead that makes a forty-four mag look like a fuckin' paintball gun. Wanna stop a train? Here's the conductor, my man."

Ray picked up the revolver. "If that one's King Kong—"

Mac smiled to himself at the inadvertently apt comparison.

"—this one is freakin' Godzilla. The Smith and Wesson model Five Hundred. Biggest, baddest, most powerful handgun made, period. Pushes five hunnert 'n ten grains at seventeen hunnert f-p-s. A fuckin' nuke-yew-ler hand cannon. This will kill a rhino or a polar bear, dude. And that's no shit."

Mac gestured at the automatic pistol. "That carries more rounds, right?"

Ray nodded. "Seven plus one versus five."

Mac pointed at the Desert Eagle and Ray laid the immense weapon into his hands. Mac's arm sagged slightly, it was so much heavier than his current weapon.

"Course, you'll have to get used to a safety again," noted Ray. "Plus this ain't no double action like your Sig."

"How much?" asked Mac.

Ray looked around like he was about to break policy and make this Mac's lucky day.

"Twelve-fifty. But for you, tonight? Eleven even."

Mac hefted it and snapped the huge slide. He popped the clip out, then rammed it back in. He said a short prayer to himself that he wouldn't have to use it.

"Throw in two boxes of ammo," he said.

Ray balked. "Uh, hey pardner, that's twenty-eight bucks a box . . ." Mac's look told him to shut up. "Oh hell, why not?" caved Ray. "I mean you're gonna use it to protect the citizenry, right?"

Mac dropped the hammer and it made a solid click. "Yes, I am."

Ronnie was at her wits' end after getting Ty's call from the sheriff's department in Everett. She told Greta she had an errand to run and jumped in her Lexus. She'd heard the reports of the missing men over the last week but had never imagined that they might relate to Ty. Until now. Ty was backsliding, she could see that.

At the sheriff's department she paid his bail with cash. Knowing computers like they did, she and Ty had long ago decided to keep some cash in the house in case the computer systems governing the banking system crashed.

Ty was led out in handcuffs and unshackled in front of her. She bit her lip, suddenly wanting to cry, but not here, not in front of these people. Ronnie was scared. She was scared for her husband, her children, and their future. If he started this behavior all over again, this time he just might be beyond her ability to save him. That's what scared her the most.

With Ty's truck impounded, they had to drive home together. As they walked silently to the car, Ronnie handed Ty the keys and got in the passenger side. She had kept her cool for too long; her strength was gone. She took a deep breath and cut loose, bawling like a baby. Ty drove half a block and pulled over. He leaned over to hold her and she pushed him away.

"What is wrong with you?" she sobbed. "Are you starting this again? Are you?"

Ty knew he had to come clean. He had another bombshell to drop on her: he had quit the Forest Service that afternoon. He quickly decided it was probably not the time to tell her.

"Honey, I'm not crazy. Do you believe that?" he asked.

She turned and looked out the window, having labored over this same ground before. She tried to compose herself, sniffling as she rummaged in her pockets for a tissue.

"Ty, you can't do this. I don't know why you're dragging us through it again. I won't do it," she said, her voice firming up. She turned to him and even in the dark car he could see her swollen eyes and beet red cheeks. His heart sank over the pain he was causing her.

"If this is what you want, you'll do it without us. The kids are older, they have more to lose, and I won't stand by and watch you disintegrate looking for something you can't find. Do you hear me?" she asked, choking back snot and tears.

He wanted to put his arms around her but that was off-limits. He put the car in gear.

"Yes, I hear you."

They said nothing more the thirteen miles back to the house.

The next morning as soon as Ronnie's car disappeared down the driveway, Ty climbed up to the attic storage room and started searching for buried treasure. As he moved boxes, he hoped Ronnie hadn't tossed the items out in the last two years. Behind a wall of other boxes Ty found his prize, four boxes marked "Ty's books, stuff."

There were other boxes of books but these four cartons were special. They contained research materials, books, pamphlets, Internet downloads, invoices, tape recordings, and videotapes and disks of his previous quest. Ty had sealed the issue in the boxes and exiled them to the attic after Ronnie's dire predictions about the destruction of their family.

Now with a new promise of bad things to come if he stayed on his current path, he gazed at the boxes for a moment, as if they contained some terrible poisonous reptiles and he had to think through whether he should release them. He did not want to hurt Ronnie, but Ty was in the throes of an uncontrollable urge to continue. He acknowledged that the feelings he was experiencing were tantamount to addiction. That being granted, and safe in the belief that he was not yet ready to confront his addiction by any twelve-step method, he steeled himself, grabbed the first box, and hefted it to his shoulder.

37

As the news van made its way to the scene of a story, Kris had time to think. She knew one thing they never taught in journalism classes and that was that the illusion of a story could be just as good as the real thing. Sometimes it was called hype, sometimes misinformation, sometimes just misreporting, but however you labeled it, the illusion of excitement, danger, or controversy drew viewers like a moth to a flame. While in school Kris had been mesmerized when she'd watch national news anchors, usually on the cable networks, speculate on a story. This was everything she'd been taught not to do. If a man had just taken the patrons of an electronics store hostage, or was simply driving erratically, they would debate whether he was suicidal, psychotic, bipolar, a wife abuser, drug abuser, gang member, fleeing felon, or child molester, and the ratings would skyrocket.

Kris saw this precedent as her license to conjecture wildly, that is until the truth was revealed, at which time she would shift gears and report that which was known. In her current situation, she was convinced that whether there actually was a killer was unimportant. If she could keep the ball in the air, the story of a *possible* killer could reap her ratings as well as credit for having uncovered the story. And a story this big would get national attention. *What if this is another*

Green River Killer or Ted Bundy? She got a chill for all the wrong reasons.

"Here's another. I think that's it," said John Baxter, handing Mac a thick green Pendaflex folder. "In there is everything we've got on those three stories."

Mac had read coverage of all their missing person cases in the local paper and saw some facts the department did not have. He had convinced Carillo it was worth the five-minute ride over to the paper to check out their files and see if they offered anything fresh.

Mac nodded, removing a manila folder and handing the rest to Carillo.

"Do you mind if we take our time?" Mac asked.

Baxter gestured toward a conference room that was rarely used. "Not at all. You fellas want some coffee?"

Mac shook his head, but Carillo looked up. "Yeah, where is it?"

Baxter didn't mind helping the police. As a newspaperman he knew a lot of cops in the area but not these guys. He was a friend of their boss, the sheriff, and getting to know Schneider and Carillo might be helpful someday. "I'll get it," he said.

When Baxter left, Carillo noticed something in Skip Caldwell's file.

"Okay, here's something bicycle guy's girlfriend mentioned," explained Carillo. "Caldwell's supposed to be in a world-class bike race that's coming up. Favored to finish first or second. We need to look into the guy favored to finish third."

Mac flipped through the folder. "Thought you didn't think much of bicycles."

"I don't," Carillo continued, "but there's no denying a possible motive. I guess they pay these jokers pretty good money just to ride bicycles." He hefted Jack Remsbecker's file. "And the lawyers?" Carillo snorted. "Who needs a motive to kill a lawyer?"

Baxter heard the last sentence as he entered with the coffee.

"If you're looking for motives," he offered, "and I don't know if this has any bearing, but I've had a guy poking around, asking lots of questions."

Baxter handed Carillo his coffee and left the office. Carillo and

Mac looked at each other and shrugged. Baxter returned a moment later carrying another folder.

"Like I said, this guy may be harmless, but he's asking the same questions you are. He's with the Forest Service and said he was investigating these disappearances. Thing is, I checked him out and his bosses didn't know anything about it. Also, FYI, the other night your people arrested him for trespassing. It'll be in our police blotter tomorrow." He handed Carillo the file.

"Thanks. We'll check him out."

As Baxter left again, Carillo flipped through the file. "This is the guy . . . You gave me some articles on this guy, Greenwood, right?"

Mac looked up, thought for a second, and nodded. "Yeah."

Carillo continued reading.

Mac looked up again. "I figured maybe Greenwood could help us—"

"Shit!" said Carillo, "Bigfoot? This guy claims he saw Bigfoot? What were you thinking?"

"What do you mean?"

"He's the guy!"

"What guy?" asked Mac.

"The guy who's making all these people disappear," said Carillo.

J. D. Watts was only now coming out of the drug and liquor catatonia he'd been in for three days. His life had turned from shit to worse, much worse, in less than seventy-two hours. He killed a guy in a fit of rage, then he and Errol were attacked by a fucking Bigfoot, which killed Errol and ran off with him. It was the most horrible nightmare J. D. could ever imagine.

Now he had some decisions to make. First, how was he going to deal with Errol's parole officer? As soon as Errol didn't check in, the guy would come out to snoop around. That J. D. was also on parole and the PO didn't know they were roommates didn't look good for him. Second, if someone found either Errol or Newburg's bodies, J. D. was completely fucked. As J. D. visualized being tied down to a gurney, like Sean Penn in that *Dead Man Walking* movie, he lost all strength. He didn't want to die.

Finally, the whole Bigfoot thing complicated everything by a hundred times. If they hadn't been dumping a body, they'd have the story of the century. They'd probably be rich and that would solve all of their problems. But Errol was dead now. In his mind's eye J. D. Watts saw over and over the face of that thing, staring at him, its horrid red eyes sparkling in the glow of the taillights, and he shivered. *Poor Errol. Poor me.* Sure, he'd been a little loaded at the time, but what he saw . . . well, it was totally real. Now what?

He couldn't exactly call the TV people with his big discovery, given the dark reason he and Errol had been in the mountains. But he knew someone would figure out Leon Newburg was missing, and also that Errol Rayburn was missing, and that the common element was probably J. D. Watts. And pretty soon, a few days, a few weeks maybe, someone would come around with questions he couldn't answer. J. D. looked at the fresh bottle of Jack Daniels he had cracked the night before, just before he passed out, and gagged.

He grabbed the remote and changed channels to watch the noon news and see if anyone had found the bodies yet. He regularly watched Channel 7's news because of that hot babe Kris something or other. As he gazed stonily at the object of his arousal, it suddenly occurred to him what she was talking about and he sat up. Missing men? Murders? J. D. realized she was describing pretty much the same area where he and Errol had gone to dump Newburg's body. If people were disappearing, he had a fairly good idea why.

A grand plan began to form in his mind. He would go public, solve the whole thing, become a media celebrity, then get a big, fancy lawyer who would get him off the hook for killing Newburg. Then doubt threw a blanket on his grand plan. What if he was wrong? What if that thing didn't kill anyone else? What if as soon as he came forward, the missing men either turned up or it was discovered they had been knocked off in a more conventional way?

J. D. sat back and took a long toke of reefer. He had time. So far, no parole officers had called for Errol, and for that matter, nothing else out of the ordinary had happened. Errol didn't have many friends, so J. D. figured so far, so good. He watched the beautiful blond newsgirl and pictured the scene as he told her his story. He allowed that maybe something would develop between them. He took another toke and fantasized about that.

* * *

Carillo threw the folder down on the desk. "This is him, Boss, Ty Greenwood."

Sheriff Barkley picked up the folder.

Mac shook his head. "I doubt he's the guy."

Carillo shot him an ugly glance. Mac hated contradicting his partner, particularly in front of their two bosses, but he was pretty sure Ty Greenwood was innocent.

Undersheriff Tom Rice closed the room's louvered blinds to give the four men privacy. "Why do you think it's him?"

Carillo was exasperated. "It's a no-brainer. This guy was taken apart by the press a couple years back when he swore Bigfoot chased him around Idaho when he was on vacation. I did some digging on him. At least several publications said he was on antidepressants and seeing a shrink, and I did find out he orders illegal painkillers by mail . . . Hey, the guy even shitcanned a high-paid career to go work for the Forest Service. Total fucking nut. We arrested him the other night for trespassing on a guy's property who had a truck turned over. I mean that's something Bigfoot might do, right?" he chuckled. No one else as much as cracked a smile and he continued. "Anyway, Greenwood's got the money to pay somebody to do that, tip a truck over. I'm tellin' you, if this guy doesn't have a motive to make people think Bigfoot's real, then nobody does."

Barkley looked to Mac. "You're not convinced? Why?"

Mac stared at Barkley for a moment. He wanted to tell them everything he'd discovered but they just weren't ready to believe him. If he spoke up now, he'd only ruin any chance to bring this out when the timing was right. Anger flashed over his face briefly, but it was anger at himself for being afraid. "I dunno. Maybe Karl's right."

Carillo clenched his jaw. "Fuck me runnin' I'm right."

Barkley pushed the file back to Carillo. "Okay, this is how we'll play it. You find what you can on this guy. If he's got that much money, we just can't roust him like some crackhead. We need our shit together if we're gonna build a case. Get prepared, then go interview him, tomorrow. See if you can get him to break but don't push too hard. If he's the guy and we don't have all our ducks in a row, then he'll lawyer up and walk."

38

That evening Mac sat in front of the television with the sound muted. He had been making a point of watching the eleven p.m. news on Channel 7 for one blond reason. Though they hadn't spoken since just after she ambushed Carillo, Mac had watched her reports over the last several days and marveled at her unfounded speculation. It also frustrated him that the news media were giving the story so much attention when they didn't really get it. What bothered him most was waiting. What if this thing found another victim? But Mac couldn't identify any pattern to its behavior, and even if he could, who'd believe him?

After watching Kris's report about a slipping landfill in Mountlake Terrace, Mac went for a night run to blow off steam. He did three miles in a little under half an hour and headed for the shower. Afterward he donned some gym shorts and a T-shirt and sat down to read. A knock at the door surprised him. It was a few minutes after midnight and he guessed it was an older neighbor who often came to him when raccoons raided her trash.

He swung the door open and Kris stood before him, holding out a bottle of champagne.

"Peace offering," she said. "Sorry it's so late, but your light was on."

"You can only see my lights from inside the complex," he said, trying to be aloof.

She shrugged. "Okay, I'm nosy. I'm allowed that, right?"

"It's trespassing. I could take you in," he said, his tone just light enough to encourage her.

"Can't you just take me into custody here and I'll plea bargain?"

Mac shook his head, took the champagne, and stepped back. She came inside.

"You want an interview?" Mac said, keeping an even face. "See, we caught the murderer this afternoon. He's in lockup as we speak," he said, wanting to see if there was even a flicker in her eyes.

She smiled sweetly and dropped her coat over a chair. "So, you got some glasses?"

"Champagne at midnight? On a school night?" he asked as he went for the glasses.

Kris casually surveyed the place like it was the first time she'd seen it. "Sure. It's the best time to drink champagne."

"You've been busy," Mac noted. "I'm surprised you have time to drop by. Why am I being honored?"

Kris busied herself pretending to look at a shelf of mementos.

"Oh, no reason," she said, "I just felt bad I haven't talked to you all week. That's all."

Mac's bullshit meter pegged. She wanted something but he wasn't sure what. He wanted to believe, telling himself the big lie that she was attracted to him but knowing it was probably a delusion.

He handed her a glass of bubbly. They touched glasses.

"To us," she lied, and Mac knew it, sipping his champagne impassively. He motioned for her to sit with him on the sofa.

She threw out a non sequitur. "Why did you get into this business?"

Mac hadn't considered that one for a while.

"I was going to be a lawyer," he started. "At first I wanted to be a criminal attorney. Then I changed my mind. I wanted to be a prosecutor."

"Why a prosecutor?"

"I don't know. Maybe laying blame was easier than defending people who might be guilty. By my third year in law school I realized what I really wanted to do was solve crimes, not deal with the aftermath. I wanted something that was in the moment, more hands-on bringing criminals to justice."

Sipping her champagne, she looked into his dark, soft eyes. She had been right, he was different. Could have been a lawyer.

"Big difference in earning power," she noted.

He tipped a shoulder in deference. "Maybe, but I think I've done reasonably well. How about you? Why a reporter?"

Kris thought a moment before answering. "I was a big fan of Nancy Drew when I was a kid. I loved mysteries. I also loved getting into other people's business. I found a job where I could do both."

Mac half believed her but saw something else in her eyes. "I think you like the attention. I think for you it's less about news and more about image. I think if someone offered you two choices, best news-woman or superstar, it's no contest, you'd go with the latter."

Another time, another man, and she might have been offended, but he was absolutely, uncannily correct. She chose to be flattered that he saw her true ambition. He didn't seem put off by her lust for power.

"Maybe. Maybe so. I got into this business to be Nancy Drew, but I ended up realizing it was better to be Bette Davis."

She reached past him, grabbed the champagne, and filled her empty glass. His needed only a splash.

"I'm thirsty," she said, off his bemused look.

Mac indicated her glass. "I do have water. You don't have to slug down fifty-dollar champagne to quench your thirst."

She was impressed he knew it was good champagne. The wine had started in on her brain. Though she had few inhibitions, her mood was quickly winding down from the intense pace she had maintained the last fifteen hours. Ready to settle in for the next seven or eight hours, she decided it would be here.

She ran a playful finger over Mac's forearm. "I'm sorry I had to leave the other night."

Mac knew where this was going and let it. "I was too."

She coyly fixed her eyes on his, then looked away. "I don't have to tonight."

With that, Mac slipped his hand into her silky blond hair and moved her face and full lips to his. They kissed. Again. And again.

* * *

He came down from his mountain, moving swiftly through the trees, the moonless night not slowing him at all. A night traveler, he preferred the dark time, when his senses were keener, more focused.

Hunger drove him toward the flat land, the place of the small two-legs. Revenge and the pleasure of the kill were secondary now to the search for sustenance. Crossing a black trail, he moved away from the prying night-fire eyes of a hardshell as it passed. He knew a small two-leg was within and he kept to the old ways, the teachings that said let no animal know of your presence until you are moving in to make the kill.

From his vantage point above the valley he saw the controlled fire coming from the openings in the wood caves of the small two-legs. He thought of the thunder unleashed by the small two-leg he had stalked. He had never before heard the thunder of the small two-legs and had forgotten the warnings of the old ones, but now he knew their teachings might be true: the thunder could kill. He felt the small two-legs probably kept thunder in their wood caves, so he needed caution approaching them. Any challenge to his power caused him anger but he knew he could use surprise to defeat them.

He also knew from his encounter with the small two-leg that though they carried the thunder, they were still afraid. So the thunder might not be as powerful as he had been told. But he would take no chances. He was a hunter and he was wise. If his prey had sharp teeth, he would avoid those teeth.

Kris lost her blouse in the living room, Mac his shirt. Ten feet down the hall, her pants fell. Up against the wall, outside the guest bathroom, Mac fumbled with her bra and she helped him free her breasts. Kissing her furiously, Mac worked his way down her neck, across milky shoulders, down the curve of her breasts to her nipples.

As he tugged gently on her left nipple with his teeth, Kris's eyes rolled back and she brought the back of her hand to her forehead in rapture. He edged her panties over her hips, revealing downy blond hair between her legs, then dropped them to her ankles. She stepped out, now wearing only her calf-high socks, wristwatch, and an expression of total abandon.

Mac, on his knees, moved his tongue down between her flawless breasts to her navel and below. Reaching the upper line of her perfectly coiffured pubic hair, Mac's nose told him the area had recently been perfumed, and he smiled inwardly that she had had this all planned, probably to the beat. As his tongue lathered her belly and thighs, his left hand pressed against her naked bottom and his right one-handed his gym shorts down and off.

Running her hands through his hair while his tongue wandered south, she let out a slight, almost controlled shriek when he found his mark. She opened her stance for him. Her head rattled a picture on the wall as Mac tortured her with slow swirls of his tongue.

39

Sometimes when Burt Krinkel heard his dogs barking at night, he'd get out of bed and check on them. There was really no reason to do it except it gave him an excuse to get up. At seventy-five Burt didn't sleep as well as he used to. By moving around he found he could go back to bed and sleep better. Why not? It wasn't like he had to get up early, though he mostly did. He'd left his job with the railroad seven years back and still couldn't break that habit of waking at four thirty.

His wife, Ada, never woke up that early, but she hadn't been in the habit for years. When their four kids were growing up, she was always up before them, cooking breakfast, doing last-minute laundry and such. But when the last one left home twenty-five years ago, Ada slowly settled into a more leisurely pace. In bed at ten thirty, up by seven, just like clockwork. Burt envied her that unbroken sleep.

At around one a.m. Burt sat up in bed. He had tossed and turned for a couple of hours, so when the dogs started yip-yappin', he figured he'd investigate. He slid into his slippers and donned the big wool robe that his grandkids had given him the previous Christmas. He assumed some possums had gotten into the trash or the dog food, but the dogs suddenly quieted, so maybe they'd chased the possums out back of the property. He decided to check anyway. He stopped in the kitchen and poured a glass of milk. A walk and the milk were guaranteed sleep aids.

The digital thermometer indicated the outside temperature was thirty-eight. He grabbed one of his coats off the hook in the mud room and went out the back door. Slightly misty, the chill air invaded the loose cuffs of his pajamas. Though it was pitch-dark, Burt knew the way by heart, aided by residual light from his porch lamp. He had a small flashlight in his pocket but didn't need it until he got to his destination. Some called Burt a frugal man but he considered himself efficient.

Kris grabbed aimlessly for the curtains in front of the sliding glass doors to the patio and missed, knocking over a tall standing lamp. Finally, her fingernails found fabric and she held on tight, afraid her knees would buckle from passion as Mac positioned himself to enter her standing up.

She leaped up and straddled him, her legs twining around his waist. The change of position was all he needed. Suddenly she felt him slide inside, full and very hard. She cried out as the deep probing sensation fired all her circuits. Their mouths found each other, their tongues entwining. Mac pumped up and down, in and out, and she broke the kiss to gulp air as she expressed her ecstasy in a very loud moan, a moan that rose and fell with each thrust.

Mac had never made love to such a breathtakingly beautiful woman. His heart, against all reasons, wanted to keep this one, and not just because she was stunning, but for the aura of excitement and danger that surrounded her. Coming to his home in the middle of the night, after attacking his partner and his department, was risky at best. Yet here they were.

Slamming her bare ass against the glass, he began to feel the rise of a climax.

Burt got to the shed and called the dogs, "Zoe, Sophie, Simon? C'mere!"

No answer. Burt opened the front door of the old clapboard building and that's when he knew there was trouble.

He shined the light inside and found the glowing crimson irises and white faces of his three dogs, huddled together in the back, all on Zoe's blanket.

"Hey, what the heck's wrong with—"

Then he felt something that made the ruddy, wrinkled skin on the back of his neck crawl. It was the sensation of . . . a presence. Someone was there. But the dogs would have been barking. Heck, they even barked when the chipmunks—

He felt it again, palpable but odd, almost like static electricity. He couldn't quite place it. He shined his weak flashlight around the front of the shed but saw nothing. Then his old nose caught a stench, just a whiff, but a very sour smell. Wondering if the dogs had killed something that was now going bad, he decided to leave it until later. He had an uneasy feeling and suddenly wanted to get back to the house. He sniffed again but smelled nothing, then turned back to the dogs.

"You kids do your job, you hear m—"

Before poor old Burt could complete the word *me,* a closed fist, concrete hard and the size of a milk pail, arced down, instantly crushing his head onto his shoulders. He was dead before his flashlight hit the damp grass.

Examining the corpse of the small two-leg, he saw it was old with not much meat on it. He would eat it but needed another. He considered the dogs. He had eaten dogs but did not like them. Their lean flesh tasted different from small two-legs; their bones were smaller and more of a nuisance.

He turned to the wood cave of the old one. Maybe there were more inside. He left the old one where he had fallen and headed for it.

Now on the bed with Mac on top, Kris threw her hips at his to heighten the power of their coupling. Up and down they went for fifteen minutes. She'd already had two minor orgasms but was anticipating a big one, one that was building, the others just foreshocks to her coming San Andreas climax. She hadn't been fucked like this ever. Most guys came like jackrabbits, but this guy . . . She'd been right when she met him: not a normal cop.

He walked around the wood cave, looking in the openings covered by warm ice. Through one of the openings he found another small two-leg,

asleep. This one was old like the other, and female. Its mate. He was learn-
ing more about the small two-legs and was finding they were unlike other
animals. Any other animal would have felt his presence and fled. This one
continued to sleep.

He touched the warm ice and it felt less solid than the warm ice of the
hardshell he'd turned over. He ran a finger over it, gauging the distance to
the old female that slept. He wanted food, not pleasure or revenge, so he
decided to make it quick.

His hand pushed easily through the warm ice and it made a cracking
sound like cold ice. The old one awoke, confused more than scared. Then
he felt her terror as he reached through the opening and got his hand
around her throat. Pulling her small body through the opening, he let her
live for a moment, allowing the fear to overcome her. Then he squeezed
and her life force flickered out. Walking back to the other, he put them
both under one arm and returned whence he came.

40

Kris sat up in the bed, tucking a pillow between her back and the wall. Still breathing hard, she felt sweat trickling down between her breasts and she wasn't sure if it was his or her own. She was impressed he'd paid so much attention to pleasuring her. Her magnitude nine orgasm had been so strong her jaw still hurt from the contortions. Mac lay next to her, spent.

"Wanta go again?" he said half joking, and when her face told him she momentarily took him seriously, he burst into laughter.

"Can I smoke first?" she retorted.

Mac pretended to think for a moment, then rolled next to her and wrapped his lips around one of her nipples. "You can suck on a butt if I can suck on this."

"Deal. Let me get my purse," she said, then got up and walked to the hall. Mac followed her perfect sweat-shined glutes as they bobbed away. *Why is it the bad girls are always so good?* She reappeared, this time giving him the reverse view. Her tits were works of art—natural or man-made, it didn't matter to Mac—bouncing saucily as she approached.

Lying down as she dug through her purse, she casually looked over. "Yeah, they're real."

Mac smiled. She'd read him like a headline.

She pulled out a cigarette, lit up, and set the handbag on the nightstand.

"You dating anybody?"

Mac wasn't sure if it was just an informational inquiry or she was staking a claim.

"No. Not for a while. A few here and there, but nothing interesting."

"You said I was strong. But am I interesting?" she asked, taking a drag.

Mac slid up her body, moving in for a kiss. She held her cigarette away long enough to allow a quick one, then went back to inhaling carcinogens.

"Yes, you're interesting."

"Good. I hate being otherwise."

"You're also beautiful and dangerous," he observed.

"I'm dangerous?"

Mac rolled off and lay next to her. She was on her back, blowing smoke into the air. Mac put his finger in her navel and she jumped, laughing. "Don't do that! It tickles!"

She recomposed herself and Mac put his hand to her flat belly, this time caressing her.

"Yeah, you're dangerous. Self-centered, narcissistic, egomaniacal. It's what makes you good at your job."

Allowing herself a very slight, self-satisfied smile, she enjoyed the knife-edged context of those terms. They frightened the average person. She embraced them, the power they gave her over weaker, "sensitive" people. She liked that he had identified her power base and yet was still beside her, now fondling her right breast.

"Yeah, you're right," she said, the pride shining through.

"Does that make you lonely?" he asked.

She pondered for a moment, never having considered that simple question. She wasn't sure what lonely really was. She had no friends in Seattle and didn't really socialize with any of her coworkers, although she'd only been in town a few months.

"Lonely? I don't know. I don't think so."

She was getting too vulnerable; time for a subject change. "How about you?" she asked. "You like being a cog in the wheel?"

Mac rolled over and looked at the ceiling. "I get satisfaction from my job, usually, but the job doesn't define who I am. A job can pressure a person to conform, but my situation allows me to do my thing and still maintain my individuality. I don't have to be just like everybody, but they trust me because I've proven myself."

"Trust, huh? Sit up, I want to try something," Kris said, motioning for Mac to move. He turned and knelt on the bed in front of her.

"What do you have in mind?" he asked, unsure of her suddenly devilish look.

The corners of her mouth curved upward, seductively, a scheme in the works. She reached over and cupped his scrotum, then slid her hand up to his penis, wrapping her thumb and forefinger around it. With her other hand she moved her cigarette slowly toward it, her eyes moving between his face and the tip of his organ.

"I doubt you got this trust exercise at a corporate retreat," Mac joked rather nervously.

She raised an eyebrow. "You'd be surprised."

With the burning tobacco a half inch from contact, Mac caved, pushing her hand away.

"Chicken," she said. "You don't trust me. See?"

She'd made her point. She set the cigarette on the nightstand and rolled toward him. Bringing her face close to his penis, she unfurled her tongue and licked it, then slid it tantalizingly into her mouth. Then she let it drop out.

"See, I could have chomped down right there, done a Bobbitt—"

"She used a knife—"

"Yes, but the point is you trust me to a certain extent, right?"

Mac was getting aroused again and readily agreed with her object lesson. "Sure. To a certain extent." Despite the clouds of stimulus fogging his thoughts, he wanted to trust her, although he knew it was a bad idea.

Now that he was nearly erect again, Kris positioned herself to get a better angle to finish what she'd started. She teased him with her mouth and wondered for a split second if he really liked her or if he just wanted to chalk up a conquest. She went with the latter as a defense against her feelings. She was starting to feel attachment and that bothered her.

Ten minutes later, Kris stretched out on the bed, having brought her partner to climax once again, this time with her oral skills. She reached over and pulled a box of Tic Tacs from her purse. She popped two and offered them to Mac, who took one. He was on his back next to her, completely spent. She lit another cigarette. After her first pull he took it out of her fingers and also drew on it, inhaling deeply.

"You smoke?" she asked.

"Years ago," he said, handing it back to her.

Kris took the cigarette and let out a deep, satisfied sigh before taking another pull.

Mac nodded slightly. "My sentiments exactly."

Despite the fact it was 3:15 a.m. and he was due at work in about four hours, he didn't care. He was savoring her company. Then a crazy thought crossed his mind.

What if I tell her? What if she keeps my name out of it? Then I can go around Barkley and Rice and Carillo and let people know this could be a lot more than just some random disappearances. Or conventional murders. Who's going to know?

Mac rationalized to himself that his was a big department. The list of possible leaks could go on and on. Outside of himself and Carillo and their two bosses, Suzy Chang knew, and probably her boss, and then the list widened after them. Even that young deputy, Bill Alexander, seemed to know, or at least suspect, that more was going on than met the eye. He didn't want to get Suzy in trouble, but if Barkley's hunt for the leaker could buy Mac time to explore the stranger side of this case, then it just might be worth it. But probably more important than anything, it might just help Mac heal the guilt he was feeling for keeping his mouth shut. Of course Barkley's hunt for the leaker might be very short, given Mac had already expressed some doubts. But his desire to find the truth outweighed the potential consequences.

"I do trust you," he said, giving a slightly displaced answer from earlier but using it as a setup for what he was about to say.

"Okay, good. So a blow job was all it took? I'll remember that."

Mac smiled at her frankness. "No, I actually do. Trust you, that is."

She puffed away, wondering where he was going with this.

"What if I said I might have a lead for you? On the missing persons case."

Kris almost dropped her cigarette. She had really just come over to fuck the guy, figuring anything she might get in terms of the case would be gravy. She had been formulating an introduction to that very subject that wouldn't raise a red flag, but now he'd saved her the effort. She reached over to her purse and fiddled for some more breath mints.

"You mean the *murder* case?" she said, trying to sound indifferent.

Mac paused a moment. Although they had shared intimacy over the last three hours, he didn't fully trust her. But this woman had a television station at her disposal.

"If I tell you something, a pretty important piece of information, will you keep your source confidential? What I'm saying is, the department would come down on me like, well, it would get ugly. Probably end my career there. So you've gotta keep me out of it. I'll give you the information and you do what you will with it. Get it out there. Deal?"

Kris stuck the cigarette in the corner of her mouth and held out her hand. "Shake hands with a naked lady. Deal."

Mac gathered his thoughts for a moment. "I'm convinced there is a killer at work. But not in the . . . normal sense."

She ignored the qualification. "So you're confirming the fact, what I've been reporting now for more than two weeks, exclusively, that there is a killer at work? You're saying that?"

"Yes, I believe so. I'm ninety percent certain."

"Do you have a suspect?"

"Yes and no."

"What does that mean?"

"Carillo thinks it's a former computer guy named Ty Greenwood."

"Ty Greenwood . . ."

"Right."

"But . . ."

"But I'm pretty sure it's someone else. I don't think Greenwood's involved at all. And whatever you do, don't mention his name. I shouldn't have told you. I think he's clean. But if his name got out in the wrong context, he'd sue you and your station and me and the department and he'd win. He's got the money to bury us all. Forget him."

Kris leaned in slightly. "Interesting. But okay, forget him, so who really did it?"

Mac struggled with this next sentence for a moment. "Actually, it's more *what* than who."

"Huh?" She was confused by the word game.

"The department has a piece of evidence from two of the scenes and we're holding it back. It's pretty unusual evidence and we've kept it quiet, mainly because my bosses don't believe what it is. Or at least what I think it is."

"What is it?"

"It's a piece of evidence that leads me to believe that the missing men were not victims of any kind of normal abduction."

Kris held her breath in anticipation. *Not victims of a normal abduction?*

"I think they were taken away by an unknown species of animal."

"What?"

"An animal very closely related to human beings. A hominid."

"A what? A what? I've never heard of such an animal."

"A hominid is a type of animal. Humanlike. Walks on two legs. We're hominids. Only this thing's bigger than us, a whole lot bigger."

Kris narrowed her eyes. "You're saying the killer is *not* a human being?"

"Exactly. And we have a twenty-one-inch footprint to prove it. "

Kris took a puff and blew it in his face. "Bigfoot? Like a Sasquatch? You're saying Bigfoot took these people? That's really fucking hilarious," she said with irritation. "So I'll bet space aliens have something to—"

"I'm not joking." Mac's face and tone were dead serious. "I've researched this thing. Read up on it, talked to experts . . . and I'm almost completely convinced they exist." He paused for effect. "I think I even came close to meeting one—maybe the same one that's taking people—the other day in the forest. Up where the cyclist disappeared. It was there, right behind me on the trail, swear to God."

His face told her he either believed this or was the best liar she had ever met.

"Okay . . . ," she said deliberately. "You saw it?"

"No." But Mac pressed on because she hadn't started laughing. "Let me get the casting."

He leaped up and went down the hall, coming back with a huge plaster foot. He held it out as she looked at it.

"It's big," she said hefting it with both hands, then setting it on the bed. "So you're saying there's something running around out in the woods, carrying people off. Something with a foot this big? How big is it? This thing?"

Mac sat back down on the bed, the casting between them. "I went to the U-Dub. An anthro prof over there, one of the world's leading experts on these things, he said the casting's absolutely authentic and whatever made it is probably more than ten feet tall."

She looked suspiciously at him. "You got this casting on eBay, right?"

Mac was deadly serious. "We pulled it from where the lawyers went missing. There were three or four of these where the biker disappeared. This is no joke."

"'We' pulled it? The department knows about this?"

"Just my bosses, the sheriff and undersheriff, also the forensic tech and Carillo. Maybe a few others. That's it."

"But Carillo thinks it's this computer guy?"

Mac nodded. "He and our bosses just aren't all that open-minded about my theory. They're looking right at this huge-ass footprint and not seeing it for what it is. Truthfully, it took me some time to accept it too. But we need to get the word out and soon. People will accept it if they hear it enough, especially on TV. Maybe they'll think twice about going into the woods."

"'Cause the bogeyman'll get 'em," said Kris with a smirk.

Mac didn't smile. "Look, I know this sounds crazy, but there's too much evidence to ignore. And if making this public loosens up my department, then maybe we can stop this thing, or at least protect people. The department's keeping this quiet mainly because they don't believe it. On top of that, they think they'd look like a joke and, worse, have hundreds of kooks knocking on the door. They're probably right about that."

"Ya think?" she remarked sarcastically.

Mac grabbed her forearm for emphasis. "You've got to take this seriously. People's lives are at stake. And this could be an amazing scoop for you. Are you on board?"

She looked into his eyes for a long moment, trying to see what was there. "You're not making this up? You really think this is real?" she asked, now seeming to believe him.

"Are you on board?" he repeated.

Kris nodded. "Okay, yeah, I'm on board, I believe you. So now what?"

"You might be able to interview this guy, the anthropologist. He's a little gun-shy, but maybe we can get him interested. But there are others, scholars and plenty of people who have seen them. I don't know why, but I have a feeling he'll hit again."

"He?"

"The guy at the U-Dub, he says it's a male."

"And the Snohomish County Sheriff has been keeping this quiet. A cover-up?"

"I wouldn't call it a cover-up, but yeah, they have. We have."

"I was really hoping you'd tell me this is some kind of psychotic, deranged serial killer."

Mac's eyes fixed on hers. "Trust me, this is absolutely a psychotic, deranged serial killer. He's just not human."

Kris kept her cool as she planned her next moves. She asked a few more questions, then rolled off the bed and went down the hall to retrieve her panties.

"I've gotta get on this, it's big. I'll give this to my news director, see how to proceed."

"You have to go now? It's close to four a.m.," Mac said like a little boy who was just told to quit playing and come in for dinner.

"Yeah, sorry," said Kris, returning with her panties and stepping into them. "I've got a lot to do on this before nine. By the way, will I be able to interview you?"

Mac squirmed. "No, not until things blow over at the department. By the way, how are you going to approach this? Say something like, 'a source inside the Snohomish Sheriff's Department'? Like that? You've absolutely gotta leave me out of this."

"I'll figure it out. Either way, I'll protect your little secret."

Kris got the last of her clothes on, and Mac, still naked, walked her to the door. They kissed and she gave him one last fondle.

"Don't get me started," he said. "We might have to go again."

She quickly kissed him and whispered, "Stud," then stepped out the door. "We'll talk."

Kris disappeared up the walk. Mac closed the door and wandered back to the bedroom, suddenly unsure of his decision. She seemed to believe him, but he felt uneasy about her reaction. He straightened the bed and climbed in, hoping to get a couple of hours before reveille.

Kris sat down in her car and lit a cigarette. Reaching over, she plucked a tiny item that was clipped to the strap of her purse—a miniature microphone. It's wire trailed inside the bag to a tiny digital tape recorder, which she switched off. She was proud of herself although not quite sure what she actually had. Now she just had to figure out how to play the hand. She was both angry and elated. Elated that she had some tape that just might be solid gold, but furious that Mac had tried with such conviction to sell her on that total bullshit story to make her a laughingstock. But she was about to get even in a way he'd never dreamed of.

Kris drove away thinking of her childhood heroine and how she'd just gone one up on her. Nancy Drew never would have fucked a cop for a clue because Nancy Drew didn't have the balls.

41

When the nightmares returned, they were different. This time Ben watched as the beast pursued others. He didn't know the people, but he worried that the visions weren't so much dreams as previews . . . or worse, live action. He saw an old couple and the beast consuming them. The sight was so horrible, it woke him up. He then slept fitfully the rest of the night and finally got up around six.

In the hotel coffee shop he sipped fresh-squeezed orange juice and sifted through the material from his nephew. One item that got his attention was an article and photos of the broken Weyerhaeuser trees. Ben guessed the Web site's creator must be local.

He left his table and found a phone in the lobby. Ben was strictly old school and did not have a cell phone. Though it was early, his nephew David was up. Ben asked him to find out the source of the Web site. David promised to poke around online and call after work.

Ben returned to his booth and ordered oatmeal, prudently opting to forego the ham and egg special. He had a sudden wave of desire for a cigarette. He took a deep breath and focused on making the desperate craving go away.

Purity, that voice inside said. *Purity.* He listened.

*   *   *

The fluorescent lights in the department burned a little too bright for Mac that morning as he wandered in and headed for the coffee machine. As usual, Carillo's coffee sat steaming on his desk while he made his first trip to the men's room. Mac was downright punchy from lack of sleep and now fretted that Kris might run with the story without first consulting him. He blamed himself and the champagne for his telling her, but it was too late: now the ball was in her court. He had no idea how she'd play it but assumed she'd open a door, and once the smoke settled, Mac would lobby the department to at least examine the possibility they weren't looking for a person.

Carillo appeared and grunted his good morning. He sat and picked up a file folder, which he waved at Mac. "This guy Greenwood. He's the guy, gotta be. I can't wait to see his face when we grill the shit out of him."

"Just remember what Barkley said."

Carillo winced. "I know, I know, but fuck this asshole. The guy gets egg all over his face and now I swear to Christ he's killin' people and blaming Bigfoot. How lame is that? You look at his Web site?"

Mac shook his head.

Carillo leaned over the desk for emphasis. "I had one of our computer guys do some poking around on Greenwood and we got a little bonus, a Web site this guy just started. He doesn't have his name on it, but its source is his home address, and whoever's running it is actually *saying* Bigfoot did it. Can you fucking believe it? Gotta be Greenwood. I mean who else, his kids? His wife? No."

Mac was surprised.

Carillo shook his head in astonishment. "Fuckin' idiot's doing our job for us. By the way, he's saying the department's probably hiding evidence. He's gotta know we saw his fake footprints." Carillo looked hard at Mac. "What's with you, you look like shit."

"Mind if we stop at Taco Time? I need some hangover food."

Carillo's eyes went wide. He laughed. "You? Mac Schneider the Boy Scout? Hangover food? Holy shit, man, whaddya been doin'? You gettin' some?"

Carillo actually seemed proud of him, and Mac was sorry he'd mentioned it.

"No," said Mac, "nothing to get excited about."

Carillo didn't believe him and came around the desk, wanting details. "C'mon, man, you're gettin' some trim and holdin' out on old Karl, you fucker. C'mon, partners share. Talk to me."

"No."

He knew if he told Carillo anything—and it wasn't Mac's style to kiss and tell—Carillo might start prying and that could spell trouble. Because if Carillo somehow discovered the identity of the woman who had shared Mac's bed a few hours earlier, he would have an aneurysm and the department would spontaneously combust.

Carillo swigged his coffee in resignation. "Cocksucker. See if I ever tell you any more about the strippers I'm bangin'. Let's roll. If we gotta get you a gutbomb, then we better move. You're gonna need your energy to help me beat the shit outta this Greenwood."

The station's audio studio was empty when Kris arrived and arrayed her stuff on the back counter. Sitting at the mixing console, she pulled out her audio tape and popped it into a DAT deck to dub to disk. With her hands-on technical experience gained between school and small markets, rearranging the tape's contents would be a breeze. As she dubbed off the damning tape while making notes, an audio geek, with the requisite scrawny beard, long greasy hair, and Buddy Holly glasses, stuck his head in.

"Hey, Kris, whassup? Need some help?" he asked.

Kris didn't look up, giving the impression of being perfectly at home. "No."

"I mean it's no problem, if you—"

"Do I look like I need help, dipshit?"

"Uh, no, sorry."

The audio geek left. Kris didn't like it when people were too familiar. Just because she was on television was no excuse to act like you knew her.

By ten a.m. Milt Nelms was ready to phone his tardy employee, Russ Tardif. Russ's two-week vacation had technically ended and he should have been punched in and on the CNC bed mill no later than five minutes to seven. Russ was never late and that irritated Milt all the more. The red second hand taunted Milt as it swept the face of the wall clock in his cramped little office just above the floor of Boeing's Everett machining plant. Milt's big decision that morning was trying to make up his mind when he should call. If he waited until noon, Russ would have no excuse. Traffic or not, he should have called to tell Milt he was running late.

Anyway, how much traffic could he run into between the plant and his house? He heard Russ lived way the hell out in the east end of the county, but so did a lot of people at Boeing's assembly plant and they got to work on time. Milt decided to wait until noon, and then Russ better be dead because that's the only thing that would save him.

By eleven a.m. Kris felt she had created a masterpiece. Her editing was seamless. She had been forced to record some supplemental voice-over, but she knew enough about acoustics and mixing to make the presence in the sound booth closely match Mac's bedroom. She was also very curious about the man Mac mentioned, Ty Greenwood. She needed to check him out, despite Mac's not thinking he was involved. Perhaps Mac's practical joke hadn't gotten her any closer to figuring out who did it, but at least it would take some heat off her while adding to her credibility. She wrote out a Post-it to look into Greenwood. As she pored over her notes, the anchor Jerry Vance appeared.

"You're in early," he observed.

"You're early too. Why?"

"The anchors had a meeting. We've got a new look to some of our features and bumpers. We had to approve 'em. Whaddya got?"

"Something I'll give you for the five. It's big."

"What is it?" he asked.

"Oh, just information confirming the existence of my killer. Straight from the police. It's a recording of a Snohomish County Sheriff's detective telling all. Other than that, it's nothing," she added smugly.

"Shit . . . ," Jerry said under his breath. "Is this for real?"

"Of course. And it's white-hot."

"So when can I hear it?"

"At five."

Jerry looked skeptical. "Has Doug stamped it?"

"He will. It'll blow your mind and confirm I've been right all along."

Jerry wandered away. "I hope so. Just let our news director in on it. Now."

Feeling all-powerful, Kris lit a cigarette and *fuck anyone who tells me to put it out. When this tape hits the airwaves, nobody will be able to touch me.* Kris took a long, satisfying drag and exhaled into the atmosphere of the newsroom. She knew something Jerry didn't: that news director Doug Gautier was out of the office for the day at a Puget Sound broadcasters roundtable in Tacoma and her tape would already have aired on the five and six o'clock newscasts before he found out.

42

After stopping to get Mac two deep-fried burritos, Mac and Carillo drove east to question Tyler Greenwood.

"Now," said Carillo, his brow narrowed in anticipation, "like the boss said, let's go sweat this jack-off."

"You honestly think he's involved?" Mac asked.

Carillo steered the car toward the Greenwood home. "C'mon, connect the dots, Mac. Who's got an axe to grind? Who'd love to blame Bigfoot for his problems? A guy like this is just the kind of crazy fuck who'd kill these guys and then leave fake prints to make it look like his worst enemy did it." Carillo chuckled. "I'm tellin' you, this guy thinks this thing is real. Total fuckin' wackjob."

Mac shrugged. Maybe he wanted Carillo to be right.

Although they couldn't see the house from the road, and the large green mailbox was not identified by a name, Mac confirmed it was the Greenwoods' by the address in the file. Across the street through the woods came a strange, throaty honking.

"What the fuck is that?" said Carillo, rolling down his window to identify it.

"Sounds like emus," said Mac, ever the font of information.

"Okay, I give. What's an emu?"

"A bird, indigenous to Australia."

"Noisy."

"They're as tall as we are."

Carillo was actually impressed. "No shit. Wow, that's a big bird," he said, turning the car up the stone-paved drive. As the sprawling, majestic home came into view, the men's eyes widened. Carillo whistled. "Fuck me runnin'."

Mac's hangover was consorting with his emotions to make him slightly irritable. And his irritation for Ty Greenwood—though he'd never met the man—had been building in direct proportion to his own failure to come forward with what he thought to be the truth. While Mac analyzed his own encounter over and over, as well as the information he carried, he still couldn't conjure up the faith of an apostle. Like Ty Greenwood. Whether or not Greenwood really saw that thing in Idaho and it chased him like he'd said, Mac resented the way the man simply came out to the media, with seemingly no qualms. Mac was angry with Ty Greenwood because he just couldn't summon the same courage.

Carillo gaped at the enormous residence. "What do you think this place is worth? Three, four million?"

Mac shrugged. "I'm not a real estate agent."

Mac realized his partner had a problem with Greenwood from square one. Karl Carillo had a bilious disgust for people with money. He had joined the military as a young man and then later had become a cop, but when life taught him he didn't really have the kind of power he'd hoped for, he became bitter, railing at those with means. And Mac knew that as Carillo got older, that tape loop in his head would irritate Carillo more and more, every time he ran into someone who had an intimidating wallet.

They parked and Carillo pulled out the keys, then drew his gun. He checked to make sure he had a round in the chamber of his Beretta 9 mm.

Mac looked over. "What? You think this guy might try and kill us?"

Carillo looked back matter-of-factly. "You are hung over. A murder suspect with four possibles? Get real."

They got out and crossed to the towering hand-carved doors inlaid with elaborate stained glass. Carillo rang the bell and appraised the doors. "There's this restaurant in Shilshole, forget the name. Took Kelly for our anniversary. Doors look like this."

A moment later a tall, exotically lovely redhead answered.

"Mrs. Greenwood?" said Carillo.

"Oh no, I'm Greta. I'm their au pair. May I help you?" she asked.

"We're with the Snohomish County Sheriff. We'd like a word with Mr. Greenwood."

Greta invited them in and they waited in the entry while she fetched their subject.

Carillo stared at the distant ceiling. "This place is as big as the theater I take my kids."

Mac recognized big money, *new* big money. A moment later down the travertine-tiled hall appeared a tall man, in jeans and flannel, his youthful looks accentuated by longish sandy hair. Mac's instant read of this impassive, tired face was of a man carrying a burden. Could he have killed these men? Ty held out his hand but neither Mac nor Carillo took it.

"I'm Ty Greenwood. What can I do for you?" Mac detected a hint of the South.

"I'm Detective Carillo and this is Detective Schneider. We're with the Sheriff's Department."

Ty gestured toward the living room as Carillo took out a small notebook.

"We're investigating the disappearances of several men," Carillo continued, as they entered the room, "and you've been asking around about them. What's your connection?"

"Just curious. Is there a problem?"

"Yeah, there is." Carillo's antagonism surfacing. "Especially when you harass family members of possible victims. You work for the Forest Service, right?"

"I did until recently."

"Oh yeah? Can't hold a job, huh?" Before Ty could answer his sarcasm, Carillo plunged on. "So as an employee of theirs you were operating outside any official capacity when you used your uniform to gain access to information held by the local newspaper."

"My uniform had nothing to do with them giving me that information." Which Ty knew was a little white lie.

Carillo knew better. "Not according to the publisher," he said, flipping a page in his notebook to confirm Ty's deception. "He said you represented yourself as an employee of the Forest Service and were investigating disappearances. What's interesting is you told him that only a few hours after some lawyers went missing in the mountains less than twenty miles from your home. And at that point, the most the public could have known was that one guy, a logger, had actually been declared missing. The hikers, for all anybody knew, weren't even missing yet. So how did you know?"

"I didn't, it just happened that—"

Carillo flipped a page in his notebook and interrupted. "We're also aware you were arrested for criminal trespass the other night at the residence of Donald R. Allison. Explain what the hell that was about."

Mac thought Carillo was getting too emotional. Mac always felt better sizing up a suspect, even developing a connection, before moving in for the kill. It gave him a better chance to read someone, while lulling them into a false sense of security. And if they were hiding something, it often caused them to make mistakes.

"I was out hiking and got lost," said Ty. "I wandered onto the guy's property. It's an honest mistake. They only arrested me because they had some previous vandalism and Allison and the cops were jumpy. No big deal."

Carillo checked his notes. "You're lying. Allison had good reason to be jumpy. He reported to us you'd been there once before and he asked you to leave."

Before Ty could respond, Carillo shifted gears. "Where were you on the morning of the twenty-first, a Saturday. And on the previous Tuesday?"

Ty was angry with himself for getting caught in a lie. He didn't like Carillo's attitude and understood this was not a casual call. These cops seemed to be casting blindly for suspects, and Ty's behavior had given them fuel for those suspicions.

"I was home on that Saturday morning," Ty lied again, not seeing an option.

How could he explain he was in a drunken stupor, driving around trying to kill himself? Ronnie and the kids had been asleep and had hardly known he was missing.

"Can you corroborate that?" asked Mac.

"Yeah, my wife and kids, they were here."

"Your nanny? She corroborate that?" fired Carillo.

"She didn't work for us at that time."

"That's convenient," said Mac. "How 'bout Tuesday?"

"Probably at work."

"Forest Service?" Carillo asked.

"Yeah . . ."

"Also convenient, that you're not employed there anymore. But we'll check their records." Carillo swept his eyes around the space. "Boy, the Forest Service paid good, huh? Shit, Mac, whadda we doin', runnin' shitheel killers down for chump change? We should be trimming trees for millions."

"I'm no longer employed there," Ty calmly answered, "but to answer your inference, I was in another business. One that paid a little better."

"Like I said, can't hold a job, can you? What was the other business?"

Ty ignored Carillo's belligerence. "Computers. Software."

"Why'd you leave?" Carillo pushed. "Fired?"

"No. I left."

"What? Bigfoot got promoted over you and you quit in protest?"

Ty stared the man in the eyes for a moment and got his temper under control. "Is that why you're here, to subject me to your bad jokes? If you give me a few minutes to explain some things to you, I think I might be able to change your mind that Bigfoot is just some joke."

Carillo stared right back. "Why did you leave your job?"

"There were various reasons. Job stress . . ."

Carillo wanted to shake his head in disgust. *Fuckin' stress? With all this asshole's money? He doesn't have a freakin' clue about stress.*

On the other hand, Mac was looking at a ragged man. Despite Ty Greenwood's lineless face, Mac saw a spirit under attack from too little sleep and too much booze. Mac could read people fairly well and he knew a desperate man when he saw one. *But is he desperate enough to kill? Pay someone to do it?*

Ty turned. "I've got something that might help you. Hold on, I'll be right back."

He left the room.

Carillo looked to Mac and nodded in Ty's direction. "I can't stand this smug dickhead. There's something wrong here. I'm not letting him out of my sight." Carillo followed Ty.

In his office, Ty reached into one of his desk drawers and sorted through a few of the images of the broken trees. Carillo, with Mac right behind, entered, surprising Ty.

"Greenwood!" Carillo shouted as he drew his gun. "Step back! Keep your hands in view!"

Ty was shocked and quickly complied. Mac thought Carillo had overreacted and remembered Barkley's advice to be careful, especially around a guy who could hire an entire law firm to prosecute a harassment suit.

Mac reached out for Carillo's gun arm. "Karl, it's not really—"

Carillo barked, "What the fuck are you doing in that drawer?"

Ty gave Carillo a level stare. "I was trying to help you. I have—"

"Don't fuckin' help me, pal. Just answer my—"

"Just look in the drawer." Ty cautiously stepped back.

Carillo holstered his gun and stepped past Ty. He looked down into the drawer. There were color printer copies of photos. "What's this shit?" Carillo demanded.

"Broken trees. I shot those up the road where Joe Wylie's truck was found. I found a Weyerhaeuser memo suggesting the official cause of damage be blamed on the wind. It's probably just bureaucracy coming up with a tidy answer, but it's possible they're hiding something."

Carillo had heard of the broken trees, but they were meaningless. As far as he was concerned, some windstorm had absolutely nothing to do with anything. *Greenwood's trying to confuse the issue, throw us off the scent.*

Ty pointed to the photos. "If you'll allow me to explain, many anthropologists say that a creature like Bigfoot, if they were to exist, might mark its territory by—"

"Enough of the fucking Bigfoot stuff." Carillo picked up the photos.

Mac watched Ty's face during the exchange. *Resignation? Frustration?*

Ty sat on the credenza. "Look, I saw a lot of trees, broken off high up, taller than any of us. Some a lot taller. Can you explain that?"

"No. So what?" said Carillo impatiently.

Ty said, "I just thought the photos might be useful."

"They're not," said Carillo, dropping them on the floor.

Mac wanted a better look at the broken trees but didn't want to scoop up the photos and interfere with his partner's role of bad cop.

Mac's eyes moved over the desk and credenza, and he recognized some of the books and Internet materials from his search at the library. Mac glanced up and his eyes met Ty's and an ever-so-brief understanding passed between them. Then Mac quickly steeled his gaze and shut Ty out.

Carillo's eyes also ranged over the desk and walls. "Kinda obsessed with Bigfoot? Huh?"

"They exist," answered Ty.

Carillo laughed derisively and looked to Mac for agreement. Mac nodded impassively. "So, Greenwood, where are those fake feet you used to make the tracks? Will you hand 'em over or will I have to get a search warrant?"

They have footprints. This was good news for Ty. "How many footprints did you find?"

"How many did you make? Just make this easy on yourself, shithead, and tell us where the bodies are."

"You're going in the wrong direction," said Ty. He looked to the other cop. There had been a flicker of recognition in the man's eyes. Ty knew he didn't feel the same way as his partner.

Ty's glance made Mac uncomfortable. "All right, thanks for the information, Mr. Greenwood," concluded Mac, easing toward the door. "We'll be in touch."

Carillo was ready to spit more venom but saw they had nothing and would have to go back to the drawing board. He turned to leave.

"I'll be back with a warrant, Greenwood. Count on it."

In the car Carillo angrily keyed the ignition. "Fuckin' rich asshole. If he didn't personally do it, he knows who did 'cause he hired 'em."

"Maybe," said Mac distantly as he looked at the house.

"Maybe? Fuck maybe, he did it," said Carillo angrily.

Mac sighed. "Regardless, we need to solve this before anybody else disappears."

43

Carillo insisted on one more related interview, and though Mac didn't think it would provide anything of substance, he kept quiet. Thirty minutes later they entered the private drive of Digiware Microsystems Corporation, where Veronica Greenwood was listed as senior vice president. Located on a verdant three-acre plot in Redmond, the high-tech campus blended concrete and cedar with the earth in a tribute to green-conscious, cutting-edge architecture. Carillo hated it.

"Looks like they're sinking into the fuckin' ground" was his assessment of the structures.

"Yeah, but it's energy efficient," Mac said, occasionally delighting in pressing one of his caveman associate's hot buttons. Carillo winced because he hated wimps, and wimps worried about wasting energy and protecting whales and owls, how much mercury was in their tuna, and saving fucking soda cans. Carillo was only thirty-three but his sensibilities resided comfortably in the twelfth century.

A bubbly young acolyte of the computer age escorted them to the reception area of Veronica Greenwood's office, where they were offered a choice of bottled water, natural soda, fresh-brewed Starbucks, or fresh-pressed organic juice. Mac requested a water. As they were ushered into Ronnie's office, she crossed the large room and greeted them.

Carillo got down to brass tacks. "Mrs. Greenwood, we think your husband may know something about these disappearances lately. We need to ask a few questions."

Ronnie had been scared by Ty's recent arrest but had assumed it was just harmless curiosity. She had seen all the materials Ty had pinned and taped to the walls of his office, but she'd let it go, assuming it was better for him to be open with it than hide it. But as the shorter, more muscular detective with the flattop and mustache began describing Ty's alleged fascination with the missing men, she could feel her face flushing. Her knees went suddenly weak and forced her to sit.

One of the cops asked about that particular Saturday, and with little prompting suddenly Ronnie was admitting that Ty had been up early, taken a drive, and later looked hungover. They asked about other days and behavior but all the questions and answers blurred together. Ronnie's belief that those who have nothing to hide hide nothing suddenly seemed at loggerheads with the inferences of the two cops.

"You say he might be involved. How?" she asked.

"We don't know yet, ma'am," said Carillo. He looked at Mac, then turned back to her. "Have you ever seen any . . . uh, I'm not sure how to say this. Big feet? Big fake feet, like you'd strap on your shoes and make prints like . . ." Carillo hesitated.

Ronnie shook her head slightly. "Like Bigfoot." Mac thought she sounded tired.

Carillo nodded. "Right. He has some?"

Ronnie didn't know what these men were trying to imply, but they'd gone too far. "My husband may be a bit eccentric, but he doesn't run around making big footprints. No, he does not have any such thing. He has castings, plaster castings, of what he says are real footprints, but that's his claim, not mine. He does not make fake tracks."

Her secretary's voice over the intercom broke the tension in the room.

"Ronnie? The call from Fujioka Electronics is ready in the conference room. Everybody's waiting."

She headed them toward the door, feeling shaky but trying to cover. "I'm sorry, but that's all I know. I have to take this call."

Carillo handed her a card. Mac felt his partner had actually been pleasant to this woman, but Carillo was always transparently pleasant if they were attractive and Veronica Greenwood was definitely that.

As they exited the building, out of earshot of the employees, Carillo slapped Mac's shoulder and whispered, "See what I told you? Fuckin' guy's lyin'. Not only lied about the Allisons, but his own wife just blew his story out about being home on that Saturday morning. When the lawyers bit it, Greenwood was AWOL."

Mac doubted the connection. "He went for a drive at three a.m. He was back around seven. I don't think that left him enough time."

"Four hours. Anyway, a drive at three in the morning? C'mon. The lawyers disappeared sometime after five or so. No one saw them after that. And another thing, he's got those feet somewhere. Wife isn't in on it, but he's got 'em, for sure. I'm getting a warrant."

Mac didn't think Greenwood was their man, but if Carillo wanted to chase his tail with a warrant, he'd let him. That might just give Mac time enough to turn up something real.

Mac and Carillo returned to the department around quarter to five. Mac quickly checked his messages, grabbed some paperwork, and left. Wiped out after his late night, he told Carillo he was heading home. Once on the road, he plugged in a Pat Metheny CD and started to relax. He tried putting all of his current problems out of his mind and zeroed in on regaining focus. His plan was to nap, shower, then do a little light reading. At the first stoplight, he turned off his pager and cell phone.

A few minutes before the five p.m. newscast, a sound technician rigged Kris with a lavalier microphone and she took her place at the end of the news desk, just out of sight of camera one. Sitting closest to Kris, an impeccably styled Jerry Vance made some notes while Trish got a last-minute face powdering from a makeup assistant. While Kris whipped over her page of notes, Jerry reached out and touched her arm.

"I wish you'd been able to clear this with Doug. But good luck."

His falsely soothing tone sounded like he was speaking to the condemned. Kris forced a smile and briefly wondered again how she would get rid of him. She was feeling strong. She caught Jerry's eye again and smiled like a shark. *Yeah, you're next, shithead.* Kris smiled brightly as the theme music for the newscast began. *The population in the cornfield is heading for a growth curve.*

44

Mac entered his condo and ignored the blinking light on his answering machine, turned down the volume, and switched off the phone's ringer. Then he tossed off his coat, shoes, and pants and fell across the bed. During the next three hours, while he slept soundly, he received fourteen messages on his pager and his answering machine screened out ten more calls.

It had become a habit for Ben to watch the local news, hoping to get some sort of clue. Just as the five o'clock news began, the phone distracted him. It was David.

"I got some info on your guy, the one with the Web site. Interesting stuff. Also, turns out your hotel has a fax. They're getting it as we speak."

"Thanks. Whadidja find?" Ben asked.

"You might want to meet this guy. I had to do some hacking, but I tracked down his address. He's definitely looking for the same thing you are. About two years ago he quit looking. Now it seems he's back at it. Hey, you need anything? You're only about forty minutes from us and—"

Ben cut him off, "No, David, I'm good. You've been a huge help."

"Okay. Good luck, Uncle Ben."

"Thanks, David."

At the front desk a clerk handed Ben the sheaf of fax pages. Walking back to his room, Ben was so engrossed in the information, he collided with a huge potted tree, bringing snickers from a couple waiting outside the restaurant. Ben laughed too, knowing they recognized him.

"That plant did that on purpose, didn't it?" he joked.

They shared another laugh.

Ty would have been very interested in the content of the five p.m. news, but he left the house promptly at four thirty in his Forest Service uniform and drove away in his truck. He'd been doing so since he quit. Every evening he'd wait until he was sure Ronnie was home before returning, then he'd make an entrance like everything was status quo. On the days she was going to be late, he came home, quietly changed, and checked in with the kids. When Ronnie got home, he carefully avoided any discussions about his day, not wanting to turn the lie into a major project. But his best chance in the last three years to prove himself right was in his lap and he couldn't let it go this time.

He popped a few Oxys before he left the house. A few was three or four and that was two or three more than he'd been prescribed, but hey, they worked. One was okay, two were good, three better, and four, well hell, four were goddamn wonderful. He was feeling blissful at that moment but also a little fearful because he knew a crash would follow. He put that dark prospect out of his mind as he arrived at the local building supply. Climbing out of the truck, he planned in the next hour to wander through the aisles, trying to gather his thoughts and strategize his next move.

The police questioning him that morning had irritated him but it had also energized him. He was glad Ronnie didn't know about that. Ty resolved to tell Ronnie he'd quit his job and was going to work full-time on his project. *This thing is so close, practically in my backyard. She'll have to understand.*

Susan Hunter's eight unanswered phone calls to her parents between seven thirty that morning and now, thirteen hours later, had her worried and upset. She, more than her three siblings, was close to their folks, Burt and Ada Krinkel. She knew they were creatures of unfailing habit and never ventured anywhere without a minimum two months' planning and fanfare. A routine drive to Arizona the previous year had seen her dad working out the details six months prior.

Susan couldn't fathom why they weren't answering the phone. The telephone operator told her the line was in order, which only fueled her anxiety. Susan lived at the water's edge on Mercer Island with her husband and two kids. A lushly forested enclave of architectural fashion in the middle of Lake Washington, The Island, as locals called it, was forty miles from her parents' place. Susan's husband told her to quit worrying and let her parents live their lives, but Susan sensed trouble.

The idea of driving way out there was nixed when her husband pointed out it was nearly nine p.m. He advised her to check on them the following morning if she still couldn't reach them. She wandered down to the lake, flopped onto the dock, and lit a cigarette. She always did that when she was stressed. She didn't want the kids to know she smoked but they did anyway. She blew out a large cloud and resolved to start calling at four thirty a.m., precisely the time her dad got up.

Ronnie rolled up the driveway at quarter to ten. Busy wrapping up pre-Christmas break projects, she had had a very long day, not made any easier by the visit from the police. She had eaten at the office, so after changing, she made some tea and went to Ty's office. She still had an energy rush from the day's activities and decided she'd better use it to get through this. She tapped on his door, then entered.

"Hey," she said, as she crossed and kissed him.

"Hey," he said, quickly clicking the mouse to escape from his own Web site. "You had a long one."

She nodded and sat on the corner of his desk. "Yeah. Ty, the police came to my office today."

Ty's face froze, the blood draining from it. Ronnie saw the effect her sentence had. She continued. "You're in trouble. They think you have something to do with these men disappearing."

Ty opened his mouth but Ronnie held up her hand. "No, hear me out. Look, I know you don't." She paused and fixed his eyes with hers. "Right?"

Ty blinked with surprise. Ronnie waved her hand. "I had to ask. You're just not you when it comes to this thing."

"Jesus," said Ty, clenching his lips. "Even you? You—"

She raised her voice and stopped him. "Ty, listen to me. I know you had nothing to do with any of this, but I thought maybe you had an idea of what was going on."

"I do."

She sighed. "Okay. I know, right. This is out of control again. But this time the stakes have gone up. I don't care what you do or how you do it, but you have to let this go. Get some therapy. I'll go with you if you want me there. Ty, Christmas is in ten days. I want you to be here, with us and celebrating it."

"What does that mean?"

Ronnie stood. "It means I'm putting my foot down and hard. Give this up or move out." She headed toward the door, then turned. "I love you but I have to protect the family, and you too, if you won't. That's my decision but it's your choice."

45

Ahot shower revived Mac's brain. Pulling on some fresh sweats, he tossed some leftover pasta into a bowl, threw in some vegetables, and popped it in the microwave. It was a little after ten when he decided to check his messages. The digital counter on his pager seemed to have malfunctioned: he never got that many calls on the busiest day. But the same level of activity on his answering machine turned his stomach because it confirmed that something was very wrong. That many messages couldn't be good. Either it was friends calling to tell him an asteroid was headed toward earth . . . or it was something worse. His first sickening thought was of Kris. He punched the playback button. The first message was from Carillo saying he'd "heard that Channel Seven bitch was at it again."

Mac's heart sank, his worst fears confirmed.

Then his boss had called, asking, "Was that you on the tape?" Another call from a friend asked the same. Then it was Carillo again. "Hey, bro," his voice wary, "what the fuck is this rumor about you telling that cunt we know who the killer is? Tell me you didn't talk to her. Tell me it's bullshit. Call me."

Mac felt gutshot. He didn't need to tune in to Kris's report—which would be on again in less than an hour—to know what she'd done. But he had to watch if for no other reason than to know how bad the damage was. After a dozen messages ranging from congratulations to mostly confusion, the last was from Sheriff Barkley himself.

"Schneider?" he said. "Be in at seven. I want to talk to you."

Mac dropped into his chair while the answering machine rewound for the next two minutes. She'd laid him away. But how? What tape? The only time they spoke about it was when they were in bed. He wondered why no one mentioned the big point of the story, that the killer was not a human being.

His spirits sank further. Editing. *Of course.* If she made a tape, she could surely edit it—cut out what she didn't want, keep what supported her case. He prayed she hadn't been vicious enough to have done that. But if she had made a tape, she apparently hadn't electronically altered his voice because everyone recognized him. But that detail aside, it still didn't sound like she named him. His brain whirled for forty minutes, piecing together what had probably happened. At five to eleven, the phone rang. It was Carillo, sounding subdued. "You watchin' this thing?"

"Yeah," Mac answered warily. "You?"

"Yeah." He paused. "Was that you?"

Mac couldn't lie, but he could buy time. "I don't know."

That was enough for Carillo. "Okay. Tomorrow." He hung up.

Mac knew he was in trouble. At best he'd look stupid or deranged, and at worst . . .

He paced furiously. The frustration of being trapped had him trying to scrub off nervous energy. At two minutes to eleven he punched the remote and found the channel. The newscast started as usual with the anchors introducing themselves. When the lurid graphic, "Murder in the Mountains: Exclusive Report," was superimposed behind the male anchor, Mac's vision narrowed as if he were peering down a tunnel. After watching Kris do her setup, Mac wasn't quite ready when his own voice came over the speaker on his TV, a written transcript overlaid on an illustration of a man in silhouette:

> "If I tell you something, a pretty important piece of information, will you keep your source confidential? What I'm saying is, the department would come down on me like, well, it would get ugly. Probably end my career there. So you've gotta keep me out of it. I'll give you the information and you do what you will with it. Get it out there. Deal?"

"Deal."

"I'm convinced there is a killer at work. I think they were taken away by a killer."

"So you're confirming the fact, what I've been reporting now for more than two weeks, exclusively, that there is a killer at work? You're saying that?"

"Yes, I believe so. I'm ninety percent certain."

"Do you have a suspect?"

"Yes."

"So why hasn't an arrest been made, what's the holdup?"

"The department has a piece of evidence from two of the scenes and we're holding it back. It's pretty unusual evidence and we've kept it quiet. It's a piece of evidence that leads me to believe that the missing men were not victims of any kind of normal abduction."

"And the Snohomish County Sheriff's Department has been keeping this quiet. A cover-up?"

"Yeah, they have. We have."

"You said, not a normal abduction. This is some kind of psychotic, deranged serial killer."

"Trust me, this is absolutely a psychotic, deranged serial killer."

Mac was numb, wounded. It was so flagrant, first taping him, then cutting it up like that. After shots of the search areas were shown, the camera came back to Kris in the studio, who acknowledged that the statements were from *"a detective with the Snohomish County Sheriff's Department who obviously requested anonymity."* Mac shook his head in disbelief. Crushed by the viciousness of the betrayal, his mind tried to deal with practical questions like how he could defend himself. Considering everything from strong denials to legal action, he knew it was a waste of time because the bell had been rung and couldn't be unrung. She'd really screwed him twice that night.

Ten seconds after they went to the next story, the phone rang. It was Carillo again.

"I can't fuckin' believe it, man," he started. "I thought I knew you. What the fuck was that all about?"

Mac started to explain and his partner—probably ex now—hung up. Mac fell back into his chair and began mourning the end of his career.

Channel 7 General Manager Lyle Benson eased his BMW 760li into his reserved space next to the elevator. He was irritated. It was nearly midnight and he had been getting ready for bed when his wife, Claire, handed him the phone. It was his news director, screaming bloody murder and demanding he fire Kris Walker "immediately." Doug Gautier said he would meet him at the station in fifteen minutes. Benson and his wife and four kids lived in a lovely old Victorian mansion at the foot of Queen Anne, five minutes from the station. Benson slipped his keycard in the elevator slot and rode right to the private entrance of his office suite in the station's penthouse. He flipped on a few lights and unlocked the door to the outer hallway. Gautier was already there fuming.

"She's out, done! That's it. Did you see her reports? That tape was as phony as a three-dollar bill. Outrageous!"

Benson went behind his large desk, the panorama of Seattle at Christmastime sparkling behind him. Lyle Benson was forty-eight and balding, and his slight paunchiness didn't look so sleek in his designer workout sweats as it did in his usual Brioni three-button. Benson calmly gestured for Gautier to sit but he paced instead.

"Doug, I haven't heard her report—"

"It's the most flagrant piece of phony journalism I've ever—"

A woman's voice interrupted, "Maybe, but I pulled a nine-one, twenty-three yesterday and tonight . . . well, I'm betting I'm at least a ten-five, twenty-eight."

Both men stopped and turned as Kris entered the room. Benson looked at the plasma monitor on his desk and clicked a few keys on his computer. "She's right. Yesterday in her quarter hour she pulled a nine-one rating, twenty-three share. The instants spiked during her report." Benson's eye returned to Doug Gautier, whose face flushed with anger that numbers alone were her defense. His rage flashed at Benson and he clenched his jaw.

"She goes or I go."

Benson sighed. "Doug, don't be so dramatic, her—"

"She goes *or I go.*"

Benson gestured. "I want you two to sit down and talk this—"

Doug Gautier spun on his heels and headed to the door. "You'll have my resignation in your box downstairs in ten minutes." He exited, slamming the door.

Benson leveled an angry stare at Kris. "He was an excellent news director, top-notch, and you caused him to leave. What do I do about you? How about I fire you?"

Kris confidently moved across the room and came around his desk. "You won't."

"Oh really? You're fired. There."

Kris only snickered. "A nine-one, twenty-three? I'm too good."

"No reporter is worth losing one of the best news directors in—"

Kris knelt before him and swung his chair to face her.

Lyle Benson didn't like being manipulated. "What do you think you're doing?"

"What I do best," she cooed. She reached under his desk and pressed a button that locked the door. "Making you relax. Either with my fantastic reporting . . . or this."

She put her palms on his thighs and then curled her fingers around the elastic waistband of his pants. Benson tried to resist but it was a weak effort.

"Work with me, Lyle."

Benson pretended to be put out, but he stood. She pulled down his pants.

"And see?" She observed, "I'm understanding. I know you have to get home to Claire, so I'll make this quick. Or should I say, I'll make *you* quick." Benson rested his hands on her blond head and closed his eyes.

46

At six fifty the next morning, Susan Hunter's silver Accord wheeled down the driveway of her parents' secluded home. One of her terrible expectations was to find her parents debilitated by some unknown illness and waiting to be rescued. True, they were healthy but they were also old. The other crises spinning through her mind were everything from power outages to fires—any event that could overwhelm them before they could contact relatives.

But she found something else: quiet, a house intact.

None of the usual reassuring sounds of her parents' home greeted her—a television blaring to compensate for her mother's poor hearing or her dad's chain saw as he bucked scrub around the property or the dogs barking. Just . . . silence.

With her hand on the front door knob, she noticed something to her left, at the corner of the house past a clump of rhododendrons. It looked out of place in their tidy little estate, a pink something against green grass. Walking toward it, she made out a piece of fabric, cottony . . .

Her stomach dropped when she recognized it as a sleeve from her mother's pajamas. She picked it up and saw it had been ripped from the garment. And it was streaked with dried blood. As she looked down the side of the house, the sight of the gaping, ragged aperture, previously occupied by the bedroom window, was far too much for Susan. She fainted dead away.

When she recovered consciousness a few seconds later, she found herself sprawled on the wet grass. Rising shakily, she staggered to her car and placed a sobbing call to the police. Their warning to stay in her car was moot. Fearing the worst, she was too rattled to move.

Ronnie entered the front door of her company amid waved hellos and passing small talk with coworkers. She was unaware of the whispered office scuttlebutt as to why two sheriff's detectives had come by the day before to question her and she also had no idea that the same brush-cut detective with the mustache was, at this moment, rolling up her driveway, followed by three other sheriff's cruisers and armed with a search warrant.

Kris sat in her car, deep in the underground parking facility at the television station, inhaling the last inch of a cigarette and sipping her Starbucks double caffè doppio, essentially *two* double espressos. She was reveling in how satisfying it had been to send her news director to the cornfield. She thought of Lyle Benson and how their relationship had returned huge dividends to her. She recalled that in many primitive cultures, having sex with someone was believed to transfer some of the life force of that person to you. Kris smiled at that.

A tap on her window startled her and she dropped the glowing butt into her lap.

"Goddamn it! Shit!" she raged.

The apologetic young face in her window belonged to one of the newsroom interns. Kris had never bothered to remember his name. She cracked her door and erupted. "Do you do this in your spare time? Scare the complete shit out of people?"

"Sorry, Miss Walker, but I think they were, uh, looking for you in the newsroom."

"I'm two hours early, why would they be looking for me?"

"I mean I think they were calling you."

In her mind's eye Kris suddenly saw her pager, sitting on her bathroom counter. Then she realized she'd also turned off her cell phone, partly out of concern Mac might call. The upshot was she'd been out of the loop all morning. She downed her coffee and got out of the car.

"What's going on?" she asked.

"I dunno," said the excited intern, "but I think it has to do with somebody else missing."

Kris hoped this kid, who was only five or six years younger than she, wasn't wrong.

They entered the elevator area and Kris impatiently punched the button while lighting another cigarette.

"Uh, I don't think you can smoke in—"

Her withering glare sealed the young man's mouth. He stole furtive glances at her painfully beautiful face. He was both smitten and scared to death.

Kris felt his fear and reveled in it. If he was frightened, then so were others. Kris wanted everyone to know she didn't play by the rules. For if what the kid told her was true, then her stock had just gone up again. *Please let it be true. Give me another missing person. A body, if I'm really lucky.*

Kris took a couple of deep, luxurious drags on the cigarette before putting it out on their floor. Former assignment editor Janey Murkowski, who only that morning had been made acting news director after Doug Gautier's abrupt departure, met her on the way to her desk.

"Kris, thank God you're here. There's been another abduction, this time a little west of the mountain biker. Old couple, signs of a struggle. Take a crew and go, ten minutes ago."

Kris nodded as the woman sped off to marshal more forces for the story. She slowly, deliberately organized the stuff on her desk. Taking her time, she wanted to savor the moment. *Abduction? Signs of a struggle?* And *a couple,* not just one. It was an early Christmas for Kris Walker. She floated to the motor pool, barely believing what she had just heard.

Ty watched the sheriff's officers going through his stuff. They searched his office, with Carillo overseeing every moment of it. They were respectful of Ty's things and Ty wasn't angry. He even offered them coffee. It took them a while to search the entire house, then they moved to the garage. Ty followed them outside, and when they were done, Carillo strode angrily over to him.

"I know you hid those fake feet, shithead. I'm gonna find 'em or find a connection to pin this on you and you will go down hard."

Ty's calm demeanor infuriated Carillo. "You do whatever you think is best, Detective, but I'm not the guy and I think you know it. I'm pretty sure your partner knows."

Carillo stepped toe to toe with Ty, despite Ty's five-inch advantage. "He's not my partner anymore. What he thinks doesn't mean shit, and what you think doesn't mean shit."

Since Deputy Bill Alexander had been involved in the missing persons cases from the outset, and now that all the disappearances had been tied together by the media, he was included in the group dispatched to the Krinkel home. He was given instructions to report to Carillo about anything he might find. It also helped that he had met the old couple the previous year when one of their dogs was missing. The dog had been found but now they were missing. Bill hoped they were as lucky as their dog.

He arrived to find four department vehicles—a crime scene investigation van, two other patrol units, and an unmarked. He waved to Carillo and noticed a distraught, fortyish woman being questioned by two other deputies. He walked over to a group of deputies and CSIs examining a ragged hole in the side of the house where there once had been a window. The nature of the damage shocked him. He hoped the old couple had disappeared by "conventional" means, but suddenly it wasn't looking that way.

"What happened?" he asked.

One of the deputies pointed at the hole. "Looks like the old lady was either pulled out or thrown through. There's actually evidence of both, a break-in and then a blowing out. It's almost like whoever kidnapped her just reached in the window and pulled her out."

Bill looked at the splintered opening and mentally discounted the other deputy's modifier "it's almost like." *No, that's exactly what happened.* Though he felt a rising guilt for knowing what probably caused this, he kept his mouth shut because what might come out of it was just too outrageous. His internal conflict was growing: now it wasn't trucks being turned over, it was people being snatched right out of their beds. Old ladies even. His stomach churned.

"You okay?" one of the cops asked.

Bill came back from his nightmare reverie to find the others looking at him. His numbed expression gave him away.

"Somethin' wrong?" queried another. "Got any ideas? 'Cause we don't."

Deputy Bill shook his head. "No, just wondering what happened. That's all."

The other cops went back to examining, measuring, and speculating. Bill looked around for footprints.

"Any fingerprints?" Afraid to ask the question he really meant, he paused for a moment and tried to sound casual. "Any footprints?"

One of the men gestured to where Carillo was standing. "Over there. Looks like a smeared boot print or something. No identifying tread."

Bill walked over and looked at the crushed grass. He looked at Carillo. "What do you think that is?"

"It looks like some asshole who didn't know how to make a decent footprint." Then Carillo walked away. Bill not only didn't understand Carillo's comment but wondered what had pissed him off. The deputy walked back to the other cops.

"Where was the old man?" asked Bill. "Both in the bedroom?"

One of them turned to him. "We're pretty sure the old man was out back, by the dog kennel. We found his slippers about twenty feet apart. We also found a flashlight nearby, still on, batteries dead. Found the dogs too. They're okay, but whoever did this made an impression on 'em."

"How's that?" Bill asked.

"They were hungry but scared bad. Wouldn't come out of their shed. They were out of food but it took a while for them to come over to their bowls when we filled 'em. I got boxers and pit mixes and I've never seen hungry dogs act like that."

All heads turned as the Channel 7 van arrived. Bill had seen Kris Walker's story with the so-called secret tape of the detective. He watched Kris alight and made a point of staying away from her.

47

The coffee shop less than a mile from the department wasn't really just a coffee shop. They served mostly food there, breakfast stuff all day and night, but Mac dubbed it "the coffee shop" for the breaks he and Carillo took. When they were partners. That was now history. Mac had spent a very uncomfortable morning and a few hours into the afternoon taking care of paperwork and handing some of his active cases over to other detectives. Few would look at him, let alone talk to him. Finally, he escaped out the front door and headed for the coffee shop.

Mac had occupied the same booth for several hours, deep in thought. Sheriff Barkley was furious that one of his top men had made such reckless remarks that had become so public. After a lot of wrangling, Barkley agreed not to fire Mac when Mac offered to take some of his accumulated vacation time, with the caveat that there would be an investigation. Mac felt it was going to be like Old West justice: "Let's gimma fair trial, 'n' hang 'im." Mac knew his career now hung on proving what was pretty much unprovable.

Forget trying to clear yourself. There's no way you're going to catch that thing, and that's the only way you could explain what you said to Kris. So the only decision was when to resign. Hell, he was only forty-one and had saved up some money, not to mention a small pension he got from the City of Los Angeles. He tried to tell himself he had options, he could do a lot of things.

As he wallowed, Shelly, the fiftyish, bouffant-tressed waitress, jogged his attention.

"You okay, honey?" she asked. "You look kinda wore out."

Mac looked up. "Oh, probably too much coffee, that's all. All that caffeine'll probably give me heart failure."

She smiled slyly. "Oh, honey, I switched you tah unleaded 'bout fifteen cups ago. Sumpin' a sympathetic ear could help on?"

Mac appreciated the kindness. Shelly had served him many times but he knew nothing about her.

"Where you from, Shelly?"

"Arkansas," she said proudly, then launched into her stock joke, "but no, I never slept with Bill Clinton, don't even know 'im."

They both laughed.

"There now," she grinned, "that's the first upturn on that handsome face o' yours all day. Want sumpin' tah eat?"

"Nah."

Mac looked to the television bolted on a rack above the counter. The five o'clock news was about to begin and he wanted a diversion.

"Mind turning up the TV? I want to watch the news. Channel 7?"

"Anything for you, hon."

Shelly obligingly jacked up the volume and switched to his station. She felt sorry for the guy. She knew he was a cop but he wasn't like the other cops she'd known. She thought he might be having women problems. Shelly'd been around.

Moments before five o'clock that afternoon, with the apparently violent abduction of the Krinkels, television newscasters all around Puget Sound were preparing to validate what Kris Walker had been saying for two weeks: that there was probably a serial killer at work. Ty's Web site logged nearly a hundred e-mails that day, and despite having an unlisted number, he fielded, and turned down, five phone calls for interviews during the afternoon.

Ty's charade of pretending to go to work had been going on a week and was taking its toll on him. Between Ronnie's remarks the

night before about the cops, and the search by the police this morning, Ty needed to come clean and do it quickly before things got completely out of control. Ty decided to stay home that afternoon and face
the consequences. But Ty also knew Ronnie did not bluff and that he
stood the real risk of being thrown out of the house.

He passed through the kitchen as Greta prepared dinner. "Would
you like a snack?" she asked.

He shook his head and headed for the TV room. As the five o'clock
news shows rolled their openings simultaneously, he scanned for a
channel and settled on seven. The male anchor set up the lead story
and the camera cut to a lovely blond reporter, bundled against the chill
in front of a farmhouse, a big grassy yard between herself and the
home. Above her on the screen was supered the graphic "Murder in the
Mountains: Exclusive Report."

"Jerry, I'm here in the mountains above Monroe at the home of an
elderly couple, Burt and Ada Krinkel. This morning their daughter reported them missing and police moved in to investigate."

The station cut to a tape of an interview with the police. Ty
cringed when he saw Carillo's face in the background, but the reporter questioned one of the other cops on scene. They showed the
badly damaged window and speculated on how Ada Krinkel actually
went through it. Mesmerized by the report, Ty drank in the details:
the frightened dogs, the flashlight, the slippers, the torn sleeve. He almost jumped in his truck and zoomed to the site but thought better
of it. He didn't need to risk another trespassing rap. Though he
wasn't sure it related to his quest, the story was so tantalizing he immediately started writing in his head how he would portray it on his
Web site.

Shelly watched as the good-looking cop threw down a bill as he left. He
must have made a decision about his wife or girlfriend, because his
whole attitude changed just like that. Might have been the TV. He
watched about five minutes and it probably got his mind off things
enough to think clearly. She wished him well. When she bused his table
and found the twenty bucks, she wished him really well.

*   *   *

The camera returned to the blond reporter, but Ty's concentration was broken when he overheard Ronnie talking to Greta. Home early. *D-day.* The news report ended and Ty turned off the television and walked into the kitchen. Ronnie was pouring a soda, her coat still on.

"Hi," he said, "how was work?"

"Not bad. Well, actually terrible."

Ronnie was trying to juggle her purse and assorted items, as well as her drink, so Ty stepped in, grabbing the glass. She was headed upstairs, which Ty figured was a good place to talk. In the bedroom Ronnie disappeared into her commodious walk-in closet.

"By the way, the cops yesterday . . . ," she shouted, almost offhandedly, as if being in different rooms would soften the subject.

Ty set her soda on one of the dressers and sat on the end of the bed.

"Yeah?" he asked calmly. "What about them?"

Ronnie came out in jeans, pulling on a red cable-knit sweater.

"One of the things they asked was where you were a week or two ago," she said.

Ty leaned back on the bed, his body language unconsciously defensive.

Ronnie continued, "I told them you took a drive early that Saturday morning but came home later. A few hours later."

"Okay, no problem." He ran his hand over the stubble on his chin. "They came back this morning."

"Who?"

"The cops. They had a search warrant."

"What?" Ronnie stopped and turned to Ty. "They what? They had a search warrant?"

He kept his cool. "They found nothing. They were here for a few hours, that's it."

Ronnie was frozen in place. "They searched *my house*? The police searched my house?"

Ty nodded. "It's not a big deal."

"Not a big deal? Oh, I'd say it's a huge deal. So what were they looking for?"

"I honestly don't know." Ty knew what he was about to say might hit a nerve but he plunged in. "I think it's out there—"

"Oh for God's sake, Ty—"

"—making people disappear and the cops think someone's laying footprints. And they must think it's me. Hey, why not, I'm the go-to guy for kook shit, right? The guy everybody loves to blame for being either deluded or, now, homicidal? Jesus Christ!"

Ronnie came back at him with her own anger. "Don't blame anybody but yourself. But if the cops are intent on coming after you for some reason, we need to bring in some major legal help and now. We have to protect you. I'll talk to Bill and see if we can get our house counsel to find—"

"Forget the lawyer. The police will be off me soon enough."

"Right. And you're a psychic now?"

With the conversation rapidly degenerating, it was now or never for Ty. "I quit the service. A few days ago. I was going to tell you sooner, but . . ."

Ronnie was devastated. She looked at Ty, then leaned against the wall, all the fight suddenly gone, her face completely numb. She didn't know whether to scream or cry. She did neither and just stared. She felt her lip quiver but there was no stopping it. One therapist had told her it was like living with a junkie, just like anyone with a destructive compulsion.

He crossed to her but her outstretched hands kept him at bay.

"No," she said, barely containing her hurt and anger. "Don't touch me."

"Honey, I need time to—"

"No, not this, not this whole thing all over, the . . ." She trailed off, tears flowing. "You said you . . . wouldn't. You promised."

Ty touched his wife's hair but she batted his hand away, her eyes awash, head lowered.

"Go, leave me." The depth of her pain startled Ty.

He backed off and looked at his wife with her head buried in her hands. He knew her well enough to leave her alone. As he moved to the door, she said though her tears, "You sleep downstairs tonight."

Ty took a deep breath and exited their bedroom.

Concern was etched onto the white trash mug of Mr. J. D. Watts. Concern that the pretty newsgirl was going in the wrong direction, and bigger concern over the phone call he'd just gotten. It was Errol Rayburn's parole officer. Now J. D. wished he had that thing the phone company gave you that could tell who was calling. He'd been expecting the call, knowing Errol hadn't checked in because he was dead but was hoping Errol's PO would just forget. He took a deep toke of Sinaloan bud and sat back in the torn Barcalounger he had found by the next-door neighbor's trash. *No fuckin' chance o' that.*

He'd been fooling himself and now the pot had him focused on the events that would take place next. The PO would come out, he'd find Errol gone, J. D. would get hauled in, and the shit would hit the fan, which meant they'd eventually tie him to Leon Newburg's murder and probably Errol's too. J. D.'s blood pressure went up as he recalled something about the State of Washington still using hanging. If it came down to it, and he had a choice, he would definitely go with the lethal injection. The pot sent him off for a few moments on a bizarre reverie about various methods of execution and how they must feel. Then he slammed the brakes on his morbid speculation. *I'm callin' the girl.* It seemed to J. D. she'd be interested in his story. And if she used it, he felt the publicity would give him some protection from his bad deeds. He saw lots of famous people on the news all the time who did all sorts of terrible things and they seemed either to get off or get lighter sentences because of their celebrity. He reasoned that coming out with the Bigfoot story would make him famous and pretty much save his bacon.

But J. D. realized if he just phoned Kris Walker, he'd probably get blown off. He had no education and didn't talk real smart, so he knew a call was out. On the other hand if he just showed up, maybe she'd take him seriously. He took another toke and decided to sober up and go down to the TV station the next day.

48

reta was setting places on the table in the family room when Ty entered and quietly informed her, "Mrs. Greenwood isn't feeling well. She'll eat later."

Chris grabbed a juice and invited Ty to watch some funniest home video show when Ty heard the doorbell chiming. He motioned to Greta that he would get it.

Anticipating a neighbor kid hawking candy bars—or worse, more cops—he steeled his expression. Yet when he opened the door, his resolve to dismiss the intruder disintegrated as he looked into a face he knew . . . yet didn't know.

"Tyler Greenwood?"

Ty nodded. "Yeah, I'm Ty Greenwood."

An old, weathered hand was offered. "Ben Campbell. Course you may know me better if I go by my movie name, Chief Ben Eagleclaw."

Ben was wearing his "uniform" buckskin jacket to aid recognition. Ty eagerly shook his hand. He'd been a fan since he could remember. Chief Ben Eagleclaw inspired a positive reaction wherever he went.

"Please, come in, come on in," said Ty enthusiastically.

"Am I interruptin'?" asked Ben. "I don't wanna impose. I just thought you might be somebody I'd like to talk to. I think we're interested in the same thing."

Ty saw both a gentleness and a power of conviction in the old

man's deep brown eyes. Ben paused in the doorway as if he were crossing more than just the threshold of Ty's home. His face was suddenly
serious. "Above us, in the woods, the mountains . . . he's up there. I
wanna find him. Wanna help me?"

Ty's eyes brimmed instantly as Ben's three words cut right to his
soul. To have Chief Ben Eagleclaw come to his home and offer to join
him in his quest was a godsend. Ty giddily ushered him in.

"We're just sitting down to dinner. Join us, please. I would be honored. And my kids will think this is better than going to Disneyland."

Ben smiled and took in the scale of the home. He'd been to plenty
of movie parties and this place was big even by Hollywood standards.
Ty guided Ben to the rear of the house.

"So, are you doing a movie around here?"

Ty had quickly decided they could get down to real business after
dinner.

"No, just here on a sorta vacation," answered Ben.

When they entered the kitchen area, Greta smiled and said hello,
half recognizing the tall old Indian but not sure who he was. She had
never been a big moviegoer, even in Sweden. As they walked to the television room to surprise the kids, Ben nodded back toward the kitchen.

"Your wife is very pretty."

Greta overheard and blushed.

Ty quickly said, "Oh, I'm sorry, she's our au pair and sort of house-
keeper. My wife is upstairs. She's not feeling well. Maybe she'll be down
later."

Greta may not have known Ben, but the kids went wild, as if their
dad had brought home both Santa Claus and Pikachu at the same
time. Ty had spent a lot of time introducing them to his favorite films,
so they were cinematically literate for their tender ages. It also didn't
hurt that Ben had played the wise old Indian shaman in a recent series
of hit films that they loved. Dinner was a delight, with Ben regaling
them with his adventures, on screen and off. Ty wished Ronnie would
come down. She would like Ben, but he knew she was in no mood.

After dinner Ty showed Ben to his office, indicating two leather, high-
backed chairs that rarely saw any use. When Ty offered a brandy, Ben
refused with a wave of his hand. "No thanks. Not much of a drinker.

Probably seen too many relatives turn into alcoholics. I think my people have some kinda genetic thing against it."

There was a soft tap on the door, and Ronnie opened it. She had an armful of blankets and a pillow. She smiled softly at Ben, who stood. "Hi. Ty, I thought you might need these."

"Thanks. Honey, this is Ben Campbell. You probably—"

Ronnie suddenly recognized Ben. "Oh. It's really a pleasure to meet you, Ben." They shook hands. "I hope dinner was good. Sorry I missed it."

"It was real good, thanks. I really appreciate your hospitality. How you feeling? Ty said you were a little under the weather."

Her glance at Ty and the armload of bedding told Ben it was more complicated.

"I'm much better, thanks. I won't interrupt. Very nice meeting you, Ben."

"You too, Ronnie."

She left and Ty poured himself a tumbler of Scotch. Ty could tell Ronnie had calmed a bit, but they had unfinished business.

"How long you and Ronnie been married?"

"Twelve years."

Ben nodded. "Great wife, great kids . . ." He paused. "Not a bad house either."

They both smiled, then Ben got into it. "I know you're looking for it, Ty. Me too. This one, the one here? He's a killer."

Ty felt gooseflesh on his neck and arms as the old man said it so matter-of-factly. Finally someone with conviction to match his.

"I've been following what I thought it's been doing," Ty said. "But I wasn't a hundred percent sure. You definitely think there's only one?"

Ben leaned forward. "Yup. He's a rogue. I felt he came from the south. He's alone. He hates us, people that is, and he's stakin' out his turf."

Ty reeled. "How do you know all that?"

Ben knew what he was about to say might test even the faith of an apostle.

"When I was a boy, my grandfather raised me and taught me the ways of our tribe. I'd been away from that for so long I forgot. That is until recently. Many, many years ago, as a young man, just before I went to war, I met one in the forest near where I was raised. It chased me, just like it chased you in the articles I read. I believe to this day it meant me harm. I'd forgotten it for years until suddenly, about six months ago, the dreams came back, the dreams of that day. It's always chasin' me and just before it gets me, I wake up. But it's been gettin' closer and closer and . . ." Ben trailed off, realizing his fear of being seized in his sleep might be too far-out even for Ty.

"Anyway, I'd been feelin' this one, don't ask me how 'cause I honestly don't know, but I've been sensin' him more and more in the past coupla weeks. Then the other day I decided to try and find him, first in a dream, sorta. I reached out with something my granddad taught me years ago, a way to travel without physically goin' anywhere. Anyway, when I did that, I saw him. And I felt his heart. It was dark."

Ty was trying to sort through all the old man had just told him. Ty wasn't sure if Ben was nuts or the greatest find he'd made since starting his quest three years ago. He chose, for now, to believe the latter. "You know where this thing is?"

Ben sat back and sighed deeply. "Not exactly. Sometimes I can getta sorta fix, but it's fleeting."

Ben paused for a moment and gathered his thoughts. "All living things give off energy. Even plants have these auras. People, they have brain waves, electricity, that goes out like radio signals. Now this is my theory . . . but didn't you ever have a feelin' someone was watchin' you, or have a sense someone you cared about was in danger?"

Ty nodded. "Yeah, sure."

"Well, this thing, this Oh-Mah—"

"Oh-Mah? I've read that name."

"It's from my ancestors' language, Hoopa. Sorta means 'Boss of the Woods.' Anyhow, Oh-Mah, they're like radios, they pick up the signals we give off. But we can pick up theirs too, only we aren't used to 'em so we don't know what to make of 'em."

"So, this thing reads our minds?"

"Not exactly like a psychic does. This Oh-Mah, he feels our thoughts. But I'm not so sure all Oh-Mah do. The one who chased me? And others my tribal elders told me about? They could. But not all."

"And you've felt this one?"

"Yeah. He's strong. His mind is strong. And I'm pretty sure he enjoys killin'."

Ty was trying to picture the nemesis he'd been chasing. "So why does he kill?"

"This one? I think now he kills for revenge, but why I don't know. He also eats his victims, I'm pretty sure. See, Oh-Mah's not an animal, not in the sense of a bear or a deer. He's more like us. But this one, he's different. He's a Shadowkiller."

"What's that?"

"My granddad, he told me a lotta things. When we talked about the creatures in the forest, he talked about Oh-Mah with respect, even reverence. Most of 'em are good, just like people. But then you got the bad ones, the ones who have a taste for killin'. My granddad called 'em the Shadowkillers, the worst of the worst. They track you quiet like a shadow; they're there but they're not. The greatest hunters in the world. And they don't let you see 'em till it's too late, then . . ." Ben clapped loudly and Ty jumped slightly. "That's all she wrote. The one who chased me? He was a Shadowkiller."

Ben decided to lay out his cards, feeling that Ty was receptive. "I'm an old man. In my dreams, the one who chased me, maybe sometimes it's this one, I don't know . . . Either way, he's been getting closer and closer. It sounds crazy, but if he catches me in my dream . . ."

Ben paused and Ty filled in the blank. "You won't wake up."

With that, Ben nodded, knowing he was talking to the right man. Together, maybe they could find this thing, perhaps even stop it, and put an end to both of their demons.

Ty poured a liberal dose of Scotch into his glass. "So, how do we find it?"

Ben stared at the floor-to-ceiling windows, seeing the blackness beyond the glass as a metaphor for the next step. "I don't know."

Ty and Ben whiled away the evening in the office, then moved to the kitchen to get Ben a glass of water. Ty poured another slug of whisky, his fifth by Ben's count, and they went outside for air and atmosphere. Ty buttoned his coat against the misty night chill and motioned toward a pair of deck chairs by the pool.

"Where do we start?" he asked the older man.

"I know he's not far from here," said Ben. "He's up in the mountains, probably comes down at night to hunt and eat."

The night air was still, and a few silent moments passed as they considered the discussion of the last few hours.

"I saw his track," said Ben.

Ty was surprised. "Where?"

"Up above here. Some people had a truck turned over . . ."

Ty nodded. "The Allisons. Yeah, I know. You saw a track up there?"

Ben nodded and held out his hands like a fisherman extolling the one that got away.

"He's big." Ben sat back and looked at the few stars winking behind the patterned clouds. "I don't think this Oh-Mah's gonna leave. I also think he's pretty mad about somethin'. Plus, he likes killin'."

Ty responded with a healthy pull off his Scotch.

Ben tipped his head toward him. "Don't take offense, Ty, but you drink a lot."

Ty looked at his glass. Had anyone else said so, he would have been angry, but Ben was his new best friend and the only other constituent of a club that now boasted two members.

Ben continued, "I think you're a good man, but I feel tension in your house. This thing has taken its toll, huh?"

"Yes. Yes, it has," Ty said softly.

"And the whisky isn't your only crutch, is it?"

Ty was a little surprised, but Ben's guess that he had other means of dealing with the pressure convinced him all the more that this old man might be in touch with a side of the mind Ty didn't understand.

"No," Ty admitted, "it's not."

"Doesn't matter what it is," Ben said, "but you gotta quit, all of it, for now."

Ty looked at him. *What does this have to do with our problem?* He started to object, but Ben held up a hand and smiled kindly.

"I'm not trying to tell you how to run your life, Ty, but I know we're gonna need everything we got to win. We're up against somethin' neither of us are ready for. He's fast as the wind, strong as a plow horse, and has a taste for death. We're just men. So we gotta outthink him, be ahead of him mentally, 'cause he's got all the other cards. If we're gonna do this, go after him, then we'd better be sharp, 'cause if we aren't and make a mistake . . ."

Ben paused, leaned over, and touched Ty's arm.

"The one that chased you? How tall?"

"I don't know, maybe seven feet."

Ben's old eyes focused on Ty's for effect. He liked this young man but needed a partner he could depend upon.

"That one?" he continued. "Yours? Probably a teenager, maybe even a youngster. He chased you for fun. This one? Ours? He's half again as tall and more'n twice as big. If we go onto his land, we're gonna be in a lotta danger. He'll know we're there and he'll be ahead of us. So if we're gonna have any chance, I need you clearheaded. Okay?"

Ty nodded somberly. "Okay."

Ty held out his hand and they shook. Ty tossed the remains of his Scotch. Ben looked over the half-covered pool.

"Don't swim much, huh?"

"Not much. The cover's supposed to retract automatically but it broke and we can't get anyone to fix it until after Christmas. Water's like ice. My wife . . . uh, Ronnie wanted it when we built the house. We use it about a month a year, maybe two. But the deer and the raccoons like it; they drink out of it regularly."

Ben considered the neglected body of water. "Well, forgot my trunks anyhow."

49

A round midnight Kris entered her Eastlake apartment, sorted her mail, checked her machine, then decided on something completely uncharacteristic—a hot bath. Generally a fan of showers, Kris regarded baths as time wasters but tonight she felt like pampering herself.

A floor-to-ceiling window in her bathroom looked out over Lake Union and the surrounding city. Because there were few neighbors who could see inside, she usually kept the curtains open. She lit a cigarette and started the water. Kris was aware of a guy a block below who liked to watch her in the bathroom. Sometimes she let him. Her pet name for him was Peeping Bob. She'd seen him in his window a few times, with and without binoculars, and even passed him in the small local grocery down on Fairview. She knew he knew who she was, but she was pretty sure he had no clue she was on to his peeping.

She poured a glass of wine and came back into the bathroom. She noticed Peeping Bob's light had gone off, a sign he was on duty. Suddenly the success of the day made her feel powerful, and since discovering that power was her new turn-on, she decided to give him a show.

Slowly undoing her blouse, she let it hang open, then moved out of the window to build his tension. A moment later she reappeared and tossed her blouse to the floor. Next she teasingly fiddled with her bra, then unsnapped and dropped it. Cupping her bare breasts, she wanted to make sure he was painfully aroused. Then she took a leisurely sip of her chardonnay.

She unzipped her skirt and let it slide off, kicking it into her bedroom. She loathed panty hose: she unsnapped her stockings from the garter belt and dropped them into the hamper. Now that she was wearing only panties, it was time to cut Peeping Bob off, since it was her policy to never let him see her completely nude. But as she reached for the curtains, she suddenly felt the wine flowing over the pleasure center in her brain. Her day had gone unbelievably well, thanks to those two probably dead codgers out near Monroe.

The stock in Kris Walker, Inc., had shot through the ceiling after Doug Gautier's banishment and the impossibly lucky validation of her series on the murders. Until Mac's admission on tape, pressure had been building on the station to explain why they were calling the disappearances murders. Everyone from local radio pundits to national news organizations were asking the big question: what does Channel 7 know that nobody else does? She gave Lyle credit for running interference for her, even with the conglomerate's head office in Provo. And now everyone from *Newsweek* and the *Wall Street Journal* to *People* was calling her for interviews. She checked out the media blogs, where it seemed her dazzling looks were a far bigger priority to the public than whether she was just winging her coverage. And closer to home, she was glowing after the word quickly got around the station that Sales Manager Howard March had proclaimed to his staff that Kris was "becoming a one-woman industry with her coverage of the missing people." Kris suddenly felt invincible.

Standing squarely in the window, she dropped her panties and kicked them away. As she sipped her wine, she performed a slow, naked pirouette for her admirer. *Enjoy looking, Peeping Bob, because you can never touch it.* She leisurely combed her hair for a few minutes, then decided Peeping Bob had seen more than he could handle. She fired up another cigarette and slipped from her stage into hot water.

It had been three hours since he looked at the clock. It was now three a.m. and Mac shut the 1961 book *Abominable Snowman: Legend Come to Life*, authored by the learned British zoologist Ivan T. Sanderson. He didn't have to get up early, but he closed the book because a subconscious notion had elbowed its way into his frontal lobe and was now screaming at him. Dr. Wade Frazier was going to help him pull everything out of the fire. Despite the man's claimed reluctance, too much had happened for him not to break his silence. Mac envisioned himself, armed with the casting, Dr. Frazier at his side, holding a news conference that would set the media on its ear. He proudly mulled over this new idea and resolved to act first thing in the morning. Despite his career's falling apart in the previous twenty-four hours, he had fresh hope, a new plan. Reassured, he climbed into bed and slept like a baby.

50

The morning shift at Boeing's Everett plant started bright and early, and once again Russ Tardif didn't show. Russ's supervisor, Milt Nelms, came unglued. *Damn near a week now and the man's a no-show.* Milt was pissed for several reasons, not the least of which were the twenty calls he'd made to Russ's house and the fact that, despite Russ's being ridiculously late, firing him would be problematic because of the union.

After questioning all of Russ's coworkers on his whereabouts, Milt came up empty. He asked that pack of lazy shits if one of them would drive over to Russ's place and check on him. No one lived out that far—and none volunteered—so Milt decided he'd have to do it himself. That morning was going to be spent twiddling thumbs anyway while engineering came up with new specs on the latch tolerances for some cargo door hydraulic assemblies they'd just completed—and now apparently had to remachine—so Milt figured he had at least four hours to kill. He grabbed his underling and drinking buddy, Brian Windham, and they jumped into Milt's F-150 and headed for points east, namely the home of Russ Tardif.

It took almost an hour for Milt and Brian to arrive at Russ's residence. They missed his driveway twice before spotting the anonymous little rutted dirt road with the foot-high grass growing down the middle. They rolled up in front of Russ's home, hoping not to see Russ's vehicle, an old Aerostar. The fading blue van told them Russ was home, and Milt felt a welling uneasiness that the situation was about to get complicated, if not ugly.

Without a word they got out and listened. They had no idea whether Russ had gone AWOL and for some crazy reason might come out guns blazing—employers never knew these days—or maybe he was dead drunk, or just dead. The only loud thing about the old farmhouse was the peeling green paint. Far below came the faint rushing sound of moving water. The thick forest that approached within fifty feet of the house was dead still.

Milt rang the doorbell and knocked for a minute or so, then walked around the house, peering inside. He saw no sign of Russ.

"You see anything?" he called to Brian.

"Nothin,'" Brian yelled back from the other side of the house.

Sizing up the sloping backyard and its knee-high grass, Milt saw a semblance of a trail leading down to the creek.

"Hey, didn't Russ say he had a workshop or something?" he yelled.

The creek's white noise masked Milt's question from Brian's side of the house.

Milt started down the trail.

Brian rounded the house, following. "I don't think he's around here," he said, warily measuring the steep, grassy grade. While he enjoyed the time away from work on the clock, Brian hadn't planned on engaging in any real detective work.

About twenty yards from the end of the trail they both saw the same thing and stopped.

Brian whispered, "Oh shit."

Milt continued toward the burned wreckage. It was hard to tell if Russ had met his demise here but it sure looked like it. They circled the pile of blackened lumber, hoping to catch a glimpse of anything that either confirmed or denied their awful suspicions. Brian picked up some lumber but Milt stopped him.

"Leave it. If he's in there, he's dead. The fire department'll need it in one piece to figure what happened."

Brian dropped the wood. That's why Milt was the boss, always thinking.

* * *

Mac hesitated, phone in hand, suddenly feeling that his great revelation at three that morning didn't seem as brilliant in the light of day. He dialed anyway.

A moment later came the crisp voice at the other end, "Wade Frazier."

"Dr. Frazier, Mac Schneider."

"Detective Schneider, what are you doing?" the professor asked with urgency. "I've heard no mention of your discovery."

"That's why I'm calling. More people are missing and I think it's to blame."

"Indeed, and you are calling to enlist me in lending scientific credence to your assertions."

"In a nutshell. Will you?"

"No, and I will tell you why I cannot. Unless things have changed, you have a casting and no other evidence. I have been watching the newscasts and reading the accounts, yet no one else seems to be aware of what you and I suspect. Unfortunately, to support your rather provocative theory, you do not have the incontrovertible proof that you need to gain acceptance. And as a yardstick of that proof, I submit to you the case of Roger Patterson, who shot actual footage of one: forty years later people still debate whether it's a man in a suit. Furthermore, to engage in a bit of psychoanalysis, I can also divine that your silence thus far indicates a diminution of absolute certainty on your part. Fearing for your career, Detective?"

Mac didn't need to get into how his career was probably already over. He didn't want Frazier to think only one of them had something to lose.

Frazier took Mac's silence as a yes. "So, Detective, you can empathize with my position. I can say this, however: should you obtain the corpse, or a living specimen, I will be delighted to catalogue it and assist in presenting it to the scientific community and, I presume, the world. Other than that, I am sorry."

"Any suggestions?" asked Mac.

"Look for it. Like us, they are probably creatures of habit. Divine a pattern to his actions and comb that area. But I advise you to do so in the possession of some considerable weaponry. This one seems to be rather ill-tempered."

"What, you don't want a living specimen?" Mac added with a wry smile.

"I would love it, but I don't think it's at all feasible. I suspect a being such as this can be contained in only one way and that does not involve a net. Good luck, Detective Schneider."

Mac set the phone down and looked at it for a moment, lost in thought. Then he picked it back up and punched in some numbers.

"Suzy, hi, it's Mac."

"What happened?" she said, lowering her voice. "You're a total pariah around here."

"I know. It's a long story."

"You'll have to tell me when we can talk."

"I will. I need a favor."

"Whatever you need."

"Anything out of the ordinary, disappearances, whatever, copy the files and send them over here."

"Done. Anything else?"

"Just be careful. You're aiding and abetting the enemy."

She chuckled sadly. "I will, and you take care of yourself."

"I will. Thanks a million, you're the best, Suze."

Mac spent the rest of the morning puttering around his condo, cleaning and straightening. The busywork required no thought and allowed his mind a clearer path toward finding options. Then another idea hit him. It was certainly a much further stretch than calling Frazier. He retrieved a folder from his office and skimmed the contents.

The Channel 7 receptionist glanced up to see a rangy, unshaven man of around thirty, clad in torn jeans, a very faded Iron Maiden T-shirt, and a tattered army fatigue jacket. She instantly wondered which of the local messenger companies had let their standards slip.

"May I help you?" she asked.

"I gotta talk to Kris Walker, the reporter," said J. D. Watts. Then he immediately recognized the need to qualify himself, based on the judging stare he was getting. "I know something about the killings she's been doin' the TV stories on," he added awkwardly. As soon as the words came out of his mouth, he realized how they sounded. "I mean I don't know the killer or nothin', but I think I got an idea 'bout who's doin' it." Chronic marijuana intake and a lack of practice in formal communication had already crippled his approach.

"Miss Walker is not in. Would you like to leave a message?"

It was nine a.m. and it hadn't occurred to J. D. that Kris might not be at work.

"Shit. Oh, yeah, well . . ." His mind raced to come up with the words that would intrigue this high-powered reporter. He failed. "I'll come back."

He walked away, then turned and asked, "When'll she be comin' in?"

The receptionist consulted a schedule. "Probably around one."

J. D. nodded and walked out. The receptionist reached for a notepad and started to write Kris a note about the encounter with the stoner kook but thought better of it. Had it been any other reporter, she would have given the warning, but Kris's reputation was getting around and the receptionist didn't want to get her attention, even by trying to do her a favor.

51

The fire department and police investigators carefully photographed the wreckage of Russ's shop after determining, through cursory invasion of the charred rubble, that neither Russ nor his mortal remains were present. They concluded that the building had partially collapsed prior to burning and that the front door—with most of the attached wall—had caved *out*. No one could explain that type of destruction, nor could they even speculate as to what really happened to Russ Tardif. The fact that it took three men to right Russ's sizable table saw merely confirmed that, according to an assistant fire chief on scene, "whatever went on here was pretty goddamned weird."

Because of the growing frenzy over the "serial killer on the loose," the statement released to the press simply said there had been an unexplained fire. Pending an outcome of the investigation, as well as notification of next of kin, information that the building had been ransacked, and that the resident was missing and presumed dead, was withheld from public consumption.

Ronnie had not spoken a word to Ty as she readied for work. Ty knew that whatever came next was Ronnie's call. He said a prayer that she wouldn't lower the boom. After she left for work, he breathed a sigh of relief. Having a bad chemistry day, he stared at his drawer, the location of his magic mood elevators. But what stayed his hand was his promise to the old man. In just one evening Ben had become his best friend and a father figure. Ty's own father had died in a car accident years ago. Ty wanted—*needed*—to find relief from the horror show in his head. His mind was telling him bad things, running awful images on his inner screen, and he cringed with despair over everything's going up in smoke. His marriage, his family, everything . . . *phhht.* Gone.

So he stared at that drawer and parsed his words to Ben as a lawyer might, looking for an out. But a promise was a promise. As a reward for being so steadfast, the lucid part of his brain told him his rebuke of temptation had just made him stronger. Hopefully strong enough, because Ben said he'd need all his strength for what was coming.

And what was coming? He didn't know and neither did Ben. Track it down? Then what? Shoot it? Drug it? Throw a sheet over it and hit it with a five iron? Could they even find it? Ty's inclination was to swarm the problem with technology and money. Break out all that dusty gear—the infrared sensors, the army issue night vision goggles, the motion detectors—and send as much data feeding into computers as needed to boil the problem down to one answer: *here it is, go get it.*

But Ben, that crafty—or crazy—old actor, had a different plan. He said the thing could evade them if they went after it en masse, bristling with the science of a twenty-first-century army. Ben wanted to take the approach he knew or, as he admitted, the approach he only recently reacquainted himself with. Ty emotionally understood Ben's "inner eye" concept, but he just couldn't get an intellectual handle on it. He was as open-minded as the next person, but the idea that Ben could contact this thing via ESP was a challenge to him. And then what if he could? Use it to locate it like a homing beacon? Or maybe somehow get it to come to them? Ty didn't know and wasn't so sure Ben even knew.

But he decided to shake off his skepticism and accept that Ben was not full of crap. Something about the man, actually many things, told Ty that Ben Campbell, a.k.a. Chief Ben Eagleclaw, was not only a good actor but a real Indian. Ty had always been intrigued by Native American mysticism. Now he might be staking his life on it.

52

Ben arrived at Ty's home just before ten a.m., and they set up shop in Ty's office. After taping Ty's maps to the wall, they used the information they had acquired to determine where each person disappeared. They stuck a pushpin in each of those points. Around one p.m. Greta knocked and asked if they wanted lunch. Having lost track of time and suddenly feeling hungry, Ty told her they'd be right there.

Ty looked at the map, which now had a pin at each known vanishing. "It's moving west."

Ben eyed the pins, trying to divine a pattern. "I think maybe it's settled in. He could range an easy twenty miles a night. I'm not sure, but I think he's probably staked out his territory and is movin' out from there."

"Where?" asked Ty.

Ben's creased brow deepened. "Don't know. Tried callin' him up this mornin'. Nothin'."

Ty visually measured the area in question. "Probably twenty, twenty-five miles by fifteen miles. That's three, maybe four hundred square miles. Where do we start?"

Ben patted Ty's back. "Let's eat on it."

As they walked down the lofty hallway to the kitchen, the doorbell chimed. Ty motioned for Ben to continue. "I'll get it," he said.

The double front doors had ornate stained glass panels but other than a profile they obscured any view of the visitor. As he approached, Ty assumed it was another reporter. He swung it open and was immediately wary. This time the man extended his hand to Ty.

"Mr. Greenwood? Mac Schneider. Remember me, from—"

"Yeah, I remember," said Ty, cautiously taking his hand. "What can I do for you? Want to search my house again?"

Mac looked chagrined. "That was Carillo's doing, not mine."

Ty impatiently held the door half open and made it clear he was not going to be as solicitous as the last time. "What do you want?"

"I'm here unofficially. You might be interested in what I've got. And the reverse may be true. I need help in finding this thing and I think you could give it to me."

Mac saw curiosity on Ty's face, but it was also mixed with some skepticism. Mac tossed out some more bait. "I know you're interested in it," he said. "I'm pretty sure it's out there. It's gotta be stopped. I need some backup so I can stop it. Interested?"

Ty stepped back and gestured him inside. He was both surprised and suspicious but decided he would observe the man's actions, then maybe they could talk. Ty could also rely on Ben's radar to decide if he was friend or foe.

"You hungry?" asked Ty. "We were just sitting down to lunch."

"Okay, sure. Thanks."

Mac was impressed that Ty Greenwood didn't seem to hold their somewhat hostile first meeting against him. But Mac had no illusions and understood intense curiosity was feeding much if not all of Ty Greenwood's hospitality.

On the way to the kitchen Ty noticed Mac's grocery sack. "What's that?"

"Something you'll find interesting," said Mac with a slight smile.

When a surprised Mac saw Ben, the detective excitedly launched into a recitation of Ben's filmography as well as career highlights. Ben was flattered, though a bit embarrassed by the level of detail Mac went into. Nevertheless, Ben let him continue, as he'd taken an immediate liking to Mac. They spoke no business during lunch.

Afterward the three men went into the office and settled into chairs. Ty opened the discussion. "Ben is also looking for it. We've just teamed up to find it. So your timing's perfect."

Mac nodded when Ty mentioned teaming up to "find it." Mac hadn't told them yet, but he had to be the guy who found it, not them. He had correctly guessed that Ty was going to look for it, but he hadn't planned on Ben's involvement. This was going to be harder than Mac had planned.

Ty turned to Ben. "Mac was one of the detectives I told you about."

Ben was surprised, since Ty had described the cops as unpleasant.

Mac read his expression. "My partner and I were a little aggressive. I apologize."

Ben pointed his finger and exclaimed, "Hey, that reporter on TV, you're the guy she interviewed. That's it. That's how I know the voice."

Mac sighed. "Yeah. Only that tape she made was butchered. She cut out the most important part of what I said."

"Which was?" Ty asked.

Mac pulled out the huge foot casting and handed it to Ty. "That this is who did it."

Ty's jaw dropped. "God almighty . . ."

Ben looked at it, less awed. "Yup. That's him. For sure."

Mac gave Ben a curious look.

Ben pointed at the casting. "I saw his track the other day. A partial. Same as that, left foot too. Favors his left. He's a lefty."

"Where did you get this?" asked Ty.

"Up where the lawyers disappeared," said Mac. "I saw a heel print first then looked a little off trail. Found this. This is what Carillo is convinced you're making."

Ty understood. "The search. He was looking for what made this."

"Right." Mac knew he had to gain their trust and quickly. "I think I had a close encounter with it. Last week. I swear it was right behind me. Fired my gun a few times to try and scare it off, then got into my car. Strange feeling, like . . ."

"A warm breeze?" Ben continued, "Or like that feelin' you get when somebody comes into a room and though you didn't hear 'em, you know they're there?" Mac was nodding in total understanding, so Ben continued. "Or maybe like sunlight, just a ray or two that makes the hair stand up on your neck? Something like that?"

Mac was fascinated how the old man knew so much about this thing.

Ben tipped his head toward Mac. "Oh-Mah. He was near you. You were real lucky."

"Ben, is that what you were talking about?" Ty asked. "Being able to feel him?"

Ben ventured an explanation. "I think it's some of that undeveloped extra sense we've got but don't use. His mental energy on the other hand is real strong . . . It's focused, like a beam of light and we can actually feel it. That's when we know he's there."

"And he senses that we know?" Mac asked.

Ben nodded. "I think so."

Ever the technician, Ty asked, "What's the range, any idea?"

"I don't have any idea," Ben said. "But like I said, I felt him in Portland. And that's what, two hundred miles? Yet, I can't conjure him here, at least not clearly. You know, I've read stories about psychic stuff. People know a loved one's in danger from across the country. Or a dog travels a thousand miles and finds its master. Or somebody knows somethin's gonna take place ahead of time and it does. There's lots of crackpots to muddy things up, but real psychic experiences happen for sure."

"So you have a sense of him around here?" Mac asked.

"Yeah, but like I said to Ty, I couldn't tell you where."

Ty pointed at their taped-up maps.

"We're plotting his path, but we don't really see a pattern. Ben thinks he's made a camp and is operating out of it. We're trying to figure out where that is. That's where we'll start."

Mac realized they wouldn't be content with anything less than actively looking for it. Ben Campbell might be old as well as an actor, but he knew a great deal about it and also seemed resolute. Ty Greenwood had a history of searching for it and came across as a driven man who could throw his vast finances behind his quest.

As the discussion continued, Mac's brain went into overdrive to come up with an option they would go for. But whatever it was, it had to have one result: Mac absolutely had to be the one who found this thing, because he was convinced that was the only way he could save his credibility and career. But Mac felt desperation disrupting his thoughts and remembered the saying his training officer drilled into him when he was an LAPD rookie, "Never play poker with scared money, kid. You'll lose every time." Mac knew that advice had nothing to do with poker and everything to do with life.

"The old couple. Think that's related, Mac?" Ty asked.

Mac continued staring at the maps for a moment, lost in thought. "Huh? Oh, yeah, the Krinkels. I read the report. Old man Krinkel was missing and it seemed his wife was *pulled* through the window from her bed. Investigators also said their dogs seemed pretty spooked. The forensics people are totally stymied, probably because they have a lot of answers but don't have a clue as to what the big question is."

Mac took a pushpin from the box and stuck it in the map.

"Russell Tardif. Probably happened last week, they're not sure. They just discovered the man's workshop, fifty percent burned, but he's missing. According to a report, which was not released to the media, it appears his shop was smashed before it caught fire."

"It broke in?" Ty guessed. "Maybe a short caused the fire."

"Maybe," Mac said. "They're not even sure he was in the shop when it went down."

Ben stood abruptly, went to the window, and stared, glassy-eyed. "This shop's by a creek," he said, his voice hollow, distant, as if in a light trance.

Mac, momentarily confused, looked to Ty. "Yeah, he's right. It is."

"Happened coupla weeks ago. Fella was sawin' wood. 'Bout thirty years old, I'd guess. It was rainin'. Come in and got him. Oh-Mah," he nodded, just as if he'd seen it on TV.

The two men looked at Ben. Mac was so taken off guard, he recited from memory parts of the confidential file Suzy had faxed him.

"You're right. He was thirty-one. They found an overturned table saw with the power switch in the on position. And the saw being over-turned wouldn't happen in a fire. This saw was a big industrial model, weighed several hundred pounds."

Ben nodded thoughtfully. "Yup. Wrote it off as a bad dream when it happened. Just another scary movie in my brain starrin' somebody I never saw before. Guess this one happened, huh?"

Mac was astonished by Ben's accuracy. "You had any other . . . dreams?"

"Nope," he said, turning back, the distant look gone. "But I'll let you know when I do."

*   *   *

Mac had waited more than half an hour for his opportunity to state his case. Ty was discussing the details of how they would conduct their search and specifics like which trailhead would be the best starting point. Finally Mac couldn't stand it anymore and interrupted him.

"Guys, listen to me, I appreciate what you're doing here, but you can't really go after this thing on your own. I know you know that."

Ty, his brow furrowed over this out-of-left-field comment, looked to Mac. "What?"

"I'm serious. This is not a job for laypeople. You're talking about tracking down something that will require manpower, and more than that, expertise."

Ben was intrigued by Mac's sudden turnaround and leaned back on the couch. He could see Ty's body language change and figured he'd let Ty address the situation.

Ty was baffled and slightly annoyed. "Expertise? What are you talking about? I mounted several formal expeditions to find this thing. I know what I'm doing."

"And did you find it?" asked Mac.

Ty leveled his gaze at Mac, trying to understand what the hell had happened to this guy in the last twenty seconds. Ty felt his irritation welling and realized his surprise and growing anger would be pretty easy to read. He forced himself to calm down. "So what are you saying? You want our help, but you want the police to do the actual work? Hell, they think I'm the guy running around planting fake tracks. They're idiots."

Mac shook his head. "Listen, I know, what I . . . If you can funnel me all you know, act behind the scenes, sort of run the unofficial command, I'll lead the investigation. I have some autonomy on what I can do, I have resources—"

"So do we," Ty responded. "Frankly, I probably have more money than your entire department does for this kind of investigation. You're suggesting we plant ourselves in this office and let you run the thing down?"

Mac appealed to Ben. "With all due respect, Ben, you plan on hiking all over the Cascades looking for this thing? You're damn near

eighty. And you're an actor, not a tracker. And Ty, I know you've put together searches, but it really isn't what you do. It's what I do."

Ty was exasperated by Mac's jarring about-face. He wasn't about to
leave this task to someone else. He realized they were at an impasse. He
also knew that if Mac had the department behind him, he would not
have come unofficially. There was something that Mac was not telling
him, but it didn't matter. Ty and Ben needed this man because he was
a cop, he had the casting, he may have encountered the thing, and most
important, he believed. But Ty had to do this on his own terms and
could not have anyone, not Mac Schneider, not the press or public
opinion or, truth be told, even his own wife, stop him. Ty held out his
hand to Mac. "Good luck."

Mac had been hoping his gambit would appeal to their logic, but it
was apparent that Ty was very emotional about this and was going to
proceed on his own terms. Mac reluctantly shook Ty's hand, knowing
that it marked the beginning of their rivalry.

Mac drove away wishing things had gone better. He knew he had
not been clearheaded lately and ticked off his lapses in judgment. They
were mounting. He had very few chances left to exonerate himself. Mac
desperately wanted this animal or ape or whatever it was to be real.
And if it was, he would be the guy to take it down.

53

Over the last two days Kris had been very busy. On top of calls from other media to interview her, she had begun receiving phone messages from a guy who claimed to know "what was doing the killings," but he wouldn't leave his phone number. Finally the receptionist copped to an actual encounter with a scruffy man who came in wanting to talk to Kris in person. After hearing a description, Kris dismissed him as one of those crackpots who was just trying to meet her. And there were lots of those now that her face was suddenly popping up everywhere. The media cockroaches had come out of the woodwork because Kris was now the It Girl, having turned the disappearances into high visibility for herself and her station. Her reports had evolved from hard news to stellar showmanship and thus drew audiences like sharks to chum. And because she'd been the first with the story, the frightened public turned to her for the latest on the crazed murderer.

Kris noticed Gwen, her intern, walking nearby and called her over. "What have you gotten on that Greenwood guy?"

Gwen nervously did a mental inventory. "I've got like a pretty good-sized file. LexisNexis, lots of articles, property records, credit stuff . . . He's like really rich, uh, lots of stuff."

"Does he look guilty?"

Gwen was perplexed. "Guilty of what?"

Kris dismissed her. "Nothing. Bring me the file."

Once again Kris was being forced to spin gold from dross because from the beginning she lacked one essential element to her tale: no bodies or other physical evidence. But unbeknownst to her, that was about to change.

A Boy Scout troop engaged in a search organized by a determined Karen Roberts had, only hours before, found something. It wasn't much, a piece of yellow fabric, but it featured one thing valuable to both Kris and the Snohomish County Sheriff at the moment: blood. The fabric, from the Gore-Tex shell of a jacket like the one Mitch Roberts wore, had been lying next to a creek and was picked up by an eleven-year-old Scout. The alert kid gave it to his troop leader and within a few hours Carillo had personally carried it to the crime lab for a battery of tests. Despite the fact it had probably been in or around the creek now for three weeks, a large-enough clot of blood had congealed and clung to the surface to allow for a typing.

While working on the blood typing, Suzy Chang gave Carillo a quick lesson in Gore-Tex.

"Normally, Gore-Tex is water resistant because it's tight enough to keep out water drops, but its breathable structure is loose enough to allow water molecules to pass through its barrier, like sweat. Blood cells, on the other hand, are small enough to cling to the microscopic matrix."

Carillo craned his neck to look at the fabric. "It looks . . . I dunno, it looks . . ."

Suzy read his confusion. "No stitches. There aren't any stitches. Since they don't want to penetrate the fabric with a needle, otherwise it wouldn't be waterproof *and* breathable, Gore-Tex is assembled with superglue, not traditional needle and thread."

Carillo arched a brow. "No shit. You learn something every day."

"Another thing," Suzy added, "this fabric is very tough, and since it's also superglued, the force necessary to separate this piece from the whole must have been significant."

A few minutes later Suzy prepared some of the dried blood and made a solution, which she applied to a test card. After a moment she looked up at Carillo. "It's type B positive."

Carillo was grim. "Mitch Roberts is B positive. Okay, at least now we can give the bloodsuckers in the media something. Since they think we're hiding everything else," he added with venom.

"Do you really think Mac would hurt the department like that?" Suzy asked.

"He already did." Carillo turned and left.

Among Suzy's other forensic tests, a DNA screen was also pending, but the matching blood type tended to bolster the theory of foul play. When the word went out, Karen Roberts was shattered, but there was certainly exultation in the Snohomish County Sheriff's Department. Her bad news was their good news.

Ty watched Kris's report that evening and called Ben at the hotel.

"You see the news? They found a piece of the lawyer's jacket."

"Yeah," said Ben. "You put it on the map?"

"Just put a pin in. We need to get out, start looking."

"Yeah, it's time. I tried to bring him up again but just can't do it. We'll have to use the maps. That and a good guess."

"I've sort of triangulated a starting point, based on the other incidents," Ty offered.

"That's where we'll start," said Ben. He paused for a beat, then asked, "Neither of us have mentioned this, but do we have a gun to take along?"

Ty was momentarily taken aback, for in all the conversations he and Ben had had, they had never actually discussed killing it. Or for that matter, how they might stop it.

"I've got a tranquilizer rifle. I had it from when I looked the last time."

Ben visualized their quarry. "Okay, but how 'bout a real gun? A big one."

There was a long pause on Ty's end of the phone as he thought of his stupendous rifle and its solitary round. "Yeah, maybe."

"Maybe?" repeated Ben.

"Okay, yeah, I have something. It's too big to carry, though."

"Then I hope you can put him to sleep."

Ty changed the subject. "I've also got a choice of cameras. I've got a mini DV for motion, and for stills I've got this little point-and-shoot, either that or we could use this pretty high-end digital—"

"Bring the little one and put it in your pocket."

Ben's abrupt answer stopped Ty. "Okay . . ."

"We might just see him at a distance and get a nice pretty snapshot. But if we get worried 'bout snappin' his picture—and let's say he's fifty feet away—well, I'd suggest shootin' him with somethin' a little more potent than megapixels, or whatever you call 'em."

Ty got Ben's point. "The little one. In my pocket."

The men agreed to meet the next day and begin their actual search. After they hung up, Ben restlessly fumbled through some newspapers and clicked on the TV to find some news. He was tired but feared sleep. He'd had some dreams the past few nights that were quite disturbing. He saw a chase through a forest, only he wasn't the pursued, it was two others. He saw it all with disturbing clarity: the two were running and one was hurt, limping, and behind them, in the shadows, came their huge pursuer. Then the thing was upon them and—

Ben would wake up. He had the dream twice and both times he awoke at that moment. He wanted to know the outcome but wasn't completely sure if this dream represented prescience or just his over-active imagination. He prayed it was the latter.

Desperately needing to rest, Ben suddenly didn't feel safe alone in his hotel room, so he slipped on his shoes and wandered down to the lobby. Off to one corner, a big potted fern offered cover, and behind it, an overstuffed chair beckoned. Snuggling himself in, out of view of the quiet late-night lobby traffic, he shut his eyes. There was something about being in a public place that made him feel it wouldn't come here and get him. He hoped. He also hoped the latest dream wouldn't come back, for if it did, it would seem to confirm itself, as if future reality could be cultivated like growing a plant. Ben cleared his mind and immediately fell asleep.

His back against a two-hundred-foot-tall cedar, he closed his eyes to sleep. He was hungry, but more so, he was tired. The old small two-legs he had killed in the dark time had provided a meal, but they were lean and bony. He would rest now, then go down to the flat land and look for food.

He had discovered that the small two-legs often left their food outside their wood caves. He did not know why, but if its smell attracted him, he would eat it. Their food was strange and had many more tastes than he was used to. Some he liked, some he did not. Often the things the small two-legs left the food in made noise when he looked inside, and sometimes the small two-legs would come out to investigate. He would hide nearby in the shadows because he did not want them to see him. One small two-leg came right at him and he was going to take it, but then its mate cried out to it and it went back in its wood cave. He did not understand why they left their food outside their wood caves.

54

Dawn found sullen clouds scudding across the horizon. The temperature actually dropped as the sun came up, and weather forecasters all over Puget Sound divined a coming storm. They just disagreed on when it would happen. Some said two days, others said three to four, with the latter estimates putting it on the doorstep of Christmas Eve. While many forecasters saw a simple rainstorm on the way, some predicted that rare thunderstorm in December.

Ty and Ben had spent three days in the woods, hiking and searching but to no avail. Having already combed the forest area below where the mountain biker disappeared, they returned to try it again. Gazing up at the sweeping clear-cut slope, an indecipherable tromp l'oeil of stumps, tortured tree wreckage, and plowed ground, the men understood that even Ben's competent tracking abilities would be taxed.

Two hours later, after trudging most of it uphill, Ben plopped onto a four-foot-wide stump and took in the ragged hillside.

"He hides his tracks," he explained. "They all do. They learn that young."

"How do you know that?" asked Ty.

"My grandfather told me. Makes sense. Most inhabitants of the forest cover their tracks unconsciously. This one, all Oh-Mah, they do it out of habit. Tracks, stool, their shelters—all covered. They're smart."

"What about the broken trees?" Ty wondered.

"That's different," Ben said, thinking for a moment. "For instance, you got a mailbox with your name on it, right? But when you travel, you don't leave your wallet lyin' around or your car door open. Same idea. You cover your tracks, keep it quiet, but let others know where your territory is. We're all territorial. Us, him."

"My mailbox," Ty said wryly, "doesn't have my name on it."

"There you go," said Ben with a smile, "you're even more secretive than he is." He pointed at the top of the hill, far above them. "He may be up there. They like hilltops. They can be defended and Oh-Mah can drop down to hunt too."

Looking for a way up, Ty pointed to a dirt scar traversing the face of the hill from the top.

"That's gotta be the trail. Probably the one the mountain biker was going to come down. We'll need to go up there."

Ben sized it up. "Darn near vertical. How we gettin' up there?"

Ty shrugged. "Hike."

Ben shook his head, grinned. "I'm 'bout thirty years past that one. But I'll watch you."

Ben motioned toward the binoculars around Ty's neck. "Check out the top. That fella Mac said he thought he saw broken trees up there."

Ty scrutinized the area and saw some twisted trees but couldn't tell if they were wind-damaged.

"I don't know, nothing conclusive. What do you think?" he said, handing the glasses to Ben, who focused on the mountain.

"Dunno," said Ben. "Maybe. My old eyes ain't what they used to be."

Ty pulled out a map. "I got an idea. Since we came up here last time, I did some checking and there seems to be a way around this slope, to the top, but it's from the back. It's a serious trek but it's not straight up."

"Where does it start?" Ben asked.

Ty gauged the map. "Seven, maybe eight miles down the road, then up the trail. Trail forks, then take the left side." Ty looked at Ben and it hit him that his companion was pushing eighty years old. Ty was angry with himself for being so absorbed with their hunt that he hadn't stopped to consider Ben's lack of endurance. "Tomorrow. We've done enough for today. We'll go back to my place, have something to eat, and plan tomorrow."

Ben was too tired to argue but didn't want to hold up the show. "You sure?"

Ty nodded, shouldered his tranquilizer rifle, and headed out. "I make some pretty scary sausage gumbo. Got some in the fridge. Pour it over a little steamed rice? Whaddya say?"

Ben smiled as he watched his young partner move off. He knew Ty had cut things short on his account. "I'm in. Sounds good. That southern soul food?"

Ty laughed. "You people got, what, pemmican? I'm from Mississippi. Our tribal food is crawdads, gumbo, and red beans and rice."

Ben mused, "Pemmican. Hmmm. Never had it."

Ronnie sat in her office, gazing out at the line dividing the green and gray of terrain and sky. Depressed, she yearned for bright colors in her life again. The muted green seemed like just another shade of gray. The world was varying shades of gray. She kicked off her shoes and massaged her feet. She had been both wounded and worried by Ty's admission he had left his job.

The previous day, Ronnie had arrived home early and taken it upon herself to do a little recon in Ty's office. It made her physically ill to snoop in her husband's business, but she told herself it was for the good of the family. The maps and pins told her he and Ben were probably somewhere out there, looking for it. Then she found the Holland & Holland gun case and her lips tightened. Ty might have been surprised at her reaction at that moment: it was relatively impassive. She hefted the case out of the closet and set it on the floor. Ty did not know she knew the combination. Ronnie had an amazing head for numbers, and when she'd first seen the invoice, the lock code was on the slip. She remembered it now, three years later. She spun the dials and snapped the hasps. She stared at her nemesis and shook her head. "You ridiculously expensive bastard. What a waste of money you were."

Ronnie had been raised by a family of gun owners, so she understood why people chose to have guns and was even familiar with their use. A pretty decent shot when she was around twelve, she hadn't shot a gun in more than twenty-five years. Her issues with Ty's massive gun transcended the traditional debates on gun ownership. She picked up the single, huge cartridge and examined it. For a moment she considered throwing it away, or at least hiding it, but thought better of it. Even though disposing of that cartridge would emasculate the large rifle, it would really accomplish nothing but making her look petty. That Ty had brought the gun back in the house told her he was over the edge again. That he had hidden it from plain sight told her he was still within her reach. She shut the case, spun the three cylinders, and put it back in its place. Then she saw the box filled with high-tech gear, including the infrared night vision goggles, and cringed at what those must have cost.

As she stared out the window, remembering, her secretary's voice over the intercom shattered her reverie to tell her a tabloid reporter had tried to get past her. He wanted to ask Ronnie her opinion on the people who were disappearing in the mountains, as well as get her comments on "her husband's involvement." With that, Ronnie felt the circus was in full swing again. If the media were calling, it was only a matter of time before they invaded the sanctity of her home.

She contemplated a separation to jar Ty back to his senses, but that was a last resort, a sort of moral jumping-off point before divorce. And divorcing Ty was out of the question because he was a great man and a wonderful, loving husband. He was just sick. You don't divorce someone if he's sick. Then she thought *unless they can get help and refuse it.* So she was back to square one. Then she pondered the concept of tough love and wondered if that might be exactly what Ty needed. Ty was pretty stubborn until something just this side of catastrophic persuaded him to change course. Ronnie needed to get his attention back. She sighed, feeling tired and a little lost.

Ty saw the unfamiliar Chrysler Sebring in the parking plaza while he waited for the garage door to open. Backing the big red Suburban into its space, he thought it might belong to one of the many people who performed services on his property. Ben climbed out and exited the garage while Ty moved some of the kids' toys lying on the garage floor.

Ben offered to make another attempt at "sending out his inner eye." Ty found the notion fanciful but would indulge him because, based upon his own experience, he felt pretty much anything was possible.

"Ty, you've got company," Ben yelled from outside the garage.

Ty exited the structure to find a woman walking toward him. She passed Ben and nodded greetings to him.

"Tyler Greenwood?" she asked.

Ty nodded, feeling the presence of a reporter. "I'm Ty Greenwood."

Though Tyler was his given name, he preferred the less formal version. Usually only his mother called him Tyler.

"I'm Judy Elder of *The Rumor*. I just wanted some comments for my magazine."

She held out her hand but Ty warily stood back. He hated *The Rumor*. They had helped to crucify him once before.

"Sorry, but I have no comment." He headed toward the house.

"Isn't that Chief Ben Eagleclaw, the actor?" asked the reporter. "What's his involvement in this situation?"

Ty kept walking and the woman followed.

"Did you know any of the victims?" she persisted. "Are you looking for Bigfoot or is that just a smokescreen? Do you know who the serial killer is? Are you involved in the disappearances? The sheriff's department thinks you're involved. What did they find when they searched your house?"

"How did you know that? That they searched my house?"

"I have the contents of a confidential police file saying so."

Ty stopped. "Bullshit."

The reporter pulled out several sheets of paper. Ty grabbed them and examined their contents.

"We also know about your arrest at the scene of the truck incident, as well as information about the Boeing worker who disappeared from his workshop, and also details about the old couple who disappeared so mysteriously."

Ty quickly handed the papers back and angrily stormed toward his front door.

"You can have them," said the reporter. "They're copies. Why is Chief Eagleclaw here?"

Ty entered the house and closed the door. He went to his office, picked up the phone, and called the Snohomish County Sheriff's Department. After chewing out the undersheriff, Ty told him, suspect or not, they had better quit releasing his private information to the media or he would sue them.

A few moments after his irate phone call, Ty left Ben to work out the next search area and went to the front of the house.

Why did the sheriff release that file?

Ty couldn't believe they'd done that. It was totally incompetent. He looked out the living room window and saw the reporter still in her car, chattering on the phone. He smelled trouble. If she had that report, then others did too. He feared her publication would run an article on them now, tying him and Ben in some grotesque way to the killings. Right now he was worried more about Ben than himself. Ty gritted his teeth, anticipating the firestorm that awaited them. *Here it comes, Part II of* The Crucifixion of Ty Greenwood, *costarring Chief Ben Eagleclaw as Ben Campbell, the friend who happened to be in the right place at the wrong time.* It was only several days to Christmas, so he hoped they'd leave them alone at least that long.

Undersheriff Tom Rice hesitated before phoning his boss, who he knew was in Seattle for a political luncheon at the Westin Hotel.

Sheriff Rick Barkley answered his cell phone. "What?"

"There's a leak in the department. That fella Greenwood, who Carillo's been looking at? He just called and chewed my ass, said some tabloid showed him some of our internal documents, the case file I guess."

Sheriff Rick Barkley cast a glance around his table and realized he couldn't talk. He got up and walked to the edge of the Grand Ballroom. His voice was barely above a whisper. "You saw them?"

"No, but I think I believe him."

Barkley made sure no one, not even the waiters or busboys, was within voice range. "How did they get the fucking case file? Was there anything about those goddamn footprints?"

"I don't know. I doubt it. Unless Mac got pissed and let the cat out of the bag . . ."

Barkley came to Mac's defense. "He wouldn't, not Mac. I reamed him good but he's still a team player. I just don't know what he was doing with that reporter . . ." Barkley trailed off briefly, then reeled it back. "The governor just asked me what was going on. I said we're working the case and he told me his office is getting lots of scared calls. I don't want the media turning this into a big old panic fest. Get Carillo somebody to replace Mac along with whoever and whatever else he wants. Let's hurry up and find this psycho before he does it again or we're gonna be clearin' room for an FBI command center. And find out who leaked that file and rip his nuts off."

55

In less than four hours, Ty's dream of getting through Christmas without hassles evaporated. Three cars and a van congested his parking plaza as a cable news truck rolled up the driveway. The mysterious dispersal of documents from the Snohomish County Sheriff's Department concerning their chief suspect, himself, among other juicy details, plus his apparent teaming with that beloved old Native American actor, was whipping the media into a frenzy. Ty instructed Greta that if she decided to answer the door, she should inform them "Mr. Greenwood is unavailable for comment."

Ty then warned her, "Make sure you don't say anything else, because they'll use your words against you and make up whatever they want," which properly scared her. Ben stepped next to them in the living room window and took in the gathering throng.

"He's right. They're just like wild dogs, they'll eat ya."

A wide-eyed Greta quickly exited, terrified of the role of spokesperson.

"Here's a nutty idea. How about a news conference?" Ty suggested.

Ben looked at him quizzically.

Ty continued, "Tell them we're going to hold a news conference. That'll get them out of here for the time being. Then we'll actually have a news conference and announce what we're doing. Maybe I'll call that cop, see if he'd bring the casting over. That'll be our centerpiece. We'll show it off as evidence."

Ben shook his head. "First off, he didn't wanna work with us. I think he's got ideas of bringing the thing in by himself. Plus, we need a body 'fore anybody'll believe us. What you're talkin' about would hurt us worse than lettin' 'em make stuff up."

Ben patted Ty's shoulder and continued, "And you're the one with something to lose. You gotta family. Now you're hangin' out with some old Indian who went AWOL from his movie. Who knows what kinda hay they'll make offa that."

Ty looked out the window at the reporters milling around. Some were pointing cameras in the windows, but he and Ben stayed back far enough in the living room so they couldn't get a good shot.

"I can take it," Ty grated.

Ben looked him in the eye. "But can your family? You don't wanna make Ronnie a joke in her own company, do you? How 'bout the kids? They go to school and kids can be mean."

Ben's words weighed heavily on Ty, but he rationalized that his end result would exonerate them all. They headed to the office. Ben worried about the toll on Ty. He knew the depth of Ty's commitment and feared that he was betting the farm on it.

"What do you think our chances of finding it are?" Ty asked Ben.

The old man's solemn expression answered him.

Kris's life had officially changed. It was only two weeks since her first reports on the missing men, and in the seven short days since airing her tape of Mac, Kris had become a media darling, seemingly everywhere. The night before, she had ascended to the national news stage when the network had called and had the national anchor throw it to Kris for a live update on "Murder in the Mountains" for the evening news. Since then, everyone from the TV news magazines to the actual tabloids had been either calling or digging into her past. Kris thought of the littered trail behind her. She swelled with pride that there would be no shortage of talking wounded.

Kris had been changing her assignment schedule to fit in interviews for her series as well as something new, interviews of her conducted by other media. The demands on her time, as well as her growing celebrity, were starting to cause problems with the other reporters. Many were finding themselves shuffled over to assignments Kris had dropped at the last minute. But none of them made any formal complaints because rumor had it she was protected by someone big. Many had their suspicions but no one knew for sure. But the fact that Doug Gautier, a highly respected newsman, had gone down in flames battling Kris was all they needed to know.

Mac clicked the TiVo and froze Oprah in midsentence. She was five minutes into a home makeover segment and Mac was bored. Mainly he was stir crazy. In the last two days he'd been to Top Foods five times. It wasn't that he loved grocery shopping so much, but it was a relief from sitting around at home thinking about what he should really be doing. He had driven into the mountains every day for the last three days, and the first day he'd sat in the car unable to get out. He would pull the big Desert Eagle pistol out of its shoulder holster, set in on the seat, and think about his last encounter up here. He wondered what he'd have seen had he turned.

Mac always began these moments with his mantra *if this thing is real, then this gun should kill it.* But the same doubt always snuggled back up to him and squashed his resolve. This doubt was in himself, he was convinced of it. His encounter that day in the woods had left him rattled. On the second day of his one-man search he'd had a hard time just getting out of the car, and when he finally managed it he couldn't venture more than a few hundred yards up the trail. That day he drove home and cleaned his new gun even though he had yet to fire it. *Gotta be ready.*

Mac wandered into the kitchen and opened the fridge. He stared at the contents for more than a minute, not seeing anything. Then the phone rang. Lately the phone had brought nothing but bad news, except on the few occasions when Suzy Chang called to give him covert updates from the department. He had a better phone in the bedroom, with caller ID, but the kitchen phone was a no-frills wall unit.

"Mac Schneider."

"Detective Schneider? Ty Greenwood."

Mac had to admit to himself he wasn't disappointed to hear from Greenwood. But he played it cool. "Yup."

"You and I know this thing is still at work."

Mac said nothing and Ty paused, waiting for a response. He continued, "Ben and I've been out looking for it. I think it's just a matter of time until we find it."

Mac's anger rose because here you had two amateurs, one of them eighty years old, and they were actively looking for it, and he instantly hated himself for not even being able to get out of the car. But he remained silent, partly because he knew what was coming and wanted desperately to resist. Mac needed to buy a moment to think through what his response might be. It rattled him a bit that Ty had managed to find him. That was supposed to be his job.

"How did you get my number?"

Ty sighed. This guy was playing hard to get. "I hired my own detective, who found out all about you. I know you were a cop in L.A. and had some tough times, so you've had your back up against the wall before. I also know you've been released on vacation pending an investigation into what happened with that reporter. You need us as much as we need you."

Mac's neck and face flushed with anger. "My life is none of your goddamn business."

"Now you know how it feels," Ty said calmly. "Anyway, it doesn't matter. We need each other."

Mac's head spun and his emotions overwhelmed his logic. Ty's prying infuriated him, and probably more so, he hated himself for his fears. "I'll think about." He hung up.

Mac was angry that he was angry. He had always been able to keep his emotions in check. Was he cracking up? He thought about calling Ty back but didn't want to appear weak or indecisive. But after a moment he admitted to himself that Ty was right: he did need them.

Ty set down the handset and shrugged. "Guess I'm not the salesman I thought I was."

"You made him mad."

"The hell with him."

Ben ran his hand over his thick, steely gray hair. He almost always tied it into a ponytail with a band woven by one of his grandnieces.

"He's a proud man." He fiddled with the band as he thought. "But maybe we haven't heard the last of Mac Schneider."

"Why's that?"

"I saw it in the man's eyes. He wants to know more than anything."

"Know what?" asked Ty.

"If it's real."

56

Ronnie drove down her road and the news van parked just outside the driveway got her attention. She pulled up the drive and saw nearly a dozen vehicles, including a few television satellite trucks, choking the entrance to her garage. She felt her blood pressure rising. Parking next to the porte cochere, she ran a gamut of reporters' questions as she hustled to the door. Without even removing her coat, she went directly to Ty's office.

Having already seen Ben a number of times, she dispensed with greetings or small talk and summoned Ty into the hall. She wasn't angry, just supreme in her resolve; her husband knew well that mode.

"Go out and make them leave or I will call the police," she promised.

Ty had hoped they would eventually go away, but Ronnie's ultimatum settled it.

"Okay, they're out of here," he said.

Ty left to broom the media riffraff and Ben went to the front of the house and looked outside. *Oh boy,* he said to himself, *I can see it now, "Old movie Indian seeks career advice from Bigfoot."*

* * *

Later that night after Ben left, Ty climbed the stairs to his bedroom. Ronnie was in bed reading. She set her book down as he entered. "What if I quit my job and we moved? Started over," she said.

Ty was surprised. He went into his closet to remove his shoes and shirt. He reappeared a moment later.

"No," he said. "You can't do that. You've worked too hard."

She sat forward, serious, pained. "I've worked even harder to keep this family together and I won't see it fall apart."

Ty sat on the bed and put his hand on hers. "You and the kids are everything to me."

"Prove it. Give this up and let's go," she said with hope. "We'll sell this place, take a loss if we have to. We're set for life, Ty, we don't need to do *anything.*"

Ronnie touched his cheek with her hand, her earthy eyes mirroring love, hurt, and fear.

"Honey?" she said softly. "We could do that. We could. Just say the word."

It was tempting to Ty. Ronnie and their two beautiful kids were all he really needed. Or were they? He kept coming back to the terms under which he held these things that were so dear to him. If the terms weren't right, then nothing was right.

Ty kissed his wife lightly on the lips and got up. "It's a big decision. I'll think about it."

Ronnie sat back, realizing Ty was stalling. *Tough love.* "Don't wait too long," she warned. "We're running out of time."

Ty heard her words as he went around the corner to shower.

Dave Christie was lulled by the chatter of a late-night radio talk show as he motored down McSwain Road, a dark lane high on the mountainous side of Snohomish County. Dave was a mechanical engineer who enjoyed his job in Woodinville as a designer of air-conditioning systems for office buildings. He had also just enjoyed five beers with his fellow engineers after a hard day of calculating cubic air volumes and BTUs. Thus hammered, he was the last person wanting to report a car accident.

So when his headlights illuminated something big walking out of the trees and onto the roadway, Dave's brain froze momentarily. Whatever it was crossed the road in two steps. When it turned toward him, his lights kicked back two shining rubies. Torn between the brakes, the gas, and sawing the wheel, Dave finally mashed the brakes and slid his Camry into the shallow ditch, where it kissed a tree, lightly crunching the front end. But Dave wasn't worried about the car right now. That thing, that shape, had vanished into the black thicket on the opposite side of the road. But it was nearby, that was for sure.

Despite the refuge of his leather-lined import that was actually made in America, the animated political babble issuing from his speakers, and the heater whooshing, Dave didn't feel too safe. If that thing wanted to get him, by the looks of it, it would have no problem.

Dave jammed the transmission into reverse, said a microsecond prayer to the gods of traction, and stepped on the gas. All he got was whining from his tires about the mud they were in. The car didn't move. He gave it more gas and whipped the wheel. After a few agonizing seconds at full throttle, the Camry slowly skipped and spun itself back onto the roadway. It was as he put the shift into *D* that he was most afraid. He visualized the thing crashing through his window and grabbing him. Flooring the accelerator again, he plowed two ruts before his rubber bit down and launched him.

Dave had always considered them just a quaint forest legend, but in the last twenty seconds that had changed. He remembered stories of shy, maybe even kindly creatures, but this one sure didn't look like that. No, not hardly.

57

From inside their shelter, the four rottweilers heard a sound far off in the woods. To a human ear it was at an impossible distance, but to the dogs the sound was crystal clear. With the snap of a twig, Queenie, the alpha dog, sprang to her feet and began a chorus of barking.

Their master, Carlin Arial, a very successful fifty-four-year-old artist, was crafting an oil painting in his studio a hundred feet behind his sprawling home. As much as he loved his dogs, they drove him crazy every time a squirrel farted. He looked at his canvas and decided he had too much of a mauve thing going and reached to his palette for a blob of ivory.

As Queenie continued to lead the cry with her hacking bark, she suddenly felt a shadow over her. All animals have an instinctive fear of being spirited away from above that has been genetically passed down from prehistoric times when huge, soaring raptors had the power to carry off even relatively large animals. But Queenie didn't see a shadow, she felt it. And she fell quiet. Her cohorts followed suit, also feeling the dark presence.

The dogs sensed that whatever was coming their way was neither deer nor human. Its fearsome size became apparent from the delicate vibration in their rubbery foot pads, and that's what actually shut them up. Their natural reverence for unequivocal superiority, a reverence with which Mother Nature imbues all animals, was a device for self-preservation. The dogs heard and felt it, then humbled themselves, huddling together, heads bowed. In the distance they could see their master through the studio windows but there was nothing they could do for him.

Carlin looked up when the barking abruptly ended, but the large windows that opened into empty darkness revealed nothing. Setting down his brush, he went to the door. Just as he was about to open it, his wife, Joyce, buzzed on the intercom.

"Honey, how late do you plan on working?" she asked.

He crossed to the makeshift system he had installed to communicate with the main house.

"I'll be a while," he replied. "Go ahead and go to bed. I'll be in later."

"Okay," she said, then added, "Are the dogs all right? They were barking."

"They're always barking. I'll check. 'Night."

Carlin Arial walked back to the carved mahogany door, and just as he was about to open it, he felt a strange premonition. He ignored the feeling and pulled the door open. The massive shock caused such a toxic rush of stress-induced catecholamines that his heart literally stopped.

As he climbed into the mountains with the limp cargo under his arm, he thought of the dogs. He felt the small two-legs used dogs to warn them. They relied on the dogs but twice now dogs had failed to save their small two-leg masters from him. This showed him that all animals saved their own lives first.

In the hills above the last wood cave, he stopped to eat. The small two-leg from the wood cave with the many warm ice openings was dead. It had died without his having to even touch it. He had never seen an animal simply die. As he ate, he thought of the old one his mind had seen at the creek. He had felt the old one that time and looked around, thinking he was there, daring to stand in his shadow. But he was not there.

He knew the old one was searching for him, sending out his mind voice to seek his. When he felt him, he did not allow his mind voice to an-

swer. He had felt the others too, but they did not have the clear mind voice like the old one.

While he ate, he thought of how he had defied the charging hardshell, knowing its small two-leg master's fear caused it to fall from the black trail. He had almost reached into the hardshell to pull out the small two-leg, but felt something was wrong with it, some sort of slowing or disturbance of its thoughts. As he walked away, the hardshell had fled in fear.

His forays into the flat lands of the small two-legs were increasing. He had no fear of them but was cautious not to go among too many. He knew they feared him and possessed the thunder. He respected the thunder for it might hurt him.

Saving what was left of the small two-leg for later, he buried the bones and continued upward.

At four fifteen that morning the police got a call from a woman in the far northeast corner of the City of Snohomish frantically wailing to the operator that her husband had been in his artist's studio and was now missing. The operator asked if there were any signs of foul play. The hysterical woman said no, but it just wasn't like her husband to disappear in the middle of the night.

The police operator resisted for nearly ten minutes, not wanting to waste a patrol car on a husband who probably just went for an early morning nature walk, but ultimately she relented, based entirely upon the emotional outpouring from the wife. She agreed to send a car to investigate but added, "Should he reappear before the unit gets there, ma'am, call us immediately."

Joyce Arial turned on all the lights around their large home, giving it the appearance of a grand opening, then wandered from window to window, looking into the forest. Her husband wasn't some kooky eccentric. He was a well-known and respected artist and she knew he was in trouble.

Nearly two hours later two City of Snohomish police officers arrived and found no evidence of foul play, other than the open door to the studio. They took down the info, comforted the wife, and left.

In the patrol car one of the cops turned to the other. "Think this has anything to do with those other disappearances?"

"I doubt it," the other cop said. "This guy took a hike, looks to me.

She said the dogs quit barking before she last talked to him. If there was an intruder, the dogs woulda went nuts."

"Yeah, you're right," said the cop, closing his notepad.

If the two officers didn't think much of the Carlin Arial disappearance, the Snohomish Sheriff's Department certainly did. By nine a.m. Carillo, three deputies, and two forensic techs were on scene, dusting for prints, taking pictures, and performing a full investigation, presuming that this was another possible homicide.

Since the heat had been turned up a few days before by Rice and Barkley, Carillo had put a tail on Ty Greenwood. So far he was spending a lot of time in the mountains in the company of a tall, old Indian. When Carillo found out it was Chief Ben Eagleclaw, the movie actor, he was puzzled. The chief had always been a favorite of Carillo's and now he was running around with the guy who probably had something to do with these crimes. Carillo's current theory was that Greenwood was paying someone to kill people and leave the fake tracks. The problem was they had really only found four or five distinct tracks and at only two of the scenes. That was it. Carillo tried to imagine why Greenwood wouldn't leave clearer tracks when he or his henchman struck. It just didn't make sense.

Carillo didn't have all the answers about Ty Greenwood but he was working on them. Even though his head told him Greenwood might not be the one, Carillo's emotions told him he was. Since gut feelings had worked for Mac Schneider so many times, Carillo decided this time he was going to follow his own. If that traitor Schneider could make instincts work, so could Karl Carillo. In a way he felt liberated. He was now in charge of this case and knew that a bust could bump him a lot closer to a promotion. But he also understood there was a clock ticking, and if more people turned up missing, he'd lose control of the case. Carillo needed to come up with the best suspect as soon as possible and find a way to pin the connection. So far Tyler Greenwood was it.

58

Three days before Christmas Eve, Ronnie sat in a meeting to discuss the big rollout of a new version of her company's wildly successful office software suite scheduled for the day after New Year's. She heard none of the discourse. Her mind was on her own high-risk venture, one designed to save her family. It was during that meeting that she settled on her plan. Now she just needed to summon the courage to follow through on it.

High in the mountains, just before noon, Ty and Ben pulled off the road in Ty's Suburban. The two men got out and went to the back to get their gear. Neither noticed the sedan pull slowly past, then park fifteen yards ahead of them. Ty opened the side-by-side rear doors and handed Ben the lighter of the two packs, then opened the case containing the tranquilizer rifle.

"You ever shot that thing?" Ben asked.

"No. But they guaranteed it would work," answered Ty.

"I haven't shot this either, but it's guaranteed to get someone's attention."

Ty and Ben turned to see Mac standing nearby, his sizable pistol in hand.

Ben was not surprised to see Mac. "I seen one o' them on a movie once. Big gun."

Mac and Ty regarded each other for a moment. Ty wasn't convinced of the man's motives. "How did you find us?"

"I'm a detective. I've been following you guys since you left your house. You also had an unmarked tail but I think they must have gotten a code three because they broke off a few miles back. I hope you two are better in the woods than on the streets. Otherwise this thing'll be on us before we know it."

"Us?" asked Ty.

Ben jumped in. "I'll take three against one any day. Plus he's got that big ol' gun."

Mac looked to Ty and slowly held out his hand. "How 'bout it?"

Ty looked into Mac's eyes to find the truth. "You really want to work with us to find this thing? You ready for that?"

Mac nodded. "Yes."

Ty lifted his arm and their hands clasped. "All right. Welcome aboard," said Ty. "Now let's go find this motherfucker."

An hour into their steep trek into the mountains, Ty and Mac could see it was exacting its toll on Ben. His breathing became more like gulps and his feet weren't as steady in overcoming obstacles on the trail. Ben was experiencing slight heart arrhythmia, so he spotted a log and sat.

"You okay?" Mac asked.

Ben nodded, wheezing to catch his breath. "Give me a minute. I'm fine."

Ty noticed the color had washed from Ben's normally ruddy face, the opposite of what one would expect from hard exertion. He gave a concerned nod to the old man. "Let's go back."

"I'm okay, really," Ben objected. "Just need a sec. Then I'll be whippin' you young pups, no problem."

Nor was Ben's pallor lost on Mac. "Ty's right. We can come back tomorrow. Or wait until right after Christmas."

Mac studied his map. He had a feeling Skip the biker had come this way and he wanted to search the top but didn't think it was wise to push their fragile companion. "Yeah, we'll come back," he said. "I'm not so sure this is the right trail anyway."

Ben knew they were protecting him, but at that moment he just wanted to crawl into his bed in the hotel. He was now feeling the sixty-odd years of cigarettes more than ever before. Ben had often worried about his heart, but despite his smoking—which his doctor always got after him over—his doc told him he was in pretty good shape. When Ben was home he would try to get up into the nearby mountains of the coastal range for a hike. He could easily hike five or six miles but those trails weren't as steep as this one. He swallowed his pride and erred on the side of common sense.

"Okay, let's go back," Ben agreed.

When her desk phone buzzed, Kris knew by the sound of the ring it was an internal call. She answered brusquely, "What?"

"Hi, it's Brenda at reception. It's the guy who says he has information on your story."

Kris looked at her watch. It was 7:10 p.m. "That same guy?"

"Yeah," answered Brenda.

"I'll be down in a minute."

She normally would have blown off anyone who came by unannounced, but this man was persistent, having already called and dropped by a number of times. Maybe he really had something. But as she approached him in the lobby, she had doubts. He was unshaven and dressed in threadbare clothing. As Kris got closer, she spotted a tattoo on his wrist. She hated tattoos. Nevertheless, she extended her hand.

"Mr. Watts? Hi, Kris Walker."

J. D. stood and his mouth dropped open. She was amazingly pretty in person. "Uh, I, uh . . . I wanted to, I mean I . . ."

Kris pointed to a glassed-in conference room at the edge of the lobby. "Let's go in there."

He followed and she closed the door. "So," she said, "what information do you have on the murders?"

"I, uh, I think I know who did it."

Kris leaned against the corner of the long table and folded her arms expectantly. J. D. had hoped for more of a buildup, given the incredible nature of what he was about to tell her, but he'd take what he could get. He was just having a problem getting past how beautiful she was. He wasn't used to women who looked like that. She almost didn't look real. On top of her looks she was so healthy and well groomed, compared to most of the women he knew, who were pretty much heavy abusers of drugs, alcohol, cigarettes, and junk food. He figured someone this pretty must be nice and very smart. Though he hadn't smoked any dope since that morning, he just couldn't seem to get his brain in gear, so he just jumped in.

"Bigfoot did it," he blurted.

Kris kept her eyes on his but said nothing. Her intent silence and lack of reaction prompted him to continue.

"Uh, I was up in the mountains with, uh, some other guys and, uh, this big fuckin', 'scuse me, I mean this big old thing jumped out and just grabbed 'em. I think it must be the one who's doin' all these murders."

Kris narrowed her eyes and just stared at him, and J. D. for the life of him could not figure out what she was thinking. Sure, his story was pretty crazy, but unlike most stories J. D. had told in his life, this one was true.

"How big was he?" she finally asked.

"I swear to God he musta been, I dunno, ten, twelve feet or somethin'. He was bigger'n any bear I ever saw, by a long shot."

Kris seemed to hang on every word. "Did he have really big feet?"

The question stopped J. D. for a second. "Uh, yeah, I'd guess they musta been huge too."

"Wow. That's Bigfoot, all right." Kris held up her finger for him to stay put and stepped toward the door. "This is big. I need to get a notepad and quickly alert some people about this. Would you wait a minute?"

"Uh, yeah, sure," said J. D. That was enough to relax him. He was thrilled she got it so fast. He'd been terrified she wouldn't take him seriously. He was so relieved, he even rifled through his jacket hoping he could find a roach to spark up, if only for one quick toke.

Kris stepped over to a magazine-covered reception table and picked up the house phone. Pausing for a moment to recall the number, she punched in the digits. She got Mac's voice mail.

"Real funny. Your little plan to get back at me just backfired. Let's see how you and your buddy like this, asshole."

She hung up and walked to the receptionist. "Call the police," she said calmly. "That guy just threatened to kill me. Make it fast. Before he leaves."

As Brenda dialed 911, Kris pretended to look around for a notepad. She made eye contact with J. D. and nodded to indicate she would be right back. He smiled stupidly.

"Don't let him leave," she warned Brenda.

Kris walked to the side of the lobby and used her keycard to enter the secure, employees-only area. Kris delighted in how she had so decisively turned the tables on Mac and his coconspirator. This Watts guy didn't look like he was an actual friend of Mac's, so Kris surmised Mac was extracting a favor from some miscreant for some sort of leniency. But it didn't matter now. J. D. Watts had made enough phone calls and visits to lay the groundwork for his looking like a stalker. No one would question Kris's version of the story, which she would soon tearfully relate to the police, about how this dangerous nut made a sexual advance and threatened her with a death most foul when she rejected him. It was perfect.

59

At the entrance to his driveway, Ty stopped the Suburban at the large cyclone fence he had ordered erected to block all traffic. It was manned by two private security guards.

"Checkpoint Charlie," Ty said to Ben.

Despite—or because of—the fence and guards, there were even more newshounds lining the road than the day before. Their flashes were popping, but Ty didn't give them a chance to take a good picture as he wheeled past his men, with Mac following in his car.

Mac was impressed by Ty's security measures. The fence and guards had not been there that morning. As they walked into the house, Mac remarked, "Man, you act quickly."

"All it takes is pesos," said Ty.

After dinner they looked over the map in Ty's office and plotted in red pen the path they had explored that day. Ty logged onto his computer to check his Web site and waded through a bunch of e-mails. They were useless, save for one from a local, ConspirAC, who had zealously been following all the events. ConspirAC mentioned the abrupt disappearance of the noted artist Carlin Arial. ConspirAC, also an ardent monitor of his multiple police scanners, passed on some helpful information, like Arial's address, and his theory that the sheriff's department might be tailing Ty.

"Check this out," Ty said.

The others gathered around the computer as Ty punched Arial's address into a map site.

"That's nearby," Mac said.

"Damn near my neighborhood."

"Ben, you get any more bad dreams last night?" Mac asked him.

Ty began searching the Web for news stories on the artist.

The old Indian shook his head. "Nope. Slept in the lobby, though. Think the staff's beginnin' to wonder."

Mac patted Ben's back. *No wonder he looks so tired.*

Ty got some hits and clicked on one. "Look at this. The dogs. See? His wife said the dogs didn't bark. Mac, didn't that old couple have dogs too?"

"Yeah, but the closest neighbors were too far away to hear any barking."

"They didn't bark," stated Ben. "If it was Oh-Mah, the dogs didn't bark."

"I read that," said Mac. "Supposedly dogs don't bark, the forest falls silent. Is that true?"

"It's true," said Ben. "That's why Oh-Mah is Boss of the Woods. All animals know it. You ever see a squirrel and a bird eatin' together? Birds and squirrels, they're sorta on the same level, they can break bread, no problem. But send a dog in and they both run. The instinct is to fear what can kill you. With Oh-Mah, the animals get quiet 'cause instinct tells 'em so. If you're a forest animal, Oh-Mah may not eat you that day . . . but he could."

Ty began, "Then why don't people—"

Ben stood suddenly, raising his hand and cutting him off.

Ben quickly walked out the French doors into the backyard. Mac and Ty fell in behind. Ben walked to the pool's edge and stopped. His head moved back and forth as if scanning with his eyes, but it was his mind that was searching. The others stepped behind him.

"Ben, what—," started Mac. Ben shushed him.

The three just stood there—two of them, eyes wide open, the other, eyes shut—saying nothing for several minutes. Ty and Mac felt the cold creeping through their light clothing. Ben stood motionless, unaffected. Another few minutes passed.

"He's here," Ben whispered softly, "watchin' us."

Ty and Mac looked at each other. The image brought a chill to both.

"Where?" whispered Mac after a few moments.

Ben shook his head and turned, speaking in his normal voice, "He's gone."

As the old Indian walked back to the warmth of the house, Mac and Ty exchanged another look, this time wondering whether their old friend was drawing on acting skills or if he had really sensed the thing. Maybe Ben's imagination had him truly believing in what he just experienced. Nevertheless, they shrugged it off as an exciting, if not completely rewarding moment and went back inside.

The old one had been searching for him, and except for the time at the creek and this brief time, he had not allowed the old one's mind voice to find his. But he was too close to stop it.

He watched the three go back into the big wood cave, the biggest he had seen. The idea of rushing in on them flashed through his mind, but the size of the wood cave and the many small two-legs he sensed, both on the other side of the big wood cave and inside it, stopped him. He needed time to look it over, time to see inside the big wood cave. And most important, he needed to come when they did not know he was there. The cave seemed to have many hiding places and ways out. If he made his move now, they might escape.

He needed to plan. So he just watched them. This time.

In Ty's office, the three men discussed the incident. A knock at the door caused them to jump. Ronnie leaned in. Though harried, she still smiled at Ben and Mac, then turned to Ty. "Hi."

Ty looked impatiently at his wife. "Hi. What's up?"

Ronnie motioned toward the hallway. "Can we talk?"

Ty got up and followed her. After they left the room, Mac shook his head. "The worst three words a woman can say to a man. 'Can we talk?'"

Ben smiled. "You have women problems?"

Mac thought about his answer for a moment. "No, not really."

"I heard you talkin' on that reporter's story. She had you sayin' there was a serial killer and all. You said she doctored up a tape she made?"

"Yeah, she took the tape, which she made secretly, by the way, and then edited it to make me say whatever she wanted. I told her the whole truth and she screwed me."

Ben stared at Mac for a moment, trying to decide if the detective was gullible or had just been blindsided. "Man, she really screwed you."

"Yeah." Mac shrugged. "Literally too."

Ben raised his eyebrows and made a face of mock seriousness. "I see."

"So I kinda dropped my guard."

Ben nodded. "I would say so."

They caught each other's eyes briefly, then laughed.

"She's a looker," remarked Ben.

"Yes, she sure is."

They laughed again.

60

Ronnie wanted privacy, so they went upstairs to their bedroom. Ty knew whatever she had to say was big, but he decided not to prepare an argument in advance. He'd just play it by ear. Ronnie closed the door to the bedroom, which Ty took as a bad sign. She folded her arms, which he interpreted as a second bad sign.

"I love you," she started. "You know that."

Yet another bad sign. Ty leaned on one of the dressers.

"I love you too," he answered with some wariness.

The normally soft, pretty features of her face were strained into flat planes and lines that hadn't been there a month ago when this all started.

"We need to make a change. We went through this before for nearly a year and I can't do it again. If you won't get help, I have to take a step."

Ty braced for impact.

"I want you to move out," she said, then added, "for a while at least."

Ty didn't believe the actual words, yet the message was what he had been expecting for some time. He just felt numb. He knew he should fall at her feet and beg her to stay.

"When?" he asked coolly.

Ronnie almost broke down over his quiet, unruffled response. *When? When? That's all you can say? Like you're asking what time lunch is?* She reminded herself he was ill. He was not the man she married, he was a pod person. The real Ty had been stolen in the night like in *Invasion of the Body Snatchers.*

"Now. Tonight," she said, reining in her desire to cry. *Two can play this game.*

"It's Christmas Eve tomorrow. The kids . . . ," he said weakly.

"Don't bring them into this," she cautioned, standing her ground. "You give this up, right now, tell your friends it's over, and we're okay."

Ronnie saw the hurt on Ty's face. She knew how precious being around his family at Christmas was to him. But Tyler James Greenwood was a stubborn son of a bitch, and when he had a goal, he pursued it, no matter what the consequences. He had been that way all his life.

Ty turned to his closet. "I'll get a few things."

Ronnie put her hand to her mouth as the tears welled. She'd made her big ultimatum and he'd called her bluff. But she knew he would. And for the first time since this all began three years ago, she realized what it really meant to him.

Ty reappeared in the office about fifteen minutes later, carrying an overnight bag. Ben and Mac guessed the significance. Ty swept the room with a hand gesture.

"Get the maps, the files . . . I'll be right back."

Mac and Ben started gathering their command post.

Ty walked down the hall to the TV room. The kids didn't need to know anything other than he was "leaving for a little while." Meredith was too young to remember the past, but Chris would certainly recall his father's absence and realize it might be happening again. Ty held it together with all his strength, not allowing his emotions a millimeter of leeway, for if he did, he'd fall to pieces.

The clock was ticking. Her throwing him out two days before Christmas told him he had little time before the rules would change for good. If he stopped this madness, it all ended and they would be back together. But he couldn't just yet. Ty muted the TV and the kids looked up.

* * *

With Ben in his rental car and Mac in his department-issued Malibu, Ty took up the rear in his Suburban. They moved down the driveway and the guards let them through the gate. Ty stopped outside, rolled down his window, and summoned one of the many media hounds.

"We're moving down to Bellevue, the Red Lion," he said. "Tell everyone the show's over and to leave my family alone."

The reporter ignored Ty's request to alert the others, but as soon as he jumped in his car to follow, the rest quickly followed suit, pulling the zoo away from the house and attaching it to Ty, Mac, and Ben's caravan.

61

The midmorning din of the newsroom was so distracting Kris gathered the files she was studying and went outside to the deck on the third floor. Reserved for summertime employee and client get-togethers, it was now damp from the morning rain, the glass tables collecting puddles. Kris lit a cigarette, shook the water off a plastic deck chair, and sat down, her overcoat protecting her from residual wetness. The top of the Space Needle, two blocks away and six hundred feet above her, was barely visible through a misty shroud.

She smiled at the vision of the Seattle police spiriting J. D. Watts away the day before. The officers were particularly motivated by Kris's spectacular rendition of what had transpired. She had no problem lying about the encounter if it meant Watts would pay dearly for trying to pull a very bad joke on her. She was angry that Mac Schneider would have gone to such lengths to perpetrate such an idiotic prank to get back at her. And for his trouble, Mac's friend the Tattoo Man would now do a serious stretch in prison. No big surprise, turned out the guy was on parole, so he'd be out of society for quite some time.

She opened the file on the mountain biker. She had been pleased with the mileage she got out of the interviews with Skip's girlfriend, Nikki, what with their impending engagement and Skip's ascendancy in the mountain biking world. But then, in an embarrassment of riches, fortune presented Kris with yet another victim with a marketable story, a well-known Northwest artist who had gone missing in the last twenty-four hours.

Kris juggled the files on the artist and the biker. While the artist was perfect for a story, his world was very well insulated and gaining access to his wife was proving difficult. Carlin Arial must also have had friends in high places, because the police weren't releasing his address and she couldn't find it through any of her sources. On the other hand, the mountain biker had been on the verge of entering the biggest event of his career on this very day, Christmas Eve, and Kris seized on that as a hook for tonight's story.

She visualized the potential theater of doing her piece live from the place he'd disappeared, a gloomy, dank forest. It would make a sorrowful—and brilliant—contrast to what would have been the glory of a world-class, nationally televised competition, "the race of Skip Caldwell's life . . . one he was destined to never finish." *It's inspired.*

The overnights had given her a sizable lead over all the other stations in her quarter-hour time slot. And as each report got more sensational, those numbers were actually building. Kris knew this was the stuff that got you to Fox or CNN, or better yet, one of the broadcast networks.

Kris pulled out another file marked "Tyler Greenwood." She looked through it and brainstormed an angle. There was a five-year-old photo of Greenwood at a software convention. She thought he was a very handsome guy—*not your typical software geek.* She had thought Mac had thrown in his name to confuse her, but apparently he really was a primary suspect in the case. On top of that, Greenwood said Bigfoot chased him in Idaho. But he wasn't your regular nut; this guy had made millions in software. Mac had said he didn't think Greenwood did it and she now believed him.

She toyed with the idea of using some of the unused part of Mac's tape to bolster an interview with Greenwood, but there were two potential problems: Greenwood probably wouldn't allow an interview and Bigfoot could absolutely kill her credibility. Then a thought crept in that the interview could be done as a companion piece, almost as comic relief to her main series. But she had to be careful, particularly about the Bigfoot element. She had to meet with Greenwood. But how? Then she reminded herself. *When Kris Walker wants something, she gets it.*

62

Ty was preparing to spend his second night at the Red Lion, two doors down from Ben. As they planned their next move, Mac and Ben observed that Ty seemed to take his banishment well, not exactly upbeat but certainly not as depressed as he should be considering the circumstances. Ty admitted to Ben he had been using OxyContin, but he swore he was off it. Ben watched Ty furiously hammering the keyboard of his laptop and thought if there was ever a time Ty needed the stuff, it was probably now.

Mac looked at his watch. It was almost five thirty. "You guys hungry? Why don't we get an early dinner. Or we could just knock off for the day, get some rest, regroup tomorrow. Unless you want to wait till the day after Christmas."

Now that he had been tossed out of his house, Christmas was just another day for Ty.

"No, if it's all right with you, let's keep at it," he said. "But I am up for some dinner."

Ben slowly pulled himself out of the chair. "You two eat. I'm gonna rest a little."

As soon as Ben left, Mac turned to Ty. "You think he's okay? I mean he looked like he was about to code up there on the trail."

"Yeah, I agree," said Ty. "He's not going in the field anymore. If he wants to point us in a direction, fine, but we can handle it without him."

Despite their past conflicts and the fact they had only had that day to get to know each other, Mac already deeply respected Ty's brains, humor, and perhaps most of all, his humanity. In that short time Ty had impressed him as a man of great character, regardless of the torment he was in.

"You okay?" he asked.

Ty looked away, shuffled some files, and stacked them on the round dining table.

"I'm fine. We need to go back to that trail, the one Ben and I gave up on the other day. If the guy at the bike store says the trail continues, then it may be up there. Like Ben said, it likes mountaintops, difficult access. We need to check it out. I'd say tomorrow. We'll give Ben Christmas day off. Let's go eat."

Mac opened the door to the hallway. "Sounds like a plan."

Down the corridor in the television room, Greta heard voices that weren't issuing from a program. She wandered past the kitchen and overheard Ronnie talking to the kids.

". . . so he'll be gone for just a little while, but he still loves you both very much. We both do," said Ronnie. "We'll have a big Christmas sometime after the first of the year."

Little Meredith seemed confused. "So how come Daddy isn't here anymore?"

"Because . . . ," Ronnie began, then ran out of words. She really didn't know how to explain it to herself, let alone to her children.

"Dad has to go away and figure some stuff out," Christopher said to his sister. "But he'll be back soon," he added, then looked to his mother for confirmation. "Won't he?"

"Yes, of course he'll be back, soon," Ronnie answered, knowing Chris was aware of what was going on. At nine he was pretty damn smart. Just like his father.

Greta came around the corner. "Hey."

Ronnie looked up. "Greta, listen, I'm going to run an errand. Can you take over for a bit? When I get back, you can take my Lexus and drive over to Everett, maybe see a movie. I think you need to get out of the house."

Greta eyes widened. "Oh yeah, Ronnie, that would be great, thanks."

Kris got back from her afternoon report by six to begin planning the live report on Skip Caldwell for the eleven. After roughing out her copy for the voice-over, Kris went to the production department to assemble the footage and lay in the voice tracks. By ten forty she planned to be in place in the mountains. At five after eleven, the tape she was now assembling would roll, making what they called a doughnut to her live intro and live close.

After her audio dub session, Kris assembled her crew. Jess was an adequate soundman who she was pretty sure had a crush on her. Gwen, her twentyish sorority girl intern from the University of Washington, was along to keep track of everything from paperwork and cables to makeup and hair. Gary was the guy Kris had her eye on, a cute, sandy-haired cameraman only a few years her senior. She told them to meet her on the Eastside at nine.

The phone jarred Ben from a pleasant, dreamless slumber. It was his agent, Jay, wending his way west on Sunset to his home in the Palisades.

"Ben," said Jay, "the production company saw the piece they did on you on *Extra*. What the hell are you doing? Tell me you aren't really chasing some ape around Seattle? Is this Greenwood fella involved in these killings? Are you nuts?" Jay didn't even wait for Ben to respond. "Anyway, they're replacing you on the picture if you're not back the week after Christmas. I had to work my ass off to get them to make that concession, given all this crazy press on you. They're on break now, but they're pissed you lied. So am I. You lied to me."

"Sorry, Jay," Ben said.

Even over all the cellular relays and the twelve hundred miles between them, Jay heard Ben's sincerity and suddenly felt a twinge of remorse for landing so hard on an old man.

"Well, listen, I don't know what you're doing, it's your business. I'll try to run interference with them for a little while if you need more time. Truth is, they have to replace the DP. He's got back problems or something. Anyway, that might buy us a little more time. When are you coming back?"

"I really can't say. I gotta see this through," Ben said.

"Okay, just, uh, just take care, buddy, you hear me?"

"Yeah, I hear you. Thanks."

They hung up and Ben put on his shoes and wandered down to Ty's room. Ty left it cracked in case Ben needed to get in. Ben tapped on the door and Ty shouted for him to enter. Ty was at his computer, the screen glowing with a page from an Internet search engine.

"Find anything?" Ben asked.

"I'm just looking up some stuff on the missing artist. Ronnie and I have one of his pieces in the dining room."

"Maybe we should go up there tomorrow and look around," Ben said.

"Let's break tomorrow. It's Christmas. I've got things to do and so does Mac," Ty said offhandedly.

Ben knew they had planned something without him because they were worried about his condition. He appreciated their compassion but his mission was as important as theirs. Taking the expression "face your fears" literally, Ben knew he couldn't do that in a hotel room in Bellevue, Washington. But right now he was concerned about Ty. The man had accepted being thrown out of his house far too easily.

"You wanna talk about anything?" he asked Ty. "Like yesterday? Movin' out?"

Ty clacked the keyboard, pretending not to hear Ben's question.

Ben persisted. "You know, you got everything you could ever need right there."

Ty knew he couldn't avoid Ben's concern but he didn't want to discuss it.

"Right where?" he said, knowing perfectly well what Ben meant.

"Your home," said Ben.

"I know that," said Ty. "I do."

"Do you? You're like a man playin' the fiddle while the house is burnin'. Your family needs you. Go home and make up, get your family back."

"I'm working on it."

"Are you really?"

"Yes, trust me. Now let's leave the subject."

"Runnin' away won't help," Ben persisted.

"Oh, so that's what I'm doing?" asked Ty, his irritation rising. "Running away?"

"Yup."

There was a very long pause but Ben wouldn't let it go. "They need you."

Ty slammed his palms hard on the desk on either side of his laptop. "I know they goddamn need me! I know! I know! Don't you fucking get it? That's why I'm doing this!"

Ty jumped up fuming. He glared at Ben and walked past him. He kicked the wall. Ben said nothing. After a few moments of hyperventilation, Ty turned back to Ben. "My family is fine. I just need some time, that's all."

"You're kiddin' yourself."

"Oh Christ, Ben, nobody understands, not Ronnie, not even you apparently."

"And what will make it better?" asked Ben. "When you catch this thing? Kill it? That may be harder than we think. We may be lookin' for years. It could hide from us. We could try and get it to come to us, but how would we do that? The point I'm makin' is we may never find it. That's a real good possibility."

Ty paced, frustrated. "Well then, what the hell am I supposed to do?"

"Go home. Mac and I can find it. More or less he and I got nothin' to lose."

"Yeah, right," said Ty. "I just found out you're in deep shit over our little project here. You split from a movie and the producers are pissed. I read they're even talking about suing you. Who's got nothing to lose?"

Ben smiled, impressed Ty had found out. "They're not gonna sue me. Don't believe everything you read. Anyway, I'm tired of actin'. And if I don't figure some way to get outta these bad dreams, I'll probably die of sleep deprivation," he said, punctuating his comment with a slight chuckle to take the curse off, but Ty knew it was no joke.

"Well," Ty added, "on top of all that, you're in no shape to be running around in the mountains. Mac and I are worried about you."

Ben shrugged. "I'll be fine. I'm a tough old Indian. It'll take a helluva lot more than traipsin' around some little hills to get me down."

Not wanting to argue anymore, Ty fell into his chair. His emotions were right on the surface, partly owing to his having to face reality stone-cold sober. He wanted a drink and a handful of pills but struggled to stay strong. He sighed deeply.

"You don't need that," Ben said, reading Ty's craving. "You need the love of your children and your woman next to you in your bed. Don't lose that."

Ty bolted from the chair, once again infuriated that Ben was right. He stalked around the room for a moment, seething at Ben for bringing it up but understanding that Ben was just the stand-in: Ty was really angry at himself. He kicked the trash basket, ricocheting it off the wall. Then he went to the window and stared, seeing only the whirlwind of his thoughts. He took deep, measured breaths to contain his emotions. He wanted Ben to leave but knew Ben wasn't going anywhere.

When Ben felt Ty had calmed a bit, he took something from his pocket. "Here. I want you to have this."

Ty turned slowly to see what Ben wanted to give him. It was an old cigarette lighter, adorned with two enameled bathing beauties in glamour poses, one on each side. Ty approached Ben, disarmed of his rage. He took the lighter. Its kitsch style amused him.

"It's a symbol of addiction," said Ben. "I got it in 'Frisco the day I hit shore comin' back from the South Pacific. I've used it to light 'bout a million cigarettes, I'd guess. It doesn't always light each time, but it's yours."

Ty sank into the chair and examined the worn old firemaker. Looking to Ben, he smiled softly.

"So what's this? Like the tribal elder passing down the amulet of knowledge?"

Ben nodded. "Yup. Just like that."

Ty was tired. He couldn't live in a hotel for long if he was to keep his family together. He knew Ben was right.

"Okay, I'll give it till the first. Then I'll bankroll you and Mac, that is, if you want to continue."

Ben looked hard into Ty's eyes. "I half believe you. You promise you'll quit?"

Ty leaned forward, his voice filled with enthusiasm. "Look, I have a plan. I already put out feelers on the Net looking for sightings, evidence, anything. What I need to do is convince Ronnie. I just need to make it sound rational to her and I think I can do that. We have Mac's foot casting and whatever else we can put together. With all these disappearances, there's bound to be more physical evidence. You found a footprint too, so there's got to be others. Maybe even hair or stool samples. We'll look for a few more days, like I said, through New Year's. If we get nothing, I'll propose to Ronnie that I hire a team to go after this thing. I just need a little more evidence, that's all. If we find something tangible in the next week, I can make the sale."

Ben worried that Ty's plan sounded almost reasonable but depended upon a lot of ifs. He didn't want Ty to make the same mistake he'd made so long ago, only for Ben the obsession had been a movie career, not devils in the forest. He got up and laid a hand on Ty's shoulder.

"I'm goin' to bed, gonna try and read a bit. Your plan's okay, just don't leave it open-ended. Be with your wife and kids for the new year. They're what count. Look at that lighter once in a while and think about an old man who missed out on so much. 'Night, Ty."

"Good night, Ben."

Ben closed the door and Ty replayed his words. Maybe Ben was right. Maybe he was putting unrealistic conditions on dropping the quest. His head started playing the tape *but we're so close, we're so close . . .*

63

e had been traveling awhile, moving through the trees between the wood caves. He was restless and hungry. A dog had raised its voice to him and he had caught and killed it but had not eaten it. Now he moved on, driven by his appetite and the need to bring sorrow to the small two-legs.

Passing the wood caves, he could feel small two-legs inside but none of the sensations drew his attention. He was now associating pleasure with the hunt. With the surplus of prey he could afford to go hungry until he discovered the right victim to torment, then kill, one whose mind voice appealed to him.

About twenty minutes after Ben left, Ty heard a knock at his door. He felt bad about their confrontation and had more to say to the old man. He was sitting at his computer. He yelled to Ben, "C'mon in." He turned and got a surprise.

"You're much better-looking than your picture," said Kris from the doorway, holding up Ty's file.

Ty stood, then froze.

"You probably should invite me in," she said. "I think it's in your best interest."

Her eyes moved over the maps and items strewn about the room. "Bigfoot Central. Cool."

"Why is it in my best interest?"

"Well, I see it going two ways. Scenario one, 'Nutty Bigfoot hunter may be the killer, but he had no comment,' and we know how that would look, or two, 'Wrongly accused software guru—'"

"Former software designer."

"'Wrongly accused former software designer sets the record straight.' If you ask me, I'd go with the latter."

"How did you find me?"

Kris snickered. "You're the hottest story in town. Finding you was easy. Getting you to talk . . . now will that be hard?"

"The press and I aren't so close anymore. Why are you different?"

Ty wasn't thrilled when Kris took off her coat and threw it on the bed. "You're not staying that long," he remarked, putting some edge in his voice.

Kris ignored him and sat on the bed. She smiled expansively. "You need me. You've been arrested for trespassing in the last two weeks, the police have searched your house, you've got some heat on you." Kris leaned back on the bed. "When politicians or televangelists fuck up, what do they do? They go on TV and tell their story . . . or confess. Do you have a story . . . or a need to confess?"

Ty saw her as the worst of the worst. He reached down and grabbed her arm to pull her up. "Okay, that's it. You're outta here."

Kris resisted. "So let me tell your story if you're not guilty."

Ty got her other wrist and pulled her up. "Leave. Now."

As Ty struggled with her, Kris turned the tables on him by suddenly offering no resistance. The result was she fell into his arms. Their faces were inches apart. For a moment Ty forgot why he was trying to throw her out. It was like being offered a ride in a stolen Ferrari: you knew you shouldn't, but it was sure hard getting to the part where you say no.

"Let me help you," she said seductively.

"I don't trust you. At all."

"You should." Kris pulled slightly and he let go of her wrist. She ran her fingertips across his chest. "I want to tell your story. Let people know you're not the wackjob they think you are."

"Nice pitch. It's awfully compelling, but no."

Ty whiffed her perfume and it was subtle . . . intoxicating. Maybe it was just her—

"I think you're innocent, Ty." She ran her hand up his arm.

"How would you know?"

"I can tell. I have really good people instincts."

"I thought I did too," said Ronnie.

Ty and Kris turned to see her in the doorway. Ronnie turned away in disgust.

"Shit," grated Ty and went after her.

Kris took a moment to process what had just happened. She snickered. "Oops."

Ty ran down the hall and caught Ronnie at the elevator.

"Honey, please, it's not what you think."

Ronnie turned to Ty, her eyes fiery. "Oh really?"

"No, my God, no, it's . . . She came over to get a story out of me and I was trying to throw her out—"

"I could see that."

"No, you've gotta listen to me, I—"

The elevator arrived and Ronnie quickly stepped on. Ty tried to follow and Ronnie's hand shot up, palm out. "No! Don't follow me."

The elevator door closed and Ty slumped. After a moment of grief he walked back to his room. Kris had her coat on. "I could call her and tell her it was harmless." She sized Ty up and thought there just might be the slightest chance the guy needed consoling. "Or was it?"

Ty's cold eyes answered her.

"Okay," she said, "I should go. I've got a report at eleven. But I'll call you tomorrow."

Ty walked past her, almost in a stupor. "Tomorrow's Christmas."

"Just another day for working stiffs, right? Later."

She walked out, and Ty marveled at his dumb luck that Ronnie would come over with an olive branch just as the hot reporter was putting the make on him. Ty angrily kicked at the bed and caught the frame instead, stubbing his toe. "Ow, shit!" That made him even madder. He evaluated good targets in the room, then some part of his rational mind told him to calm down. He sat on the edge of the bed, feeling about as broken as he'd felt in a long while.

* * *

He had become less careful because of his familiarity with the terrain and broke the rules more often. The old ones taught that you must cover your presence and move in and out of another's territory without leaving a trace. Feeling his total superiority, he walked boldly, occasionally leaving his tracks where they might be seen, his two-thirds of a ton easily etching the impression of his feet.

He moved close as he passed the wood caves, peering through the warm ice openings, waiting to lock eyes with a small two-leg, its waves of terror his reward. While he was looking into one opening, a female passing by inside saw him and let out a tiny, high-pitched cry. He suddenly felt her sexuality and it made him curious. Small two-legs were similar to him in some ways. He felt a pang of his own sexuality and realized it was something he missed. But the small two-legs were too small, too fragile for his kind of mating. Her second scream brought him back from his thoughts. He responded with a thunderous bellow that shook her small dwelling. Then another small two-leg, a male, probably her mate, entered that part of the cave and met his gaze. The male's fear poured off him like a warm wind, even more than the female's terror, and that is when he made his move.

The sides of their little cave were soft, like a thick wall of branches. It gave easily. As he entered the cave, their pitiful cries, both from their mouths and their minds, made him want to silence them quickly. Their cave was cramped and he had to bend down to fit inside. He struck the male with his open hand and the little body flew through the wall, its life-light snuffed. The female tried to run past him, to go through the hole he had made, but he grabbed her around the neck. Stepping back outside so he could rise to his full height, he held her up to his face, his grip just enough to silence her mouth cries.

This one had only one thought and he could not decipher it immediately. Then he knew what she was thinking. His iron grip clasped her throat, sending blood rushing from her mouth, nose, and ears, and popping her eyes out of their sockets. He dropped the corpse and moved around the wood cave. Through one of the openings he saw a slowly spinning wash of controlled fire on the wall in patterns. He recognized the patterns as the shapes of a deer and a rabbit. Lying next to it in the shadows was the object of the female's last thought, her cub.

It was lying in a small nest. He tore away the wall and pulled the nest closer to him, not wanting to enter the restricted little cave again. The cub awoke and cried. He sensed only the most basic thoughts from it, no fear, just simple anxiety. It was pure and unconfused, unlike its elder small two-legs. This cub had thoughts like other young animals, the sense of fear still undeveloped. He examined it and thought it was much like his own cub—the one the small two-legs had killed with their fire. Leaving the ruined remains of its parents, he held it in the palm of his left hand and moved toward the trees.

64

The drive north to Snohomish County was surprisingly enjoyable for Kris. She liked her new, younger crew. The soundman, Jess, was quite a card, and Gary, the cameraman, it turned out, operated outside the box. Gary even pulled the van into a little grocery on the north side of Monroe to pick up half a case of beer for their "wrap party." Their intern Gwen was a pliable little mouse who exhibited the proper respect for Kris.

High spirits prevailed because it was Christmas Eve and they were doing a remote shoot high in the mountains, far from the prying eyes of the public. After finishing their feed at five minutes after eleven, they planned to spend a little time soaking in the ambience of the woods, as well as celebrating Christmas with a few Buds. Gary and Jess each hoped to get lucky with Kris, or at least open the door for a date. If Kris said no, there was always Gwen, the winsome little coed from the UW, and each had lusty preconceptions of how sorority girls could be. Jess tried to break out the brew before they even arrived, but Kris quickly kiboshed that. Gary figured that rebuke gave him a leg up with Kris.

Kris liked this crew because they didn't bitch about her smoke in their eyes. She gave them points for being afraid to stand up to her. She made brief eye contact with Gary, her glance promising him a chance.

She noticed her message was received as he settled back, happily inhaling her smoke. *It's just too easy,* she smiled.

Bob Hoagland was about to pack it in for the evening. He bid his wife, Janet, good night and had turned out his Christmas lights when he heard something outside his home. Bob and Janet were retired on ten remote acres northeast of the city of Snohomish, and the only sounds they heard at night were raccoons or possums rooting around their trash cans. This was very different, a soft, plaintive crying.

Bob flipped on the light and opened the front door to one of the strangest sights he'd ever beheld. A baby was lying on one of the stones of their walk, several yards from the porch, clad in Disney pajamas. Blinking his eyes in disbelief, Bob looked around the yard, then walked into the cold night air and picked up the whimpering infant.

Janet was in the rec room watching the end of a news magazine show. When Bob walked in, the baby let out a wail that sent her out of her chair. Bob looked at her quizzically.

"It was just there, out on the walk."

Both felt a chill from the utter weirdness of it. Janet walked over to examine the baby.

"Want me to call the police or will you do it?"

Bob whiffed. "Whew, I think it's had an accident."

Janet smelled it too, but after four kids she knew her business. "That's not baby poop."

They both sniffed, trying to identify the strange, foul odor. Then Bob called the police.

After getting lost twice, Gary the cameraman steered the Channel 7 van up a narrow secondary road, the headlights cutting a little tunnel of light through which to crawl. The high energy of the crew had dimmed somewhat at the prospect of not finding the location where they were supposed to broadcast. Kris held her watch close to the instrument panel to read it, then lit a cigarette.

"Stop here," she commanded. "It's ten forty-five."

Gary glanced at her but continued searching for the turnout described by the Snohomish County Sheriff's PIO.

"Look, what difference does it make?" she asked. "It's dark, it's the fucking forest. We're anywhere we say we are. This is it. Stop."

Her three comrades suddenly realized why she was a rising star: she made her own rules. A turnout beckoned at a bend in the road and Gary pulled in. They piled out to set up. Kris looked around and could see no lights from homes. She knew the darkness assured them that the viewing audience would believe they were right next to Skip Caldwell's bike trail. Jess raised the microwave dish, linked their feed with the station, and ran a test.

From the station, a technician's voice crackled over both Jess and Gary's headsets, "Okay, I've got bars, now give me a picture."

Gary hefted the heavy Ikegami HDK-79E hi-def camera to his shoulder, connected it to the battery pack on his belt, then to the base station in the van, then switched on the camera light. Back at the station the bright image of Gwen helping Kris adjust her hair winked onto a bank of standby monitors.

The assistant studio director pressed his talk button. "Okay, we've got you. We've got a grocery store robbery in progress in the Central District, so we'll probably lead with that. Air Seven's en route, so you might get bumped to between seven and ten after. We'll advise."

Gary chopped his light and hit the standby button on his Iki. The enthusiasm of the group returned, now that they were going to meet their deadline. Kris puffed away on a cigarette, bathed in the light from the open van, whose shadows melted into the boundless black void around them. She looked at Gary and took a drag. "Ready?"

Gary gave her a thumbs-up. "Let's knock this out and have a brew."

Gwen liked this crew. They were younger and hipper than some of the others she'd worked with. And Kris Walker wasn't the dragon lady everybody said she was, although on the drive up Kris had blown some smoke in Gwen's face, making her cough. Except for the smoke, Gwen liked Kris.

At five to eleven Mac, skimming through the newspaper, read that Dr. Wade Frazier had not only received a sizable research grant but had been made head of his department. He smiled to himself, now realizing why Frazier had been loath to help him: *would have blown his big grant and even bigger job out of the water.* The phone rang and Mac set the paper aside.

"Schneider," he answered.

"Mac . . ." It was Ben, sounding sleepy and slightly out of breath.

"Ben, what's up? You okay?"

"Just had a dream . . . one of those dreams . . ."

"Yeah," said Mac. "The one where the thing's after two people? That dream?"

"Not that one, another. This sounds strange, but I think you know her."

"Who?" asked Mac, suddenly very curious. "Know who?"

"A blonde. I think it was your reporter. Real pretty."

"Yeah, sounds like her. Why? What did you dream?"

"You got her number?"

"Yeah, but she might not—"

"Warn her. Now."

65

When Kris felt her cell phone vibrating, it was two minutes before she was to go out live to all of Puget Sound. She glanced at the phone's display and recognized Mac's number. She figured he was probably calling to bitch at her for either stabbing him in the back or having his buddy thrown in jail or calling him an asshole on his voice mail. *Guilty as charged.* She shoved the vibrating device deep into her pants pocket and positioned it close to her crotch. She figured Mac was still good for a thrill.

With his eyes nervously on Channel 7's newscast, Mac took a break from phoning Kris and punched in the numbers for the television station. Twice he got a recording that routed him to a voice mail. He got an emergency number but that too went to voice mail. He wracked his brain, trying to decide how far he should go to warn her. Ben had certainly been right a few times, but this was quite a leap of faith.

Mac took a chance and called his own department. He got a rookie operator and told him to find a working emergency number so he could speak to an actual person at the television station, saying it was "pretty important." Had Mac insisted it was a dire emergency, he might have had better luck. The rookie had heard all about Mac Schneider.

He told Mac he'd check it out and promptly forgot after a lengthy domestic violence dispute call moments later.

As Mac waited for the callback, he saw Kris appear on camera, somewhere in the foothills, to report her story on the mountain biker. Ben's premonition had Mac on the edge of his seat, electrified with anxiety, his imagination inventing a giant hairy form crossing the scene from the shadows as she spoke. He didn't need that kind of proof. No, he really didn't want that at all.

Kris ended her poignant piece on the ace mountain biker with "Robbed of his dream, today could have been the highest point in his young life, but here I stand, in the lee of a dark peak somewhere above me, quite likely the last place Skip Caldwell ever saw."

As soon as she finished—"Kris Walker, reporting live from the mountains in Snohomish County, back to you in the studio"—since there were no questions from the anchors, Gary cut his floodlight.

Elevated by the end of a long day and the atmosphere of this coal black nowhere, Jess quickly coiled his audio cables, unhooked Kris's microphone, and reached for the beers.

Gary held up a hand to stay the party. "Leave 'em till we've struck all the gear," he advised. Then to bolster his argument, he added, "We don't need to forget a thousand-dollar lav or something."

Jess abandoned the beer and pitched in stowing equipment. Kris, as usual, stepped aside and lit up. As her crew busied themselves in their pre-party prep, she walked a few steps from the zone of light radiating from the van. There was a cold, light breeze, and though she could hear leaves and needles rustling, she could see nothing but the van and the ground around them.

Kris took rapid, nervous puffs to come down from the high of being on the air, but soon there was something else, another anxiety crawling up her back. It wasn't waning postperformance stress, it was more like apprehension. It was odd, like the vaguest energy, so faint it was hard for her to define. She suddenly had the creeps and wanted to be somewhere else. She stubbed out her cigarette and walked over to the crew.

"Let's go," she said, reaching for the passenger door.

Gary didn't understand her abrupt attitude shift. "Hey, we're done," he encouraged. "Let's have a beer." In the uneven light from the interior of the van, Gary thought Kris's face seemed oddly stricken, but he still pressed her, "C'mon. Let's have one."

"I said let's go," she said, irritated. "I don't want to be here anymore."

Gwen looked at the Stygian curtain around their little cocoon of light and immediately felt what Kris had just felt. "She's right," she said. "Let's hit the road. We can drink on the way."

Jess already had a beer and was two big gulps into it. "Fine with me. Gary's driving."

Gary didn't understand the mood crash. "Look, let's just—"

Gary's words were interrupted by a soft snapping sound close by. They all looked as Kris opened the van's passenger door.

"That's it," she commanded, "let's get the fu—"

Suddenly the damp atmosphere shuddered as an impossibly low animal growl ushered forth from the blackness next to them, freezing them in their shoes. Then that deep bass, guttural sound rose to an impossible amplification, a shredding, metallic animal scream that sent adrenaline pumping into their systems like the spillways at Hoover Dam. They flew into accelerated motion. Gary ran around toward the driver's door and Kris leaped into the open passenger side, while Gwen and Jess swan dived through the portal of the sliding door.

Behind the van, Gary was the first to meet their gigantic antagonist, a dark living tower blocking his path to safety. He screamed in horror and it struck him open-handed, bashing his head against the back end of the vehicle, ejecting a mass of gray matter and vital fluids through the side of his breached cranium.

From the passenger seat Kris reached across and twisted the ignition keys and the engine came to life. She scrambled over the console, not knowing who or what was attacking them but thinking of nothing but escape. A motion caught the corner of her eye and she saw Jess fly out of the middle of the van.

Gwen's continuous scream was so shrill and powerful she went hoarse before finishing. Just as she drew another breath to scream again, Gwen too was whisked from the van. Kris fumbled to get the vehicle in gear and then backed up. As she did, she heard both Jess and Gwen emit bloodcurdling wails of piercing agony. Then a squishing sound ended Jess's cries.

She floored the gas pedal. The van's wheels spun but Kris felt no sensation of movement. She whipsawed the steering wheel and realized the van wasn't moving because their assailants were *holding the van in place.* Gwen's screams quieted to bubbling whimpers, all in the space of a few seconds.

Kris wrenched the steering wheel back and forth with the throttle full out, and the engine strained toward blowing apart. The tires merely buzzed like dull saws cutting dirt and gravel. She still couldn't see the aggressors but suddenly realized it wasn't a group of people. That's when it occurred to her that the attacker might not be human. Mac's words reverberated in her head but she still rejected the idea as too fantastic, too absurd, despite the insane events occurring. Gwen's strained gurgles ended abruptly.

Kris smashed the gas pedal again, raging the engine. Then the van keeled over sideways, crashing onto the driver's side, shattering the side windows on impact. What looked to Kris like a surreal, animated black tree limb knifed down from above. On the end of the appendage was a black, humanlike hand big enough to palm a beach ball. It clutched her roughly and she was pulled out the passenger window, hitting her shoulder and legs as she passed through.

The dead van's lights still threw illumination as Kris now stared eye to eye with a real monster. Alone, her companions having been destroyed in mere seconds, her feet dangling five feet above the ground, she looked with uncontrollable horror into its subhuman, apish face framed by a huge spray of matted hair. Holding her by the back of the neck, it sniffed her, the nostrils on its flat nose flaring slightly, its stinking exhalations sounding like wind in a deep cavern.

As terrified as she was, Kris had a sudden ray of hope that it wasn't going to kill her. If it wanted to, it would have done so by now, she reasoned. Along with her transcendent fear, the scale of this creature and the easy power with which it held her one hundred twenty-two pounds overwhelmed her with a life-draining awe. It snorted and turned. Keeping its grip on her, it picked up something else. Kris saw Gary's lifeless body dangle from the creature's grasp. Then it carried them into the woods.

66

gain and again Mac punched redial and kept getting the recording that the subscriber was out of range. He figured she must be moving because the phone had rung through just two minutes before and now it defaulted to voice mail. He vowed to pester the hell out of her until she answered and confirmed she was safe. He hit redial and this time the phone rang. His heart racing, he closed his eyes and visualized her answering. It rang and rang and rang.

After an interminable fifteen minutes bouncing up over logs and through brush, the giant's hand encircling her slender waist, Kris felt her hopes fade with each mighty step. As the monster climbed farther into the mountains, her stark terror, combined with the bobbing motion, made her nauseous. But she resolved to live, somehow. She heard a sigh from Gary and realized it was just air escaping his lungs. She had caught a glimpse of him by the van and was positive he was dead. The beast had Gary slung under his other arm as if he were carrying a rolled magazine.

They traveled deeper and higher into the forest. Kris had felt the phone vibrating in her pocket since the abduction and tears stung her eyes. She made several tries to retrieve it from her pants but just couldn't get her hand inside the pocket. Then the creature shifted her slightly and she got her hand on the phone and felt it vibrating. She pulled it out and managed to open it just as it went to voice mail. Then she fumbled the phone and nearly dropped it. Terrified of losing it, she clutched the phone as if it were her last hope. And it probably was. Kris never cried, but this seemed like a good time to start. She had to escape. It would be the greatest story ever told—if she lived. That last thought caused her to hiccup and more tears rolled out. She tried to keep silent, but her chest shivered and she sniffed involuntarily, the pain of the beast's vise grip around her midsection almost too much to bear. The jostling up-and-down motion made using the phone impossible, especially in the dark, so she waited, squeezing it tightly, occasionally feeling it vibrate, but fearing she would lose it if she tried to open it.

After a very long while they ascended a mount and the ground leveled. Somewhere off in the impossible distance Kris saw a pinpoint light. She knew it was miles and a valley or two away, but she made up her mind to run for it if she got the chance. Nearly blind in the intense darkness, she heard Gary thud and then the thing lifted her again. She felt it grab her jacket and pull, tearing the fabric. Then her blouse and pants were ripped off. After sniffing her all over, it tore off her panties and tossed her to the ground.

She heard it mangling Gary's body and noticed that the beast's stench had dissipated slightly. It had moved away from her. That's when she took her cue. Phone still in hand, she jumped up and ran, back from where she sensed they had come, to that light so far away. She knew that by catching it off guard, she could lose it in the dark. Naked except for her bra, kneesocks, and shoes, Kris sprinted down the cold mountain. She couldn't see a damn thing, but she convinced herself she would escape. With tears streaking her face, she resolved she would tell her story.

As the small two-leg female fled, he began to eat the dead male. Tearing off the soft, tasteless outer skin, he bit into the still warm flesh, its blood providing a lubricant to wash the meat down his throat. He ripped an arm from the male and gnawed, its tiny bones cracking like twigs under colossal molars.

Crouching, he filled his gut. The female could not go far. She was ready to mate. He could smell her.

Kris raced into the abyss, stumbling over rocks, brush stinging her flesh, but the scratches and nicks were nothing compared to the alternative. In less than ten minutes she reached open ground. Ahead lay a rocky escarpment, its outline barely visible in the dim illumination from the spotty cloud cover. She flipped open her phone and the lighted pad beckoned. Despite her hands shaking terribly, she managed to retrieve the number that had last called her. She punched the button and heard the phone ringing. She looked above her, hoping the beast had abandoned interest in her but still fearful it might be coming for her.

"Hello" came the most welcome voice she had ever heard, Mac's.

"Help! This thing is—"

That's all Mac heard as her cell cut out. "Hello? Hello?" he screamed into the phone.

"—after me! Help me, Mac!" Then she realized she had lost the signal. Two sobs burst forth before she got her emotions in control. She looked around and tried to find a way down the steep mountain in near total darkness. She picked the best line and continued but didn't get far before stumbling, rock knives savaging bare knees.

Picking herself up, she moved on. She managed to get to a run again and tried phoning Mac but tripped on a root or rock and pitched headlong into a boulder, viciously shattering her jaw and reducing most of her front teeth to a mouthful of hard chips floating in saliva and blood.

Taking a moment to regain her bearings, she spat out her wrecked teeth and staggered to her feet. Miraculously she had not let go of the phone. Then it buzzed. Disoriented by the fall and her injury, she fumbled and dropped it, knocking off the battery.

"No! No!" she slurred through her broken jaw and ruined dentition.

She picked up the phone and tried to find the battery. After a long moment she grabbed it and floundered to reinstall it. She pressed redial and prayed for a ring tone. She heard it.

"Kris!" came Mac's voice. "Where are you?"

"I'm in the mountains, I'm . . . I'm . . ."

Her speech was heavy, as if she were speaking with a mouth full of molasses. She sounded drunk. Or hurt.

"It's coming! Your monster! You should have told me!"

"Told you what?"

"That it was real!" she cried and broke down.

Mac's blood ran cold. "Kris, where are you?" he screamed.

Then her voice really frightened him because she sounded so much like a wounded little girl. "Mac, I'm scared! I'm scared!" she whimpered thickly.

Kris looked off into the impossible distance where safety lay and saw that lonely little light, her homing beacon. In that one instant it was so sadly clear to her that Mac couldn't help her. She was also sad because she knew she would never get to that light. But she had to try. For the briefest moment she felt very, very sorry about many things. Sorry because this fleeting phone call was her last chance to touch a fellow human being before whatever fate awaited her. And she was so terribly sorry for not being a better person. She knew she was cruel and had drifted to the side people jokingly called "dark." Like Darth Vader. For the first time in her life she didn't resist the feelings of guilt, didn't try to desperately crush them down before they made her soft. She had crossed the Rubicon a long time ago and once again, in a different way, not too many minutes ago. But if she had any chance at all, her life would hinge on what she, and only she, would do in the next few moments.

Mac yelled into the phone again, "Kris, you've got to tell me where you are!"

He waited for her response and could hear her crying softly. After a long moment he heard her sigh and say, "I'm so—"

"—sorry." Mac didn't hear that last word as her cell cut out.

Kris's phone beeped to indicate a lost signal.

And then she heard it. Coming down the hill, its breath a chuffing steam train somewhere above her, zeroing in as if she were wearing a flashing sign. Her legs went wobbly as dizziness nearly sent her tumbling headfirst onto the rocks. She regained her legs but was instantly disoriented, suddenly unsure whether she should go uphill or down. She turned and ran downhill but immediately fell again, this time backward, tearing a large patch of skin from her bare buttocks. In the fall, her forearm hit something, sending her phone clattering away. Stunned and weathering searing waves of pain, she slid more than ran, her exposed legs and ass bouncing off the rocks as one of her shoes fell off.

Despite her battered state, she gamely continued onward, spurred by the sickening knowledge that her inhuman kidnapper was still after her. She ran two or three steps, then slammed into some razor-edged stone, flaying her calf. Her resolve was almost gone, her reserve of hope nearly empty. The clatter of rocks above her told her the monster was close, but she reasoned that if she couldn't see it, it couldn't see her. She decided to gamble and stopped running, opting to roll into a fetal position and hope it passed her by. She did her best to stifle her rushing breath, her mind flashing on stories of Holocaust victims hiding in attics from the Gestapo, smothering their crying babies to death to keep from being discovered. She felt a stab of remorse that she'd never had much sympathy for them until now.

It was close. A rock rolled nearby and she heard its deep, powerful respiration, then whiffed its sour primate smell. If she could hold out and it gave up, she would walk out of here alive. She was absolutely rigid, moving not an eyelash, despite the shield of blackness. She allowed her eyes to tilt upward, and rimmed by the faint light of the overcast was the treelike beast, standing over her. Suppressing a scream with her remaining life force, she closed her eyes and prayed it would not find her.

It started to step past and for a moment she felt she was home free . . . then came the softest sensation, a bit of hair brushing her shin . . .

And it had found her. Kris screamed as one huge hand thrust down and pinned her. It leaned close, its hot, rancid suspirations assaulting her nose. Then its hands moved down her bare body. That's when she realized it was not going to kill her, just yet, for it had something else in mind.

Kris's terrible suspicion was confirmed seconds later as it spread her legs and its huge, stubby, engorged member jammed into the delicate flesh of her inner thigh, trying to find its mark. Kris suddenly understood, as Russ Tardif had, that there really were things worse than death. It tried again to enter her, and though Kris Walker had never been a screamer, she summoned a wail that challenged the top of her lungs, giving voice to her most profound final wish to provoke a quick end. But it was not to be.

The beast tried to enter her for an exquisitely agonizing few moments. She could feel its rigid animal-thing probing her, but her all-consuming terror had dried up any possible lubrication to help it. Then she felt its hand down there and its giant fingers probing pitilessly to enlarge the opening. She squirmed as best she could, but the beast's other hand held her as if a car rested on her chest. Then the pain shot through her like a white hot blade as it tore at her intimate parts. The blood flow provided enough viscosity to allow it to gain entrance and her eyes snapped wide when it slid its hideous organ home. Kris let fly with another scream that seemed to go out to the cosmos. She screamed and hit at its arms and body. It allowed the feeble onslaught for a few moments, then it put its hand to her throat.

Kris had begged for death to be swift, but now that it was here, the fear of what was next enveloped her. Its hand pressed hard, then the fingertips touched the palm as it encircled her neck. She thought she would black out quickly but it was not quick enough. As her air was cut off, her body began to spasm. She felt her vision going as her tongue lolled out involuntarily. Then, with the crushing pressure on her brain-case increasing, she saw streaks of colored lightning as her eyeballs squirted from their sockets and her optic nerves essentially shorted out. She was aware of her bladder letting go, and her last sensation was of being first in a beautiful green field with blue skies and cotton-ball clouds, and then, as if by a cut in a horror movie, in a hellish wasteland of fire and black skies populated by faceless dark beings.

67

Mac phoned Kris back a dozen times, trying hard to hold off the sense of helplessness and panic that threatened to overpower him. Once he decided he had lost contact, he called the department and told them to dispatch cars to her location, the base of the mountain where Skip Caldwell disappeared. He thought about calling Ty but knew there was nothing he could do. He pulled on some shoes, grabbed his coat, and headed for the carport.

The Channel 7 dispatcher looked at the clock in his office and wondered what the hell had happened to Kris Walker and her crew. He tried them again on the two-way and got no response. Whenever a crew wrapped a story, it was standard procedure for them to call in, but he hadn't heard from Kris's crew since their live feed. It was already one in the morning, but it was common knowledge among dispatchers that cameraman Gary Taggart had been reprimanded for stopping off for beers after late-night assignments when technically the vehicle and all the gear were checked out to him. Station policy not only prohibited drinking when in possession of company property, but the prompt return of the van, with its many hundreds of thousands of dollars of equipment, was imperative. The dispatcher decided to wait a while longer before calling the big guns and putting Gary's ass on the line. He rationalized two reasons: they had gone to the far reaches of Snoho County and it was Christmas Eve. He figured that they had turned off the radio and celebrated a little—both strictly against company policy—and would probably be rolling into the barn any minute now.

At a little after one a.m. Mac's car rolled up to the turnout at the base of Skip's mountain. There were no patrol cars. He picked the Desert Eagle off the seat and racked the slide to chamber a round. He radioed to the station and gave the dispatcher directions to relay to the patrol cars. But even though this was their beat, because of the large area, remoteness, darkness, and organic nature of the roads—not to mention that many of them were not well marked—patrols sometimes got lost. Their GPS systems were only so effective in identifying many of the tiny side roads that sprouted from the main roads like so many spider veins.

At ten minutes to two a patrol car pulled up next to him. Mac threw a fit over his radio because they'd only sent one car and yelled at them to order backup. The confused deputies weren't even sure of what they were responding to, other than they had been told Sheriff's Detective Mac Schneider had reported an abduction.

Mac apologized, then patiently explained to the deputies the details of Kris's panicked call, carefully leaving out who—or rather what—he thought the assailant was. He feared that if he got into that now and hurriedly tried to explain, they would be calling for backup to help bring *him* in and the search effort might come to a screeching halt. The three men grabbed their flashlights and walked up and down the road, shouting for Kris. In his panic to find Kris, Mac did not think to ask the station to check with the phone company which cell relays had been used during her calls with him. This would have told him the general area she was in. He mistakenly assumed the crew had been where they said they were during their newscast. What he didn't know was that Kris and her crew had taken the wrong road and had been halfway around the mountain from where Mac and the deputies searched.

At precisely three a.m. Kip Chalmers, operations manager for Channel 7 and the name at the top of the list of people to alert in an emergency, received a call. Chalmers did not appreciate being roused from a sound sleep on Christmas morning and ordered the dispatcher to call the police. As his head again found the pillow, Chalmers decided the whole crew of that van was in deep shit. After Christmas they'd be fired or written up, he thought, drifting back to sleep.

The dispatcher placed the call to 911 and within ten minutes the desk sergeant at the Snohomish County Sheriff's Department now had another source to corroborate Mac's story. He ordered all cars in the vicinity to look for the van and the crew. The television station gave the sheriff's office the frequency of the van's GPS tracker, but no one could raise the frequency. It was either damaged or too far out of the area.

Several hours passed before a patrol car found the frightful battle scene, a tossed-over vehicle and two slaughtered people. More patrol units arrived, and a bleary-eyed Carillo pulled up to the scene just as the sun rose. The position of the van and the two yellow nylon tarps, hands and feet protruding, woke him up. He approached one of the uniformed cops.

"Whaddya got?"

The young cop looked at his notepad and recited it like a grocery list.

"Two DBs, lots of upper-body trauma including dismemberment. The van was pushed over by unknown assailants, and according to the TV station, there are two additional individuals missing. Merry fuckin' Christmas, huh?"

The van's Channel 7 logo answered one of Carillo's questions. He knew they had lots of employees but hoped the blond witch was under one of the covers. He walked over and knelt by a body, pulling back the fabric. It wasn't her, but a chill ran down his back as he looked into the open, milky eyes of a dead girl, young, probably early twenties. The skin of what had been a pretty face was putty gray, her neck crushed. What struck Carillo was the way it was crushed, with her head turned forty degrees too far, a crust of blood ringing her mouth and nostrils. Livid strangulation marks stood out all over her neck like amorphous tattoos from her throat to below her ears. Carillo had never seen anything like it.

"Christ," he said, throwing the cover back over the poor girl. "What kind of sick fuck would do that?"

"We don't have any idea who or why they did it," said the young cop, standing behind Carillo. "The other one, his neck's broken too and his arm is separated, but not just like a regular separation, but actually off his body. It's still in his sleeve. Really weird. You're right, whoever did this is one seriously fucked-up puppy."

At the edge of the clearing Mac walked out of the woods. Carillo saw him. Mac looked tired. He approached Carillo.

"Find your girlfriend?" asked Carillo.

Mac was in no mood to argue. "No."

"Mac, get the fuck outta here. You look like shit. Let me do my job. I'll find her."

Mac knew that was as close to kind words as Carillo could manage. Mac was dead tired after tromping around the woods all night with various deputies in tow. He nodded his assent to Carillo and headed for his car.

A Channel 7 helicopter buzzed overhead, then drifted down and landed in the middle of the road fifty yards from the crime scene. Several men emerged. Even casually dressed, they looked like executives. One of them, a solemn, crisply manicured man Carillo guessed to be in his late forties, approached.

"Are you in charge here?" he asked.

Carillo nodded and held out his hand. "Detective Karl Carillo, Snohomish County Sheriff. And you are?"

The man shook Carillo's hand. "Lyle Benson, general manager of the station."

He draped an arm over Carillo's shoulder, a gesture from which Carillo normally would have recoiled, but this guy was a big cheese and seemed about to let him in on something. They walked out of voice range of the other police.

"Detective Carillo, something very, very terrible has happened here, and though it is news, it has happened to some of our family. I need your help."

Carillo stopped, indicating his irritation at the familiarity of the man's arm on him. Benson removed his arm.

"What do you want?"

Benson, a soft man in Carillo's eyes, assumed a solid set to his face that surprised Carillo.

"Detective Carillo," said Benson with a quiet intensity, "we want to keep this quiet for a little while, at least until we can ascertain if there is some sort of, shall we say, organized aggression aimed at our station."

"Like a terrorist plot," Carillo summarized.

"To put it bluntly, yes," agreed Benson. "Our reporter who vanished was running a series on the missing people and we are examining any possible links."

That confirmed for Carillo one bit of good news, but he shrugged deferentially. "Look, you're the media, there's not much I can do to stop any of you."

Benson looked down into the reflection off his Italian loafers. "We just need you to hold off any statements to the press or any of your normal contacts, for a few hours, perhaps the rest of today. Most importantly we want to avoid a public panic. Given all the disappearances, and what with the crew doing a report on that very thing, well, I think it would be in both our interests to make a determination of what we have here before making this public. I would advise against using police band radios to transmit critical information. Simply put, this situation requires a blackout. That will probably require you to cordon off the area to all traffic and unauthorized personnel."

Carillo nodded assent. Normally he would have cleared such an action with either the sheriff or the undersheriff, but he had tried them on the way and then remembered they were both skiing with their families for Christmas.

Benson continued, "We have members of an elite private security firm en route to take stock of the situation and advise us. The governor approved our request and I'm merely informing you as a matter of courtesy, as well as in a spirit of collaboration."

"Fine with me. Just don't let your people get in my way," he added, making sure Benson knew who was boss. Benson's plan worked for both of them. The lack of reporters poking around would take the pressure off him to get a handle on the situation. Carillo was still trying to process what had happened to the news crew. He thought of Ty Greenwood and was suddenly at a loss to explain how the man could have pulled this off. His main worry right now was that the FBI would bump him out.

Benson motioned for them to stroll back to the area of activity. "Thank you, Detective, and don't worry about our consultants. They are highly regarded. Their clients include both the FBI and CIA and I've asked them to make their findings known to you as well."

Carillo grunted, "Yeah, okay."

Back in his car, Carillo used his cell phone instead of his radio to call in a preliminary report to the department. Then he called his surveillance team at Ty Greenwood's hotel.

"He's been here all night," said the plainclothes deputy who had sat in the parking lot the whole time. "Something weird, though."

"What's that?" asked Carillo, who thought nothing could top this crime scene for weird.

"Mac Schneider was here, at the hotel. We aren't sure, but he may have been with Greenwood."

That stopped Carillo cold. "What?"

"And this may be even weirder, but that missing reporter, the blonde? She was here last night too. We checked and she asked for Greenwood's room. She was there maybe ten, fifteen minutes, tops."

Carillo was speechless. The deputy waited a moment. "Carillo, you still there?"

Carillo snapped out of it. "Yeah, yeah, I'm here. Okay, I'm on my way over."

68

The night had not been kind to Ty. After the misunderstanding with Ronnie, he stayed up late working, mainly to bury himself in some mind-occupying task rather than think about how he would explain to her what happened. He wondered if she would give him long enough to reason with her, because he was sure she'd feel her eyes provided far more compelling evidence than his testimony. Ty reached for the phone but pulled back. It was not quite eight a.m. and she might be sleeping in. As he stared at the phone, debating whether to call his wife, it rang, almost as if he had commanded it to do so.

"Hello?"

"Ty, Mac." His voice was stressed. "Get Ben, I'm almost there. Something's happened."

"What?"

"Just get Ben." Mac hung up.

Ty dressed quickly and knocked on Ben's door. A moment later Ben answered, dressed but looking sleep-starved.

"More dreams?"

Ben lips were drawn. "Yup. Bad one last night. Called Mac, figured he knew the girl."

"Who? What girl?"

"Mac's TV reporter . . . in my dream. Oh-Mah was there. It was bad."

"Mac's on his way," said Ty, "says something happened."

Ben turned and walked to the window, wanting to shield Ty from the stricken look on his face. He knew what Mac would say. His dream had been too vivid and horrible not to have happened. There was no question in his mind it had been real.

The door was open when a breathless Mac walked in several minutes later. He closed it.

"It killed a news crew."

Ty exhaled, "Oh my God. Where? How many?"

Mac and Ben locked gazes.

"It was her," said Mac.

Ty instantly knew. "Kris Walker."

Mac nodded and Ben's face was full of questions.

Mac's eyes conveyed his agony. "I talked to her. I called her over and over and finally she called back. She was . . ." Mac paused, trying to visualize Kris's ordeal. He shook his head. "It was after her. She said so."

Ty admitted softly, "She was here last night."

Both of his companions looked to him. "She came to get my story. It was probably around eight or so. She wasn't here ten minutes. She kinda came on to me and Ronnie showed up and . . . there was a misunderstanding. You think . . . it . . . got her?"

Mac's head nodded somberly. "Yeah. It was . . . it was after her. It was real bad."

Ty asked, "Where was she?"

"Around the mountain from where I felt it." Mac turned and looked out the window.

"You gonna be okay?" Ben asked.

Mac stood for a moment, took a deep breath to gather himself, then turned back to them. "There's a tail on Ty. I think Carillo is going to come after you. We need to take the back stairs. I'll go out and get my car and drive around back and pick you guys up."

"He's up on that mountain," said Ben.

Mac's eyes had the fire of revenge in them. He pulled back his jacket and displayed the butt of his huge pistol. "Not for long."

Ronnie awoke and rolled over. As her consciousness rose, a feeling of emptiness washed over her. Even on the drive home from Ty's hotel she had had regrets about her reaction to the reporter in Ty's room. Just as she knew Ty would never hurt anyone, despite what the cops and the media were saying, she also knew he would never cheat on her. Her emotions had just gotten the better of her.

She didn't know Kris Walker but what she'd seen of her gave her the impression of someone smart and ruthless. Looking at it from Ty's point of view, she saw how he could be right. She warmed to the idea she'd made a mistake, and she wanted to correct it. She admitted Ty needed help, but more so, right now, she missed him and his children missed him. And it was Christmas Day.

Meredith cuddled against her shoulder and Ronnie nudged an amber lock from the little girl's cheek. Looking at her innocent baby's face, she noticed a thread of drool tracing down from her tiny mouth and Ronnie's eyes filled with tears. She couldn't savor the moment: it only punctuated the mistakes she felt she had recently made.

She softly kissed her daughter's forehead and slid from the bed. Even though it was Christmas, it just didn't seem like it with Ty gone, so Ronnie rationalized the few hours she absolutely needed to spend in her office as okay. After that her plan was to spend Christmas evening with her family, and that would include her husband. She picked up the phone to call Ty, but Christopher was on the line talking to one of his little buddies. She decided to call Ty later, on the way home from the office. Then she'd be clearheaded enough to be firm yet loving.

Later she found her Lexus in the garage, locked, and remembered that Greta had taken it the night before. Contrary to their practice of leaving the keys in their cars, the Lexus's keys were in the house, so rather than walk back, she took Ty's Dodge pickup. Though cumbersome and inelegant, the truck connected her to Ty. As she made her way to Redmond, she resolved to call him when she got home that afternoon. She didn't think it would take any pleading to get him to come home. But if it did, so what? Ty always said she was the strong one.

Before they left the hotel, Mac and Ty had argued with Ben about whether he should try the ascent or wait below, perhaps manning a cell phone back at Mac's car. Ben would have none of it and stubbornly insisted on full participation. With great resolve he told them he needed to be there, on the trail, not waiting for word. The truth was if there was a ghost of a chance they might encounter it, he needed to look the thing in the eye. There was no alternative for him. Ty got angry with him, as a son might with a stubborn father. Mac understood both points of view. He also felt a warmth for Ben, but as a colleague and friend. In the end Ben won.

His activities during the dark time had tired him. First foraging, then killing the mother and father of the small two-leg cub, then killing the four and destroying their hardshell. Unlike most of the other small two-legs he had encountered, that last female had tried first to run, then fight. He wondered if small two-leg females were stronger, at least in instinct. The small two-leg mother had thought of her cub as he killed her, and the other female with the hair like sunlight had run, then fought him to the death. He respected such spirit.

He arranged some cedar boughs under a tree and prepared to sleep. Looking past the top of the tree, he saw dark clouds and smelled rain. His belly full, he made himself comfortable under the tree and closed his eyes.

As sleep stole over him, he thought of the old one, the small two-leg who had been trying to find him. That one had a mind voice that was strong. He heard it even now. He was coming.

As they quietly assembled their gear, Ty sized up the misty mountain before them.

"So the news crew was on the other side?" he asked.

Mac tightened his shoulder holster and nodded. "Near where I was."

Ben handed Ty the tranquilizer rifle. "He's up there, I've felt him," said Ben solemnly. "He's probably there now 'cause it's day. The night is his time."

Ty shouldered the rifle. "You said you hadn't been able to conjure him, you weren't sensing him. At least until the other night at my house."

"That feelin' was strong for a moment," Ben said, "like from Portland. The other times he's been faint, kinda far off. I haven't been able to really get a fix, almost like he's tuned me out. I can't explain it, but I just have a feeling he's around . . . up there somewhere."

Ty readied a small rucksack, stuffing some energy bars into it along with two small bottles of water. The largest thing that went into his pack was a flat, hinged plastic box. He opened it and checked its contents, the five remaining tranquilizer darts.

Ben looked on. "That juice still good?"

"Should be," Ty said.

"Don't much matter. You're not gonna need 'em," commented Ben.

"Why? You think one's enough?" Ty asked, wondering what Ben knew about tranquilizer darts.

"Don't know, but if one don't do, our boy's not gonna wait for number two."

Ty tipped his head toward Mac. "That's why Mac's got the cannon. If the thing won't come peacefully, then Mac will arrest him. Posthumously."

Mac drew his gun, popped the clip out, and thumbed the cartridges onto his palm.

"What are you doing?" asked Ty.

Mac inventoried the thumb-sized fifty-caliber rounds, then started pressing them back into the magazine. "Making sure they're all there." He flipped the safety on and reholstered the gun.

Ben looked at the sky. "It's warming up. Weather's gonna get worse." Then with a twinkle in his eye, "Guess that's why I live in California, 'cause down there warmer is good."

Mac and Ty smiled, hoping the day would end on an upbeat note, maybe even success. They were defiant and frustrated, chasing a killer none of them had seen and the rest of the world didn't believe existed. It was almost as if they were daring it to be real, like kids playing with a Ouija board, not sure of the forces they were meddling with, but hoping for a thrill. They also realized that if they met their quarry, they might still not be ready. Between Mac's casting and Ben's visions, along with the mayhem this thing had apparently wrought, their opponent was both fearsome and hateful, and in their hearts they knew the three of them might not be enough.

A few ridges over from Ty, Ben, and Mac, an intensive search was under way for clues to the killing of the news crew. The team hired by Channel 7 comprised former FBI, NSA, and CIA employees as well as retired SEAL and Delta team members who were available on a moment's notice to anyone who could pay their hefty fee. Aided by local law enforcement and a growing contingent of antiterrorism operatives from several government agencies, the massive search was being conducted down roads cordoned off from the media.

By late morning Channel 7 and law enforcement, with the governor's blessing, had not yet released the real story but were expecting to do so by late afternoon or early evening if nothing else was found. They all knew there might be repercussions from not letting the public know immediately, but the savagery of the attack on the crew, along with the other disappearances, had them all trying to figure out if this were some sinister larger plot. That the attack had happened in such a remote area allowed them to more easily manage the release of information.

69

Three hours and nearly five miles later, the three men reached a T in their path and tried to use visual clues to determine which trail would take them to the top. They had long since passed the Y where they had previously abandoned the climb. Ben's raging heart rate told him he'd better take it easy or they'd be signaling one of the helicopters orbiting five miles away for a medical evac. Ben knew he would be forced to turn around soon, whether they reached the top or not, so he decided to push it a bit further and keep the problem to himself as long as he could. But as he leaned against a tree, his deeply hitching breath drew the attention of his partners. Mac looked at Ty, who imperceptibly nodded his agreement. Mac turned to Ben and threw some weight into his words, "Okay, that's it, we're going back."

"Mac's right," said Ty, "you're no good dead."

Ben wanted to fight but at that moment he just needed to sit and let his lungs catch up on oxygenating his blood. He found a large round rock by the trail edge and took the weight off his legs.

"How far to the top?" Ben asked Mac.

Mac unfolded his map and tried to decipher it. "Don't know," he said. "The map doesn't even show this T. According to the elevation contours, we should be right below the top, maybe an eighth of a mile. Looks like not even a hundred feet vertical. Either Ty or I could scout ahead and see if it's that close."

Ben shook his head. "We shouldn't split up, especially here."

As Mac looked at the map, Ty shifted his focus up the trail and his eyes gave away his surprise. He pointed. "Look."

Mac and Ben followed Ty's sight line. Perhaps fifty yards away, a few dozen trees, from saplings to second growth, were broken or torn off. Mac whistled softly at the chilling sight.

Ty unshouldered his trank rifle and turned to Ben.

"Hey Ben, do you see . . ." Ty trailed off, causing Mac to switch his eyes from the trees to Ben. The old man was now on his feet, squinting as if in pain, but more like he was listening intently.

Mac started, "You—," but was silenced by Ben's quickly raised hand.

It had all become clear to Ben in a split second. His suspicions were confirmed. Just as it had been doing with its tracks, it was hiding its thoughts as well. Mac slowly drew his pistol and Ty checked to make sure his rifle was cocked. Ben knew his radar had let them down, robbing them of a warning.

"Damn . . ." Ben pivoted on his heels, already knowing what he would see.

Ty and Mac spun and what they saw striding rapidly down the hillside above them was staggering—a dark, shaggy titan, rage spitting from its golden eyes.

In that instant, the poison of fury in Ty's system overwhelmed his natural fear, Ben accepted what he saw, and Mac was just plain scared shitless, his policeman's brain automatically measuring the onrushing monolith against Dr. Frazier's estimate. In less than one second Mac knew he should have listened to his instincts. *Of course it was real . . .*

With no time to react, Ty quickly raised his rifle and fired his dart—slightly wide. Mac unfroze, drew down on its chest, and squeezed his trigger. Nothing. The trigger was immobile: the safety was still on.

"Split up! Run!" Ty yelled, wanting to draw the beast away from his friends.

Mac instinctively pushed Ben toward the downhill trail, then followed the only other route, up the hill with Ty. As Ben took off downtrail, Mac hoped it would come after them.

It did.

* * *

When the old one saw him, there seemed to be less fear than recognition in his mind voice. With the other two, one felt fear, as he should, but the other had a mind voice filled with hate, strong like his own. But while his own hatred was based on revenge and drove him to hurt the small two-legs, this one had another hatred.

He turned to the hating one and his companion. The old one could wait.

Ben ran, his dream real again after sixty years. This terrain was different from his long ago encounter, but what disturbed him most was that he knew this place. It matched his dreams of the past year. His old dreams of the lush forest of Humboldt County had been alternating with the new dreams of this sparser, rockier landscape, enough so to cause him to doubt the authenticity of the original encounter and to question whether it had really happened. Now he realized this place was familiar because it was always something that was *going to happen.* Ty and Mac were being chased—just as he had dreamed—and he was on his own. Ben knew how this dream ended and he needed to change it.

Ty and Mac had no hope of losing their pursuer, given its size and speed. Sprinting away from it, Mac replayed the image of its impossible dimensions, shoulders as wide as a car, telephone pole arms and legs, and a spectacular mane framing its frightening man/animal physiognomy. Ty had dropped the dart rifle and Mac was racing to stay two steps behind. Mac still gripped his huge handgun but didn't dare stop, knowing the beast was breathing down their backs. He thumbed off the safety and visualized how he would turn and fire, but he just couldn't come up with the two seconds he needed.

The lumbering giant was not ten yards behind, its steps measured and patient. Mac knew it was just toying with them. Flashing on Ben's saying how some could feel your thoughts, he felt sure that what he felt in the forest the other day was definitely this thing. Mac quickly resigned himself again—if it came to that—to go down in a blaze of fifty-caliber gunfire.

* * *

Trotting behind, ready to strike when he tired of the chase, he kept them a few paces away. The other reason he held back was that he felt one of them carried the thunder. He was not sure how they let it loose, so he stayed just behind them, biding his time.

He thought the one closest, the frightened one, might have it. He could easily reach out and end him but did not know if that would un- leash the thunder. He realized from its mind voice that this was the same one who had had the thunder before, below on the trail.

Then that power feeling of hatred from the mind voice of the one in front welled up and taunted him, so he decided to strike. They were defy- ing him, which summoned his own power feeling and rising hatred. He feared nothing, not even the thunder.

Ty was furious they'd been ambushed despite all the preparation. He couldn't believe the déjà vu: he was helpless once again, only this wasn't a playful teenager. This malevolent giant was going to kill them in an unspeakable way. His anger over that prospect drove his legs faster.

As he crested the summit, Ty had a split second to choose between two descents, one bad, the other worse. To one side was the rocky, stump-clustered clear-cut where Skip Caldwell and Kris had met their deaths. To the other was a ragged precipice.

Knowing they were no match for the beast on a reasonable down- hill, Ty picked the cliff and went over the edge, with Mac following. Both men assumed they were about to die as they ran down an almost- vertical rock face that on any other day they would never have at- tempted to even crawl down. An eons-old remnant of a landslide, the incline was pocked with stones and boulders and its countenance had been scoured of most vegetation by unrelenting north winds. Ty fixed on the river coursing at the cliff's base far below. Their speed increased too quickly and Ty and Mac simultaneously realized they were out of control.

Mac fell first, his toe catching a crevice. He went over, hitting his side hard and continuing his tumble, the gun flying out of his grip. Ty, in the lead, heard Mac fall and lost it a second later, unable to brake his forward momentum. He took the spill better, slipping onto his butt and bumping up and over some rocks only to find a sort of natural

chute, which he rode for a good thirty yards before stopping. They had
no idea if they were still being pursued, and Ty's only consolation in
falling was that he didn't think it could possibly be behind them.

Ty turned to see Mac falling toward him. He tried to catch him but
missed, then saw the gun skitter by just within his reach and grabbed it.
Ty looked up and saw the beast leaning over the ridge, apparently sizing up the feasibility of pursuit. Before he lost sight of it, Ty steadied
and aimed. Squeezing the trigger, he felt the huge gun explode with a
kick he hadn't anticipated, sending him over sideways, the gun slapping a rock and leaping from his hand. Ty skidded and bounced another fifty yards, then managed to stop. Several feet below, Mac had
come to rest. A few rocks peppered by, following him from the top. Ty
slid down to Mac. One look into his chalky face told him the man was
hurt and in shock.

"I think I busted my leg," Mac gritted.

Just below the knee of Mac's jeans, the blood-soaked fabric bulged
ominously. Ty recognized a compound fracture and queasily looked
away to scan the ridge a hundred yards above. Nothing. The slope was
so barren he could have seen a cat moving, let alone their monster.

Mac turned to look, paying with brief but blinding pain. "Ohhh.
You hit it?"

"Don't know," answered Ty. "The recoil knocked me off balance. It
was a long ways off. I doubt it."

"Where's the gun?" asked Mac.

"Lost it," said Ty, pointing, "Down there. Sorry."

As Mac's pain subsided to a dull blur, he voiced another worry,
"Ben."

Ty pulled out his phone and punched in 911, trying to put Ben out
of his mind. No signal, out of range. He folded the phone and looked
around. "We've got one way out of here."

They looked down from their rocky perch to the river, several
hundred yards below. Ty gestured at Mac's leg. "You've got a compound break. I can help some, but you're probably going to have to
walk on it."

Mac laughed. "Walk? Shit, it'd be a lot easier if I just fell the rest of
the way, less weight on it."

Ty admired the man's guts. It took courage to face death with a
hearty chuckle.

"Or I can get out of here and call for help," Ty offered.

Though agonized, Mac smiled. He shook his head. "And I sit around and wait for Junior to come eat me? I'll goddamn flap my wings and fly before that happens. Let's go."

The small two-leg's thunder had lashed out and hurt him, like the claw of a bear. It had cut into his shoulder, not deep but the red flowed, like the red he saw from those he killed. He now knew the thunder attacked like an animal and could wound but not necessarily kill. He respected the thunder but did not fear it.

The place where the two escaped him was steep. He could have followed them but the effort would have been high and the threat of the thunder was real. He wanted the hating one who had let loose the thunder. The hating one was special.

He let that one go for now but would return and find him. He knew the hating one lived with the old one in the big wood cave. He watched the red trickle from the raw rut. He would find that place again, because this small two-leg with the power voice, this one who had let go the thunder—this one would die. But first, the old one was below on the trail.

70

Ben covered a quarter mile at top speed before hearing the thundering report of the gun. He prayed Mac's aim had been true. He wanted to go back but had a feeling he should keep moving. He paced himself, and though his heart was chugging hard, he knew he was going to make it. He would get back to Mac's Malibu, break the window, and use the police radio inside to call for help. He wondered if the radio worked without the car key.

As he stopped to catch a breather, his old ticker was screaming, but Ben felt no signs of danger, from his body or from the thing somewhere out there. He was less afraid of its running him down than he was of his body's failing him. Instead of spitting into its face and dying like a warrior, he was afraid he might just pucker up like a seventy-nine-year-old rag doll. In his dream he was always running, a young, strong brave, the thing nearly upon him. But of course in the dream he always woke up right before it caught him. He didn't have the luxury of that particular escape now. He began moving again, wondering how his partners were. Part of him hoped they had slain the beast, but another part wished for his own resolution.

A moment later he knew he would complete his dream.

It was behind him, moving fast. He knew it, could feel it. Its mind found his and they locked. It was not going to let him go. Ben trotted, stifling his panic, knowing that's what it wanted—panic, fear. He didn't want to die. *Eighty's a good, long life. Yeah, tell that to the guy who's seventy-nine.* Then he saw Doris at home, worrying about him. She'd be okay, he'd seen to that . . .

Now he knew it was going to happen and that he was really just a frail old man with a crazy notion of facing a sixty-year-old ghost, and—

It was behind him, not far. Fifty yards, a hundred? Five hundred? Didn't know, it didn't matter. There were five or more miles between Ben and the car, and even then—

He heard it now, its locomotive breaths . . . Oh-Mah . . .

Ben tried to speed up, but his lungs were inadequate, not keeping up, not enough air, feeling dizzy, his arm, left arm, feeling numb, bad sign . . . know the signs . . . bad one. He ran harder, knowing it was all or nothing. It was right there, felt it, warmth on the back of his neck . . .

He kept moving, trying to quicken his pace, but his worst fear was being realized: his body was letting him down. He pushed the throttle but was out of gas, *no oil in the crankcase.* His chest heaved in consort with his open mouth to grab air, but it wasn't working anymore. His legs were getting rubbery but he kept forward progress, he could do it, he'd been to war, this was nothin'—

Suddenly pain radiated out from Ben's chest and in no time it became one of those huge fireworks displays, the biggest he'd ever seen . . . beautiful blooming, sparkling stars in his eyes, cascading rays of light, it was stunning, the best fireworks he'd ever seen . . .

And after what seemed to be the longest pause . . .

Almost like a lazy afternoon spent lying in the sun . . .

He was floating, drifting . . .

Or was it running? No, he was . . . flying. Now he could see everything, soft, glowing, dreamy. He saw himself, on the ground, on the trail, lying there, his eyes open, but he was here . . . How could he be there *and* here?

Drifting up, he felt no more pain, no more fear, no more bad things, just a warmth, a feeling of . . . love? He saw it, Oh-Mah. It was huge, running, and it was hurt . . . its shoulder . . . blood. He felt its pain and he felt . . . compassion. He didn't need to beat it anymore, to look into its eyes . . .

Then it was upon him, or rather that crumpled shell at the side of trail, the empty husk that looked like Ben, but couldn't be because he was here and then . . .

A hand, not on his shoulder exactly, but more on his soul, touched him, and he knew the hand.

"Granddad?" he asked, though he somehow knew.

It's okay, Benjamin. It's okay.

Ben knew the voice and now he understood. Of course it had been familiar, his inner voice, his inner Indian . . .

"I know," said Ben, and they drifted higher, watching this Oh-Mah as he frolicked with the old carcass that had been Ben. After a moment, or an eternity, it all got very white . . . blinding but not hurting a bit . . . so beautiful . . .

71

After half an hour of inching down the cliff, Ty and Mac reached what appeared to be an impasse. The slope actually got steeper and now they reached the top of a rampart that was going to require either ropes or wings to continue down. Ty heard Mac's anguished grunts as each little bump and slide produced breathtaking pain. Ty surveyed the drop and knew he courted serious injury even without the impossible burden of a wounded comrade. He measured the slope above and dismissed returning to the ridge. Lying on their backs, they clung to the rocks, trying to keep gravity from pulling them any farther.

Mac saw the same thing Ty did. "We're stuck."

"I'm going ahead," Ty said.

"Okay, then I can do it," said Mac, his desperation palpable. "I've got to."

"Look, you're hurt, you can't walk. This section is a very tough climb down even in the best of conditions. You stay. It won't come back."

"I'm not taking that chance," Mac said. He saw what lay below and knew he wouldn't make it, but he wasn't going to stay on the mountain, a vulnerable morsel waiting for that thing to come down and get him.

Ty tried a different tack. "What if it's circling around? It's certainly smart enough to figure that out. What if we get to the bottom and it's waiting for us?"

"Then I'll distract it and you'll run," Mac said wryly.

Ty put his hand on Mac's chest. "Stay here, I'll be back in a few hours with a chopper."

Before Mac could object, Ty went over the edge, sliding as best he could. Mac's pain was coming on strong, now that he was past that first half hour, the golden time when the body in shock doesn't let on how much damage there is. He watched Ty sliding away, and the sudden mental image of that thing above them overcame his nauseating hurt.

Gingerly pushing off, Mac began a controlled slide to the edge of the precipice, then went over. For the first ten feet he was fine but then he started rolling sideways. He tried to compensate, his shattered leg firing beams of pain into his brain, giving him instant tunnel vision. Then he lost control and began tumbling.

He flew by Ty, almost taking him with him, then continued down, his arms flailing in vain to find a purchase. Ty was sliding but had some semblance of control, despite the rocks shredding the seat of his pants. He braked and watched helplessly as his comrade brutally caromed off all the obstacles in his path, making his descent the fast and hard way.

When Mac disappeared over a lip, the crackle of loose rock below indicated he was still plunging, so Ty didn't have much hope for him. He sadly resolved to locate the body when he got to the bottom and return with a crew to fetch it. He closed his eyes and said a prayer for Mac—whatever was left of him.

The light in the old one went out just before he caught him, and that frustrated him. He angrily tore the body to pieces, throwing the limbs and torso into the forest. Then he thought of the other two, climbing down away from him, and his rage flared.

They would go to the water. He knew where their black trail was, the one which they probably traveled to get here. It was far from the river. He thought of a route that would put him between them and their hardshell.

He wanted to kill the two, particularly the hating one, the one who did not fear him. He moved away quickly. He would find that small two-leg and make him feel fear.

* * *

When Ty eventually slid down and reached Mac, he found the detective's body wedged against a large outcropping three hundred feet above the river's rocky shore. Ty knew he was dead. Savaged by the hillside, Mac's face was an almost unrecognizable pulp. His right eye was smashed shut, his nose was broken, and his face had numerous cuts and scrapes. The compound leg fracture had escalated, the bloody bone spear now poking several inches out of the hole in his pants, and one of his arms had been twisted impossibly. That's why Ty was shocked to find a weak pulse.

Not giving Mac much more than an hour or two to live, Ty had no choice but to somehow get him out. Getting a grip on Mac's coat, he pulled his limp form off the rock shelf and plotted his path as he went. Ty saw that the final obstruction between them and the river a hundred yards below was another outcropping, seeming to offer no avenues around its jagged projections. As they gingerly descended, he desperately looked for a course around it.

Pulling and sliding the deadweight of his companion, Ty managed to move around the rock. Twenty minutes later—and more than an hour after their initial plunge—Ty's feet hit flat ground. Shouldering Mac in a fireman's carry, he set off toward what he hoped was salvation.

If he moved across the open ground during the light time, he knew that other small two-legs might see him, but right now stealth was unimportant. Revenge was.

He knew where the river flowed and headed toward the place where the black trail and the water met. He was certain that was where the two were going.

The red had stopped flowing but the sting of the thunder was in his mind. His hatred grew as he raced over the terrain, moving as fast as a hardshell on the black trail. When he found them, they would suffer.

Ty staggered with Mac's one hundred eighty-some pounds on his back for nearly a mile down the rocky river bank until it narrowed into a small, bankless gorge. He knew there was only one way through and that was the water. The river was swollen with snow runoff. Ty put a hand in to test the temperature. Ice water. He thought of the least lucky of the passengers on the Titanic and gave himself maybe fifteen minutes in the river before he would be too cold to continue. At that point they'd both drown.

Ty set Mac down and reconnoitered, determining that the gorge opened into a wide gravel bar after another fifty yards or so. After wolfing a power bar and slugging a few gulps of water, Ty hefted Mac and waded in. When the frigid water poured into his shoes, it jolted his eyes wider. When it hit waist level, it took his breath away. He managed to hug the shallow shore for a while, but then the gorge steepened and his footing began to go deeper and deeper, until he was chest deep in the freezing water. The only positive was that Mac's limp mass now felt more manageable because he was partly floating.

In less than two minutes Ty couldn't feel his feet anymore. If he slipped on slime-covered rocks, Mac would go under and he himself would drown as well trying to save him. This thought panicked him but he steadied himself, putting that ugly vision out of his mind. He hung on, setting his mind on one step at a time—just as with quitting drinking or pills.

Suddenly they plunged underwater, betrayed by a loose rock.

Ty scrambled to save his unconscious cargo while struggling to get his own head above water. The lazy current grabbed them and twisted Mac out of his hands. Fully submerged, Ty fought back, trying to find Mac but losing him, digging his numb feet and legs into what seemed like solid bottom. In a moment Ty's head broke the surface and he gasped for air, fighting to reach Mac, who was floating away, face down.

He lunged for Mac's limp arm, and his fingertips grasped an area of fabric the size of a postage stamp. Tweaking hard, he moved Mac a few inches closer. Then he grabbed for a firmer hold and flipped Mac over, getting his face out of the water.

A very long five minutes later they reached the other side of the rock and Ty dragged them out of the water. They were soaked and cold; incipient hypothermia started a new clock of doom ticking. Ty laid Mac down for a moment to gather his strength. The moment their body contact was unlinked, he felt the rush of cold on his back and shoulders and started to shiver. He took out his cell phone, hoping the water hadn't done it in and that he was within range. Amazingly it was still functioning, but still no signal. Packing Mac onto his back, he set out again, this time feeling like he would run out of energy very quickly, his body heat dramatically more depleted than just a moment before.

For the next fifteen minutes, Ty reached deep inside and hauled his burden, stopping more and more often as his strength waned, but spurred on by a creeping anxiety. He imagined it coming out of the bushes at every bend, and his emotions played tricks on him. Every wind-rustled leaf was the harbinger of their deaths, every thicket veiled a giant subhuman assassin.

After a seeming eternity Ty spotted a small bridge a few hundred yards away. At exactly that same moment he felt something behind him, an eerie sensation that crawled down his back. Afraid to turn but knowing he had to, Ty wheeled far enough around to get a view of the forest and hillside above. The naked ridge a half mile above was where they had had their encounter. They had taken the most direct route right down the steep face, but the ridgeline and slope to his right could also deliver you to their current location if you were willing to go the extra distance. It was tough terrain but he knew the thing would have no trouble traversing it.

That was when he glimpsed a dark streak passing through a small clearing, heading down toward them. He was astonished how fast it was. Despite the soaking wet weight on his shoulders, Ty was newly motivated, widening his steps, heading for the bridge, its road their only hope. During the next few moments Ty visualized the huge strides the thing was making as it descended. He focused on his goal, trying not to think that it might be upon them before they even reached the bridge.

He had once wondered what it did to its victims but had put the thought out of his mind. Now that particular horror bloomed in his imagination with scenarios of death most foul. Then rage pushed his fear aside, as once again he was running for his life and one of these things was the cause. If he could have killed it with his bare hands, he would have. He thought of Mac's big pistol and how he would happily give his entire fortune for it right now.

Less than twenty yards to the bridge he looked back. Nothing.

He estimated the river to be a hundred feet wide but knew that thing wouldn't even break stride, taking it like a ditch. He reached the bank supporting the bridge and climbed it, using every bit of his strength. He hadn't checked Mac lately and wasn't even sure he was still alive.

Ty felt the thing again, behind them, coming . . . somewhere . . .

Reaching the cracked asphalt roadbed, Ty felt his heart sink as he saw it for what it really was, just a lonely road miles from anything. It probably didn't see a car a day. He looked several hundred yards down the river, and his knees nearly buckled as the creature blew out of the trees and crossed the river in a few huge splashes. It saw them and moved like a freight train. Ty knew they were dead men. He was completely exhausted and couldn't move another yard.

And then Ty learned what a miracle looks like. It came in the form of a rusted '71 GMC pickup, sporting a rifle rack laden with fishing rods and driven by a grizzled old angel named Roland Simms. Roland was scouting for a good piece of white water to haul out some rainbows for Christmas and instead found two guys on a bridge, one carrying the other, something he hadn't seen since he was an eighteen-year-old kid on Guadalcanal.

Ty waved, trying to look distressed but not hysterical.

Simms pulled up, unequivocally confirming to Ty the existence of God.

"Jumpin' Jehoshaphat, what happened to you fellas?" asked Roland.

"He's badly hurt. Had a fall hiking, need to get him to the hospital," Ty said, assuming the sale by laying Mac onto the truck bed. Simms was surprised by the way that Ty took over and hesitated becoming a taxi. "Well, I guess I could go call—"

"Sir, the man's hurt. I'll pay whatever you want, but we need to go. Now."

Ty opened the passenger door, and newspapers, a smelly creel, a few crushed Burger King bags, and used Styrofoam cups cascaded from the seat as he slid into Simms's old truck.

"I'm Ty Greenwood, this is Mac Schneider. He's a Snohomish Sheriff's detective."

Ty knew if he told the guy what was closing on them, the old man would make them leave or, maybe worse, stop to look.

As Simms dutifully—and methodically—put the truck in reverse, Ty glanced behind, down the bank, saw a flash of movement below, and guessed they had less than ten seconds. Simms got the truck moving and gave it a little gas—not enough—and they idled slowly away.

"Guess it's a good thing I came along. Your buddy's lookin' pretty banged up," blithered Roland. "By the way, name's Roland, Roland Simms. Whad'you say yours was?"

Ty looked back. The angry behemoth had reached the roadway and was only two or three steps from catching them.

"Behind you! Hit it!" Ty screamed, "Punch it! *Go, go, go!*"

Roland Simms looked in the rearview mirror, choked, "Holy Jesus and Mary!" and his foot nearly slammed the gas pedal through the rusty floorboard.

Fearing it would get its hands on Mac in the truck bed, Ty watched helplessly as it gained on them, but in a few seconds the old truck—its pollution-control-free V-8 singing—put distance between them. For a quarter mile it gave chase, then disappeared into the trees. Roland Simms's eyes were bigger than saucers, his chest pumping like he'd just carried the truck himself.

"Jesus H. Christ, mister, what in the blue blazes of perdition was that?"

Ty gloomily looked back into the truck's bed at Mac, a mass of crumpled bones and clotted blood. "Let's get to a hospital, ASAP," he said, feeling his wet clothes again but not caring. He looked at the blurred scenery. After a moment, he answered Roland Simms.

"That, Mr. Simms, was what we were looking for. And he found us."

72

Once they were far enough away from the beast, Ty had Roland pull over and together they managed to heft Mac into the cramped cab. Ty turned the heat up full blast. He knew Mac's injuries were life-threatening and keeping him warm just might save him. On that hurried drive to Bellevue, Ty's phone finally made a connection. He reached 911 and was advised that the hospital would be ready and that they should drive all the way in instead of rendezvousing with an ambulance. After learning the injured man was a cop, the dispatcher told them to carefully use whatever speed was necessary and that the police would try to divert or control traffic.

That done, Ty explained to his new best friend Roland Simms what it was that had nearly ruined their day. By the time they reached the emergency entrance to Bellevue's Overlake Hospital Medical Center and Mac was laid onto a gurney and raced into the ER, Roland was a changed man. He'd driven faster than he'd ever driven and his system hadn't felt so much adrenaline since he'd been under enemy fire more than sixty years before.

Ty shook Roland's hand. "Thanks, Roland. And watch out for the press. They're as bad as that thing."

* * *

While being treated for cuts and bruises, Ty tried to locate Ben on his cell phone. Failing to find him at the hotel, he called the office of the security firm guarding his home and had them dispatch some men to Mac's Malibu to wait for Ben.

"Send at least three," he said, then added, "and make sure they're armed, heavily armed."

Then he called the police to report Ben missing and drew an immediate response. He was told that they "were currently a little overtaxed" but at least one search and rescue team would be dispatched. Ty wondered if the "overtaxed" part had anything to do with their quarry and its handiwork from last night. He assumed most police departments had been alerted after the Channel 7 slaughter and were now being more responsive to missing person reports.

Ty checked in with his hotel's switchboard and got a message to call Ronnie. Then he noticed his cell phone had registered a voice mail from Ronnie from hours earlier. He checked it and all she said was a cryptic, "Call me." His heart leaped at the thought she might be opening the door, but he didn't want to worry her that he was in the hospital, so he decided to wait until he was discharged. He could tell her everything in person, that is, if she really wanted to see him. Knowing his wife, he thought she might be regretting her decision to throw him out as well as not believe him about Kris Walker. A brief vision of Kris crossed his mind, and a chill shot across his shoulders as he saw her in the grasp of that thing. He hoped it had been quick.

Ty wanted more than anything to see Ronnie and his kids. As he sat bundled in a blanket on the examination table, waiting for the doctor to return to sew up a four-stitch cut on his cheek, he had a life-altering revelation: he was free. He realized that the last three years of hell hadn't really been about clearing himself, or proving anything to the press, or even retaining his credibility.

Ty realized it had all been about one thing: proving to himself he wasn't crazy.

That incident in Idaho had set off a chain reaction of other events, but its essence was always about convincing himself he had seen what he'd seen. He felt like Wilbur Post, trying to get Mister Ed to talk to someone—*anyone*—when even he didn't believe Mister Ed could really talk. Were they voices in his head or was that goddamn horse really saying something?

He felt like he'd had a fever that had been building for three years, then the things that happened this day caused it to break, and just like that it was gone. He couldn't believe his salvation was that simple, to just see it again and go on about his life. He wondered briefly if he was simply in shock and the obsession would return the next day, but Ty searched his feelings and found nothing inside. The madness had passed. He was more certain of that than he'd been of anything in the last three years.

While the doctor stitched him up, two men pulled back the curtain. "Mr. Greenwood?" one of them asked. "We're with the Bellevue Police Department. We have some questions."

As dusk settled in over the Greenwood home, wind began to whip their one-hundred-sixty-foot cedars with the promise of a storm. Ronnie strolled down their driveway at four p.m. and gave each of the security guards a bottle from the wine cellar and merry Christmas wishes before sending them home early. Then she called the Red Lion and asked for Ty. She also had the desk ring Ben, assuming he'd know where Ty was. Neither Ty nor Ben was available, according to the desk clerk, "though Mr. Greenwood did call in for his messages a while ago." She left him a message to call.

Hitting their problems head-on was a concept both Ty and Ronnie practiced in business but not in their personal lives. Ronnie couldn't explain why she had spent so many years mastering avoidance and denial in her own affairs. If she conducted business that way, she would have been lucky to have risen to stock clerk. She asked herself why it was so hard to talk to her own husband.

She also wondered why Ty hadn't responded. Ronnie overflowed with regrets at tossing him out, then storming off in a fit after finding Kris Walker in his room. She turned on the TV in the kitchen and was surprised to hear Kris's name all over the media, not just on her own station. Lurid rumors were beginning to fly on the national media that Kris and her news crew had been the victims of everything from a group of angry survivalists to an organized team of serial killers. Ronnie wondered if there was a relationship between the incident from last night and this startling news. She kept an open mind and expected Ty would be able to explain.

For now, she anticipated his call and mentally practiced her apology. She resolved to change things for the better. Then doubts formed that perhaps he was enjoying his freedom and maybe what she saw had been the Ty she didn't know. So what had happened to Kris Walker, and was Ty somehow involved? She forced those thoughts from her head. She didn't believe Ty had changed. Lately he may have become weird and unpredictable, but he was still Ty, wasn't he?

"Ronnie? You want to eat now?" Greta asked, having held their Christmas dinner per Ronnie's instructions.

Ronnie had expected to have spoken with Ty long before this, so she finally gave in. "Yeah, we might as well. The kids are probably hungry."

The two cops were considerate enough to stop at Ty's hotel so he could be questioned in dry clothes. Ty's apprehension about Ben grew after the desk clerk told him Ben hadn't appeared yet. On the bright side there was a message from Ronnie to call her. Unfortunately the cops had taken away his cell phone. Ty also didn't need to tell Ronnie once again that he was in the custody of the police. He would wait until they were through and call her on the way home.

Even now, most local police agencies were getting their information about the killings from the television as news leaked out. The Bellevue cops were very curious why Ty Greenwood was investigating the series of murders with a Snohomish County Sheriff's detective who had been removed from the case. They also knew Ty's name had been all over the media as a suspect in the case. Yet it appeared to the police that Ty had saved Mac's life, which didn't really match up with his being a suspect. Why would a suspect save the guy who had been investigating him?

They entered the station and the two detectives took Ty to a locked but windowed interrogation room. One of the cops sat while the other leaned against the wall.

The sitting cop began the interrogation. "So what were you doing up there?"

Over the next twenty-five minutes, Ty unfolded his tale in an orderly and calm fashion and took them through the main events, from the time he saw the article about the broken trees to being rescued by

Roland Simms. The cops occasionally looked at each other with poorly concealed smirks and eye rolling, which Ty noticed but ignored. At one point the station lights flickered. Leaning cop looked at sitting cop. "Lightning."

When Ty felt he had given them all the salient details, he sat back in his chair. There was a long pause and leaning cop chuckled. "So, Mr. Greenwood, when we arrest Bigfoot, do you think you could ID him in a lineup?"

Sitting cop cracked up and Ty sighed patiently. Ty figured it was only a matter of time before his story was corroborated. He assumed Roland Simms would be talking soon, and certainly DNA from the scene of the news crew slaughter would prove something other than a human being had been their killer. Ty's thoughts turned to Ben and he said a prayer that the old man would be all right. Then it occurred to Ty that every time he tried to think about Ben, his thoughts seemed to automatically go to Mac. It was as if he did not have control over his own thoughts, as if something were bending his concerns for Ben and pointing them back to Mac. Ty didn't understand it, but he was feeling a growing anxiety about getting to Mac.

The two cops shook their heads, got up, and left the room, figuring a few hours of cooling his heels might soften Ty up to telling the truth. Ty glanced at his watch—almost seven. He was beginning to worry he wouldn't get home, until he reminded himself that he hadn't even spoken to Ronnie and wondered if his returning home was what she had in mind. She had not said that in her messages. He wanted to call her, but the cops had not yet allowed him a phone call.

73

The unseasonably warm yet powerful wet front off the Pacific collided with the cold, weaker dry air out of Canada, and the resulting battle of air masses created a growing electrical storm and spotty downpours throughout Puget Sound. Five miles above Ronnie and Ty's home, Arlo Westmeyer looked out the window into his backyard and saw rain streaking through the illuminating floodlight. Occasional flashes and thunder in the distance grew louder and more frequent.

"Honey," he yelled to his wife, "I'm goin' out to cover up the mower."

Arlo grabbed his parka and exited the sliding glass door toward his workshop. He had mowed their acre that day and had been called into the house before covering his baby, a deluxe Sears Craftsman twenty-two-horse riding mower. Arlo found the plastic cover and wrapped it around the mower tighter than usual because the winds were forecast to get worse.

As the wind beat him with spitting rain, he had a sudden terrible dread come over him. It was as palpable as the wind. He instinctively melded into the lee of his large shop to conceal himself. He stood motionless for a moment and looked around into the dark woods nearby, then at the warm glow of his house. Just as he told himself it was silly and was about to step out and head to the house, something came out of the shadows and passed him less than three yards away. Arlo shrank back as the tremendous form drifted by, momentarily blocking his view of the house. Its stench permeated the wet air and Arlo nearly fell to his knees, his face tightening with fear, his breath bottled up. And then it was gone.

Petrified and fearing any movement would call attention to himself, Arlo managed to unlock his legs and run hard for the loving womb of his home. That night Arlo's wife called her sister in Cleveland with news that Arlo had fallen off the wagon.

"On Christmas night, can you believe it?"

Karl Carillo had spent all day trying to make heads or tails of the scene in the mountains. His CSIs were even baffled over what had happened when they couldn't really find fingerprints on the van where prints should be. They also couldn't figure out, even from an exacting field investigation, what had killed the crew members and how. There was blood and evidence everywhere, but they literally had never seen anything like it. The head of their crime lab, Brett Miller, told Carillo they would have to take everything back to the lab and run further tests to tell him anything of value. Carillo finally went home around six to have what little Christmas he could with his family.

When the phone rang at the Carillos', it was Karl's wife, Kelly, who grabbed it. She summoned her husband as their children, filled with Christmas excitement, yelled in the background. Carillo took the phone, put his hand over the mouthpiece, and narrowed his eyes at his wife.

"Would you get those fuckin' kids to shut up?"

Kelly nodded dutifully and moved to stifle her children.

Carillo spoke gruffly into the phone, "Yeah?"

"Hey Karl, it's Bailey." Chet Bailey was a fellow detective. "Bellevue police just called and said they were holding a guy for questioning."

"Yeah, who?" Carillo said, not particularly excited to talk shop at that moment.

"Your guy Greenwood."

Carillo's eyes lit up. "What? Why? What do they have him on? I've had a tail on him all day. He hasn't moved."

"Well, he did. He was with Schneider, doin' some kinda weird shit in the mountains, not far from where the TV crew died. Mac's in the hospital. Heard he's bad. Can you believe it?"

"I'll be right there," snapped Carillo. His former partner's being gravely injured didn't really register on his emotion meter, nor did he wonder what his business was with the prime suspect. He'd always liked Mac, but Mac had somehow gone bad. What dominated Carillo's thoughts was his fixation on nailing Ty Greenwood. Though it was the waning hours of Christmas, he quickly put on his dress shoes and sports jacket and ventured into the windy night. If Bellevue PD had Greenwood, Carillo would quickly fill out the paperwork to allow him to transfer Greenwood for questioning. He was licking his chops to get his hands on him. He had a feeling he'd have this thing solved before he crawled into bed later.

An older gentleman in a tuxedo walked down the hall at the Bellevue Police Department to drop off a gift for his friend the chief of police. On his way to a party in Newport Shores, *Snohomish Daily News* publisher John Baxter had stopped off to dole out some Christmas cheer to his pal, whom he knew to be an aficionado of fine Kentucky bourbon. As he passed the windows of the interrogation room, Baxter saw Ty sitting alone. He cornered a passing cop.

"What's that guy in here for?" Baxter asked.

"I think they're trying to find out what he has to do with the killings," said the cop. "He was with a Snohomish Sheriff's detective today and they got in some trouble in the mountains." Then the cop added, "I think they're buying time to figure out something to charge him with."

A few days before, John Baxter had finally found the time to do a background check on Ty Greenwood. From what he had learned about the former computer magnate, Ty Greenwood possessed the funds to meet any bail they threw at him. But that wasn't John Baxter's concern. What bothered him was that he had also discovered a sad tale of a man who reported on a rather bizarre encounter in the woods of Idaho and was pummeled by the media for doing so. Happening upon Ty's Web site, Baxter had been fascinated by the detail of the reportage and the determination he read between the lines, and his newsman's senses told him Ty Greenwood was a very misunderstood man.

Baxter waited until no one was around—most of the skeleton staff was in the break room having an impromptu Christmas party—and he opened the locked door to the interrogation room. Ty looked up, surprised.

"So," said Baxter, "they think you did it, huh?"

Ty nodded. "I'm afraid the truth was a little too bizarre for their taste."

Baxter paused for a moment as if gathering his thoughts. "When I was a young man, about twenty-five or so, I was a hunter. Used to go up in the mountains every weekend—deer, bear, antelope, grouse, chukars, even gophers. Hell, I shot anything that moved. Then one day I crossed a meadow, west o' Marysville—was nothing then like it is now, it was wilderness. Anyway, I saw some movement and I shouldered my Marlin. Had a three-oh-eight and figured I'd bag a nice buck or something. I put my Leupold—a military model, one of their first—anyway, I swung my scope onto this thing, and I'll be damned if it looked like, well, it looked almost human. Honest to God, I didn't know what to make of it. I just . . . froze. I watched it through the scope for a good minute or so as it grabbed some berries and then left." Baxter stopped and his eyes seemed to unfocus, as if he were still there. Then he took a deep breath and his eyes returned to Ty. "That day I drove home, hung up my rifles, and never took another shot at a living thing again." The two men looked at each other for a moment. "I believe you, Ty." Then the older man gestured toward the open door. "C'mon, a man needs to be with his family on Christmas."

A moment later, as they quickly walked to the parking lot, Ty turned to Baxter. "Could you just take me to Overlake Hospital? My house is too far for you. I'll catch a cab out there."

Compound fractures of both legs; both the radius and ulna of the right arm broken; a cracked and dislocated right shoulder; a concussion; a fractured skull; a broken nose; one dislocated and two broken fingers; and a variety of contusions, lacerations, and abrasions was the battle tally on Mac's chart. While one team of doctors and nurses had worked to repair the compound fractures, another group examined Mac and found no internal damage, but they did find evidence he had experienced brain trauma.

After his operation, Mac was upgraded from grave to critical, as his life was no longer in immediate danger, but the chief of neurology, who had been trying to leave for a party when Mac arrived, gave him only a slight chance of emerging anytime soon from his deep coma. As the nurses hooked Mac to the monitors and IV, his absolute lack of responses caused the physician to remark, "Looks like we might have a Karen Ann Quinlan here. Page me if you see any sign of consciousness."

Later, while Mac lay in that sterile room with the lights dimmed for the night shift, a visitor drifted in. An old man in the bed next to Mac was out like a light and didn't notice the caller.

The guest spoke softly to Mac but didn't stay long.

74

Ronnie's anxiety was rising. She knew that regardless of whether Ty was reveling in his bachelor life, he would have called by now. She tried his cell phone but kept getting his voice mail.

Discarding all pretenses, she called the hotel again and left a simple message: "Come home, love, Ronnie." She hoped that left no doubts—in case he had any. She punched in his cell phone again, and just as it rang, the power in the house winked out. Since all of their phones were cordless, the base unit went out and she lost her signal. She moved to get her cell phone then remembered it was probably in the Lexus. The house was pitch-black and though the night was occasionally lit by brilliant flashes of lightning, she didn't want to try and make her way out to the garage right now. She regretted the aesthetic decision to build the large building across the plaza. The darkness gave her the urge to locate her children.

"Kids?" she called out. "Where are you guys?"

"Mommy! Mommy!" came Meredith's small voice, raised in panic. "It's dark!" She'd never seen a power outage in her six years.

Greta shuffled into the kitchen in her slippers. "You have candles?"

Ronnie felt her way to the cupboard and pulled out some candles. "Go ahead and put them around the downstairs." Then she whispered, "Just don't give the kids any."

"How come, Mommy?" asked Chris, who had just entered the kitchen. "I can have a candle, I'm old enough."

He was right, thought Ronnie, he's no longer a baby. "Okay, honey, you can have a candle but be very careful."

"I will," he said. "Just don't give Meredith one. She's too little."

"No, I'm not," said his sister, joining the three of them. "Too little for what?"

Greta lit a large decorative candle, set it on the counter, then lit three smaller ones.

"Here, Christopher, go put this in the hallway. Set it on this," she said, handing him a small plate.

Chris left on his mission and Meredith reached for a candle. In the light Ronnie saw amazement in her little girl's eyes and felt a pang of sadness that they never just turned off the lights to show the kids the simple magic of candlelight.

"Be careful with that, honey," said Ronnie. "And don't let the wax burn you."

Meredith took her candle and left the room, walking with the book-balanced-on-the-head precision of a fashion model. Ronnie lit a few more candles.

Greta took one. "Have you ever written by candlelight?" she asked Ronnie. "I think I'll go write a letter."

She left for her room, the flickering aura guiding her down the hall. Ronnie warmly accepted the joy of such a small thing as the lights going out, re-revealed to her by these three youngsters. She lit a candle for Ty, hoping he'd arrive soon.

On the ten-minute ride to the hospital, Ty offered to tell Baxter his whole story as soon as the dust settled. The two men shook hands.

"They're probably going to arrest both of us now," Baxter said matter-of-factly.

Ty sat back in the passenger seat. "Let 'em. I'll bury them with lawyers."

Ty borrowed Baxter's phone and tried his house. Unaware of Ronnie's latest message, he wanted to get permission to come home. His plan was to quickly check on Mac, then get a cab to Snohomish. His home phone responded with a fast buzzing but no ring.

"No answer?" asked Baxter.

Ty shook his head. "Phone's out of order, probably the storm."

Wind and rain swept across their car, and in the distance they saw flashes of lightning.

At the hospital entrance, Ty climbed out. Baxter leaned over. "You watch out, Ty. Don't spend too much time here, they'll be coming for you."

Ty tapped the roof. "I owe you, John. A lot. Thank you."

Ty closed the door and Baxter drove away. Ty looked around the parking lot for police cars and entered the hospital. Although visiting hours had officially ended, Ty charmed the nurse at the desk into letting him upstairs to see his injured companion. At the nurse's station on Mac's floor, an older nurse told him Mac was in a coma but was probably going to survive. As Ty entered the room, all he could see was a mass of bandages. Mac's arm and legs were in traction, a tangle of wires and tubes tracing in and out of him. Ty glanced at the old man in the other bed, whose wide open mouth revealed that half his choppers were MIA.

Ty slid the sole chair over to the bedside. That oddly pressing need to see Mac was finally satisfied and he no longer felt the yearning when he thought about Ben. The old man was the bigger problem now, and not just because Ty might have to leave home that night to help search for him. *Great. I worm my way back in, only to leave again.* But it was for Ben. Ronnie would understand.

He gave Mac another couple of minutes, then stood, gently touching a plaster-covered leg. "See ya, friend."

Ty moved to the door.

"Ty."

It was the faintest whisper, almost as if the word had come not from a mouth but directly from a mind. Ty turned around, thinking his ears were playing tricks on him.

"Ty."

Ty walked over to Mac and realized that in the mass of wrappings Mac's left eye was now slightly open.

"Mac? You awake?"

Mac's lips moved but no sound issued.

"What?" Ty asked gently.

"Home . . ."

"Listen, don't try to talk. You're pretty weak." Ty leaned close.

"Home . . ."

"Home? No, you're in the hospital, but you'll be—"

"Go . . . home . . ."

"Go home?" Mac was on the edge of consciousness and Ty didn't want to strain him. "Home? I'm going home."

"Now. Ben says . . . go home . . . now."

"Ben? He's missing, Mac. Ben's miss—"

"Ben's gone."

"Huh?"

"Ben's gone."

Ty felt something emerging and it was scaring him. "Ben's . . . gone?"

"Came . . . here. Talked . . . to . . . me. Says . . . go home. Now."

"Ben told you to tell me to go home now?"

"Now. He said . . . Oh-Mah . . . he's there . . . your house."

The blood drained from Ty's face as the cryptic words began to take on a terrible meaning. "Ben told you Oh-Mah was at my house?"

"Yeah . . . go home . . . now . . ."

75

Ty stared intensely at the bandaged face, trying to decide if what Mac was saying was true. Was it the delirium of a badly injured man or could Mac have somehow been given an urgent message by their old Indian friend? Their friend who, if Ty's interpretation was correct, was now beyond these earthly bounds. It was crazy, not possible, but somehow felt real. Ty turned, walked quickly out of the room and toward the elevator. Suddenly he stopped. *I need a cell phone.*

He looked back at the nurse's station and weighed the risk of asking one of them to loan him their cell phone, but he feared calling attention to himself. He noticed a door that said Nurse's Lounge and entered. It was an empty locker room. He frantically pulled open locker doors, and after four he found a purse. No phone. He searched five more open lockers and bingo, found a wallet, keys, and a phone. He put the phone in his pocket and cracked the door to the hall. A doctor and nurse were coming, so he pulled back and looked for a place to hide. Nothing. He braced for them to enter. He quickly rehearsed some excuses for being in there, but they passed by. When their voices vanished, he looked out again and the coast was clear.

Crossing to the elevator, he took out the phone and dialed his house. Again he got the fast ringing. He called the operator to confirm a malfunction as the elevator doors opened on the lobby.

Just as he stepped out, the corner of his eye caught dark blue, and he quickly made a turn to avoid the two Bellevue cops who had just rounded the corner. Ty dodged into a vacant waiting room and waited a moment. Mac's faint words sounded like cannons now. He carefully peeked around the corner and saw no one. Then he calmly but quickly walked out the front door, his eyes sweeping the area for any police.

He was met with a driving rain. Fortunately the entrance wasn't brightly lit, so he stood in the shadows for a moment, his mind spinning for solutions. A man came out the front door and passed him, on his way to his car. Ty followed him. As the man fumbled with his keys, Ty tapped him on the shoulder.

"I'll give you five hundred dollars to take me to Snohomish."

The startled man quickly got in and drove away.

He spotted an elderly couple in the parking lot and reworked his approach as he walked toward them. The woman was holding an umbrella and helping the old man, who appeared to have just gotten out of treatment.

"Excuse me," Ty opened, "this sounds a little crazy, but I have a dire emergency in Snohomish and can't wait for a cab. Will you take five hundred dollars to drive me there?"

Looking slightly stricken, they climbed into their car with muttered apologies about having to get home.

"A thousand?" said Ty, upping the ante.

They drove off and Ty stood in the parking lot, the rain now coming down hard, arrows of lightning strobing off the clouds and the city terrain.

When Carillo arrived at his department only to phone the Bellevue Police Department and discover that Ty Greenwood had somehow gotten out of a locked interrogation room and simply walked out of their building, he went berserk. Tired and frustrated, he had fewer answers now than this morning when he'd arrived at that horrific scene. Carillo wanted Greenwood to be involved because he fit better than anything else he had. Carillo had concluded that because of the bizarre nature of the van deaths, and the lack of conclusive physical evidence, the crime had required a very concerted effort, and to him that meant high-end organization. And money. Lots of money.

Now, armed with few hard facts and even more simmering rage, Carillo decided that Christmas or not, he had some hard questions to ask Ty Greenwood. He was also worried that the case was slipping from his fingers. Now everyone from local law to the FBI to Homeland Security was involved, and he didn't want any of them to solve *his case*.

Two miles from the Greenwoods' home, the Charnstrom family had vacated to Hawaii for two weeks and their residence was empty. So Jeff Wilson, the high school senior next door, availed himself of all the cool bachelor amenities their pad had to offer, mainly the liquor cabinet and hot tub. All it took was jimmying a window and voilà.

Now stewing in churning one-hundred-two-degree water with his current girlfriend, Snohomish High head cheerleader Kari Keelock, Jeff was in hog heaven. After he had assured her that they wouldn't be electrocuted by lightning and that not wearing a bathing suit was okay, Jeff and Kari sipped his neighbors' Black Jack and Coke in the nude and dug the light show overhead. After half an hour of soaking, Jeff—with the help of his friend Jack Daniels—worked up the nerve to slip his tongue in Kari's mouth, then immediately began working south.

Having never performed oral sex, Jeff found a willing test subject, and as his head went under the water, the spa jets sounded like five Niagra Falls. When he came up for air, Kari's dreamy look told him he was on the mark. He took a deep breath and went down again.

Just as Jeff reacquired his target, Kari suddenly jerked violently, her knee connecting with his jaw. Choking, he started for the surface when something amazingly strong grabbed his neck and held him down. Fighting for all he was worth, Jeff didn't sense Kari was there anymore and in his confusion thought she might have hired a bunch of guys to drown him. *But why?* Jeff never found out and Kari couldn't tell him, for in seconds her broken body lay sprawled on the lawn, as his floated face down in the bubbling, steaming water.

And their slayer moved on toward his goal.

76

F ive minutes had passed and Ty was losing his rationality as his desperation grew. He knew Ben had a strong spiritual side, despite his joking that too many years in Hollywood had made him a pale imitation of a real Indian. Ty also had the powerful awareness, stirred by more than just Mac's words, that Ben was in fact dead and that his warning was real, truly issued from beyond the mortal plane. Ty's mind spiraled with the surreal, mystical, and hard reality questions posed to him in the last few minutes. He knew he had to get home immediately.

For the second time that day, a mystical vehicle came to Ty, a miracle from on high, a message of deliverance handed him by powers he hadn't absolutely believed in until today. In this case it was a beat-up '87 Chevy Cavalier. A nurse got out, slammed the door, and ran inside, leaving the car idling five steps from Ty. He didn't stop to question why, he just acted.

Walking deliberately to the Cavalier, he opened the door and settled into the seat. Seconds later a Bellevue Police cruiser pulled in behind him. Ty's eyes were riveted to the rearview mirror. After a few seconds the two officers got out and walked toward the hospital's door. Ty put the Cavalier in gear and drove away as if it were his own.

With eyes alternating between the road and the rearview mirror to assure he was leaving the parking lot without detection, Ty gunned the car toward the on-ramp and onto the 405 north. He kept his speed to around seventy, a little faster than the flow, but not enough to bring the Washington State Patrol down on him. Then he dialed 911 and told the operator a group of armed men were attempting to break into his home. The operator asked if he was physically at the residence and he said he was. When the operator gave his address and it was completely unfamiliar, he remembered he was using a stolen phone. Then she informed him he was not being truthful because her computer showed the cell phone from which he was calling had just handed off to a relay identified as located in north Bellevue. After arguing for a few moments, Ty apologized for the deception, explained it was a borrowed cell phone, and convinced the woman there was a genuine emergency. She informed him she was relaying his actual address to the sheriff's department and that a squad car would be dispatched immediately.

Ty tried the house again. Same busy signal. Another call to Ronnie's cell phone also went unanswered. *Probably in her purse, or worse, in her car.* The downpour increased as he rolled north, the Cavalier's wipers feebly rubbing waxy streaks across his field of vision. Ty cursed his crappy stolen Chevy and threatened to sell his own Chevy Suburban in retaliation. He looked at his watch in a passing light. At this pace the trip would take him twenty, maybe twenty-five minutes. He decided he would run any lights he could.

The Greenwoods' neighbor, Ken Harrison, had almost forty emus on his property and they were honking away, frightened by the lightning/thunder combos striking every thirty seconds. The electrical outage be damned, the Harrison house was blessed with its own power in the form of a NorthStar fifteen-thousand-watt, twenty-five-horsepower generator. The family had just finished Christmas dinner without missing a beat and were now moving into the family room to watch a laser disc presentation of *White Christmas.* Daughter Cindy furrowed her brow. "Hey, listen," she announced.

Ken complied for a second. He heard his generator thrumming quietly from the side of the house. He continued loading the huge disk into the player.

"I hear my generator. That's all."

"I know, Dad, that's what I mean."

Kathy Harrison looked quizzically at her husband. "Cin's right," she said. "It's like somebody threw a switch on the birds."

Ken wanted to watch the movie, not investigate why his large birds were suddenly model citizens. "Maybe they just got tired of complaining."

"I'll go check," said younger daughter Jill, who started heading toward the back door.

"No way," Ken said, hitting play on Der Bingle and company. "We're watching the movie, young lady. Stay right where you are."

It was so black on the road leading to the Greenwoods' home, Carillo was beginning to wish he hadn't come. Having heard the call from the department to respond to the Greenwoods' emergency, he radioed in, acknowledging he would respond to the so-called urgent plea for help. Now that he was here, a power outage wasn't something he'd planned on. Christmas wasn't that big a deal for Carillo, but the insane events of the day had caused him to miss all the football and for that he was fuming.

Creeping his car along in the sheeting rain, guided only by sparks of lightning and the glow from his headlights, he finally arrived at the Greenwoods' driveway to find it blocked by a temporary chain-link gate.

"Fuckin' asshole," he muttered.

He remembered the long driveway and was mad that he'd left his house without a hat.

The rain blasted him as he got out of the car. Clutching at his jacket, he found the end of the metal fence and squeezed his way between it and a tree. His feet and legs were instantly soaked by wet ferns just as a ragged strand of galvanized steel tore his sleeve.

"Fuck!" he yelled, now furious that he'd ventured all the way out here. What he would never admit to himself was that he was probably driven less by his suspicions of Ty Greenwood than by his hatred of wildly successful people.

Navigating in the dim glow of the rushing clouds, Carillo found the driveway and headed toward the house. So much inconvenience only heightened his anger, so Ty Greenwood the escaped killer was going to feel every cut of his whip. Carillo felt a thrill when he visualized arresting Greenwood, then both cuffing and shackling him to enhance his humiliation in front of his family.

Arriving at the plaza between the house and garage, in the darkness and downpour Carillo could just make out the large wooden awning that extended ten yards from the front door. He headed for it. As he did, movement caught his eye—the vague shape of what appeared to be someone walking at the edge of the yard, seventy or eighty feet to his left.

"Hey, you, stop! Sheriff's officer!" he yelled in a command that was overly dramatic, dialed up to overcome the rain and wind as well as soften any resistance. But the person vanished behind the house, and that infuriated Carillo because he knew the guy heard him.

"Fuckin' dickhead!" No civilian was going to disobey his order.

Carillo headed quickly for the corner of the house, sure it was Greenwood playing games with him. As he rounded the corner, he saw the shadowy figure moving ahead of him, halfway to the next corner. What seemed odd was the size. The huge house was throwing off his yardstick . . . but he could swear the shape of the person seemed too big. He chalked it up to the darkness playing visual tricks.

He shouted another order to comply and the figure suddenly turned and came back toward him. Carillo put his hand around the stock of his holstered gun to show he meant business and advanced to meet the man with his game face set. But the scale of the house was really far bigger than he'd gauged, because as the shadow man got closer, he seemed to get impossibly larger. It was then Karl Carillo realized, too late, that it wasn't a man at all.

77

"What was that?" Ronnie said, almost to herself, not sure whether Greta or the kids were within earshot.

The faint yet disturbing screech sounded like it came from somewhere outside.

"Greta?" she called out, then headed toward Greta's room on the other end of the house, past the TV and utility rooms.

"Greta?"

Greta appeared in the hallway down from her room, candle in hand.

"Did you hear that noise?" asked the young Swede, her eyes circles.

Ronnie nodded. "It sounded like, I don't know, a cougar maybe."

"What's a cougar?" Greta asked with trepidation.

"A lion. Well, like a lion, only smaller."

"A lion?" Greta said, her voice dropping to an awed hush. "Here?"

Ronnie didn't mean to scare her. "Really nowhere near as big," she said, trying to comfort her foreign charge. "But don't worry, either way it couldn't get into the house."

"I hope not," said Greta fearfully.

Ronnie touched Greta's arm reassuringly and headed back toward the other end of the house. She was beginning to worry about her husband.

* * *

The small two-leg he had just killed was not the one that let loose the thunder on him. As he walked around the big wood cave, he searched for the mind voice of the one with the thunder, the hating one.

He didn't sense the one with the thunder inside but knew there were females and some young in the cave, probably belonging to the one he wanted. If he killed them, the hating one would come.

A few minutes passed, and when no more strange sounds came from outside, Greta went back to her room to continue writing her letter by candlelight. After determining the kids were probably upstairs, Ronnie went into the kitchen, found an open bottle of cabernet, and poured a glass. She figured if nothing else she'd have her own Christmas party. She took a sip of the wine, breathed deeply, and tried to relax.

She hoped Ty would be home soon because she not only missed him, she felt safer with him around, what with the lights off and possible cougars in the yard. Then she felt like the heat pump just blew a faint burst of warm air onto her, yet she knew there was no power. If anything, the house was getting colder.

She shook off the feeling and was about to go check on the kids when a flash of lightning disclosed an out-of-place shape by the pool. It was so fast, she reasoned her eyes were playing games with her brain. She stared intently out the window, trying to discern what she thought she had seen.

Another moment went by and she was about to dismiss it and walk away when a great sustaining bolt of lightning lit the yard like a military flare, and what it revealed, in unmistakable electric detail, caused Ronnie's hand to go limp. The wineglass crashed to the floor. In that one bone-chilling second, the hulking form and glimpse of semi-human features told her two things, that her husband had been right all along and that she and her babies were in mortal danger.

Two stunned seconds later, a short spark of sky fire showed this fearsome night demon moving toward the house. Recoiling from the window, she experienced a terrible suspicion that it knew what she was thinking. Ronnie ran for the front of the house, forcing calm over her voice. "Kids? Kids? Come here, where are you?"

* * *

Greta loved the peace of the golden light illuminating her little manuscript. She loved America but had a few aches for the taste of home. She had decided to seek solace in a long letter to a former boyfriend whom she knew still carried a torch for her. Writing in Swedish in case anyone found it before she could post it, she waxed poetic in her native language.

Pausing to gather her thoughts, she picked up her iPod, stuffed the earpieces in, then scrolled up a soulful song by Alicia Keys. Setting the player back down, she glanced up into the tall bay window two feet away and her heart stopped. In the glass a huge, terrible face appeared, animal-like yet hideously mannish, a scraggly crown of hair cascading to mountainous shoulders. Its yellow eyes met hers and she fell back in horror, believing it to be the monstrous cougar Ronnie had so blithely described.

Then this monumental apparition reared back and exploded through the polygonal structure, a spray of glass and wood framing raining inward, blowing out the candle. Greta scrambled for the door but the thing was on her, grabbing her hair and growling viscerally. She screamed as her head snapped back and she was slammed like a sack of flour, first up into the twelve-foot ceiling, then onto her dresser, sending her perfumes, brushes, and mirror spinning across the room.

Utterly dazed, she had just enough awareness to know she was in the grasp of some dreadful monster. Her mind sparked past a shred of Christopher's description of Bigfoot. Suddenly she was airborne, tossed like a puppet through the shattered window onto the grass.

The cacophony of smashing and screaming and ungodly bellowing spurred Ronnie to race to protect her children.

"Meredith! Chris!" she screamed. Then she heard it, coming down the dark hall.

Ronnie turned to see an unreal humanoid shape filling most of the fifteen-foot-high passage and moving toward her. She ran into the kitchen and fumbled around the counter in darkness, trying to locate the knife rack. In her panic she knocked it over, sending knives flying. On the floor she quickly found the handle of a ten-inch butcher knife. Keeping low, she scurried on her hands and knees, below the counter line.

It came around the counter, its breaths like steam evacuating a boiler. She could feel it, not just its sickening odor and amplified sounds, but its anger, like a malevolent radar seeking her out.

"Mommy! Mommy!"

Ronnie's blood froze. Her younger child was just outside in the hallway, unaware of what awaited her around the corner.

"Run! Run, baby! Run upstairs!" Ronnie screamed.

Then she heard it turn toward her child. Popping up from behind the counter, Ronnie saw the towering form moving to the hall. Instinct took over as she lunged at the beast, the big knife gripped like a dagger. Leaping up, she landed on its lower back and grabbed a handful of long, gritty hair. With her other hand she rammed the knife home with all her might. The ear-blasting metallic scream it emitted was something the likes of which no human had ever heard.

Meredith shrieked and ran toward the stairway as fast as her little legs would carry her. The creature whirled, throwing Ronnie across the polished wood floor. Howling in fury and pain, it reached back for the knife.

The monster danced in rage and Ronnie saw no way to get past it to protect her children. It withdrew the blade, and its jet-plane bellow told Ronnie she was about to die in a most awful way. As it came for her, she leaped away through the opening to the hallway and realized there was only one way out.

The giant came out of the other end of the kitchen, into the hall, and bore down on her. She had three seconds—her hands found the secret panel—two seconds—she pushed and the hidden door popped open—one second—she smelled it as she tumbled inside, pulling the wine cellar door shut and falling down the stairs into the blackness.

Up above she heard it, muted now but still louder than any living thing she had ever heard. Her entire body shook, the shock of the last two minutes shorting all her circuits. The momentary relief from the terrible tension, mixed with her fear for her children, made tears roll from her eyes. She squeezed them shut against the darkness, relived Greta's mortal scream, and knew the poor girl was no more.

As the creature smashed at the walls above, she feared it would inadvertently pop the secret panel, open the hidden door, and somehow squeeze its massive frame down the stairs. Dying in the dark in the hands of that thing was not a death she deserved. Her shaking escalated to uncontrollable shivers. How could this be? If this is what Ty had faced, then why hadn't she believed him? But how could anyone believe this?

78

The Cavalier's bald tires caused Ty to nearly slide off the road several times as he took corners too fast in the rain. He hurtled through Snohomish, trying not to get the attention of the police but maintaining a speed well above the legal limit.

He prayed the car's owner hadn't yet reported the theft. He flew through a stop sign outside town and nearly hit an Explorer. Inhaling deeply, he realized he hadn't taken a good breath since leaving the highway ten minutes before. *Five more minutes.*

The female was hiding and he pounded holes in the walls trying to find her place of refuge. He could feel her but could not reach her. She had hurt him and he was going to destroy her.

Then he heard small voices of terror in his head. Her cubs. They were in the cave, somewhere above. Their mind voices were clear, pure. He would find them, kill them. Then the female would come. Females were stronger than the males and more reckless when it came to their young. He gave up on the wall.

Chris and Meredith sought refuge in Meredith's room. It was farthest from the stairs and offered access to the attic. Candles in hand, they climbed the wooden ladder onto the small balcony loft overlooking the main floor of the bedroom. His sister was crying and Chris tried to be the little man, still not sure what was loose in their house but knowing his mother's screamed instructions had been pretty specific: run.

"Here," he said, handing his candle to Meredith.

Chris climbed the short mahogany ladder to the hatch in the angled ceiling that led to the space above. From a gap in the molding he pulled out his secret key, a bent hairpin.

"Is Mommy okay? What's that downstairs?" sobbed Meredith, the candles in her hands shaking.

Chris worked the lock. "I don't know, a bear I guess."

"Is it Daddy's monster?"

Chris was surprised she knew about that. He'd assumed she'd been too young to remember. "No, I don't think so," he assured her. "Couldn't be." But he wasn't completely sure. He got the lock to snap and pushed the panel aside. "C'mon, I'll boost you up."

"No, no, it's too dark, you go," she said tearfully.

"You go," he said. "Hurry."

"No, it's scary," she said, near panic.

Then they heard it, quickly climbing the stairs, *thump, thump, thump*—five at a time. Meredith squealed in terror and almost climbed up her brother's back. Her candles went flying, down to the plush carpeted floor. While Chris took a moment to heft his little sister up into the opening, tongues of flame from the carpet began to animate macabre shadows on the walls.

When it rounded the corner, in the growing firelight Chris saw the most terrifying sight of his short life, an impossible two-legged creature—so huge it took his breath away—its carbon-hued face twisted with pain and demented rage. Chris's jaw fell open as the thing ducked under the eight-foot doorway and headed straight for him. Chris knew the indoor balcony's height was nine feet and saw that the monster's head was well above that. The thing could easily reach out and pluck him from it.

It took a swipe at him, missed, and knocked the little veranda from its moorings. Chris leaped to the carpet, and as the flames swarmed around his feet, his sister's tiny scream from the attic opening was drowned out by the inhuman roar of the beast looming over him.

It grabbed for him, then charged, forcing him into the corner. Chris had only one option and took it, the way he'd seen a zillion stuntmen do in movies, only this wasn't a movie. Putting his hands behind his neck, he leaped—staying as close to a ball as he could manage—and crashed through the window.

The Cavalier sailed down Ty's street at seventy. He slammed the brakes a hundred yards before his driveway, skidding sideways to a stop directly in front of the chain fence. An unmarked police sedan parked nearby caused his hopes to soar with the possibility that the situation was under control. He climbed around the chain-link gate and headed up the driveway to the house. With no lights on, it was hard to see any detail. Rounding the corner, he could barely make out the large, dark gray outline of the house in the acre clearing. Ty headed for the front door, praying he was early. He intended to get his family out and head to the safety of Bellevue.

Several steps from the door something caught his eye, a small shape bobbing as it came around the corner.

"Hey!" Ty yelled to get its attention.

"Dad? Is that you?" Chris said, running toward Ty.

As he got closer, Ty saw his son was limping and heard his heaving breath.

Ty went to one knee. "Jesus! What happened?"

"It's in the house . . . it chased me . . . room's on fire . . . Mere's in the attic," he exploded in a breathless stream of consciousness.

Ty's legs nearly collapsed. "Slow down," he said frantically. "*What's* in the house?"

"The thing," Chris said, near tears. "Your monster."

His worst fear realized, Ty asked, "Where's Mommy?"

"I don't know," Chris said, now starting to cry. "I heard real loud noises, then it came up and went for us. Mere's in the attic and the room's on fire," he repeated.

"Where's Greta? Is she home?" Ty asked.

"I don't know if she's okay. I heard her scream real bad," said the little boy, breaking down at those last words.

A loud crashing inside validated everything Ty's son had just said. Ty held his son's shoulders firmly and summoned his calmest voice. "Go to the garage, get in Mommy's car, and lock the door and get on the floor on the passenger side. Okay?"

Chris sniffled and nodded. "Okay. Is Mommy all right?"

Ty gave his son a quick hug, then gave him a push toward the garage. "She'll be fine," he said, "we'll all be fine. Go. Hurry."

Chris took two steps, then turned back. "Dad? Are there any more . . . of them?"

"No, son, just the one. Go ahead, you're okay."

Chris headed off and Ty followed his small shadow until it entered the garage, then he moved around the house, hoping to locate the thing before going inside. The last thing he wanted to do was barge in and come face to face with it. He pushed back the horrific visions assaulting his senses, that of his wife and daughter torn asunder by this enraged man-beast.

Hugging the perimeter of the structure, Ty turned the corner and followed the side of the house. A half dozen steps later he made out what looked like a person lying on the lawn. He approached, knelt down, then to his horror realized it was headless. Sickness gripped him as he tried to make out detail in the near blackness. Then he spotted another, smaller item a few yards away. He moved toward it and saw it was the head. Too dark to make an identification, but he could tell it was a man, which ruled out the body being Ronnie's or Greta's. But who?

When he turned the next corner, he saw illumination from above: his house was on fire. The flames in Meredith's bedroom were now blazing merrily away and spreading to the roof. Ty heard nothing else and feared that calling out might alert his foe. He had to find it before it found him.

79

The fire had driven him elsewhere in his search for the other cub—not the one who jumped, but the little female. He felt she was above him somewhere, in the upper part of the cave. Some of the cave's roof was too tall even for him to reach but there were places he could. The walls were soft and easily destroyed and he tore into them, looking for the cub.

He also sensed the one he wanted was near. The hating one with the thunder was feeling fear now—for his mate and his cubs—and that pleased him.

He knew if he found the female cub, the one he wanted would come.

Meredith moved away from the attic's access door and deeper into the void while smoke poured in, filling the space and making her cough. She was completely terrified, crawling in absolute darkness, burning to death or asphyxiation now threatening her as much as the monster.

And it was after her. She heard it below, tearing at the walls trying to get to her. She moved slowly, her tiny hands gingerly feeling their way over the joists, trying not to fall down into one of the many angles that made up the attic. The only times she had been up here were in Chris's company, but she had never felt comfortable. And they had *always* had a flashlight.

Like all kids, Meredith was afraid of monsters, her imagination promising a big paw reaching out from the darkness at any second and grabbing her. Now, alone in the blackness, the prospect of it really happening caused her to shake so hard she could barely move. Suddenly an explosion right beneath her rocked her perch as a fist bigger than a canned ham collided with the walls. Screaming hysterically, she clung like a limpet to the two-by-eight joist but lost control of her tiny bladder, releasing a warmth down her legs.

Ty heard the crashing and knew the creature was upstairs. With the electricity and phones out, the hardwired automatic fire alarm was inoperative. Ty gauged the fire and guessed it would take about fifteen to twenty minutes to engulf the upstairs. He had only that much time, or less, to save his family.

Ronnie heard the monster's pounding upstairs, but the volume was so loud she couldn't estimate the distance. It could be on either the ground floor or the one above. She worked her way up the stairs of the wine cellar on her hands and knees and slowly pushed the door open. It actually seemed light in the house compared to the coal mine she'd been in for the last five minutes.

Hearing the beating on the walls more clearly, she knew it was up in the bedrooms. She smelled smoke, and the terror of fire on top of this chilled her to the marrow. She moved fast, heading toward the stairs, thinking only of her children.

She rounded the corner below the stairs, ran smack into something, and screamed. Ty wrapped his arms around her.

"Ronnie! Oh baby, I'm glad you're okay."

Ronnie almost fainted, she was so relieved to see her husband. "The kids are upstairs!" she cried.

Ty put his hands firmly on her shoulders to calm her. "Chris is in the garage in your car. Is Mere still upstairs?"

"I think so."

"Go out, get in your car, and get the hell out of here," Ty said, hammering his words firmly.

"Okay, but what about—"

"*Rrrrrraaaaarrrggghh!*"

The giant form rounded the gallery above and came down the stairs, fast.

Ty and Ronnie sprinted to the front door.

"Get out and take the car!" Ty yelled, slowing to let Ronnie pass.

Ty exited the front door and slammed it to buy a second or two. As Ronnie raced to the garage, Ty backpedaled, keeping his momentum going. The giant primate burst through the teak and stained glass door like a high school pep banner. It went for Ty, who tried to lead it away from his wife and son. But instead of staying on him, it suddenly changed directions and went for the garage. Ty realized how cunning this thing was: it wanted him but knew his Achilles heel. It wanted to hurt him psychologically first. *Go after my family and you make me suffer, make me weak, you fucking bastard.* Ty bolted for the far side entrance to the garage.

Ronnie flew through the garage and grabbed the door handle to her Lexus—locked. She banged on the window for her son to unlock it.

"Christopher! Chris, let me in!"

"Mommy!" came his voice from somewhere nearby.

"Where are you?" she said, spinning around to find him.

"Here," he said. "The car's locked."

Suddenly the articulated garage door in front of the Lexus imploded. The creature ripped the wreckage out of his way, bent over, and entered the garage. Ronnie screamed and ran for her son's voice, hoping to use her body as a shield. Then an engine fired up and one of the cars down the line exploded through the closed door in a spray of splinters and shredded aluminum.

With the spare gasoline can on the seat beside him, Ty gunned the old Mercedes and whipped the wheel, spinning the car back around to face the garage. He aimed at the huge black shape in his high beams, put his foot to the floor, and launched straight toward it. It turned to see him, eyes reflecting laser red, then tried to leap out of the way. The car gunned into the garage and Ty spun the wheel, trying to make a direct hit, but only grazed the monster's leg before crashing completely through the back wall. Behind the garage in tall grass, Ty accelerated and fishtailed the old car, cranking it around for another try.

He passed the far end of the building, just on the tile apron, and saw Ronnie and Chris run out the side door. The wall around the door burst outward, the thing coming up fast behind them.

Ty slammed his brakes and jammed the car into reverse, just as the creature turned and came toward him from the side. As Ty hit the throttle, the beast grabbed the front wheel well and tipped the twenty-eight-hundred-pound car, then heaved, and suddenly Ty was upside down, the Mercedes's roof spinning on the tiles.

He was trapped. The pinned gullwing doors wouldn't open, and the upended gas can gurgled its contents onto the ceiling of the car. Ty spun, kicked out the passenger window and was part way out before the car stopped revolving. As the monster came toward him, he grabbed the gas can and slid out.

It loomed over him on the opposite side of the car. Ty knew it had him, its powerful stench overcoming the gas smell that roiled over Ty's nostrils, its breath forming clouds. They stood for a brief moment, just looking at each other. Ty knew there was no running around the car in circles because it could easily toss the car out of the way and that would be it. Suddenly he remembered something and reached into his coat pocket. Taking out Ben's old lighter, he bent down and flicked it in the interior of his beloved classic car. The fumes ignited instantly with far more fury than Ty imagined. The blast knocked him back, but he rolled out upright, gas can still in hand, and ran to the front of the house.

Momentarily caught off guard by the fire, the creature gave chase, but Ty had enough head start to get inside. He ran up the stairs.

"Mere!" he yelled. "Meredith!"

At the top of the stairs, Ty tipped the container and let a quart or so pour over the marble steps. The thing came through the front door and quickly ascended the stairs. Ty fell back and snapped the lighter. Still wet from the earlier drenching, the lighter just clicked. No spark. *"It doesn't always light each time, but it's yours."* The monster was halfway up the stairs. Click, no spark. It was at the top of the stairs. Click . . . spark . . . *WHOOOM!*

Caught in the middle of the gas when it ignited, the beast loosed a roar that shook even that majestic residence. Ty scrambled to escape its clutches as it lashed out at him. Then, as the flames climbed its massive legs, distracting it, Ty escaped down the hall, yelling his daughter's name. Smoke clotted the air, flames now filling both ends of the hall-way.

The creature's agonized screams faded as it ran down the stairs to seek refuge in the wet outside.

Ty cried out for his daughter, "Meredith! Meredith!"

"Daddy?" came a very muffled little voice.

"Honey? Where are you?" He thought her voice was coming through an air return. "Mere! Where are you?"

"It's smoky, Daddy!" Her panicked little voice lanced Ty's heart.

"I know, sweetie," he said, trying to keep his tone calm. "Keep talking, I'll find you."

Ty couldn't figure out where she was. Perhaps she had somehow climbed into a part of the wall through one of the large holes made by the beast. Meredith kept talking and Ty kept trying to zero in on her, kicking holes in the drywall to find his little girl.

"Daddy, is that you doing that?" she whimpered.

"Yes, sweetie, it's me, I'm almost there. Keep talking, kiddo."

"I'm here, Daddy!" she yelled.

Ty looked up and realized she was fifteen feet above him in the ceiling. She was somewhere to the left side of the huge skylight that ran the length of the hall.

"Shit," he grated.

"Is it okay? Can you get me?"

"Yes, honey. I'll be right back."

Ty picked up the gas can and ran toward the stairs. He knew there was an access door at the end of the hall, but without a flashlight, or a reliable lighter, he might get lost in that huge black space trying to find her. He knew where she was, and ripping away the ceiling was the fastest way to reach her. But for that he needed the ladder. Which was in the garage.

The gas on the stairs had dripped down, and now the entry walls and the eighteen-foot Christmas tree were ablaze. Dancing through the flames, Ty sardonically thought, *At least it's light enough to see now.* At the bottom of the stairs he slowed and glanced around for his adversary. Nothing in the entry or down the hall. *Must have gone out the front door.*

A thundering explosion shook the ground and rattled the windows as the fireball from the burning Mercedes billowed skyward. Ty looked out the door, saw the blazing hulk but no sign of Ronnie and Chris. Or the thing. Stepping carefully outside, he looked around, then bolted to the garage. He hoped the fire had driven it off. The burning car provided enough light to see around the plaza. Ty entered the garage and found the large aluminum extension ladder.

With the ladder over his shoulder and gas can still in hand, he trotted for the front door. As he reached the steps, he heard something over the hiss of the rain, a fast slapping sound, and he spun in time to see the thing flying out of the woods like a monstrous smoking ghost ship, bearing down on him at full clip. Ty threw down the ladder and ran into the house. He heard it enter behind him in angry pursuit. At the kitchen, Ty turned and went for one of the French doors, trying to lead it outside. He thought about Meredith and his promise to return. Knowing the smoke would soon overcome his baby, he quickly devised a desperate play.

Out by the pool, Ty ran to the far edge and stopped. He could hear the thing somewhere near the kitchen, banging, trying to find a way out. Ty unscrewed the filler neck of the gas can and upended it, creating a semicircular puddle at his feet.

He thought of that Steely Dan song as he swallowed hard and gathered his courage.

> *Throw a kiss and say good-bye*
> *I'll make it this time*
> *I'm ready to cross that fine line . . .*

He had wanted to die that night not so long ago, but now he wanted to live. Badly. But his family was at stake and this was the only option he could come up with. If he didn't make it, he prayed Ronnie would save their baby girl. His job right now was to stop this thing, kill it.

Drink Scotch whisky all night long and die behind the wheel . . .

"Come and get me you son-of-a-bitch!" he roared.

He opened Ben's old lighter and waited.

He could no longer feel the mind voices of the small two-legs. His hate-infected rage had drowned them out. All he wanted was to get the one who hurt him, rip him to small pieces and eat him as his mate and cubs watched. Then he would eat them while they still drew breath.

The wood cave burned hot and he felt trapped as smoke seared his eyes. He was enraged that the small two-legs used fire against him yet again. The one he wanted was outside, by the small pond, just standing there, defying him. He smashed through the wall and scrambled to destroy the hated small two-leg.

Ty watched the dark juggernaut rip through the wall and come for him. In the two or three seconds he had left, he couldn't help but be impressed by its incredible size and perfection of purpose. An apparently invincible foe, like a primitive human magnified to the extreme of physical evolution by a demented Mother Nature.

It rounded the pool, and when it reached the point of no return, Ty held out the old lighter and bet everything it would work one last time. He snapped the little grinding wheel against the flint . . . click. Nothing. Click. Nothing.

The creature was upon him, then click—

Spark—

The gas fumes swirling around him ignited in a dull whooshing sound that signaled the end. Flames instantly engulfed Ty's legs, feet, all around him . . . then *all of him.*

The monster grabbed him by the neck and lifted him. Ty's arms flailed at it in response but did no damage. Ty's vision turned to fireworks, both from the flames and the huge fingers squeezing off the blood to his brain. It held him so their faces nearly touched, its fetid exhalations a nauseating tropical wind. Ty looked into its golden eyes and was able to conjure one final act of defiance.

He spit into its face.

As his brain shut down, his last thought was that he hadn't protected his family. His heart broke as he lost consciousness and death beckoned . . .

Then he felt the impact of hard cement and realized it had dropped him. Ty shook off his light-headedness and saw the gyrating thing above him, now skirted in flames to its waist. He felt heat and looked down to see he was still ablaze from his chest down. Summoning his last bit of strength, Ty rolled the two feet over the pool's lip and into its shallow end. Breaking the surface, Ty looked up and saw the dancing monster, ringed in fire. Lightning flashed as it screamed like a thousand banshees and Ty ducked back under the water to hide.

The flames tore at him, but he knew he would live by following the small two-leg into the water. There he would destroy him. As he stepped to the edge of the small pond, he saw lightning and heard thunder—

Then another thunder—the other thunder—

His eyes and mouth opened wide in numbing shock as this thunder found him, clawed at him, tore him open. This thunder cut to his heart and his strength flowed out, his powerful voice silenced, his exquisite rage and magnificence gone in an instant.

Ty broke the surface just in time to see the monster crashing onto him like a felled oak. He ducked, but the massive creature splashed down, pushing him to the pool bottom. His panic caused him to suck water.

He was under the surface, with the beast attacking him: Ty's misery was complete.

The bone-jarring recoil from the giant rifle knocked Ronnie completely off her feet. Slightly stunned, she shook off the effects and sat up to see she had made a direct hit. The beast had toppled into the pool. She tried to take a breath and found that the sledgehammer blow from the padded stock had knocked the wind out of her.

Within a second or two Ty realized the thing wasn't moving, it was just deadweight. Pinned under the icy water, Ty struggled to free himself but couldn't get his left leg out from under the beast. Unable to stifle his cough reflex, he inhaled more water. *After all this I'm going to drown.* He struggled, but the water in his lungs caused him to cough again and that was going to be the end of—

Something grabbed him, pulled violently, and his leg came free. Two hands—human hands—dragged him out of the water. He was gagging and coughing. Water poured from Ty's throat as his lungs labored to expel fluid. A hand slapped his back to help him purge the water.

"Ty! Ty! Are you okay?"

Ty continued choking and looked up to see the concerned face of his wife. He exaggerated his coughs to clear the water from his lungs, then rose unsteadily to his feet.

"The house . . . ," he coughed, "Mere!"

Ty, half leaning on Ronnie, staggered toward the fire.

81

Before going into the house and retrieving Ty's rifle, Ronnie had broken the window on the Lexus and retrieved her phone.

"I called nine-one-one," she told Ty.

Between coughs, Ty expressed the bottom line. "They . . . won't be . . . here . . . in time."

Inside the smoking house Ty and Ronnie climbed the stairs through the flames and propped the ladder against the wall. Ty started unsteadily up the ladder and Ronnie stopped him.

"I'll go. You're shaky, plus we'd have to make a bigger hole for you."

Ty resisted for a second, but as usual, she was right. Then Ronnie did an odd thing. She turned and ran down the stairs, yelling over her shoulder, "I'll be right back!"

Ty watched, perplexed and frustrated as his wife negotiated the walls of flame wrapping the stairs and disappeared around the corner. He looked up to the ceiling and screamed, "We're coming, baby. Hang on!"

A moment later Ronnie reappeared, taking the stairs two at a time. Carrying a pair of infrared goggles and a claw hammer, she scurried up the ladder, and with machinelike intensity slammed holes in the drywall ceiling. As soon as the hole was large enough, dark, thick smoke billowed forth, punctuating how short their time was. In less than a minute Ronnie had torn out a hole big enough to wriggle through. She pulled the goggles down and pushed off the ladder, disappearing into the smoking aperture. Ty held the ladder and ran his hand nervously over his face and through his hair, the tension unbearable.

Ronnie coughed hard and yelled for her daughter, the black and gray infrared images of roiling smoke and heat the only thing in her field of view. The smoke was overwhelming, and with a sense of terror she knew she could endure the noxious mix of smoke and ash for only a moment longer before passing out. She screamed and choked her words out, "Meredith! Meredith!" Her single thought of losing her daughter so terrible, she was ready to die to prevent that outcome.

Then a bit of grayish white ten feet away, rising a few inches above the joist, caught her eye. As she quickly scurried toward it, her foot slipped between the joists and crashed through drywall. For a split second she almost plummeted through the ceiling but then regained her footing and made her way to the form. It was Meredith. She grabbed the little girl and hauled her over the joists to her point of entry. Just as she got to the hole, a hand reached inside and pulled her daughter through. A choking Ronnie followed Ty down the ladder, and they ran out of the house, Ty now half carrying her along with Meredith slung partly over his shoulder.

Reaching safety, Ty set Meredith on the ground and performed mouth-to-mouth. A moment later the little girl snapped back to life, her lungs coughing out their poison. Ronnie lay down, still coughing, and hugged her baby and sobbed. Ty leaned down and enfolded them in his arms as they all cried with joy and release.

Though Chris had been ordered by his mother to stay in the garage, he exited his hiding place after figuring out the danger had passed. Five minutes later the first fire crew in their big White diesel crashed through the chain-link gate, and a procession of trucks followed them up the drive.

An ambulance arrived with three police cars, and in seconds paramedics were attending to Meredith. Ronnie held her daughter's hand as one of the paramedics placed an oxygen mask on her face. The man gently lifted Ronnie's comforting hand away and indicated they needed room.

"She's gonna be fine, ma'am," he assured her.

Ronnie smiled thankfully at him, then embraced her husband, his clothes wet and burned. Another paramedic approached and helped

Ty to the ambulance. His hair was singed and he looked like hell, but his burns were only superficial.

Then from around the corner stumbled a deeply shaken but very much alive Swedish au pair. A paramedic rushed to help Greta.

The fire department quickly contained the blaze in the upper story and extinguished the one downstairs. One of the crews had driven their rig around back, and their lights blazed over the area. Two firemen stared into the pool at the floating behemoth, one holding the huge Holland & Holland rifle that had ended its reign of terror. A young sheriff's deputy walked over and stood next to them.

Gazing down at the giant corpse adrift face down in the blood-stained water, the young deputy asked the fireman tending to the rifle, "I heard the wife shot it. That the gun?"

The fireman looked over. The deputy's name badge said "Alexander." The man nodded.

"May I see it?" asked Deputy Bill Alexander.

The fireman handed him the heavy rifle. "It's all yours."

Bill took his eyes off the extraordinary body in the pool long enough to examine the rifle. He knew his guns and was aware of both the rarity and power of this firearm.

"Yeah," he said to the fireman but more to himself, "that's about the right size."

Epilogue

The sun was about as hot as it got on planet Earth and that was just right for Ty. As he floated through time and space, his only connection to reality was the brilliant fiery orange dazzling his retina through closed eyes. A rivulet of perspiration ran down his jaw and dropped from his chin onto his bare chest. Something tickled his forearm—fingers—and they moved slowly toward his hand, a pinky hooking his.

"Where are the kids?" he asked, not opening his eyes.

"Back at the resort," said Ronnie, the soothing calm in her voice something Ty hadn't been used to in a long time. "You dozed off," she continued. "They went to some sort of swimming party with those kids from London."

"Are they . . . ," he started.

"Highly supervised. They're fine," she said anticipating him.

"How about me? You let me fall asleep in the sun, huh?"

"I've been basting you," she said, playfully squirting him with a glob of cool sunscreen.

His eyes opened and he grabbed her arm, pulling her close. The beach was sugar, the ocean an opal, all under a cloudless Caribbean sky.

"Now you've got to rub it in."

Ty was surprised but pleased that Ronnie had doffed the top of her bathing suit. "Going native, huh?" he said with a smile.

Ronnie rubbed the lotion slowly. "Hey, there's no one around, why not? I could use a little color."

Ty sat up in his beach chair and pivoted, putting his hands to her waist while she continued smoothing in sunscreen. He leaned in and kissed a bare breast.

"Hmmm. Cocoa butter."

Ronnie smiled lustfully. "Yeah. Want to taste the other one?"

He looked into her eyes. The whimsy of the moment melted away as they saw each other again with the same powerful attraction as the first time, only heightened by love that had been tempered in the fires. Ty pulled Ronnie to him and they rolled off the chaises onto the sand. It had been a long time, but they were one again. They made love while the palms watched and whispered their secrets in the breeze.

Ten days after Mac had been admitted near death, his doctor pronounced him a miracle patient and released him. Girded in three casts, he was sent home to be tended by an in-home nurse for the next twelve weeks. He'd hoped for a young, cute one, but his nurse Marlene, a stocky married woman in her late fifties, settled in quickly and amused Mac to no end with her acerbic wit.

Mac sat propped in his chair eating lunch in front of the television when a knock sent Marlene to the door. She opened it to find a Japanese news crew.

"Pardon me," said their impeccably suited reporter, "but may I have an audience with Detective Mac Schneider?"

Since the doorway didn't have a sightline to Mac in his chair, Marlene ad-libbed.

"I'm sorry, but he left this morning."

The man furrowed his brow. "But he is recovering, no? I did not know he could travel."

Marlene's civilian clothes didn't betray her role as a nurse.

"Oh, he's all fine now," she fibbed. "He underwent some sort of new electric current therapy. It's the latest thing in this country. You oughta do a story on it. It totally healed him in two hours. He went off to play racquetball, then I believe he's leaving to go scuba diving in Mexico. He'll be back in a month. I'll tell him you stopped by. Thanks," and she closed the door on the befuddled newsmen.

Mac chuckled. "You should have your own show."

"Me? No. You're the celebrity. But I can't keep doing that with all of them. Are you ever going to give any interviews?"

Mac looked away. "Maybe, yeah. Eventually."

During Mac's hospital stay, Ty had stopped by a few times, including the day he and his family headed to the British Virgin Islands for a month. They mostly talked about Ben. There was no postmortem, no guilt, just regrets that he was gone. Ty gave Mac Ben's old cigarette lighter, saying, "This saved my life. I have a suspicion it'll help you heal faster."

Mac smiled softly and took it. "You know, it may sound a little nuts, but I think Ben's still around, keepin' his eye on us."

Ty nodded. "Yeah, I feel him too."

During Ty's last visit before the trip, Mac thanked him for saving him and Ty shook it off with "You would have done the same." When Ty stood to leave, instead of shaking his hand as they usually did, he hesitated, then leaned down and hugged Mac, signifying a bond between two men who trusted each other with their lives.

Snohomish County Sheriff Barkley came by and offered his apologies for the way Mac had been treated, then chided him for not coming forward.

"Would you have believed me?" Mac asked.

The chief paused for a moment. "Hell no."

Both men laughed.

Then the mood got somber as they discussed the hero's funeral Carillo received, with more than two thousand peace officers from around the country in attendance.

When Mac found the energy, he phoned Kelly Carillo to offer his condolences.

"He really admired you, Mac," she said. "You were like the big brother he never had. He was always competing with you, but he loved you."

They spoke warmly of Karl, but Mac knew a thousand things about her husband he would never tell her. And she knew a thousand things Mac didn't know. It was left that Karl Carillo had been a good husband, father, and cop.

"Want some more soup?" asked Marlene, pulling Mac back from his thoughts.

He handed her his bowl. "Yeah, it's good. Thanks."

As Marlene went into the kitchen, Mac looked up. "You like being married?" he asked.

"It's got its ups and downs," she answered, dishing up his soup. "Maybe I do. But what do I know? I've been married thirty-six years. I don't know the difference."

She returned, setting the bowl on the lamp table, and Mac's face warmed for the first time in a while. "Yeah," he said. "You know."

Marlene's eyes smiled and she went back to the bedroom to straighten up. *He's such a nice guy, his ex must have been an idiot.*

Watching television with the sound muted, Mac sipped his soup and thought about Kris. Of all the victims spirited into the depths of the woods, she was the only one whose remains were found. They were collected by a search team, but her TV station dawdled in handling arrangements, so Mac made a few calls and had them quickly shipped to her folks.

Mac wondered, if not for a few quirks of fate, what things might have been like with her. Then, just as quickly as the musing came over him, he didn't want to think about it, any of it. He blanked it all out, turned up the TV volume, and continued eating his soup.

Greta Sigardsson, aside from chronic neck pain, emerged relatively un-scathed from her spectacular encounter. After spending a day in the hospital for observation, she had planned on taking the first plane back to Sweden, as she had had just about enough of America.

Then Hollywood called. A very well connected producer, after see-ing her interviewed on a number of shows, approached her to screen-test for his latest picture, the third in a wildly successful teen horror series. Greta balked at first, but the possibility of a $300,000 payday en-ticed her. After demonstrating a modicum of camera presence, she got the part and was off to the races.

Within five hours of getting the role, she had signed with an agent, taken on a manager, and hired an entertainment attorney. Within ten days she was dating the hottest young actor in the biz, had inked a million-dollar contract with Revlon, and had leased a bunga-low in the Hollywood Hills that had reputedly been Frank Sinatra's secret love nest with Ava Gardner.

When her new manager diplomatically suggested she change her last name, she snapped, "That's what they told Schwarzenegger." Greta was home.

"There you go," said the cheery young woman behind the table, handing former sheriff's deputy Bill Alexander his information packet. "Good luck," she added.

Bill walked away and poked through the packet. Entering the gymnasium-sized hall, one of four in session that evening at the Bellevue Holiday Inn, Bill found four hundred folding chairs, arranged in orderly rows. They were already three-quarters filled. He wandered down the center aisle and located a seat about ten chairs in.

A massive banner behind the podium proclaimed the purpose for which he and the assembling crowd were present: "Buy Homes! Zero Down!" Another banner was simply a string of dollar signs. When he had seen the newspaper ad, the concept of being his own boss had excited him. The prospect of a whole new career was thrilling. No one in the sheriff's department ever discovered he was the one who leaked that case file to the press. Only after he quit did he find out they had the casting. If he'd known about it, he might have swiped that too, and maybe sent it to the *Seattle Times*.

But right now it didn't really matter because he was dreaming of his future freedom, not to mention purchasing power. Why, he might get himself that Chevy Tahoe he'd always wanted. But what appealed most at that moment to the former law enforcement officer was being in the bosom of a large gathering of fellow human beings, all contained in a warm, very well lighted room. A very different place and situation from another night not long ago crossed his mind, and he shivered so vigorously the woman next to him looked over.

He smiled quickly. "Felt a draft."

J. D. Watts was convicted of murdering Leon Newburg, based upon evidence from the crime scene such as Watts's fingerprints on one end of the baseball bat and Newburg's brain matter on the other, as well as blood and hair from the trunk of the car. But his story, in light of what had happened, turned him into something of a minor celebrity, being one of the few who survived the monster's rage. However, some of J. D.'s prison colleagues didn't appreciate the attentions of the news magazines and true crime shows, and one morning, as he took a shower, they jammed the sharpened handle of a spoon through his heart.

By the time Ty, Ronnie, and the kids returned from the tropics in late January, the crew Ty hired had already cleared away the destroyed sections of the house and had commenced rebuilding. Sorting through their clothing and other items, Ronnie made determinations about what could be saved and what would be tossed owing to fire or smoke damage. She had also restructured her job, after gaining approval from her partners, to reduce her role in the day-to-day operations and to work out of the house via video teleconferencing. Technology allowed her freedom from the office for all but about fifteen hours a week.

Ty temporarily assumed the job as curator of what many were calling the greatest anthropological discovery of the millennium. To field requests from myriad television and radio shows, to respond to movie and book offers, to organize lectures and symposiums, as well as to schedule audiences with various scientists, scholars, and researchers, Ty set up an office in downtown Snohomish and assembled a small staff. Safely reposing in a specially constructed chilled locker at an "undisclosed location" was Ty's organization's sole asset, a ten-foot-eight-and-three-eighths-inch, thirteen-hundred-and-eighty-eight-pound cadaver—allowing for the sizable hole through its upper body.

Ty set up formal examinations and cataloguing of the creature, which was eventually christened by science, after a great deal of rancor and dissent, as *Homo gigantus benjaminus,* the third name a slight deviation in naming protocol to honor the man Ty successfully lobbied to credit as its discoverer. Of course Ty retained all exhibition and licensing rights. After careful planning as to how to administer the body and the inherent rights—estimated by *Forbes* to be worth in excess of one hundred million dollars—Ty created a trust to aid the families of all the murder victims. That done, every cent of the remaining monies was pledged to funding everything from cryptozoological research to humanitarian aid for undeveloped nations.

*   *   *

When Ty and Ronnie heard of Greta's recent success, they sent her a huge bouquet and wished her well. Before leaving on their healing trip, Ty sought out the nurse whose phone he'd swiped and gave her a check for $10,000 and a prepaid cell phone for the next five years. She was bowled over and said she wished he'd taken her wallet and keys and maybe even her two kids.

Then Ty went to the home of the owner of the woeful Cavalier, a thirty-eight-year-old divorced ER nurse with four kids, and profusely apologized for the theft. She calmly reassured Ty that she understood, which was easy to do given that Ty Greenwood had recently been featured on the covers of *Time, Newsweek, Life,* and three hundred or so other publications worldwide. But she was speechless when Ty handed her the keys to his fairly new Suburban along with a check for $100,000. "Your car saved my family" were the only words he could choke out as they hugged.

With Ronnie's blessing, Ty mulled over the notion of taking an active role in the exploration of unexplained phenomena around the world but finally dismissed it. He knew the most important job he could have would be watching his kids grow up, so he decided to stay home, do research, and read and write. He had some hard moments, even days, suffering the effects of alcohol and OxyContin withdrawal, but he was under a doctor's care and through his own iron will would be healthy again.

During the vacation Ty and Ronnie agreed to seek therapy, both together and individually. There were many walls that needed to come down and they understood the necessity of an experienced guide to help tumble them.

While the earth's media co-opted Ty's photos in their articles, Ty actually passed on all offers for direct interviews—from magazines to Barbara Walters—save for one. Turning his back on the giants of the news and entertainment world, Ty gave his only interview to his new friend, John Baxter, publisher of the *Snohomish Daily News.*

As part of her job of sorting through the wreckage, Ronnie checked all the computers in the house and ran diagnostics to make sure they were working properly. Calling up Ty's files, she was about to launch her damage-checking software when she noticed the file "Why I Killed Myself." Some mental backtracking on the entry date reminded her it was the morning he had driven off in his Mercedes. And the title told her much.

Her fingers kissed a couple of keys and highlighted the file line item. As she poised her digit on the delete key, she hesitated. She knew Ty had created the file for her to discover; she just knew him too well. So much had happened since and she knew the file was old history, written by a very different Ty Greenwood. But there was curiosity, about the whats, the whys, and maybe even the hows. Suddenly, with a terrible thought of the latter, she quickly stroked the key, and the file—and that chapter in their life—was gone.

"Hey," came that soft southern vocal coloration, "what's up?"

Ronnie turned fast and guiltily got up from the chair. "Oh, nothing," she said to Ty, "just running diagnostics. Your computer's okay."

Ty felt Ronnie's heart beating rapidly as he took her in his arms. He understood they were all still suffering from the effects of the attack. Then his eye caught the screen. Though she'd quit the directory, he remembered that one file from what seemed like so long ago. For a second he wondered if Ronnie had read it, but he knew his wife too well. It wouldn't have mattered to him if she had, because things were okay now.

They kissed and Ronnie pulled back slightly, her face suddenly concerned.

"Where are the kids?" she asked. She hadn't seen them in the last hour, so consumed was she with the cleanup. It was a question both of them had asked a lot lately, almost unconsciously. Ty looked into her eyes and smiled. For the first time in a long time Ronnie saw that strong, loving sunshine in the face of her man, the old Ty. He was back, his shoulders broad again. He kissed her softly, then put his hand to her head, bringing their cheeks together.

"Safe," he assured her. "They're safe."

Doris Campbell had not slept well since losing Ben. But it was not because she worried about her future. Ben had secretly salted money away over the years, and between it and his insurance Doris was set for the rest of her days. Ben had also arranged for an account that would pay for everything, including her Home Shopping Channel bills

("Within reason," said the lawyer). But her zest for TV shopping had waned after she'd lost the most important thing in her life.

Turning in to bed early, Doris tossed and turned but sometime around midnight passed into dreamland. So it was a surprise to hear that familiar voice, gentle but strong and very real, whisper in her ear. A sleep-dazed Doris bolted upright, the murky room's shadows playing tricks on her: a familiar tall, lanky shape appeared at the foot of her bed.

"Benny?" she said, rubbing her eyes to focus yet knowing it couldn't be. "Benny?"

Then it was gone.

Doris sat in the same place for a few moments, but nothing else happened. She knew those whispered words she imagined she'd heard had been just a wishful dream. She'd never really had the chance to say good-bye. Feeling sad, a little empty, Doris finally gave up and laid her head back on the pillow. His passing caused her more pain than she had ever felt. She had been balming her other hurt for years with shopping, but now, without him, she had to stand on her own. It scared her but she had courage. Closing her eyes, she knew Benny had always been her crutch, and although he was gone, she still felt his strength.

As she was regretting losing her chance to tell him good-bye . . .

She felt a weathered old hand lovingly brush her face. She didn't need to open her eyes, she knew that touch.

"Love you too," she answered the whispered words, then fell into peaceful sleep.

Afterword

On a sunny Friday afternoon, October 20, 1967, an ex–rodeo rider named Roger Patterson, along with another cowboy named Bob Gimlin, were guiding their horses through a remote creek bed near Bluff Creek, in northwestern California's Humboldt County, twenty miles from the Pacific Ocean. Something spooked their mounts and the men were thrown to the ground. As a large, hairy black creature strode away from them, Patterson juggled his sixteen-millimeter camera and captured some of the most famous footage ever recorded.

The film was analyzed frame by frame at the time by the special effects department of Universal Studios. Their professional opinions were that the overall effect, from the sheen of the multicolored hair to the cords and sheets of musculature undulating under that hair, could not possibly have been man-made, given the limited technology of the day, even with an unlimited budget. Since then many experts have deconstructed and analyzed the film, most recently by using the latest computer technology. All acknowledge that it is a virtual impossibility that the film was faked and that the subject was simply a man in a fur suit. In 1969, Canadian John Green, a former journalist and still one of the most respected of Bigfoot investigators, showed an executive at Disney the film and was told essentially the same thing.

* * *

So, does a North American great ape exist? And if it does, the natural follow-up question is What is it? As a boy growing up in Oregon, I had a fascination with this uncatalogued hominid that began when my parents read me a series of newspaper reports on the bizarre encounters of a road-building crew at a remote location in the mountains of northern California. The men reported a number of inexplicable occurrences over several evenings. After the workers turned in for the night, various items were vandalized, including a three-hundred-pound oil drum—carried half a mile and hurled into a ravine—and the tire of an earthmover, weighing nearly eight hundred pounds, that was rolled and hefted hundreds of yards, then tossed like a child's toy into a ditch.

The nightly visitors to the road-building crew also disturbed other equipment and, in each instance, the morning light revealed enormous humanlike footprints peppering the dust around their encampment. The possibility that the events were hoaxes was eventually dismissed given the sheer weight of the items that had been disturbed.[1]

I was particularly impressed then, as I am even now, at these spectacular demonstrations of brawn. In the last few years I've occasionally watched the World's Strongest Man Competition on ESPN, and I think of that earthmover tire back then—so effortlessly carried and rolled—as I watch men who are literally the strongest of their species exerting themselves to their limits to merely tip the same item end over end. Eventually, when people began to accept that perhaps something odd was indeed afoot, one proposed answer was that the crew may have encroached on the territory of enormous unknown beings who wanted them gone.

Not long after I discovered Bigfoot, I learned that a team led by New Zealand's Sir Edmund Hillary had just spent months searching Nepal and Tibet for the legendary yeti. To an eight-year-old kid the possibility that a different version of such a fantastic creature was practically in my own backyard was thrilling. It was then that I began a lifelong quest to determine whether these creatures existed, and if so, what they were. Years later when I was looking for a subject for my first

---

[1] In November 2002 the contractor in charge of that project, Ray Wallace, died. His family then came forth with the announcement that Wallace had created a huge hoax by faking some footprints with wooden appendages. The truth is Wallace did fake some prints but most of the evidence from the construction site was unexplained by his fakery.

novel, knowing what I did about Bigfoot, he seemed like a natural as an antagonist.

When I was all of nine, I went to my local library and checked out the book *Abominable Snowman: Legend Come to Life* by the celebrated British zoologist Ivan T. Sanderson.[2] Though much of Sanderson's technical rationale confounded my fourth-grade brain, I was mesmerized by the many anecdotes and eyewitness accounts. It was at that time that I realized these large creatures were being seen all over the world, and that the American and Canadian West counted more sightings than anywhere else. Incidentally, the term *Bigfoot* was coined by a newspaper reporter at the time of the Northern California sightings and I use that name for the sake of clarity.

The mythology of *every* North American Indian tribe includes a large creature, neither man nor animal, that walks the forest floor on two legs. Indians have carved uncounted thousands of totems in their honor. From Northern California through British Columbia and up into the Yukon, Northwest Territories, and Alaska, nearly every totem has a representation of this manlike being. According to scholars who have studied tribal mythology, these creatures from Native American legends and folk stories are seen almost exclusively as corporeal and not ethereal. That they are viewed in the same vein as other living entities such as eagles or wolves, as opposed to spirits or demons, is telling. Yet Native American tradition generally elevates these beings somewhat over their fellow forest dwellers in that they are ascribed traits that are more human than animal. Indian folklore—and in many cases, acknowledgment as fact within historical Indian culture—has these creatures possessing such advanced qualities as wisdom and even spirituality. They are often viewed as gentle protectors and the prospect of glimpsing or even encountering one is not to be feared. However, just as humans give each other mixed reviews, North American Indians acknowledge pretty matter-of-factly that while most of these beings are good, some are not so good.

A study of maps of the American and Canadian West show more than two thousand places with Native American names referring either

[2]Chilton Company, 1961.

directly or indirectly to Bigfoot. Interestingly, the locations mainly correspond to traversable ridgelines, natural pathways in the wilderness, or locations near water. Many contemporary Indians have reported sightings, but many more have not because the acceptance of the creature known as *Sasquatch, Oh-Mah, See-Ah-Tik, Tsunoqua,* or any of the hundreds of other names given it by Indians over the last several centuries, is part of their culture.

In the last century, many tens of thousands of sightings have not only been reported in western Canada, and the states of Washington, Oregon, and California, but large hominids have also been witnessed in every province of Canada, as well as in all other U.S. states except Hawaii. Widening that field, we find that such creatures have been encountered on all other continents save Antarctica. Are these encounters an elaborate and fairly consistent hallucination by many thousands of people in all walks of life, including teachers, doctors, scientists, law enforcement officers, and ministers? Perhaps. But recall William of Occam's philosophical proposition, Occam's razor, which posits that *given competing explanations for a specific thing, the simplest of those explanations, regardless of how improbable it may seem, is probably correct.* Perhaps they really did see what they thought they saw.

I've had the good fortune to spend a great deal of time in the wilds of Oregon and Washington. I've also traveled the length of British Columbia and have even spent a little time in the Yukon. I lived in Alaska for three years and most of it, like other parts of the West, is so remote, access is available only by aircraft. Those familiar with the forests of, let's say, the Northeast can scarcely imagine flying in a Cessna for an hour or two and seeing nothing but trees—not a building, not a telephone or power pole, not a person. The tracts of forest in the West may be diminishing but they are still vast, in the true sense of that word. Not to negate the majesty of the forests of Maine, or even New Jersey, those of the West have a different quality, a feeling of absolute isolation brought on simply by the great distances across them between towns and cities and the often complete lack of infrastructure.

And if much of the American West is isolated, then Canada is in its own special category. Most of Canada's thirty-some million people live within 150 miles of the U.S. border, yet Canada's area is considerably larger than the contiguous U.S. Much of northern Canada is uninhabited. And in the sparsely inhabited areas of the provinces, sightings of

large hairy manlike beings are commonplace, particularly from western Manitoba through the Plains and Rocky Mountain provinces.
Could a North American great ape exist in such remote stretches of
wilderness? It would have food aplenty and, having evolved into a creature of northern climes in the past forty or fifty thousand years (since
crossing from Asia over the land bridge that existed between what is
now Russia and Alaska) it would, it seems, be right in its element. The
only possible evidence of humans most of these isolated upper primates would have would probably be the rare jet contrail or satellite
skimming by in the night sky, neither of which they would equate with
a related race of beings.

Since the nineteenth century, curiosity about these unknown hominids
has been rising. As America expanded to the west, amazing stories
trickled out that caught the attention of eastern Americans and Euro-
peans. During Mac Schneider's research to educate himself about unknown hominids, the story that gives him the heebie-jeebies really did
come from Theodore Roosevelt's 1893 book *The Wilderness Hunter,* an
account told to him by the old trapper named Bauman. A wild and
lonely place even now, the head of Idaho's Wisdom River in the 1840s
was isolated in a way most inhabitants of our modern world cannot
begin to understand. Quite the woodsman himself, Roosevelt felt the
fear in the old trapper's words and had no doubts about the veracity of
Bauman's frightening account.

Yet another celebrated Bigfoot incident occurred at the base of
Washington state's Mount St. Helens. In the 1880s miners working on
its flank observed, then shot at and apparently wounded a "huge, hairy
beast." Later a group of such creatures returned and rained rocks and
boulders onto the miners' cabin. The creatures eventually left, but the
miners were so shaken, they abandoned their site. The miners' account
tends to support the idea that the rock-throwing creatures were merely
retaliating over the unprovoked aggression by the gun-toting humans.

In a tribute to Teddy Roosevelt's recount of Bauman's tale, I placed
Ty's first encounter in Idaho. And Idaho has personal significance for
me as well. During summer break from college, one night my girlfriend and I were camping by a babbling brook in the mountains of
northwestern Idaho. A few hours after turning in, I awoke and sensed a

presence near our tent. Just then something passed by us. The little hillock we had pitched our tent on was maybe three feet above the stream and consisted of packed pine needles and forest duff. Whatever walked next to our tent gently vibrated the soft, spongy ground with the magnitude of a horse. A stench wafted over the cool night air through our tent flap, then vanished. Although I knew whatever it was had moved on, I lay there for several minutes listening to make sure it was gone. Despite our vulnerability and the disturbing circumstance of having something so large right next to us, I had no fear. I am not sure what it was but I have my suspicions.

In this book I gave the Shadowkiller the ability to sense the emotions, and even thoughts, of humans. How much do we really know about psychic energy or such seemingly metaphysical manifestations? Having read some credible accounts that seemed to support this theory, as well as legitimate speculation by various scientists and investigators in relation to Bigfoot, I also drew on two events in my life as the basis for this phenomenon in the book. One was the incident in Idaho. I felt no fear at that time, yet such an encounter should have left me scared witless. Instead I was merely fascinated. Is it that I just have nerves of steel? No. To wit: drivers using BlackBerrys scare the crap out me. Maybe I'm reading something into this? Could I have merely speculated, years later, that whatever it was that passed me in the night gave off good vibes like a friendly cruise ship flashing a welcome? Perhaps. But the other event was just the opposite.

Many years ago while driving high in the mountains of Oregon, my family pulled off to the side of a logging road to enjoy the spectacular mountain vista before us. My sister and I played by the car as my parents stepped to the edge of the road to have a look. My folks tell me they suddenly had the most uncomfortable feeling, as if something were watching them. But it was more than that. They both told me the feeling of alarm was palpable, as if their senses were telling them to get the hell out of there. They quickly gathered us up and drove away. I never heard that story until I was well into adulthood. And if you knew my parents, you'd understand they are hardly the types to be alarmed, even in the face of danger. My dad did a horrendous tour in the field artillery in the South Pacific in WWII and is an extremely calm and rational guy. My mom grew up on a ranch in southern Oregon and handled a rifle at six. In both cases, what was it?

One form of hard evidence that is difficult to dismiss is the plaster castings of footprints. Many thousands of foot castings have been struck all over the earth, and ichnologists—fossil foot track experts— have concluded that a great many of them seem to have been formed by some sort of upper primate, a very large, upright walker, as yet to be catalogued by science. Ichnologists point to the castings and the evidence of complex structures of these anthropoidal feet, features such as intricate dermal ridges and sweat pores, as well as unique anatomical anomalies like injuries and deformations, details that would be impossible to re-create if one were attempting a hoax.

Experts also agree that faking such anatomically correct tracks, while carrying the appropriate hundreds and hundreds of pounds (to make the proper depth of impression) up extremely steep grades, is not within the realm of human performance. That conclusion was reached after investigators tried to visualize how a two-hundred-pound man, carrying an extra six hundred pounds, would walk with fifty-inch strides up a twenty-degree slope—all while wearing false sixteen-inch feet. Similar track evidence has been discovered not only on dozens of occasions, but thousands of miles and decades apart.

In the last several years exciting new information has surfaced as to the integrity of many foot track castings of alleged "big-footed" creatures. Jimmy Chilcutt, a forensic technician with one of the most extensive catalogues of primate finger- and footprints in the world, was given some footprint castings to analyze. The castings were purported to be those of Bigfoot. Chilcutt, at the time a law enforcement officer with the Conroe Police Department in Conroe, Texas, had certainly heard of Bigfoot but was highly skeptical. His expectation was that he would quickly debunk the myth after examining the casts and be on his way. Instead, his painstaking examinations revealed that the castings were authentic. He eventually acknowledged that they were far too detailed to have been faked and truly represented some sort of enormous primate that walked on two legs. Chilcutt's statement was unequivocal: the tracks were those of a North American great ape that is unknown to science. End of discussion.

Since 1967 the Patterson-Gimlin film has been scrutinized countless times. Some anthropologists have, after extremely technical computer analysis, concluded that the gait and body movements of the filmed creature were completely "ape-like" and would have been virtually impossible for humans to duplicate, even had they possessed advanced knowledge of primate anatomy and kinesiology, as well as a remarkably sophisticated suit at a time when Hollywood's best special effects people could only have dreamed of such an item. The arms were measured by computer at a whopping forty-three inches and the hands were fully articulated—that is, the fingers could be seen flexing—a feat well beyond the technology of 1967. A mere two months after *Planet of the Apes* wrapped production in August 1967, Patterson and Gimlin shot their shaky little film with an infinitely more realistic star than did Hollywood. And I'm not talking about Chuck Heston.

To further support the Patterson-Gimlin footage, the 14.5-inch plaster foot castings taken by them on the day they shot the film not only exactly match other castings taken ten days later in the same area by Bigfoot investigator Bob Titmus, but also match castings taken there by Patterson *three years earlier.* Ichnologists have determined that all the castings not only match but are the authentic footprints of an unknown hominid with a mass in excess of seven hundred pounds. A detailed computer study of the film has indicated the subject of the film was also seven feet three and a half inches tall with a chest size of *eighty-three inches.* They also measured the leisurely stride at eighty-one inches.[3] That's nearly seven feet. Hey Shaq, can you do that?

Clearly, this is one sizable individual. Additionally, the creature in the Patterson-Gimlin film is female and exhibits enormous, pendulous breasts. It is impossible to imagine that a hoaxer would have gone to such a spectacular—perhaps even bizarre—degree of detail for a hoax. Through brief correspondence I had with Patterson the year before he died, as well as information I have received since then, I know that he did not get rich from his discovery.

As to the anthropological rationale for the existence of this creature, a number of anthropologists are warming to the late Dr. Grover Krantz's theory that it may be the direct descendant of *Gigantopithecus,* a giant hominid related to humans and the great apes. Most anthropologists used to believe *Gigantopithecus* disappeared a few hundred thousand years ago, but as time passes, more and more scientists are now not so

[3]The NASI Report: *Toward a Resolution of the Bigfoot Phenomenon,* by J. Glickman, Hood River, Oregon, Diplomate: American College of Forensic Examiners.

sure. Its survival to the present would answer much that is unex-plained. According to Dr. Krantz, a respected anthropologist from my alma mater, Washington State University, by matching fossil evidence with foot castings and descriptions from thousands of sightings, we can conclude that Bigfoot is, as Dr. Wade Frazier put it in the book (and Krantz put it in real life), a dead ringer for *Gigantopithecus.*

Dr. Krantz was convinced *Gigantopithecus* was a true hominid, an upper primate that walked upright, and was—compared to humans—very, very large, perhaps more than eleven feet tall in some instances. Fossil records bear evidence that this genus of hominidae *did exist.* Incidentally, Dr. Krantz once estimated there had been in excess of a quarter million "events," that is, sightings, encounters, or the discovery of spoor, worldwide, in the previous forty years.

Other than Mr. Chilcutt's revelation, the most scientifically compelling piece of information may come on the heels of reliable DNA testing. Hair found on branches in North America, Malaysia, China, and Russia has recently been subjected to analysis. While one Canadian tester determined his sample was bison hair, if mitochondrial DNA can be obtained and sequenced, it might just put the mystery to rest.

A CNN poll from a few years ago indicates 40 percent of Americans believe Bigfoot exists, with another 33 percent unsure. An AOL poll said the number of believers was 59 percent. Yet if you asked any of those 40 to 59 percent why they believed Bigfoot was walking around the woods, you would likely get answers that were based less in fact and science and more on emotional excitement about the unknown and the possibilities of discovery in a world getting seemingly smaller by the day. I too am deeply compelled by the excitement of the unknown, but my layman's knowledge of science and my natural curiosity have caused me to seek the answer to the question. Having extensively researched this subject, I can say with confidence that I have connected enough dots to satisfy myself that there are large, primitive hominids existing in the wilds of our planet.

And why not? Most people don't know that the gorilla was unknown to the modern world until the turn of the twentieth century. The coelacanth, a rather large fish, had been considered a prehistoric casualty—paleontologists confidently concurred that it had been a goner for sixty-five million years—until one swam into a fishing net off Madagascar in 1938. In the last ten years a large and previously unknown deer was discovered in the jungles of Vietnam and an enormous uncatalogued shark, the megamouth, washed onto a beach in 1993 and caused many textbooks to be revised. In late 2005 an expedition to Indonesia discovered a remote area of jungle that was a veritable catalogue of new species.

How could Bigfoot exist so close to mankind and remain relatively undetected? To thrive in its harsh environment, such a creature would need senses that greatly transcended ours in receptivity, therefore it would be fairly easy for them to avoid us. Most sightings have occurred when the wind was carrying the scent of the people the wrong way. Either that, or the creatures were spotted from a great distance or surprised by a car. Many have asked the question, Why has a body never been found? A few years ago a poll of several thousand active hunters was conducted, and the results were that none of them had ever seen either the whole or even partial remains of a bear. And bear are presumably magnitudes more plentiful than the creatures in question.

Another possibility as to why no corpse has ever been found has precedent with isolated tribes of chimpanzees, baboons, and some mountain gorillas, and that is that Bigfoot may actually conceal, or even bury, their deceased. Such creatures would likely have long life spans, so deaths in a tribe or family association would not only be infrequent, but as these creatures possess an intellect not too far below our own, such passings might be treated with respect or, heaven forbid, spirituality.

Finally, some individuals, perhaps in the Bigfoot "community," will be angry with me for turning what by most accounts is a passive forest giant into a murderous monster. I should probably underscore right here that despite my antagonist's foul temper, I truly feel that these forest giants are indeed mostly benign, and I absolutely do not condone going after them with any kind of weapon, let alone an elephant gun. I also think that modern technology has moved us closer to finding them, and when we do discover them, they should be studied at arm's length and left as undisturbed as possible.

My answer to those who believe that all Bigfoot are just huge cuddly Ewoks is to remind them that there is plenty of evidence that every member of the great apes family—chimps, gorillas, orangutans, and bonobos (sometimes called pygmy chimpanzees)—has exhibited hostility toward its own kind as well as toward members of other species. Ask the poor fellow (Mac Schneider and Dr. Frazier discuss him) near Bakersfield, California, in March 2005, who was savagely attacked by two full-grown male chimpanzees. It's speculated that the crazed chimps went ape when another chimp simply received a cupcake. The cakeless apes literally chewed away most of the man's face and ripped off his testicles (among other grievous injuries) before being shot to death. Miraculously, the man survived.

The late anthropologist Dian Fossey documented violence within her gorilla tribes, as did renowned primatologist Jane Goodall with her chimpanzees. Interestingly, in an interview on NPR in late September 2002, Dr. Goodall, considered the world's leading authority on chimpanzee behavior, raised a lot of eyebrows when she said she believed that large uncatalogued hominids, i.e., Bigfoot and his kin, probably did exist.

As an antithesis to bold pioneers like Goodall, Grover Krantz, and Idaho State's Dr. Jeff Meldrum, to name a few, I employed the character of Dr. Wade Frazier (named after my good friend and fellow believer of the unbelievable) to exemplify the reluctance of the scientific community to embrace the notion that we don't know one-tenth or even one-thousandth of what is knowable and that risk is the cornerstone of exploration and subsequent discovery. Frazier's character is also a gentle smack in the face to those who choose doctrinaire academia over adventure and discovery. Sure, Dr. Frazier writes books on cryptozoology, but when the chips are down, he holes up in the safety of his office. Politics trumps science when Dr. Frazier's fear of losing his grant money supplants doing the right thing, particularly when he knows exactly what it is that is making people vanish and could lend a credible voice to the cause. Shame on those scientists whose knee-jerk reaction is to scoff in the face of such tantalizing evidence without really exploring it. Isn't discovery one of the cornerstones of science?

So, back to the big question: do they *still* exist, these big creatures with the eponymous feet? If they don't, then one wonders how such phenomena can possibly be ascribed to anything else. Perhaps some day years from now, not long after the San Diego Zoo opens its "Bigfoot Adventure," complete with a family of these creatures, everyone will look back and wonder how anyone could have doubted it.

Matthew Scott Hansen
Los Angeles, California